THE MOON GODDESS AND THE SON

DONALD KINGSBURY

THE MOON GODDESS AND THE SON

BAEN BOOKS

A Baen Books Original
Distributed by Simon & Schuster
Simon & Schuster Building
1230 Avenue of the Americas
New York, N.Y. 10020

Cover art by David Mattingly

1   3   5   7   9   10   8   6   4   2

ISBN: 0-671-55958-3. First printing, December 1986

Library of Congress Cataloging in Publication Data

Kingsbury, Donald, 1929–
    The moon goddess and the son.

    1. Title.
PS3561.I487M66   1985   813'.54   84-28309
ISBN 0-671-55958-3

Dedication

I was at the American Astronautical Society meeting in San Francisco in October 1977 to give a talk and to listen to other talks on the theme: *The Industrialization of Space*. A gaggle of us space nuts were sitting around drinking beer and gossiping about rockets when I muttered under my breath, "There's gotta be a better way to get up there," whereupon

Roger Arnold,

who was at the table, smiled and passed me a note: "There is." And that was the beginning of this adventure.

And to:

Robert Cornog for discussing the economics of the leoport; Jesco von Puttkamer, long-range planning analyst for NASA; James Kingsbury of NASA; and Stan Schmidt, David Hartwell, John Douglas, Jim Baen, Betsy Mitchell, and Eleanor Wood, all of the publishing world.

TIME PATROL WARNING

This time-bus does not follow a chronological tour.

There may be sudden unanticipated shifts of timeframe which may cause passenger disorientation and temporary confusion. Take your anti-time-sickness pills and always seek to locate reliable reference anchors. (In case of emergency, comfort bags have been provided in the seat pocket directly in front of you.)

We will be touring the space-vicinity of Earth and its moon during the quiet of the so-called Nuclear Peace between the Second World War and the Great Accidental War. (See abbreviated history reference manual 14-C5 in the seat pocket for handy audio/visual reference anchors.)

Although our tour will mainly confine itself to the late twentieth century and the early twenty-first century, the physics of minimal energy pathing requires that the temporal motors of your bus take us briefly through time zones which may be as much as three thousand years on either side of the Nuclear Peace. Do not be alarmed if a camel-riding Nabatean trader temporarily enters the scene or if a Mongol warrior attempts to block your way, or even if you find a strangely dressed archaeologist excavating a trench across the Washington mound. This is normal.

The staff of Time Immemorial welcomes you aboard. Have a nice century.

CHAPTER 1

VANDALIA Ill. (INS) 18 Aug 1997—Marc Errold Clifford visited his estranged wife this Sunday when she refused to allow him his weekend visit with their two daughters. He brought his shotgun and murdered his wife and then smashed down the girls' bedroom door and killed them with three more shotgun blasts—Joan Clifford (12) in the closet and Sharon Clifford (11) under the bed. Neighbors heard the screaming but before the police could coax him to surrender, Mr. Clifford slipped a broom handle into the trigger guard of his weapon, took the barrel into his mouth and carefully executed himself with a kick of his foot. Mr. Clifford was described by a neighbor as a gentle man who managed the local sandlot baseball team and who enjoyed duck hunting. His recipe for Peking Duck was a local favorite.

FROM DIANA OSBORNE'S SECRET NEWSPAPER COLLECTION.

Diana's ambition to get a job on the moon started the same day she learned from a child's book of mythology that her namesake was the moon goddess. She was six and so excited by the revelation that she laid herself across the sill of her bedroom window and, using her belly as a pivot, seesawed out onto the slanted porch roof.

There, she pulled her underpants halfway to her knees so they wouldn't get scratched if her bottom were to slip on the gravely shingles while, on all fives, she edged her way down the asphalt tiles. The prickly cushion was the lesser of two evils—granulated skin smoothed itself out, but runs in her undies would earn her an unforgettable beating. Inching caterpillar-like out along the sloping roof, heels first, then palms, then bottom, heels, palms, bottom, she worked herself to a

1

point beyond the tree branches so that she could stare at the full moon in the sky where she belonged.

The golden disk raced through scudding clouds above the flat-black housetops of her sullen Ohio town. Heaven was in the sky. Heaven had rocks and funny floating houses and heroes who didn't need to breathe air. Heaven with its spacemen was her *real* home. Heaven was beautiful and round and a brighter yellow than any crayon. And the goddess Diana could fly off roofs and fly through the forest.

"Goddamn it, Diana! What the bloody hell are you doing out there on the roof!"

She started, then cringed—her vision falling, a buckshot-blasted sparrow, the underpants around her knees tripping her as she tried to react, landing her on fingertips that bloodied themselves clawing the slanting shingles. Her thigh took the scraping blow that interrupted the awkward rise. She hadn't meant her father to catch her, knowing his easy fury. There was nowhere to run; nevertheless she eased sideways along the roof.

"You'll kill yourself, you little twat!"

Before she could get to the gutter, he reached out and hauled her over the windowsill, swinging her into the bedroom by one arm, throwing her to the floor, then jerking her upright. He slapped her. She knew enough of his temper not to scream so she merely whimpered while he lifted her off her feet and tossed her onto the mattress. He stripped her, ignoring socks and shoes. The tear in her underpants earned a head-shaking smack. He tied her to the bed frame and beat her bleeding with his belt.

In that Ohio room her body endured—the pain blotting out this man, blotting out even the pain itself—while from another mythological place her mind observed. No goddess who could fly was afraid! She saw a wild boar's charge and fiercely cast a spear toward his heart from her stance safe behind a round lunar shield. Did the point tear flesh? She kicked him. Enraged by resistance, her father struck again and again, determined to make her feel the pain, to cringe, to cry, to moan. Expertly she retreated from his rampage, all the way to the far side of the moon, leaving only her body behind to distract this boar's rough rooting.

Once the man's rage had dissipated, when the house was wholly quiet and the night supreme, a woman crept from the shadows to wash the wounds of her daughter. "Stop it!" screamed Diana. "You're hurting me!" She could scream at her mother, turn her back, sulk. Crying, the mother laid a blanket over her and tiptoed out of the bedroom.

Hours passed and slowly the trauma evaporated, leaving only the pain of being touched by a bloodstained bed that refused to stop torturing her back and legs and stomach with its prodding fingers. When the moon rose so high that her round eyes could no longer see it through the window, she felt abandoned.

In the morning she ate her cornflakes with surliness, scrunching over the table, her fist around the spoon, blond hair hanging in a way that hid her face. She said nothing, spoke to no one Her mother tried to comfort her and still she said nothing. Diana's ears were waiting for the postman—the soft clunk of feet, the opening and closing of the door, the sheet-metal sounds of a mailbox lid being lifted and shut. The only nice thing about being beaten was that she got off from school.

It came, this time as the rasp of magazine-stuffing.

She was out like a shot, following her man on tiptoes so he wouldn't notice until they were both away from her parents' house. Then she ran up beside him. "Gimme a bundle to deliver!" she demanded, a smile all over her face, her eyes flirting. He tousled her hair and turned up the next walk. She followed him. "Is it all junk mail?"

"Some people still get real letters." He held out three envelopes before he slipped them into the door slot. They were printed up at the local post office and delivered to people who were too poor, or obstinate, to own a fax-phone.

"Those aren't *real* letters," retorted Diana.

So the postman gave her a postcard. "Now don't drop that. If you're going to be my little postgirl, you have to take care of everything I give you."

It was a picture of a marina in Florida. Diana stared intently at the boats and the blue sea and the sailors and the women in bikinis. It didn't look like Ohio at all. She turned the card over and carefully read it, puzzling over some of the squiggles. Mrs. Simak's daughter had terrible handwriting and if she had gone to school in Ohio *they* wouldn't have let her graduate up to the second grade. Still, Diana was clever at squiggles and codes. For years she had had a girlfriend who owned a whole collection of Sesame Street shows on VHS.

Mrs. Simak's daughter had a tan, said the postcard. The Blodgetts had come back and wanted her to stay for another week so she was moving to the waterfront guest house. She wouldn't be back till the end of the month. Mrs. Blodgett said hello. And PS, please water my petunia jug.

Very studiously Diana correlated the address on the card and the address on the old wooden door with its cracked varnish. She rang the doorbell impatiently. Buzz. An ear to the door. No steps. Buzz, buzz, buzzzzzzzz. An ear to the door again.

White-haired Mrs. Simak peeked out cautiously to see that the two of them weren't burglars. Diana thrust the card at her, a smile covering her face again. "Good news from Dottie. She's having fun!"

"You two gossips have been reading my mail again, have you?"

"Just the good pieces!" She glanced at the postman. "Do you have any junk mail for this address?"

"Just a tax bill."

Mrs. Simak sighed.

And so the morning went. Diana followed him up and down the street along the route, sometimes chatting with him, sometimes letting him deliver his mail, sometimes cajoling him into letting her deliver it. She liked protecting him from dogs. The black shepherd was very fierce today and she had to hold his mouth closed and growl at him.

Finally the postman asked her about her bruises.

Diana only smiled mischievously, full of the things a woman hides, and gave him a mysterious glance with her eyes. "I was a bad girl. I snuck out on the roof to look at the moon and fell off. My father was very angry with me. You should see my side where I hit—it's all bloody. In a week I can make myself a nice scab sandwich." She laughed. She never admitted to anyone that her father beat her, least of all to the men she loved.

Reluctantly she left her sweetheart at the post office and began to work her way home through the back alleys. Alleys were more interesting than streets. They had trees to climb, some with decaying tree huts. She knew where there was an old carhouse without doors. Alleys had fences and tin-walled garages and garbage.

All the way home Diana rummaged through the garbage cans, peeking into plastic sacks that had been ripped open by cats and racoons. She collected a respectable haul of magazines within five blocks, plus a newspaper called *Police Reports* which she intended to check out for murder stories. The magazines were *Big Boobs*, good for the color photographs, *The New Yorker*, which had interesting cartoons about kook Americans, *Cosmopolitan*, with its coy hints, and two copies of *Nubile*.

The *Nubiles* she coveted for her imaginary life. She could visit the golden cupolas of the Kremlin while drinking superior vodka. She could sip Chivas Regal with gentlemen at a table in a space station overlooking the glimmer of Los Angeles below, or run around naked on horses with genteel cowboys who had lung cancer.

Once, courtesy of two *Nubile* full-page advertisements, she went on a ballooning adventure with sophisticated friends. Their balloon was an unreal red and blue and they had a wicker basket under it with a nice barbecue fire to cook steaks for a picnic. Diana wore Turkish pants and brought the sliced orange and onion salad and the digiphone for gossiping with the farmers below. But her friends made a big mistake because they *all* liked their steaks well done. By the time they were ready to eat, the other balloons were out of sight and they were way up in the sky above the clouds and could only see the billowy castles of the Ogre-giant from Jack-and-the-Beanstalk. Finally they settled down in Northern Canada near the MacKenzie River and were rescued by four goldminers who all carried a pint of Seagram's Finest in their back pockets.

Diana usually masterminded these adventures in the O'Connor's deserted garage. It had two openings in the rotting wall planks which reminded her of a rabbit hole with an escape hatch. The escape hole opened up on the other side of the O'Connor's fence, so she was never caught. To this retreat she brought her new armload of magazines. She cached them beside the rusty lawn mower, under the floorboards, not intending to read immediately. Reading was for quiet times and she hadn't checked out the neighborhood for adventures yet. But she couldn't resist taking a quick peek at the June issue of *Nubile*.

She opened to a color photograph of the round moon taken from low Earth orbit through a construction rig manned by two spacesuited men. For minutes she stared at it. *Her* moon. And then she turned the page to see if there were more. There was only one other photograph, that of a black-haired man floating inside a small cylindrical module, grinning at the photographer with blue eyes while hanging casually onto a giant robot-arm control panel like a swimmer hangs onto a bobbing raft.

The caption identified Engineer Byron McDougall, formerly of the Air Force, formerly a NASA shuttle pilot. He was quoted as saying that once they were finished building the leoport he had in mind to get up there and tunnel out a lunar city large enough to "show those Russians at Theophilus what a moon base really is." And what did he expect the Americans to build that the Russians didn't already have? "I think I'd start by importing the floating gardens of Babylon."

The idea appealed to Diana. She didn't know the word "leoport" and she had never heard of Babylon, but she knew that "floating gardens" would please Diana's forest nymphs. Instantly she was in love with Byron. Instantly she knew that she was going to make another scrapbook about space to hide behind her desk with her collection of murder stories.

Her moon rose again the next evening and, when she found it, beamed on her with shining pleasure. It hadn't abandoned her. Forever afterwards the night sky was her faithful companion. Often she pretended to sleep, staring out the window, dreaming. When she heard her father's snoring she was sometimes made bold enough to sneak again through the window onto the porch roof, there to wonder at her moon or watch it rise. She knew from the TV space operas that you didn't have to die to go to heaven. Men lived out there in ships and modules—and long ago, when her Americans had been bolder, American heroes had even gamboled over the lunar hills where only Russian scientists were camped today.

On her seventh birthday a high school boy took her out with his portable tracking telescope and they set up on a flat asphalt and gravel factory roof. The cratered mountains of the moon stunned her with their beauty—*her* mountains, *her* craters, *her* plains, *her* rills and streamers. Meticulously she located each of the old Apollo landing sites. She was especially thrilled when she found the Apollo 16 landing site in the roughly cratered terrain between Mare Nubium and Mare Nectaris just 120 kloms north of the crater Abulfeda and 300 kloms west of the giant Russian lunar base at Theophilus.

Sometimes at the controls of the telescope she was serious. Sometimes she dreamed. Once, with her eyes filled by the huge moon, a moment of astral travel cast her into a crater full of flowering trees, their scent enticing hummingbirds for the pleasure of the shy nymphs. It was the duty of Diana to watch over the wood nymphs of the moon. What splendid forests she could see, arching higher than redwoods in the low gravity!

The young boy showed her Jupiter and the Pleiades. He showed her the Russian space city, Mirograd, rising like the red star of Mars over the heartland of America every hour-and-a-half, as it had since long before she was born, closer to Ohio than San Francisco or New York or even St. Louis.

Another evening they followed the bright thread of the half-built American leoport as it arrowed across the southern sky at twilight—the telescope's clock machinery holding the image upon the lens while the boy and child watched as its golden thread was overtaken by the night behind the Earth. When it was gone the boy explained that they could see the leoport this far north only because it hadn't yet been nudged into equatorial orbit. Leoport, he explained after Diana asked, meant "Low Earth Orbit spacePORT." It was a necklace of rings held together electro-"magically."

Another year passed. When she was eight Diana had a temper tantrum and stoically endured five beatings until her mother papered her wall with a photomontage of the moon's surface. With a sweet smile on her face she lived in that map. Gryphons rowed her over Mare Frigoris while she held polar-bear robes about herself. Husky man-headed lions carried her in a red and gold inlaid palanquin through the Alpine Valley to the warmer regions of the Imbrium where she flirted with Neptune and raced and feasted with other immortals. Once she took astronaut Mattingly by the hand for a walk through the woods in the sheltered valley of the crater Descartes because she felt sorry that he'd never had the chance to walk on the moon like his comrades Duke and Young.

Diana kept her two files of articles hidden from her father behind a special plywood door at the back of her desk, the brown folder and the red scrapbook each growing week by week—one a well worn set of newspaper clippings about fathers who murdered their children and the other a bright tale of heroes. On the first page of the red book she had pasted a magazine cutout which she thought was very appropriate. It was titled:

The Men and Women Who Will Make America Great Again.
Our answer to the Soviet presence in space.

Underneath this title, which was embellished with eagles, the magazine page lay crammed with passport pictures of men and women printed above their names and accomplishments, ten of them in all, less even than the number of senior Soviet scientists posted routinely to Mirograd and even rotated to the moon. But the ten were Americans. They were the rabbits who were catching up with the tortoise—again—and their lives were watched enthusiastically.

Diana's favorite was Construction Engineer Byron McDougall. She collected everything she read about him. One year she even counted all the instances he had been mentioned in *Time* magazine. This was Byron, the hero of the leoport accident which had kept a continent of Americans mesmerized, horri-

fied, crying and awed for twenty hours of terrifying suspense
until he saved everybody. That was the only time Diana had
ever remembered seeing her father both drunk and happy
simultaneously.

The treasure in Diana's scrapbook was the *Omni* interview of
her Byron. She used it to practice reading. The interview
carried the best picture spread of him she had ever seen—
posing with his wife and his son in a barn in New Hampshire;
caught while he suited up for a shuttle flight; standing awash in
the Pacific Ocean at San Diego while two other photographers
also took his picture; bottled up in his small orbiting office
overlooking a house-sized shipment of leoport rings . . .

And Diana's favorite portrait: Byron as a young man.

Somewhere *Omni* had found a shot of him crossing a desert
airfield in Saudi Arabia back in the '80s, his face warmly naive,
before the world was complicated by space stations and battle
lasers, when he was still a youthful fighter pilot training Saudi's
to fly the mighty F-15. Those were the old days when fighters
were still flown by men. He looked so at ease on the desert,
pleased with his pilots and his planes and the windy desolation.

She would have tacked the portrait of this innocent McDougall
beside her moon map except that her father would have reacted
violently to a male pinup, so instead she hid Byron's picture
behind her desk and occasionally slept with it after a beating.

Byron McDougall was the love of her life.

CHAPTER 2

MOSCOW—The orbiting of an additional module to the major new Soviet Space Station from the Baikonur Cosmodrome was announced by Soviet leader Mikhail Gorbachev this morning. He emphasized the peaceful nature of Soviet space research, contrasting it with the United States' intent to militarize space, hinting that by the 1990s Soviet space science would have a permanent research base on the moon. Western military sources confirmed that the launch has provided a significant addition to the Soviets' space station complex and proves out the almost unlimited expandability of the Soviet design. The original module, called Mir, contains six docking ports which can be attached to other modules which themselves can contain docking ports. It is expected that over the next few years the Soviet space station will become a large, active complex served by the new giant Tsiolkovsky booster and a transport shuttle. British space expert R. F. Smith-Crowley estimates that the Soviets are now at least ten years ahead of the American space effort and very shortly will have a capability to prevent the United States from deploying any anti-ICBM battle stations.

Flying out of Dhahran by night, over the oilfields of the Saudi Kingdom, the Boeing 727 banked northeast toward Amman. Gas flares lit the desert, some flickering orange and red across the sands like hell's spurting flames firmly controlled by Allah's hand, others, fainter, embedded in the dark, gave the appearance of comfortable Bedouin fires kindled from camel's dung.

A young United States Air Force captain from the Dhahran Air Academy, the only American aboard, noted that the Arab seated beside him resembled a notorious rebel who, if not dead, must certainly be locked away in some prison. He wondered in puzzlement for a moment—all Saudis looked like New York Jews to him—but then Bijad ibn Jamal smiled politely to the family in front of him. The steel teeth on the left side of his face were unmistakable—souvenirs of the riots at Jubail.

Well, I'll be damned! thought the boyish American who carried the name of Byron McDougall. Who in their right mind would let ibn Jamal out of his cage?

Once, at Dhahran, the gossip had flowed about this man. A pilot spoke in grisly detail of how a friend of a friend, who had since been silenced by the King, had pushed Bijad out of an airplane over the Empty Quarter. This story was disputed. Bijad had been shot by his father for blasphemy. He had died of torture in Riyadh. The stories of his death were endless. He angered good Moslems—they wished him dead—and yet they always spoke of his death with a certain wistfulness, as if it were a shame for such a brave and charming fool to die so easily.

Byron smiled. Was he really surprised to see ibn Jamal alive and free? Though Saudis, like Americans, were capable of believing dreadful things of their government, observation suggested quite the opposite: Saudi Arabia was that part of the Middle East where Allah was most merciful. Political prisoners did not disappear and they were not tortured. The sons of Abdul Aziz, like their practical father, were not willing to make unnecessary enemies in a land where revenge is an obligation.

During a long flight one has much time for idle thought. Byron recalled the behavior of King Abdul Aziz ibn Saud when, in 1921, he finally conquered his family's mortal enemies, the Rasheeds. Mohammed ibn Talal ibn Rasheed expected death. Instead Abdul Aziz gave his captive a place of honor at a great dinner and embraced him.

"The time for death and killing is finished. We are all brothers now, and you and yours will come to Riyadh to live with me and be part of my own family." Three of the Rasheed women, widowed by the battle, were married to Saudi men.

Old Abdul Aziz knew about justice, thought Byron. You tried a bit of man-made justice and carried it as far as you could, and when that didn't work anymore you invited your enemy in for dinner and brought out the *mensef*. The founding King of modern Saudi Arabia had a genius for ending cycles of revenge. Perfect justice was left to Allah. And perhaps that was enough to explain why Bijad ibn Jamal had not died for his recklessness.

Who could account for such men?

Byron suspected that Bijad carried within his soul some ancient family obligation. He came from a devout wahhabi family whose grandfather had been a loyal member of the army of Abdul Aziz. The grandfather had helped in the capture of Mecca but later joined the Ikhwan revolt of 1929, to die charging the machine guns of Abdul Aziz's army at the oasis of Umm Urdhumah. It did not matter that Bijad now denied his clan or, that by adopting Marx, had broken with his past—an Arab's memory does not pretend to be consistent with reason.

The soul of the devout wahhabi Moslem, warrior of the desert, still shone from the eyes of this graduate of Berkeley. Grandfather Jamal would not have recognized his grandson, but Byron, whose father was a fanatic, did. Fanatics may change their beliefs like the mountains change color—but the behavior of a fanatic remains like stone against weather and time and reason—and passes from father to son in strange ways.

A Saudi family, seated directly in front of the American, had never been in an airplane before and watched through the windows with an excitement that often broke into musical Arabic. They watched even as the desert became blackness below and stars above. The Palestinian steward moved down the aisle serving coffee and Pepsi-Cola, mellon and sweet cakes. Bijad asked for a newspaper.

He's charming and full of force, thought Byron, watching the exchange, watching even as the newspaper and coffee were brought over and placed upon the little pull-down table. Bijad noticed his interest—and Arabs do not drop their eyes, like New Yorkers, when you meet theirs. He offered his coffee to Byron and Byron could not refuse. The American called over the Palestinian and ordered another cup for Bijad.

Coffee was the traditional Middle East drink of hospitality. It held all the generosity of the semitic soul. But you could never reach the bottom of the cup. Millennia of memory lay there under the politeness, every grudge, every slight—held and cherished and stirred, waiting upon the moment of justice.

As his eyes smiled at Byron, Bijad's seemed to hold his patience behind a dam built across a narrow valley. From the crotch of the valley one could not measure the size of the lake behind that dam.

We believe in a Just God, for are we not the instrument of that justice, waiting without forgiveness, even unto the seventh generation, to avenge each wrong?

Ibn Jamal, follower of a Jewish atheist, had written with Islamic fervor for the oil workers of the Gulf, rousing them in secret tracts to erase all past exploitation by the ruling classes, by the imams, by the capitalists, and the Zionist conspirators.

He began a conversation easily, commenting on the main head-line of the newspaper he held in his lap.

"Is it not beautiful that the Russians will be filling your sky? From sea to shining sea."

Byron read Arabic, and so he had seen the headline, but it didn't jump out at him like an English headline and he had to stare at it and move his lips before it registered. "Well!" And he twisted his neck to read the first paragraph of the story.

It was not news to Byron. Everybody with any knowledge of the Soviet space program had been expecting this since 1973. And though the February story about the launching of Mir's core had passed almost unreported by the press, it is only American Congressmen and newspaper editors who have to have an elephant in their bathtub before they notice that the circus is in town.

"You read Arabic?" asked his companion politely, switching on the overhead light and turning the paper so that Byron might more easily view it.

"How could I resist learning your enchanting language? I'm a poet at heart. I've always wanted to be civilized."

"You read fluently?"

"No—but I get by."

"You are in the American Air Force. Do you make much of this station-of-the-space?"

"It's going to be big. Russians have a cultural weakness for gigantism. This looks like only the beginning."

"A city in the sky. Like in *The Empire Strikes Back*. An evil Marxist city. Do you think your Russian friends will flush their toilets into the Great Lakes as they pass two hundred miles overhead?" Bijad was grinning.

Byron could tell from the pleasure in the grin that his fellow passenger was seeing Uncle Sam up to his neck in sand with camel dung in his mouth and his eyelids scissored off. He was right, a Russian base dominating the heartland of America was embarrassing, and there was no way the United States could challenge it with only three shuttles flying and the great Saturn booster, of lost lunar fame, long on the junk heap of American impatience—but the Arab's grin was overdone.

Then, as the aircraft lumbered inland, the full moon began to rise. Soft light touched the rolling landscape beyond the silver wings. To the Saudis this desert held the fascination of a womb now lost to their past, forbidden to them by their new womb of air-conditioning. To the American it looked like the view one might see from a spaceship drifting in the stellar darkness over an airless moon of rock—an interesting frontier.

Below the aircraft, under the moonlit haze, but long ago, a fragile trade route had reached across the desert, between the Persian Gulf and the Mediterranean worlds, linking civilizations barely aware of each other. From the sea at Kuwait spices and silks, musk, slaves, anything both valuable and light, were trundled by camel caravan over incredibly harsh country to the oasis at Jauf and thence on to the crossroads city of Petra. In the course of six hundred years the Nabateans built their desert empire, then vanished. They had been gone for twice as long as they had reigned. Byron wondered if someday they might reappear, trading across the dried out wadis of Mars selling the goods of distant Callisto to Soviet Centurions patrolling the borders of their empire.

Byron's journey was not a military mission. He had planned this trip to Jordan last December with his wife Junie, but quarreling had prevented them from coming. She did not like ruins, she did not like walking in the desert, she did not like Arabs, and she was afraid that some anti-semitic Arab would murder her, mistaking her for a Jew because of her prominent arabian nose. Junie had returned to New Hampshire, giving the excuse that she was pregnant, and only now did Byron feel free to indulge his wonder.

The Boeing arrived over Amman after dinner when the city was a hilly twinkle of lights not yet gone to sleep. Byron's travel books claimed that it had been founded in the bronze age, first appearing in history as the chief city of the Ammonites. It was here, during a siege, that David sent Uriah the Hittite to his death so that David might take for himself Uriah's beautiful wife, Bathsheba. Amman had been destroyed many times—and rebuilt as often. The acreage of twinkling showed it had grown, by the atomic age, to be a city of nearly a million people.

At the airport Byron and Bijad ibn Jamal continued their talk around a tiny table over more coffee, not about Saudi politics, for Bijad seemed curiously reluctant to move in that direction— as if silence had been a condition of his release. He preferred, instead, to speak about justice in general.

He hinted at American wealth. He spoke darkly of Zionist wealth. He spoke with contempt of French wealth.

Wealth was a crime. He could not mention the wealth of Riyadh but wealth was on his mind. He began to castigate the first great Islamic dynasty, the Umayyad Caliphate, which had ruled Islam, in corrupt luxury, from Damascus between 661 and 750 AD.

When the Umayyads were deposed by al-Saffah, an amnesty was announced and eighty members of the family invited to dinner. While they ate, hidden soldiers, on signal, slew them with swords. Carpets were spread over the corpses and the feast continued. Ibn Jamal grinned at the delightful perfidy of the story. His mouth said no words of treason, but his eyes saw a thousand men of the House of Saud under those carpets.

Byron was hardly paying attention. He missed his wife. If she wasn't such an argumentive fool, she could be here with him now, enjoying the quaintness of this madman. It was going to be lonely in Amman without her.

CHAPTER 3

Woman was God's second mistake.
FRIEDRICH NIETZSCHE, *THE ANTICHRIST*.

"Oh, Daddy," exclaimed Byron's very pregnant wife, "this little town has everything. I know what you think of country living, but you haven't seen the absolutely fabulous place I bought. The church is only a five minute drive away."

"What denomination?" asked Charlie Bond.

"Congregational!" Junie replied aggressively.

"Jesus, you're going to bring up my grandson as a Congregationalist?" He was appalled at the heresy.

"With your luck the baby will be another *granddaughter*. Come with me, I'll show you the town." She took his arm.

But the old fighter pilot was reluctant to move. He was watching them tow away his blue and yellow Cessna. He didn't trust the staff of these backwoods dirt airfields. Finally he resigned himself. "You really should look for an Episcopal Church," he told Junie.

"Daddy! It's half-an-hour's drive away and the rector is a little old man who is always telling stories about the good old days when he was machine-gunning Japs on Guadalcanal. I couldn't bear it! *Our* minister gives parties. He loves everybody."

"The younger generation has no *brand loyalty*," grumbled the chief executive officer of the Shantech Conglomerate as Junie led him by the hand to her Lincoln. She had been brought up on Chryslers and the family had been Episcopalian for eleven generations. He snorted. Probably she didn't even use Rinso anymore.

But as they crossed the field that passed for a parking lot, his flash of anger at his daughter shamed him.

15

"You're looking as snappy as ever, Junie," he said by way of apology.

"Thank you." She waited until he had eased her safely behind the Lincoln's wheel and had gone around to let himself in before she spoke again. "Open the windows for me, Daddy."

He hesitated, momentarily panicked by the non-Chrysler dashboard. These damn Ford's never put their buttons in the right place!

She drove him out of the flatlands up into the hills and showed him Stonefield. She stopped on Main Street and bought wine for dinner, and ducked into the bookstore for *Glamour*.

"This is boondocksville!" he grumbled when she returned.

"Daddy, will you shut up! You're a Boston grouch. This nook end of civilization is the find of a lifetime! It's a college town and has all the amenities like bookstores and even touring Broadway plays . . ."

She chattered on and on until he felt a compulsive need to shut her up. "All that and a Congregational Church, too." His sarcasm hid an uneasiness with his daughter's plans that ran far deeper than her choice of church.

"Don't forget that airfield I whumped up right in my back yard for my fighter pilot men!"

Daddy Bond was a Sabrejet pilot from the Korean War with two MIG kills to his credit. He had been USAF Reserve for many years, and his companies were deep into defense contracts. It was in pursuit of one of those contracts that he had discovered the man his daughter married.

He smiled, remembering his son-in-law. A Major General had chosen Byron McDougall to take him up for a tour of the clouds in an F-15—Bond suspected himself of running off at the mouth about Korea and that the General had been desperate to get rid of him. Byron, however, liked the stories and Bond, warming, enticed him home with a casual description of his four nubile daughters.

Unfortunately, as Bond recalled their heavy drinking, he had ungraciously passed out on the couch while telling a ribald story to Byron—and Byron, who was by then far from sober himself, had wandered off alone in search of the girls, but instead of locating them had gone to sleep in Junie's car where she found him the next morning much to her disgust. She had raced upstairs. "There's a drunken wingless chicken in the back of my car with his *feet* sticking out the window! Get rid of him!"

Junie drove her father through the hills of the local farmland, past a transformer station and the town sandpit and the fields just turning to spring. Around a corner her new house stood on a slight rise. Fieldstone fences, built on Junie's instructions in the old-fashioned way, faced the road.

But husband Byron had never seen the place and had been given no choice in the buying of it and that was what was worrying his father-in-law. Such were the ways of a willful daughter. Her judgments about complex trivia were always perfect—she knew what stocks to buy and sell, she knew which cut of meat went with which vegetables and where to buy the cheapest violin strings—but she had never been able to understand simple importances. She had no common sense.

Daddy Bond, of course, had little trouble with the simple basics. His son-in-law was an Air Force officer. There was no possible place for him in the wilds of New Hampshire, however close it was to Boston, however close it was to a dirt airfield.

"You've got to see the view out back!" Junie exclaimed.

He waited until they were in the kitchen. After mixing himself a vodka and clam juice, he confronted her. "Junie darling. You want something from me."

"How did you guess?"

He smelled the soup—and the lamb roast with curried rice. She knew what he liked to eat but never went out of her way to feed him unless she wanted something in return. He waved a hand. "Do you need money?"

"No! You got me into stocks and bonds when I was twelve and I'm doing very well, thank you. I never overspend. You know that by now! I can afford a white elephant that the real estate people haven't been able to get rid of. No, I don't want your money."

"Ugh. That means you're not going to let me off lightly."

She smiled and ladled out the soup. "I want you to get Byron out of Saudi Arabia. Goddamn it, I want him out of the United States Air Force."

"Hey . . . how can I do that? What magic powers do you think a corporation boss has? You've been reading the newspapers again. I've warned you about that."

"I have it all planned," she said cunningly. "The Soviets are set on building a huge space station."

"They've had two-man space stations up there for years. Flying outhouses."

"But now there's *sure* to be a serious program to get *us* up there," she said with the even voice of a broker riding a hot tip. "Byron says Americans always do things best on sudden excited impulse because we have short-fused assholes for brains. I mean this Mir complex isn't one of those test systems—those flying outhouses, as you call them—my sources tell me it's the real thing." She buttonholed her father. "So we're in serious trouble, right? Little American boys are too interested in the soft life to be interested in being first—but they can't *stand* to come in second—I know all about boys. Washington will be going crazy! Especially since the Challenger just blew up. I want Byron to be tapped for the super-crash-priority space station design team. That's what you can do for me. Or do I have to sulk?"

"Now Junie, give your old man a break. I've been building up Shantech for eight years now. We're in a damn good position and we have a lot of fine companies under one umbrella, but I just don't have the connections even if they put ten billion into space next week. And I'm not one of the technical men—I'm a manager. I could ask around."

"Do that," she said firmly.

"Junie, listen to me. Byron is a kid. He's a flyboy, not an engineer. He joined USAF when he was eighteen and he doesn't know anything else. He dreams but that's not ambition. He never made a decision in his life that some officer didn't hand to him. I'm not saying that as an insult. He's a fine organization man."

"He got his engineering degree while he was flying. Daddy, he's good!"

"Now don't take that mail order degree seriously. The Air Force is sensitive about its jock image. They want to be loved for their brains. So they humor pilots who read. But believe me, he's a fighter jock and he doesn't know anything else. He doesn't have any experience as an engineer. Experience is everything."

"You were a fighter pilot and you didn't have any experience running companies!"

"My father was a hot vice-president at GE."

"So fathers do have pull! I didn't say he should be top man! He won the Langford prize for his designs for a moon colony. That's something. He did better than forty other student engineers! You've never seen him work. When they assigned him to Saudi Arabia he just sat down and learned Arabic and he could already talk and read a little after only two weeks. How many Americans can do that?"

Charlie Bond mixed a little vodka and clam juice into his soup. "Maybe you're right." Soberly he thought about his daughter's goals. He knew she didn't really give a damn about space stations. What did she want? She wanted her husband out of Saudi Arabia.

It seemed unlikely to Charlie that Byron would ever be invited to join one of the space station design teams—but he *was* an extraordinary pilot and that suggested openings.

He cut himself some lamb. He chewed it.

NASA had been struggling to operate with only four of the Rockwell Orbiters, and now had only three. With Moscow moving into space in force, Charlie was willing to bet that many more spacecraft would be built, modified versions of the original machine. With normal production economies, ten space-craft could be had for hardly more than the price of a replacement for the ill-fated Challenger.

Pilots with Byron's expertise would be in demand. Too bad NASA didn't operate out of New Hampshire, but that wasn't something you could tell Junie.

"I'll see what I can do. Does your old man get a kiss?"

"Better than that. I'll name your grandson after you. Charlie Bond McDougall. How does that sound to you? You've waited long enough for a son." Not only did he have four daughters, his three grandchildren were girls. She paused for dramatic effect. "It *is* a son, you know. I had my baby tested." And she laughed. She knew how to reach her Daddy.

A son.

CHAPTER 4

Little Boy Blue Eyes, come blow your horn!
Sheep in the meadow, cows in the corn.
Pretty sweet mother sings in her dreams
Of a son's sketchpad, musical themes.
Little Boy Blue Eyes tends to his sheep
Under the haycock and fast asleep.
Father builds bridges for men to cross
Seeing his tall son rising to boss.
Little Boy Blue Eyes, wake up and fly!
For if they catch you, they'll surely cry.

MOTHER GOOSE

They named him Charlie "Bond" McDougall.

The son of Byron and Junie grew up in the years between the building of the Soviet Mirograd complex and the slow slogging return of the Americans to a serious space effort. He matured into an only child with thickly lashed blue eyes and shadow-dark hair who spent his youth escaping to the barns of his neighbors. Charlie's whole memory of life was of two giants. One of them was all of five feet two and ever there to boss him. The other stood ramrod straight, appearing only at irregular intervals to deliver orders that had to be executed on some strict schedule if Charlie didn't want to be driven crazy.

His mother shouted directly into his eardrum, yet the giant who flew down out of the sky was more terrible. On the ground his father's manner remained calm, but his grip on a little wrist was like iron and he could carry Charlie around by the hair. Mostly the fear-awe came from the quiet military voice demand-

20

ing obedience. Sassing died in a boy's throat. Any thoughts other than the one Big Byron wanted him to think got fragmented by a caution that overcame him every time he looked at that face. You could kick a cow but you didn't sass the Papa giant.

During those crucial years when most babies discover the first spark of individuality by playing with the power of the word "no", Charlie had been broken. "No" was a forbidden word that caused earthquakes and typhoons and sirens and lightning. "No" became a word he spoke only to himself. Obedience was easier. He knew there were other ways of doing things but they all seemed like horribly painful alternatives.

When circumstances left him with his maternal grandmother for weeks at a time, he began to perceive that his mother came from a long line of charming naggers who always got their way with men or boys. Gran'ma gave him candy canes and she was sweetly reasonable for about the time it took him to run back and forth across a room and tag each of the four walls—but after that it was *obedience* school for dogs.

Before he could talk Charlie had learned about fighter planes, tanks, rifles, spy satellites, and ICBM trolls living underground. He knew how to stand beside his bed for inspection by the time he was three. Yet he was four before he understood that his father was a third generation military man. That was the year he met his father's father. The most fascinating thing about visiting his white-haired grandfather McDougall, and watching that flintlock face, was to observe someone barking orders at Papa and watching *Papa* obey. Grandpa McDougall became Charlie's favorite man.

Mama wanted "sweet baby" to become the world's greatest violinist or maybe a dancer. So he learned to play the violin and to dance. Papa, who was a spaceman and away from a home a lot, wanted him to become the greatest space engineer who ever lived, the cutting edge of the Last Hope of Mankind. So he learned to play with computer toys and erector sets.

He hated the violin and he hated dancing and he hated space travel and he hated anything to do with the United States Air Force or aviation but he hated screaming mothers and "displeased" fathers even more. He loved his parents and did not even know that he was angry. Obeying was the only peace he had.

Still, while he became a fine violinist, his strings had a perpetual habit of snapping. He somehow never learned to replace them and it was always his exasperated mother who had to restring his instrument. He was invariably the best dancer in his class but he was always being thrown out of this academy or that school because of his incurably sly habit of peeking into the girl's dressing room over the plywood partition or of teasing ten year old ballerinas by pretending he hadn't pinched them under their tutus. Why anybody should make such a fuss, he didn't know—they didn't even have any breasts yet. And when he did sneak a look, they didn't even have any hair on their yummies.

For his father Charlie devised a different kind of torture to express his love. Though he dutifully slaved over his science and even tolerated the graduate students from the local college that his father hired to tutor him, he managed—without ever saying "no"—to avoid reading any science fiction. Slyly he understood that it was incredibly important to Papa that he be educated in the science fiction classics.

When his father gave him wonderful hardbacks with full color pictures of strange planets and heroes with ray guns, Charlie had the perfect way of saying something like, "Yeach! Haven't you got any good sex books with naked girls?" He knew how to look appealing enough not to get clouted. His father liked girls so it was safe to like them, too.

Once he very carefully let himself get caught reading a Doc Smith Lensman saga. But it was just a cover for some neat pictures of girl's yummies, real ones with hair—and he didn't get clouted for that either because they were his father's pictures, pickpocketed out of an old Air Force uniform, and Charlie knew enough about blackmail to stare his father down while allowing his mother a single quick glance.

There was the time Charlie, rummaging around in the attic, found a doll his father had bought as a present for his lovey-dovey Junie, carefully wrapped in plastic. It was a horrible bug-eyed monster with a battery-operated finger that glowed in the dark. Charlie had laughed for days when he discovered that his father still had a sentimental attachment to his doll and would not permit it to be hung up by its feet for the cat to play with. When Big Byron went back to space Charlie gave the creature to the neighbor's pigs, curious if they would eat batteries.

Later, when he was thirteen, Charlie even dared suggest to his father that science fiction wasn't really literature—how could it be when it substituted, with relentless predictability, bizarre plotting for sensitive intellectual content? He had just learned the words "intellectual" and "bizarre." But he only spoke that way at breakfast when his father was grumbling into his coffee, not yet in shape for an argument.

Mark Twain, Fitzgerald, Hemingway, Tolstoy, and Luke Short

were all delights. Charlie relished Shakespeare's camp mastery of cliche and Milton's ability to march through a whole universe, his sergeant beating out the same driving cadence. But Charlie put his foot down at even classical science fiction authors like Heinlein and Asimov and Silverberg and Herbert and Clarke. What a lot of silly crap. He used their works for bookends and as coasters to keep wet Coke bottles off his good furniture.

On Charlie's fourteenth birthday his father was away in Washington at a conference which meant that he was missing the final testing of the leoport he had spent *years* building. Charlie expected him to hop right back up there but when Junie started to run around the house, screaming, trying to get it cleaned up in time, he knew that the Papa man was coming home instead.

She *made* Charlie do some painting. He fumed. It was so exasperating! She gave him instructions for every brush stroke. The more instructions he got, the more stubbornly he remembered them all, obeying each one with fanatical care and attention. She could have left him alone in the sun on the grass for all the time it saved her.

Papa arrived home in a spiffy new airplane two days later. Charlie thought his father had forgotten his birthday and he sure wasn't going to mention it. But the old man came through that evening. They had a *child's* birthday cake with an icing of greenish sugar bunnies dancing around mint sugar circles embossed with stupid sayings. His mother gave him an expensive flute. He thanked her. His father produced a rare luxury hardbound copy of *Dune* with a genuine Frank Herbert signature on the frontispiece and the original John Schoenherr black and whites from *Analog* inside as well as color illustrations from the original movie. His father was all indignant that they had remade the movie, but Charlie, who had seen neither version, didn't care.

"You'll love it," said Byron McDougall hopefully.

"Hey Papa, that's a great gift. This evening I have some spare time and maybe I'll take a crack at it." When his father went out for a beer he rolled his eyes and ate a seasick bunny.

He'd heard about *Dune* at school—giant worms that burrowed underground at *fifty kloms an hour* and ate sand, converting it into oxygen without benefit of any known energy source; witches who controlled men with an inflected whip of words (like his mother); and drug freaks with solid blue eyes who tapped into the racial consciousness! The things his old man believed in! Any high school chemistry student with a knowledge of chemical kinetics could show on his computer that a worm two hundred meters long, discharging into the atmosphere as much oxygen as did ten square kilometers of green plant life, would have to be so red hot its proteins would char! Science fiction—Jesus!

That evening Byron peeked into his son's room on tip-toes to see how the first chapter of *Dune* was going, just as Charlie knew he would. Charlie was engrossed in the eighth module of Edmund Robert's *Differential Equations* from his half gigabyte math disk, setting up the ninth problem on the paralyzer, which was what the kids called their 64 node parallel processing computers.

"Have you had a chance to look at *Dune*?"

"Tomorrow. I got myself hung up on the breaking mode of long cylinders and I don't want to sleep on it." Years later, *Dune* was still on his shelf, unopened.

But his father got even. He said he had been in space too long and was getting flabby. He needed some exercise. He suggested a hike through the Green Mountains. He suggested it with the quiet military authority that told Charlie there was no getting out of going with him—but it sounded like fun. Summer was *boring*. Nothing to do but chase the pigs and practice the violin and learn differential equations and read Shakespeare.

He didn't realize then that the old man had in mind a three day, off-trail, hundred-mile forced march through the mountains with backpack. For the first thirty miles he was too occupied with surviving to notice that his body was falling apart. But at the end of the first day's march, stuffed in his sleeping bag, half roasting, half freezing in the mountain air, unable to tell whether he was dying because of the march or because of the lumps he was sleeping on, he knew he was going to have to think about how to get out of the next two days. He slept instead.

The dawn was coming through the leaves and the trees rose around him like stakes in a pitfall. His head was pillowed against a rock and his father's boot toe was gently rocking him awake. He opened his eyes and stared at a grinning face. "Come on. Let's go. I'm dying, too, but I'm not a sissy."

Could a boy so young regret his whole life? Charlie dreamed with his eyes hammered by the greens of dawn . . . wouldn't it be nice if this Byron monster were back in Saudi Arabia . . . that somehow, unborn, unburdened with the name of Charlie Jr., he was still a soul floating above the pastures of New England, mercifully legless, bent upon the quest of finding parents, testing this pregnant belly and fondling that one as it pushed a supermarket cart, evaluating, measuring, taking the utmost care to place himself. How foolish the youth of the nation were in their choices! Anything, anything but this Byron monster from outer space for a Daddy.

But it was too late. His father didn't disappear back to the Middle East. Charlie was trapped in this aching body, and Big Byron lifted him up by the hair and set him on his feet.

CHAPTER 5

PARIS—The Soviet Trade Representative to France and his chauffeur were blown up and killed by a radio-detonated land mine three blocks from their Paris residence during the early morning rush hour in an attack which wounded the new Soviet military attache. An unidentified cell of the Afghan Jihad claimed that the attack was in retaliation for a recent atrocity bombing south of Herat by the Red Air Force which itself was a reprisal for the assassination of eight high-ranking Soviet Army officers in Herat last February. Diplomatic sources in Kabul have reported that the Soviets' revenge raid killed at least two hundred Afghan civilians and wounded hundreds more.

"Al Hussein Ben Ali Street. The Holiday Inn," Byron McDougall told his tiny brown cab driver at the Amman airport.

The man smiled, all friendliness. "You from USA? Holiday Inn nice place. Was at Holiday Inn, Las Vegas once. Nice girls in show. Half nude. Comedian told us 'Check-em out.' He pinch one on bottom. She yelp." He grinned a golden smile.

Byron smiled with the cabbie, a sudden sexual craving telling him that he missed his Junie for all her complaining. Even if she never let him pinch her buttocks, she liked him to hold their round softness in his hands and squeeze while she moaned. The cab's suspension was shot, the seat uncomfortable, hot. He hoped Junie's pregnancy had been proceeding smoothly and, for a moment, wondered what it would be like to have an adoring child underfoot. But the bumps and the far moon in the sky of Amman distracted his eye.

What a peaceful world up there compared with the Middle East. But it was desolate, like the desert here. *They'll probably have to use Bedouin as lunar colonists.* Now that was a sobering thought. He tried to imagine the austere paper-mache and cardboard moon-colonies he'd built as a boy peopled by these self-reliant nomads who had no use for more baggage than they could carry with them.

Byron took a room on the ninth floor overlooking the street, slept five hours, and was out seriously exploring by dawn, camera over his shoulder, film in his pocket. The seven hills of Amman seemed to be carved into miniature stone houses, every crag holding a stunted tree. The colors were pastel—russet, dull blue, creamy gray. Rains had called out periwinkles and daisies from the cracks of a wall.

In among the newer city he found Greek ruins, a Roman theater, and a Roman fortress built atop an older fortification, Byzantine floors, churches built over temples, mosques built upon churches, an Umayyad castle—layer after layer—rock worshippers, pagans, Jews, Greeks, Romans, Nabateans, Christians, heathens, Moslems, Circassians, Turks, Bedouin, blacks left over from the Nubian slave trade, Palestinian lawyers, a British newspaper—and the Holiday Inn. The minarets of the occasional mosque seemed strangely out of place, as if Mohammed had never quite conquered Amman.

Eventually Byron noticed his stomach—*Ana ju'an*, he thought in Arabic—and slipped into a bright unassuming restaurant run by a Lebanese refugee from Beirut on a street that zig-zagged up one of Amman's hills.

His waitress ignored him. It was too late for the morning's *ftoor* and too early for the cook to have prepared *ghada*, not yet being noon. But he was in no hurry and enjoyed watching her. She was listening avidly to her Japanese hand-held radio. There was nothing unusual on the news. Some Afghan refugees in Paris had just blown up and killed some Soviet apparatchik in France and his chauffeur, badly wounding a military attache. Experience at killing Russians in Kabul was coming in handy.

The Soviets were building noble mansions in space with one hand and liquidating peasants on Earth with the other.

Byron caught the girl's eye, indicating coffee with Arabic hand gestures. She filled a cup and hurried over, smiling, apologizing that it was too early for lunch. He complimented the restaurant with his best Arabic flattery and said he was willing to wait for the heavenly *musakhan* which he had heard so much about from all their delighted clients. She giggled at his accent.

"Did I speak that right?" he asked in Arabic.

"You say well," she replied in English.

He tried to talk to her about the news from Paris but she was too shy. "Islam is one," was her only comment before she slipped away to the kitchen.

A noble slogan. He wondered how she really felt about the brutal Afghan war. Probably nothing. Given eight carnivorous Moslem groups in Lebanon, given two Christian groups who hated each other, given Syrians who were subsidizing Russian atrocities in Afghanistan with money sent to Moscow to buy arms to kill Lebanese, given angry Jews, given various assorted expeditionary forces—none of these groups knowing anything about negotiation—her family had probably been too over-whelmed by their decade old civil war to have much feeling for other far-away Moslems who were also being murdered.

Islam was *not* one, and Allah made them suffer for it.

The sudden news of the assassinations in Paris had brought on an inner rage that sometimes attacked McDougall. This Afghan war had been going on interminably since seventy-nine, far longer than the Second World War in defiance of all socialist principles of compassion and concern for peasant and working man. The war benefitted no one but the Soviet aristocracy, and in the end, as they lay in their own blood on a Paris street, not even them.

In the doorway a gangly American girl was staring at him. She was over six feet tall, dressed in faded blue shirt and jeans and cowboy boots with a band about her forehead pinned by Amman silver wrought in the Crusader style. As soon as he looked at her she pretended she wasn't staring and left to stand outside the window. Once she came back in, watched him eating his *musakhan*, and ambled back outside.

She was still out there when he finished lunch and she was still looking in and watching him so he half-decided to try his hand at picking her up. That required an "entrance." He stood in the doorway, on the stair so that he would be taller than she, not looking at her directly, but pretending to be letting his eyes adjust to the sun.

"Fishhook in your mouth, Yank?" She was smiling, and she had pretty buckteeth.

The accent was West Texas. He was surprised. He would have guessed Maine with the Bean Emporium mail order boots. "You cast a long fly for a Texas gal."

"Ah'm good at angling dry gulches. You're friendly for a Yank. Here Ah've wasted an hour screwing up my courage to speak to you and you don't even seem formidable."

"How did you know I was a Yank?"

"Your shoes, Shorty, as foot pinching as would please any Yankee banker. If you hadn't looked like such a rug-skinned Yank Ah would've had less compunctions about speaking to you. Can Ah borrow five clams?"

"And here I thought you wanted me for my body."

"Shorty, two of you might interest me—one of them sitting on the other's shoulders. Right now Ah'd settle for the one with the wallet."

"A woman in distress, far from home."

"If Ah were, Ah might fall for your blue eyes and dark hair." She smiled in a way to make him forget she was gangly and boney of face. "But for truth Ah'm just having one of those days when all don't go like it should. Ah can't even find an American man who has a five spot to spare—on top of my luggage being lost and my hotel never having heard of me." Her eyes flashed like the sun off quartz. "And the American Express office had a fire last night! If you don't have five dollars for a desperate girl, do you have a car?"

"I'm about to rent one."

"You're in luck. You're going my way." She took his arm.

So Byron found himself driving bumpily over pebbles outside Amman to an archaeological dig that was laying a trench across an eight thousand year old village. Amanda knew the whole staff and soon the director was making polite calls on her behalf over the field telephone to try to locate her belongings.

Sometime during the dawn of agriculture, the village had been destroyed by fire. You could see it in the final layer. Raiding? Carelessness? Violence? War? Who had died and who had survived?

He stayed for a supper of rice and stew cooked on a Coleman stove. Amanda told him where to go in Jordan and what to see. He tried to seduce her by asking her about herself, but it didn't work—instead of being flattered, instead of becoming vulnerable, she brought out photographs that, by Coleman lantern, looked like the undulations of ordinary desert. It was a "mound," she said, "her mound," and she was sure there was a village under it, maybe even a city. A person with trained eyes could tell. Her eyes glowed.

The average life of a city, she said, was from 300 to 700 years. Then, disappearing from the face of the earth, it fell victim of the same processes that embedded fossils in sedimentary rock. Cities like Beirut were built by men and doomed by men. Cities came and they went. On the Day of Judgment, she rattled on, when the earth opened up at God's command, thousands of marvelous cities would appear and come to life before God snuffed them out again. Oh, to be alive on the Day of Judgment when the cobblers and tailors and craftsmen, priests, and slaves, boiled from the earth to fill the temples and bazaars, to man the walls!

While she talked, Byron lazily imagined old Samarkand, devastated by the Genghis Khan, filling again with independent traders, and—not far away—the villages of Afghanistan, utterly destroyed by the Red Air Force, each rising from its rubble with a thriving marketplace, silks, and children, and busy farmers. He liked a woman who could fill his mind with such pictures.

She disappeared into the tent to bring out sleeping bags. When she became silent, and when he had nothing to add to her whimsy, they listened to the chirping desert noises lying on their backs under the stars. "What do the Soviets call their space city?" she asked in her pleasant drawl.

"It's hardly a city. Just a couple of modules and maybe within the year—maybe—the staff will increase to twelve men."

She took his hand. "But that's the way all cities begin."

"They call it Mir," said Byron. "All the papers say that means peace, but it's the old Russian name for a stockaded commune. Defended-fort and peace are the same words in Russian."

"When it dies, how long will it stay in the sky?"

"At that altitude? Maybe 300, maybe 700 years."

"You see!" she said.

He laughed.

"They'll build cities higher up, won't they?"

"Yeah."

"One of those might last itself as a ruin for eight thousand years, like our little village here in Jordan. That would be a dream for an archaeologist," she sighed.

"You have a long term view!"

"Jordan humbles a little ole Texas girl. What's San Antonio? American cities all sprang up at about the same time." She laughed with her flashing buckteeth. "They're due to disappear. Boom!"

"Boom! Just like that. You're one of the pessimists, eh?"

"No, I'm not. I'm an optimist. The Black Plague came and killed half the population of Europe. We were the survivors and do we remember that the dying claimed that the world was ending by God's Wrath? We buried them and went on building cities because survivors are all incurable optimists. We survived didn't we? The dead aren't around to caution us. So what's an atomic war? There'll be new cities and new peoples and the archaeologists will have a marvelous radioactive layer to date cultures by. Ah just envies them. It's all the same in two thousand years. Don't tell me it would be any worse than the holocaust was to the Jews or the Mongol Hordes were to Islam."

Lost at night in the country outside Amman, relaxing with a woman whose elan he instinctively understood, with the dust and the breeze and the smell of spring, the death of cities seemed very remote—but violence always seems remote between crises. Those who take pleasure in building palaces where none exist never anticipate destruction.

"And who will be around to build the new cities after a nuclear war?" he asked.

"The spacefaring Russians. They just built Mir, remember? They aren't going to stop there. They'll be on the moon and Mars when the war comes. The Russians in Moscow will die, but the other Russians won't. God, imagine being on Mars a hundred thousand years from now and digging up the first Soviet colonies. What would we find? Maybe a central Cultural Palace. Certainly busts of Lenin!"

CHAPTER 6

Supreme excellence in warfare consists of subduing the enemy without fighting.

SUN TZU, *THE ART OF WAR*

The converted Russian Orthodox Cathedral stood alone among the trees and the stream and grass, and if you approached it from the right angle the parking lot was invisible. It was built tall, on the floor plan of a stubby cross, each face rising on four thin columns for six generous stories, there to flower into precisely three circular arches. For many years it had served as a warehouse, and for many more it had been abandoned. Now its five cupolas gleamed, the stonework had been carefully restored, the grass mowed, the bushes tended.

Rebuilt inside, the Cathedral housed offices and libraries, conference and training rooms designed for a special kind of bureaucrat. A secretary waited in front of the elevator. She watched the whole Soviet delegation to the disarmament talks walk out of the main conference hall en masse, heading for the alcove where there was a spread of cakes and a pot of coffee, grumbling among themselves that further discussion with the United States delegation was useless.

The chief Soviet delegate poured coffee into a fine china cup and added sugar, then cream from an elegant stainless steel pitcher. He paused a moment before slipping a small slice of black-forest cake onto his saucer. He spoke in English. "The American proposal was as fine a compromise between the opposing positions of the State Department and the Pentagon as I've ever heard!" he muttered wryly.

"Did you see the lackey's face when we walked out?" grinned the associate.

The Chief Soviet delegate made a spastic motion of dismissal. He was handsome enough to be a model for men's clothing—as long as he didn't move. His walking and his arm motions, even the way he tilted his head when he thought, had an alien rhythm that suggested either mild brain damage or a person whose attention was so immersed in his thoughts that little was left over to control the body. "Actually I got us the hell out of there because I noticed he had eight more pages of that stuff still to deliver! Probably spent all night writing it! I hear Sam Brontz hired him fresh out of Harvard."

"It's getting too brainy for me around here," grumbled another delegate. "I feel intimidated."

"I'll have forged papers from the Moscow Institute of International Relations ready for you tomorrow."

"Hey, with a grin like that, Limon, you'll never be mistaken for a Russian."

"Grins are the new party line," snarled Limon Barnes.

"Crunch! you're having everybody for breakfast today!"

"Brontz is driving in to put me on the griddle this afternoon. I'm missing something in all this arms reduction talk simulation— it's not going well—God, it is as bad as the real thing. I need some time to think. We'll let our Harvard friend sweat it out for a while through diplomatic channels. Tass can say some horrible things about him." He paused, frowning. "Why don't we just confuse the hell out of him? We could have the KGB pick him up for overnight questioning about eleven tonight. How about it? We're short on simulation training for our KGB agents."

"Sure. I can have a *Lavrenti Beria* team ready by eleven. We'll work Harvard over all night in relays. How about a slander-against-the-Soviet-State charge? Nothing too heavy the first time. Just a warm up."

"Fine," said Limon.

"I hope Brontz didn't forget to tell the boy he doesn't have a nine-to-five job."

Limon enjoyed his little walks through the somber church and down the circular stairway into the library where he kept his office. It was such a preposterous idea, this assumption that one can train an American to think like a Russian—but twenty times as fast. Perhaps it was all illusion; certainly it was fun.

The Russian Orthodox Cathedral of Massachusetts, at the time of its greatest need, had been taken over by the industrial training firm of Stephens, Matthews, and Bennet who were looking for a large country home in which to run their world famous negotiation seminars. Bought out by Sam Brontz for the

Shantech Conglomerate, and converted into a Soviet studies institute, all of SMB soon fell under the rubric of "those guys at the Cathedral of Saint Marx the Benefactor."

Matthews was still on the Board and still directed the negotiations study group, but Brontz had elevated twenty-three year old Limon Barnes to the command of the game simulations, much to Limon's astonishment. He had never expected to find a man in high capitalist circles who could appreciate him. He supposed that he should have. Hadn't kings always chosen their jokers with the same care used to select a mistress?

Limon was an unlikely choice and his first invitation to the formal dinner table of Sam Brontz had unnerved him. He had grown up with strange people, fat boys and skinny boys and misfits, and no girls. He had had a very good social life playing games in neighborhood basements but it was never a normal social life. It had certainly not included girls like Linda Brontz, born to make men feel awkward. And it had certainly not included crazy old men like Sam Brontz who panicked if he spilled gravy on his tie.

Daughter Linda had never heard of Dungeons & Dragons and he made a terrible mistake to allude to it while passing her the celery—Limon had grown up playing D & D and tended to talk about it too much. She asked him if he had ever read Fitzgerald. Of course he had read Fitzgerald—he just couldn't remember any!

It was more fun being a bishop in the Society for Creative Anachronism and disappearing annually to the wars in Pennsylvania where the losing side of armored warriors, having been disposed of by bribery, noble combat, or perfidious chicanery, was always awarded Pittsburg. But how could he tell her about that? She had never even been to Boskone—and she lived in Boston! She didn't even know that Boskone was a science fiction convention named after an evil empire of Doc Smith's Lensmen series.

Brontz's daughter wrote on a *typewriter* which she half-smilingly hinted had once been owned by James Michener. Limon had skipped typewriters, breaking his word processing teeth on Electric Pencil after having scrounged one of the first CP/M computers out of his allowance money. She was still *getting* allowance money. By the time he was eighteen he had already made his first half-a-million dollars in the games business, a feat which allowed him to retire from the real world for a month or so before being trapped by Brontz and forced to eat roast beef and cranberry sauce and chat with a girl.

Barnes never liked to talk much except when he was playing games or designing them. His first conversation of substance with Sam Brontz, after many strange initial trials, was about a game Sam wanted to create. Even then they couldn't understand each other.

Limon was a Fantasy Freak. His idea of a good game was to sneak off from battle on a moonlit night and go skinny-dipping without his chain mail in the company of a bunch of tree worshippers.

Sam, on the other hand, thought of games as *simulations* of reality. Unlike Limon, Sam had nothing against living in reality—it was just that simulations of reality were cheaper. Think of where Hitler would be now if his generals had learned to master the rules of the Apple II games, Eastern Front and Stalingrad. So far as Limon could figure out, Sam wanted a game to teach Americans how to win while playing Nuclear Face-off. Why he wanted such a game, Limon did not know. He had never learned to understand his boss. So far as he could tell, Sam didn't even think of the Russians as the major obstacle— the Soviets were just a monster guarding a room on the way to gold in the caves below.

Limon brought down from his office shelf the apparatus of his new board game, *Face-off*, and laid it out over his desk a bit nervously. It didn't look like much but it was the first real product his group had been able to get out that played well. This was the eighth version and there were no bugs left. He was particularly proud of the unique way the game assigned character attributes, the simple style of starting play, and the very complex level of master play. He felt he could defend it.

His intercom screen went on and one of the other secretaries rushed in to tell him Sam had arrived, but when she turned to rush out again, bumped into Sam who wasn't bothering to wait on protocol.

"Well, Limon," he said, and Limon knew instantly that he had a disaster on his hands. Sam was wearing his look of stern affability. A silk scarf protected his neck, he had on walking shoes and a pedometer at his belt. "My doctor is into making me exercise, so I thought I'd take you off for a walk in the woods for our little man-to-man talk."

Man-to-man talk! Jesus! thought Limon.

In the woods they conversed about orioles. That reminded Sam of a story about fighting blackbirds. Limon said nothing, moving with the kind of spastic walk that overtook him in moments of stress.

"Your game is a nice game," said Sam. He paused.

Limon cringed. The old Brontz gun was out and aimed. *Shoot! Shoot!*

"However, Shantech is not Parker Brothers," Sam paused again.

I can't stand it! thought Limon. "Okay, I resign."

Sam looked at the young man disapprovingly. "You'll be given a few more months to do a better job. I have complete faith in your ability to come up with what we need. Let me explain myself *again* to you."

"The game plays, sir," said Limon, cringing as he heard himself speak that final word of deference.

"Of course it plays. Linda and I had a great time with it last night. Unfortunately *entertainment* isn't our goal. This is the real world, Limon. Like it or not, you're stuck in it."

"I've managed to avoid it successfully."

"You *can't* avoid it. The United States and the Soviet Union are at war. If you have been watching violence on TV for as long as you can remember, you don't realize that fact; your generation no longer understands anything about violence. The bombs aren't going off—we are still alive—so naturally this must be the peace."

"No board game is going to change anything, sir."

"Sonofabitch, I didn't ask you for a board game! Do you understand bureaucracies? Those men running the American and Soviet missile centers are the finest we have. They damn well better be. Our chosen defense policy doesn't allow for a single mistake on either side. But bureaucracies age—as our mutual boss, Charles Bond, likes to remind us. Competence inexorably erodes. One hundred years after France produced Napoleon, it produced the generals who fought the First World War. The competence of the Soviet and American missile commands is *temporary*." A single unmanaged flaw in the implementation of *Mutually Assured Destruction* assures our mutual destruction. Such a defense policy is totally unacceptable."

"Matthews makes a very good case when he says that the Soviets don't have the negotiating skills to change."

"Nonsense! Why are *you* in charge of my operation here and not Matthews? We can *force* the Soviets to alter their defense policy. It's a game. Force. That's what I'm selling, Limon. *Force!* Not negotiation."

"Force?"

"Force! And I'm not suggesting anything genteel like checkmate. I'm talking about ramming my fist into the board and scattering the pieces like shrapnel."

"It's an approach which might make the generals in the Urals just a mite nervous, sir."

"Up the generals in the Urals. A coward who demonstrates to the world his bravery by shooting at peasants from inside his tank, as in Afghanistan, is always a nervous wreck—just like we were in Vietnam. You didn't understand me when I spoke of force. Did I say nuke the Soviets? You use *force* to dig up a weed but you don't *nuke* it. What kind of force would the Soviets accept? Think."

"They're not going to accept any kind of force, sir. It goes with the paranoia."

"Wrong. A while ago they were refusing to negotiate, confident behind their superior nuclear armada. Since then SDI research has located grave vulnerabilities in their strike force and they've changed radically—they are now proposing the complete abolition of nuclear weapons and to the last Russian they think it is their idea. We can force them into a defense policy that has a fail-safe mode, especially if we continue to make them feel that it is their idea, but especially if it *is* a real defense."

"How?"

"How the hell should I know? That's what I'm hiring you to find out for me—and you give me a board game!"

"You want me to set up a role-playing game that recreates the mind of a Soviet decision-maker so that Shantech can learn how to direct it?"

"Exactly."

"I resign."

"The losers of the war in Pennsylvania get Pittsburg, remember?" said a smiling Sam as he encouragingly slapped young Limon on the back.

CHAPTER 7

Though one skilled in war can arrange to protect his people from attack, he cannot cause an enemy encampment to become vulnerable. Defense is the art of protecting what you have. But victory is won by attack. Therefore the skillful commander takes up a position from which he cannot be defeated and attacks only when his enemy makes himself vulnerable.

SUN TZU, THE ART OF WAR

From a distance and to the left, too far away to be a part of the conversation and too near to be wholly out of it, the stranger watched the physicist and his student in argument. Sam Brontz had never met the legendary Synmann before.

Joseph Synmann was doodling a mushroom cloud in the shape of the green-capped Amanita phalloides, his eyes downcast inside balding hair that dribbled to his shoulders like a waterfall in August. He was listening, not happily, to this graduate student expound, all the while studiously drawing tiny faces at the base of his mushroom sketch—cartoon Japanese faces with slant eyes—until the exact moment of impatience when his doodle ran out of yellow paper. He interrupted the boy's speech so suddenly that his lawn chair wobbled in protest.

"Unfortunately we are *not* rational!" Synmann could not stand sophistry—and he so classified an argument that demanded man's rational nature to overcome man's irrationality. Man was either rational or he was not.

"If we are not rational, then how do we build bridges?" asked the student.

"Building bridges is your definition of rational?"

"Yes."

"All right; let me accept your definition and we'll work from

38

there. Then 'rational' in the sense that you have been using the word is too restricted. Bridges get built because of logical process—but they also get built because of things like graft . . . curiosity . . . men impressing their mistresses . . . greed . . . you name it. Men are never *just* logical. They've been known to blow up the bridges they build!"

"Jesus! you run off on tangents when I'm trying to make a point! I'm talking about the creative-constructive thing in man. It can conquer the demented things he does if we educate and encourage it!"

"Bullshit! You're assuming that rationality is something akin to mathematical logic."

"It is."

"It is not. We are rational—your definition—we are able to build bridges—*only* because we have the daily capacity to deal with self-generated inconsistencies that would immobilize the best system of logic known to science. Logic can't handle inconsistency; humans can. Humans can transcend the best logician."

"Don't get supernatural on me!"

"Supernatural? Ask the artificial intelligence people what happens when you try to build a thinking machine that is confined to the axioms of mathematical logic! The damn things don't have basic common sense!"

"Humans are *destroyed* by their inconsistency!"

"No. It is logic that is destroyed by inconsistency in its basic axioms; humans apparently *thrive* on inconsistency. But we pay a price for being at home with our inconsistencies. The price we pay is that we are fools, which is what you are objecting to. The reward is that we sometimes transcend the bureaucratic mind which is rigidly logical in the very sense you so admire." Synmann snorted, and his long hair flew away from his head like from an explosion. "You can't equate logic with creativity. Logic is only *one* of the tools that a creative person uses."

He now noticed that his unwanted guest from Shantech was listening in on the argument, evaluating, appraising. Sam Brontz would have to be dealt with—but not before the barbecue. Joseph Synmann turned to Brontz, politely.

"We are arguing about the rationality of holding a knife to the throat of a neighbor's young daughter to protect ours, while the neighbor is holding a knife to the throat of our daughter to protect his. My young university friend maintains that since we are rational we *must* notice the irrationality of our act and thereby cease being irrational"—his voice was now sweet with sarcasm—"since no consciously rational beings have ever been knowingly caught in an irrational act—at least not since the discovery of LSD and pot."

"Oh, father," said a nearby young woman who was mixing the salad on the lawn table, "nobody is holding a knife to *my* throat. Now why don't you behave and leave Darryl alone."

"We were discussing the *arms* race—not your lily white throat," said a miffed Darryl.

"The arms race? Well, that's one way of putting it," muttered Synmann. "I thought we were discussing how many angels in skull-masks might dance in front of a nuclear power plant to end war for all time."

"I don't believe we've met," said Darryl deferentially, holding out his hand to Sam Brontz.

Synmann took the opportunity to introduce them. "Sam is an arms merchant who wants to buy my company for Charlie Bond's group."

Darryl recoiled. The daughter stopped beheading tomatoes in mid-motion. "Father! You aren't going to sell your company to a *defense contractor*! You're a hippy!"

Before Sam Brontz could protest, a smiling Joseph led him over to the barbecue pit. "I like to needle the little buggers," he whispered. "What other pleasures do I have?"

"Inch-thick steaks," said Brontz, mesmerized by the tray in front of him.

"It pays to have a wife whose father was a German butcher. By their glow the coals look about ready." He laid the grill in place across the bricks. "So why is Mr. Bond sending you around? Are you his chief enforcer?"

"Charlie didn't send me. I'm playing empire-builder all on my own. That saves him time."

"I was wondering how rough the play gets if I don't like your offer?"

"There has been no offer. Most of my hunches don't pay off, Dr. Synmann. We look at many companies for every one we buy."

"Good. I hope that means I'm safe."

"Your company as it stands today is a very bad buy. You will be making *us* an offer."

"Like hell I will!"

"*You* will have to make the offer because *we* won't. Bond never, never gets involved in a hostile take-over. He thinks a hostile take-over makes for bad business. It does. *All* of the conglomorates built by hostile take-overs are in trouble."

"So you want me to make you an offer, eh?" Synmann

grinned. "You could put your whole cash flow at my disposal. How's that?"

"Unreasonable. We like to think of ourselves as a mutual self-help society. We provide you with those necessities that you are too small to provide for yourself, and you provide us with those things which we are too big to understand. What are you offering for our cash flow?"

"I'm a good cook."

"Make mine rare."

"Then you'll have to wait. I start the well-dones first. Who's for well-done! Darryl?"

"Yeah."

"How many mediums?"

Four hands went up and he began to lay out the steaks over the heat. "There has to be an angle, Brontz."

"There is."

"I did some fast homework on Shantech last night—and accelerators, super-conductivity, proton-busters, maglev trains and the like don't seem to be your line."

"We sub-contracted for you on the Ohio job."

"You know what I mean. The angle."

"Charlie Bond likes brains. That's what he buys and that's why he's been successful. I do his technical staff evaluations. I'm good. I know it would take a hundred men to replace the five of you. None of you know a damn thing about running a company but technically . . . well, I'm amazed."

"Specialized brains don't help your bottom line when the bottom has dropped out of your line."

"Change your line. There's been some big changes in defense policy. Men like you are in demand."

"Yeah. The Air Force is taking on the National Guard about bolt-thread pitch standards. Yeah, yeah. I'm not interested."

"I'm talking about SDI and you know it. General Hanson gave me your name."

"So he put you onto me, eh? Yeah, I talked to him. Don't forget that was after my LTSM fiasco. I thought we were going under and I was a little bit wild in the head. I was overselling an idea—trying to cash in on the ICBM killer craze."

"You sold General Hanson."

"He's not a physicist."

"He's a cracker-jack engineer."

"Generals slurp in the trough of every super-idea they can stick their muzzles into. This one's a Crazy Eddie. I was out of my gourd."

"Then you're one of those who don't think we are bright enough to defend ourselves against ICBMs?"

One by one, Synmann turned the steaks over with a vicious flip. Fireballs leaped upward around the sudden fat drippings. "*Of course* we can defend ourselves against ICBMs! When Washington developed the Mutually Assured Destruction strategy—was that back in the fifties?—there wasn't any way to knock out a rocket. Yesterday's technology supports yesterday's thinking. And, *of course*, there are bureaucrats trained in MAD who can't make the effort to think any other way. Today it's a new game. Jesus, did you see that latest infra-red detector with silicon brains?"

"Then you have faith that a defense is possible—but no faith in your own idea?"

"I'm a super-rational man," grumbled Synmann laconically. "Many things are possible—even my own brainstorms—it's the inevitable cycle of countermeasures that discourages me. Take medieval chain mail. It was defeated with a better projectile. And then they built better armor. But somebody noticed that the armor was so heavy that a pikeman could pull a knight off his horse and slaughter the helpless man inside. Only after many innovative cycles did armor become obsolete." He sighed. "How many iterations of technical perfection do we have to go through before nuclear weapons become obsolete? I don't know. What's in this racket for you? More money?"

"You'll find that you and I have more in common than you think," said Brontz. "I know your position on defense."

"I doubt it." Synmann was growing hostile. "My position is very straightforward and very unpopular with both sides. I believe in being armed to the teeth but I'm also one of the active detractors of a defense strategy whose failure mode creates dust clouds that . . ."

". . . will cause a fimbulwinter," quoted Brontz. "I read your paper. I quote it all the time. I loved it."

In Norse mythology the gods, with the last remnants of mankind, are doomed to die at Ragnarok after three years of a sunless fimbulwinter brought on by wickedness and bitter warfare.

Later that evening, the Shantech man examined a model of a battlestation that hung from a thread in Dr. Synmann's psychedelic study. Toothpicks formed both the barrel and the mirror mount that were slung below a band-aid box which supported plastic perfume bottles serving as fuel-tanks and supply modules for the two-man crew, all appropriately sprayed mauve and yellow to match the rest of the room.

The papers on the desk overflowed onto the floor, and three computers were stacked on top of each other, the lower one no longer used. Pieces of a homemade mass-driver hung from the ceiling beside an extensive collection of Ukranian Easter eggs. The startlingly large winding of an unused electromagnet provided a stool to reach the upper layers of the bookshelf.

Since all the chairs were filled with floppies and open books and various journals—one of them so full that it was topped by a dictionary to keep the papers and disks from sliding away— Synmann sat on the floor to open out his drawings. He extracted a file from between two magazines and opened that, too.

"You've got to know before we start, that this is all just back-of-the-envelope crap. We're ready for a real study, of course, and it looks good. It's not tomorrow's weapon."

After only a moment's hesitation, Brontz joined the long-haired physicist on the floor, tucking up his trousers carefully so they wouldn't crease. General Hanson had told him that just looking at the stuff would knock his socks off.

CHAPTER 8

How lonely sits the city once so full of people!
None come to the appointed feasts,
All her gates are desolate and
Her maidens have been dragged away.

The enemy has stretched out his hands
Over all her precious things.
He has destroyed the palaces;
Laid in ruins the strongholds.

Hear how I groan; there is none to comfort me—
The Lord has trodden, as in a wine press,
The virgin daughters of the city,
Crushed the young men.

My priests and elders perished in the city
Seeking food to revive their strength.
Infants and babes faint in the streets of the city
And my eyes are spent with weeping.

Is this nothing to you, all you who pass by?
Look and see: Is any sorrow like my sorrow
Which the Lord has inflicted
On His day of fierce anger?

Vast as the sea is the ruin;
The gates have sunk into the ground;
The law is no more.
Who can restore our city?

THE LAMENTATIONS OF JEREMIAH

Byron's rented Toyota lacked a digital clock on its glowing dashboard—and so the seasons and the century had to be read, instead, from signs along the route. Behind a truck loaded with refrigerators, and thus, he supposed, still somewhere in the twentieth century, he drove into the mountains through vineyards, spring wheat, neat slopes of olive trees. Fragments and eddies of other times kept tempting him off the highway. Once for a giddy moment, when a herd of goats crossed the road, he was lost even as to which millennium he travelled. But the *place* he was always sure of—that was constant—this was Gilead.

He drifted. A hundred years spanned one valley and a thousand the next. He saw a horseback-mounted crusader riding rapidly along a ridge ahead of the dust cloud raised by frantic hooves, perhaps a scout for King Baldwin on his reprisal raid against Toghtekin. A Moslem troop laid out camp in the shelter of a great outcropping of rock. Deeper in the past he found a refugee band of Jews of the Christian schism who had fled from the Roman sack of Jerusalem and now, safely beyond the Jordan in the lands of the Decapolis, gazed back at their lost homeland.

And then, beyond Hadrian's triple-arched gateway, overlooking the ruins of Jerash, he came across a twentieth century outpost of the Time Patrol. A young policeman, disguised as a Jordanian, was on duty selling tickets for a nearby Sound and Light Show Festival as well as tickets for various Time Tours. Twentieth century ceramic urinals were available for free beyond hydraulic doors that closed automatically.

Here the armies of Alexander the Great camped and pissed before founding the city of Jerash about 332 BC where it thrived as a member of the Hellenistic explosion, prospered under the Roman occupation, survived the Jewish rebellions—until a shifting of trade-routes reduced its vigor. Declining, the city was mortally wounded by the Persian and Arab invasions, and finally died during an assault by crusaders, to be claimed by the sand and abandoned for eight hundred years. In 1878 a small colony of refugees fleeing from Russian imperialism began a new cycle beside the mound of the old.

Byron wandered through the marble columns of the Roman ruins but his feet did not feel the bleached flagstones and he stared blankly at the Byzantine churches, not seeing the past with its ghosts of traders and caravans, not seeing the Saudi tourists all about him, or the Italian tour group, or the British couple who were paying to be enlightened. Time-winds had taken possession of his soul.

He was seeing the future.

In a mesmerized trance he was transported from the ruins of Jerash to the ruins of the Washington D.C. of a millennium hence—a city vandalized, its roofs fallen in, its cellars buried under silt and dust, some of its buildings partially restored. Who were those shimmer-coated tourists who poked about curiously and from where did they come? What was that building which had lost its dome? and who the headless man gazing out over the city from his weathered chair?

It was a strange and alien future—frightening even. Byron tried to fight his way back into Gilead, tried to remember that he was standing in front of the ruined Temple of the Moon Goddess, surrounded by the power of the patroness of Jerash.

Artemis! he cried.

But she did not come to rescue him. Her century was gone and the twentieth century, where whisps of her pull remained in old stone columns, was itself as remote as fragile silk to the travelling mind of Byron. Then he found that his body was not in Jerash . . .

. . . but was slogging over the dunes of empty Riyadh half-a-thousand years after the oil was gone. An erratic breeze sifted sand through weathered concrete high-rises, sometimes burying and sometimes uncovering the marching white arches of the airfield. It howled through unused places, patiently polishing the museum pieces left in its trust. Two small brown archaeologists, hunched over collection trays, were measuring their find of Pepsi bottles, distraught because they had no theory to explain why the old Coke culture had not penetrated this far into the desert. He tried to tell them but he had no voice.

The future and the past.

Dizzyingly the sun rose in the west and set in the east, releasing him from the future. The sun had an alliance with the moon. He staggered away from the Temple of Artemis, back to the ceramic urinals of the time-station at Jerash, staggered out to the parking lot and his machine. He put the key in the lock and turned on the motor. It hummed. The sun flickered three-hundred thousand times.

After an eternal journey, after missing his target twice and circling through back roads, the crusader's fortress at Kerak appeared, majestically perched like a crown on the hilltop high above the sloping Dead Sea Valley. He hid his Toyota behind an outcropping of reddish rock and thought for a moment before changing into an appropriate persona. An air force officer in these times when only Satan could fly would be highly suspect. And so he entered the walled town like any foot soldier, greeting the mailed-men on duty, looking for a place to slake his thirst from cisterns that could hold out against siege.

The cross-vaulting of the castle led from room to larger room, to galleries, to stables with war horses and the smell of manure, lookouts, walls, apartments furnished with stolen silks. Kerak the Magnificent was one of a string of fortresses built along the eastern caravan routes to defend the Frankish conquest of Jerusalem and capture wealth for the greater glory of Christ, patron saint of European murderers and scoundrels.

Formidable, impregnable, Kerak would fail within fifty years— alone at the end.

Jerusalem fell first.

Standing on the high battlements above the awesome valley of death, looking out to the horizon where Jerusalem must be, Byron of the United States Air Force judiciously changed personalities from Frank to Syrian. The time-winds had shifted, bringing with them Syrian warriors.

Fortresses can be bypassed by war, they fall to battle, to time, to pillage, to neglect. Could the vile barbarian infidels ever have held the Jerusalem they had taken by massacring all its Moslems and by burning the city's Jews in their synagogue? What frontier fort is that strong? Vanity and greed make poor mortar. Fortress walls crumble at the command of Allah, opening the inner heart-rooms to be purified by righteous strength.

Before the final siege was over the Christian defenders had begun to sell their women to the Moslem enemy in exchange for food.

Days passed for Byron and the time-wind blew more centuries away on its wings. By Land Rover he visited the eastern desert palaces of the Umayyad Caliphs—ruins, only hinting of the pleasures of the falcon and cheetah hunts, horse races, poets, dancers, musicians. Time took him as far north as the black basalt necropolis of Umm el Jimal, and south as far as the Byzantine mosaics of Madaba.

Amanda found him again at a party in Amman in a room of beaten brass and somber drapes, standing beside a bust of the Roman Emperor Claudius. Byron and Amanda, time tourists, awed by eternity, were glad to see and touch each other's solid American fingers, wholly indifferent to the century of their meeting.

"Ah just can't believe your blue eyes, Mr. Raven Hair."

He gazed up into her specked ones. "Did you ever find your luggage?" Claudius prodded him with a plaster nose.

"No. Ah think my bags all got shipped to Shanghai."

"Which dynasty?"

"Come to Petra with me," she said impulsively. "Ah have a hankering to show you Petra in its heyday."

So on impulse he took her to Petra.

Once they were past Ma'an, the road swung into the hills over a rock-strewn waste of russet dust that folded across the dried up wadi beds until the asphalt thread vanished into a shimmering stoniness. Amanda had insisted on driving down during the cool of night but instead they had spent the night together in Amman and lingered over breakfast. Now the sun was high and cruel. The bleached land of ochre and shadow broke away into a deepening violet until the distant horizon vibrated with cobalt fire.

The land rose. They were moving up into the mountains that rimmed the great rift valley which, in its northern extension, cradled the Dead Sea and the River Jordan and the Sea of Galilee, and in its southern extension became the Gulf of Aquaba. The road twisted and climbed, too narrow to be comfortable. Amanda drove like a mad Arab to the summit of the Shara range.

"There," she said.

From behind a dynamited cutting, the land fell away into vast etherial panorama. The white walls of the village Elji lay below, embedded in trees and patches of vegetation. Terraced fields wound around the hilly contours. Farther downslope the barriers of rock that hid Petra from the world crouched beneath the gaze of bleak Gebel Haroun. Like a resting lion annoyed at the flea of Aaron's tomb in his mane, Gebel Haroun straddled the horizon, warning of the Wadi Arabah flatlands and the inhospitable Negev beyond.

The way-station to the Nabatean time-zone was another outpost maintained by the Jordanian Time Police of the twentieth century. Travellers received the usual handbills telling them tactfully not to interfere in the past, suggesting that qualified guides might be helpful, and sternly informing them that overnight visits at the site would not be tolerated.

After partying all night and driving down the King's Highway under the blazing sun, they were in too tired a mood for an immediate field trip. All they wanted was a bed. The bed was too short for six foot tall Amanda. She sat on it cross-legged, breaking a round orange and feeding slices to Byron, smiling across the whole of her boney face.

Later, in the semi-dark of pulled shades, her nose snuggled under his arms, she muttered that Americans smelled good. He patted her back, pleased to be with a woman who didn't smoke.

"My husband wouldn't approve of you. But don't you worry about meeting him. He thinks a trip across the border to New Mexico is travelling. Once he went to Phoenix."

"You didn't tell me you were married."

"Cause you didn't tell me *you* were married. Ah know the difference. Ah know you've lived with a woman. Single men don't make love like you do." Amanda punched through the bottom of the sheet so her feet could hang out over the mattress. "What's her name?"

"Junie just bought me a house in New Hampshire. I looked up Stonefield on a USAF map I have. Have you heard of Stonefield? I think she wants me to raise chickens."

"My old man thinks that something three hundred years old must be an antique. Once he found a buffalo bone from the Great Extinction and thought it was a fossil!"

Hours later, after the sun had set and the night had passed away leaving only the hardiest of the desert stars still out, after eating a dozen oranges and talking about flying and digging and weird relatives and the philosophy of freedom, after flirting and pulling the mattress down on the floor so she could sleep stretched out—all behind locked doors and pulled shades—they were ready for Petra.

Donkeys and horses and guides were available but she took him out along the trail by foot while the dawn sky was still purple. "I want you to see the Khasneh right after dawn."

"And what is the Khasneh?"

"An Awesomeness Who Crushes All Ego. You'll see."

CHAPTER 9

How did it ever come about that mankind embraces vulnerability as his only salvation—working by day and by night to perfect hair triggers that, with the first twitch, will incinerate him to a glorious martyrdom? This, our sagacious Press tells us, is a security too sacred to touch. Any change might cause a twitch!

DMK (1984)

The chief operating officer of Shantech had been thinking about his son-in-law all day, making phone calls, testing his contacts. Daughters were a damn nuisance, but it was pleasant, once in a while, to pull off a spectacular hat-trick for them.

So far Charlie Bond had not been able to do much. With a major Soviet space station a sudden reality on top of the failure of Challenger, NASA's own goals had been thrown into the confusion of rumor—a typical American crisis. Nobody knew where the United States was going, or what would happen—but everybody had a theory and everyone knew someone they were sure would know more.

Finding Byron a Stateside job in the space program in the middle of such confusion was improbable. The elder Charlie did not see a way of pulling his son-in-law out of Saudi Arabia. As usual, he would have to ask Sam Brontz to handle the matter between all the other things his aide was doing.

It was already past dinnertime. Eating sometimes got in the way of work. He picked up the phone and ordered a plate of hamburgers and salad sent up while he reviewed the Synmann file. An odd man, that one.

Military contracts per se held no interest for Bond—for one, weapons that threatened Russian civilians to Make the World

50

Safe for American Democracy while offering up American women and children as front line sand-bags did not appeal to his chivalrous side. It did not look like a sensible investment of capital.

Bond was no pacifist—but there was *defense* and there was double-speak defense. A "defense" whose keystone was the holding of Russian school-children hostage in order to restrain the behavior of a Soviet aristocracy which thought nothing of bombing and maiming and starving children in Afghanistan was somehow no better than that which it "defended" against. It lacked moral elegance.

As a fighter pilot Charlie had napalmed "helpless" Chinese soldiers in Korea, and had been curious enough about the consequences of his act to take a truck ride up to the front to look over the blackened corpses. God, through Jesus, had talked to him that day, and he had come to some firm conclusions. He knew what *he* meant by defense.

Bond was sure that a people with their hands gripped around a dead-man switch while they thought, in unison, "I'll destroy you if you destroy me," would not last more than two generations as a moral people. Who could, year after year, stay ethical if he was so stupid that the only way he could think of to defend himself was to threaten indiscriminate murder?

And so Bond was fascinated by the idea of a real defense against ICBMs, one that did not solve the dilemma by advocating the murder of Soviet children. Somewhere there *had* to be a Christian way to resist the fleets of Armageddon.

He had vague space battlefields in his mind—laser-snouted generators beaming the skins off missiles as fast as they rose out of their silos; little robot mines in the blackness of space, clicking away, spotting a school of missiles sweeping past, and launching interceptor torpedos.

Sitting behind his desk, he became a fighter pilot again, commanding a spaceplane out there, steering with his hand on the extensor lamp, cleaning up what the robots couldn't get. He made roaring noises in his throat, his tongue vibrating like a heavy weapon. And the Soviet children stayed safe even under the rain of broken missiles over American cities because the defense was so formidable that there was no need for retaliation.

His swivel chair slowly turned as he watched his mental images with a fixated fascination, knowing that every single invader he let through would mean the loss of an American city. *Pow!* It broke into pieces! *Pow!* Another one! *Zap!* They crumpled and flared crazily down through a hundred miles of atmosphere to the very bottom of his skull.

The chimes rang. *Ah, the hamburgers!* That was quick.

But it was Sam Brontz.

"I got in early, eh? Surprised you? It surprised me." Sam threw his briefcase under the table beside the tropical plants while flopping onto the white pillows of the long couch. "That pilot of yours flies in over the tree-tops like a cruise missile. You should put him on your Florida smuggling-run if only you had one. He's wasting his talents flying out of Boston for a staid old gentleman like you."

"He's my charity case. I rescued him from a grounder's life after he flunked out of the USAF's fighter pilot training school."

"God save us from charity! I would have been here earlier but I needed an hour at my hotel to shower away the sweat and clean out the leaves caught between my toes. That sonofabitch navigates his airplane by reading road signs! And the ugly sonofabitch is nearsighted!"

Sam let the white pillows engulf him while he stretched his freshly shined shoes deep into the pile of the rug.

"I have some hamburgers coming," said Bond. "You want one?"

"Do you think my stomach has settled out from making that bomb run?"

"Before it does, I have a nauseous favor to ask of you—Sam old friend of mine. It has to do with nepotism. My son-in-law. You'll have to use Krantz to help him."

"Which Krantz? Louis Krantz from NASA?"

"Your old high school buddy."

"Lou's honest—which is good for the shuttle program and pretty rough on nepotism."

Bond grinned. "I'm talking about nepotism, not *dishonesty*. All relatives aren't incompetent. We both know the magnitude of the Soviet space drive and the starved US orbital delivery capacity. It won't be long before we are forced into an upgraded shuttle program. And NASA is losing some astronauts because of Challenger. They'll need crews. Why not Byron?"

"He's that good? Really? I can't sell Krantz a lemon. I can't afford to sell Krantz a lemon."

"Byron is a phenomenal pilot; cool and disciplined and fast. He's never had an accident. He even had an F-15 fail on him one time and he brought it in for an emergency landing undamaged. His record is perfect. He's picked up an engineering degree in his spare time. He qualifies."

"Then why does he need me?"

"A lot of people qualify." Charlie Bond was still grinning. "It's nepotism that gives the edge."

"Is Junie behind your fervor?"

"How can I resist my daughter? She wants him home."

"Does she know there's no difference between Saudi Arabia and the moon?"

"No, and don't tell her. The moon she remembers fondly. It lit up her way at night when she was afraid of the dark, and space research is something she thinks is done on Earth to make jobs because her stock portfolio tells her so. Now do me a favor and speak to Krantz."

"You can't give your daughter *everything* she wants."

"I'm not. Junie wants an engineering job for Byron, but it's not in the cards. He's a pilot. I'm giving her what's possible."

Brontz sighed. "Have Ginny send me his file. I'll think of an angle."

The hamburgers and salad arrived by messenger boy. Bond opened up his bun so that he could pour sugar on the sliced tomatoes. The sugar came out of little packets he stole surreptitiously in restaurants and filed in a folder under S.

Brontz covered his lap with a linen napkin before he touched a burger, and Bond's mind returned to business. He wondered how his meticulous aide had made out with Synmann who had the reputation among his graduate students of only taking a bath in the summertime when he was skinny-dipping.

"I'm dying of curiosity. You did get to see Synmann? He didn't throw you out?" Bond grinned.

"And who would dare toss on his ear a man of my charm and financial standing? The old hippy needs money."

Charlie went to the question. "Has Synmann got anything?"

"He knows how to knock out ICBMs. He uses a very impressive mix of weapons in building his defense. Nothing escapes him. He's obviously given a lot of thought to countering every possible Soviet counterstrategy. I love his penchant for using low-tech whenever he can get away with it. But his ace card is very high tech, indeed."

Bond twiddled his glasses, reflectively. "So you like it?"

"Synmann says almost nothing would get through the site-protected areas, and if we were on our toes we'd get 90% of all the incoming missiles. That's against the present arsenal of SS-18s, SS-19s, SS-26s, SS-27s and submarine launched missiles. Evidentally those buggars are pretty dumb and vulnerable. Thin skinned. He doesn't pretend he'd do half so well against a new generation of Soviet missiles armed with counter-measures. Then we'd need his ace."

"That's an impressive claim but you don't sound impressed."

Brontz laughed. "I'm a good physicist and I spot flaws fast. I didn't pick up any flaws in Synmann's reasoning."

"I hear it in your voice, Sam. I know you very well. You have reservations."

"It's just that my worldview is different than Synmann's."

Bond was impatient when Sam got coy. They had known each other too long for that. Time was valuable. "Go on."

"Synmann is a technocrat. He sees weapons in terms of what is possible. He sees a system and he sees its countersystems and he sees the full array of counter-countersystems, and in his head he builds and deploys them all. He's still buying that old American trap—Americans are good at innovation, that's our strength, so we can keep the Soviets off balance by staying ahead of them."

"That *is* our strength!"

"Goddamn it Charlie, that's a trap! You can't run forever!"

"The status quo is a trap, too," Bond snapped. "If we point 5000 rockets at each other, in time one of them will take off because the bureaucracy will fail. Blooey. There is no such thing as error-free management. Remember Challenger and the Chernobyl fiasco. Reaction times are so short now that MAD is more and more under the control of buggy programs. Your life depends upon a Russian computer programmer's ability to write bug-free code. I thought you were running as scared as I am?"

"Just a minute, Charlie. Let's be *practical*. I'm a physicist turned entrepreneur. I see weapons in terms of what is *affordable*. Synmann sees weapons in terms of what is *possible*."

"Shit!" said Bond, annoyed. "That's what everybody says—a defense against H-bombs is too expensive."

"On the contrary. The way Synmann wants to optimize his defense it is a bargain. For 200 billion dollars we would get a system that would take them a trillion dollars to beat." Sam rubbed his thumb over his fingers. "But it is buying the *fourth iteration* of the response to the counterdefense that is not affordable, neither for us nor for the Soviets."

"Big deal. If the fourth generation isn't affordable—nobody will go that far."

"Let me tell you what happened while I was sitting there on Synmann's floor listening to the future. He's a strange cat, and I'm not used to sitting on the floor and it was blowing my mind so much I was hallucinating. Synmann was the excited kid, running around getting into everything. He was inventing a new way to kill ICBMs every three minutes. I found myself debating silently the economic choices we'd have to make. Choice. What an incredible stimulus to thought when you have choices to make! Deploying some of those fail-safe defensive systems might even generate more wealth than they consume!"

Sam Brontz folded up his napkin, so that the crumbs would stay inside. He neatly bagged the remains of his dinner and walked over to dispose of it in the shredder. Then he paced.

"Charlie, sitting there on the floor with that mad hippy I became a megalomaniac. I know how to save the world, Charlie!"

"Not on my money!"

Sam grinned. "It isn't going to cost us! We'll go with Synmann but he won't be building the weapon he thinks we want."

"He put LSD in your tea."

"He put a bee in my bonnet. Everybody, including Synmann, is asking the question: How do we knock out ICBMs? That's the wrong question. How do you design a system that allows a nation to defend itself, that can be used, even by accident, without destroying mankind, indeed, *must* be used every day, and is so effective that nuclear weapons cannot compete with it in the marketplace? That's the right question."

"I can see you've decided to take over Synmann's debts. How *far* are we going to support this long-haired freak? Will he need people to ride herd on him? A mad physicist can go through a billion dollars faster than any whore."

"Synmann we can handle. What is important is that Synmann's group is a cornucopia and I want to keep them together while I work on a couple of long-shot deals where his team are key players. I have this gleam in my eye. I have a non-military use for him."

"Something you've neglected to tell me about?"

"You know me; I never bother you with the details."

CHAPTER 10

Cast from the rock as if by magic grown,
Eternal, silent, beautiful, alone!
The glyphs rose-red as if the blush of dawn
That first beheld them were not yet withdrawn;
The hues of youth upon a brow of woe,
Which Man deemed old two thousand years ago.
Find me such a marvel save in Eastern clime—
A rose-red city half as old as Time.

DEAN BURGON FROM PETRA

The Siq gorge sliced through the multi-colored sandstone of el Kubtha like a corroded crack, the easily defended eastern gateway to Petra. It was an ancient fault in the mountain, a mile long, split open by a restless subterranean monster, its floor filled and its walls carved by sudden desert rains. In the early morning Amanda walked Byron down from the Government Rest House. She would not take one of the old horses or a guide.

He followed her silently, not sure he understood his restlessness. For a long time now he had known that he wanted to build things, to leave some more permanent impression upon history than a vapor trail at 40,000 feet. This hectic visiting of the crumbling ruins of the greatest aspirations of other men was vastly disturbing.

They entered the Siq across a recent dam built to divert the occasional floods that once had swept a party of tourists to their deaths. The Nabateans had raised the same dam, for the same reason, thousands of years ago and Byron climbed down to investigate the still functional overflow tunnel carved through the mountain by the Nabatean stone cutters.

"Once there was an arch over the gorge . . . see." She showed him the worn abutments with the spring course of stones still intact. "In 1896 it tumbled down, Ka-boom! Don't Ah remember such *useless* trivia?" she stated proudly.

As they followed the Siq, it first opened to the sky, then began to crowd its passage. Sometimes confined wadis broke through the sides, filled with tumbled stone and scrub trees and the flowering pink and reds of the oleander blossoms. The defile grew narrower as its walls rose taller. Amanda showed him an eroded votive niche carved into the sandstone, and a sky-aimed stairway that lead to nowhere but was perhaps the invisible stargate of a race which had once been curious about mankind.

The gorge became more and more impressive. He found himself staring upward with a stretched neck, like a tourist in New York. The rising walls of weathered rock glowed with pastel bands—shell whites, chalk yellow, clay gold, iron red, dusty blueberry. Sometimes the gorge zigged at an angle that brought in the light, sometimes it zagged to catch its visitors in a pre-dawn umbra, sometimes the light hid in auroral glory behind the next bend. The Siq played with light.

Then, while the Siq was at its narrowest and the sky gone, they saw the end—the dawn through a craggy slit blazing upon golden shades of peach, the Khasneh, a sudden man-made structure dramatically cut into the facing wall of another gorge. In that first narrow vision only two incredible columns were visible, supporting a second structure with more columns.

The full magnitude of the Khasneh began to awe Byron as they moved out in the open. It was six enormous columns wide, holding a triangular pediment that extended from an attic which was the base for a whole second monument of three pavilions. Obviously the Nabateans had imported a Hellenistic architect but the symbiosis was more than Greek—no Greek had ever thought to carve, out of a mountainside, a temple fully ten stories tall. It took a mad Bedouin to even conceive of such a thing.

"Wow!" said Byron with American verbal inadequacy.

"The Khasneh sure is a handsome hunk of rock even if a mite conceited. Aren't you glad Ah brought you here? Ah love this place. Ah'm tempted," Amanda bragged, "to bring the whole shebang back to Texas—as soon as Ah get my hands on some capable mules. And Ah'm going to buy Utah for a backdrop when Ah get it there so's it'll feel at home."

She lent him her canteen and they began their march up the wider Outer Siq toward the Wadi Mousa. The scenery did remind him of a desolate area of the Utah hills—until they began to come across Assyrian style tombs carved into the gorge walls, then a whole street of Assyrian facades.

Amanda told him that no one knew if these were parts of houses or were simply more tombs. The lower half of them, which might have been built up with stone or brick or wooden structures, was too eroded by water and rock-fall to provide much evidence. The location was wonderfully defensible and would have attracted the early traders to use Petra as a depot and watering point for their caravans.

Byron scrambled up and in and out of the gloomy interiors with some fascination. He nodded and waved down at Amanda. "It feels like home!" he said, somewhat mysteriously.

"I always knew you were a cave man!" she shouted up at him.

"Did I tell you that I designed a whole moon colony as my big project? You can't build on the moon's surface. You have to carve caves out of the rock." He was grinning. "These old Nabateans would have been very much at home in my future!"

The Assyrian facades suddenly gave way to the semi-circle of a stadium-style Roman theater, which the Roman administrators had cavalierly chiseled out of the middle of the older Nabatean presence, leaving sliced-through half-chambers still gaping out of the rock above the theater like prescient projection rooms.

"When did the Romans come?" asked Byron.

"About a century after Christ. By then the Nabateans dominated the trade routes as far north as Damascus and would have taken over the new trade routes through Palmyra and Aleppo if they had been left alone. As it was they were cut off."

"And died out?"

"You know better than that!" chided Amanda. "The Nabateans were obsessive traders. Don't you think the best of them just left Petra and moved to where the trading was better, to Palmyra, to the southern seaports? Do good men ever accept a trap or pretend to themselves that the world will always be as it is? They were subdued by the Romans—but when the Roman empire was dead it was their sons who returned as Moslem conquerors."

The builders versus the destroyers, with Time as the only survivor, he thought.

She took him north along the west side of el Kubtha where they clambered up a stony hillside toward the Urn Tomb. He stared out over the vista with four-dimensional senses that pierced the past. At one end of time he saw . . . camel caravans glad of the mounted Nabateans who protected them . . . goats . . . farmers . . . Edomite miners bringing in their copper ore . . . a maze of houses on the hillside, plastered and white-washed, baking in the sun . . .

And, at the other end of time . . . the restless stones and gravel and sand which are the tombstones of all effort . . . bushes twisted in starvation . . . a dried gully . . . three shards . . . the bleached desert mountains brooding around a single weathered tomb sliced from a slope. Time had spared only the tomb. Two Roman style colonnades lined an entrance that was half as long as it had once been. Still surviving were the remains of an arched superstructure of masonry that had extended the Urn Tomb's realm outward over the hillside.

Builders created magnificence, and entropy carted it away.

North, beyond this Tomb, lay more tombs. Tomb after tomb, carved by the hands of copper miners who had been bought by the wealth of traders who sought immortality. The sarcophagi of the traders were gone, their finery was gone, their bones were gone, and their souls had vanished but the tombs remained—the Assyrian Silk Tomb of batique beauty and the Corinthian Tomb which somehow failed to mate Nabatean architecture with Roman form.

It was a long morning. They followed the line of an old wall that had once guarded the northern city approaches and then wandered down the Wadi Mataba back to what had been the central city. Everywhere there was evidence of a prosperous people—Roman improvements protruding from the ground, old gates, the stumps of a typically Roman colonnade street, the massive temple walls of the totally Nabatean Kasr el Bint, everything dominated by the stoney mountains that surrounded Petra and defined it.

It took them an hour to climb to the top of Umm el Biyara, over a gently sloping rubble tossed by the rains, the obliterated remains of a ceremonial way, and up through the Couloir, which had survived, a massive double flanking ramp carved into the mountainside millennia ago to make the passage easier.

The Umm el Biyara was a natural walled castle, and it had been used as a castle. It got its name—mother of cisterns—

from deep bell-shaped caverns cut into the rock by the pre-Nabatean Edomites who had used them to store water during the summer and during siege. From the high plateau, holding themselves against a brisk, dry wind, Byron and Amanda peered down at the distant city. The desolate central area of Petra was plainly visible by the humps of old walls, and the ghostly rectangular outlines of what had once been dwellings and temples and streets.

While they were eating a late lunch from their packsacks, they were overtaken by a British pair who were hurrying through a tour of Petra during the afternoon. The two couples had chatted the night before in the Government House lobby. He was an engineer, and she a librarian, both on a long vacation to celebrate the leaving of the nest by their last child.

"A rather lovely view up here. We knocked you up for breakfast, but you were gone. How long've you been out?"

"Going on a millennium," said Byron holding a wedge of Swiss cheese while peeling away a yodeler, printed on aluminum foil, from around its sun-melted softness. He was beginning to feel the day in his feet. "What's the news from the twentieth century—or have you been there recently?"

"Rather different from this charming necropolis. Just heard on the wireless that the Red Team have sent up two more men to their space station this morning."

Byron mulled that one over. "Two more? That's a hurried pace to put up a twelve-man crew."

"You *hope* its only a twelve-man station." The British engineer grinned. His grin reminded Byron of the grin Bijad ibn Jamal had worn when he suggested that a battalion of Soviet cosmonauts would soon be pissing into the Great Lakes as they passed overhead.

Byron shrugged, trying to make light of the United States' inability to keep up with the steady Soviets. "We work our buns off getting up into orbit so the future's tourists can be amazed by the lack of decay in the artifacts. Think of all the pleasure the bureaucrats of the next civilization's Department of Antiquities will have raising money to save the first space cities from burning up in the atmosphere and obliterating all that history."

"Quite," was the engineer's deadpan reply. "Don't forget the bureaucrat who will refuse to grant a demolition permit so that a better space city can be built in the old orbit."

For a long time after their friends had left, Byron stared at the necropolis below and the lonely mountains around and finally at the sky, now brighter than all the stars, sunbright. "Unh!" he muttered.

"What?"

"Nothing. I was just being sad that the old Nabateans gave up—letting time win—and then I remembered what you said, that they didn't give up at all, that they just moved on. It made me grunt. I just realized where they are!"

"You sound left out."

"Yeah. They're up there in space building their new city and here I am sitting idly in a place, long past its prime, grunting out thoughts about human destiny." His voice was wistful. Always the better men went with the challenges and where did that leave Byron McDougall?

"And you wish you were in the Red Air Force?"

"Sometimes it is a pain-in-the-ass to be an American. Day in and day out you have to listen to people who say we should stay home." He began to mimic them savagely. "We should put our money into Milk for The Children who are *Our Future!*" he squeaked. His voice took on a preacher's boom, "We should put Our Money into iron lungs for Deserving Senior Citizens!" Amanda giggled and, thus encouraged, Byron continued to mock all that was liberal and sacred. He went too far. His good-humored mockery petered out and he became sullenly serious. "Every village has its Democrat who wants to grind up the seed corn to bake into bread for the starving children."

"*Ah'm* a Democrat," she bristled.

He smiled, absently rubbing two stones against each other. "So was my mother. She thought children were more important than the future. She poisoned us to death with her smoking while she fought against nuclear power so that her children wouldn't be poisoned. I wonder if that's what happened to the Nabateans? Keep your children fat by feeding them the seed corn."

Amanda, in spite of the fact that she was a devout Democrat, was softened by his wistfulness. "And what would you do if there were only Republicans in the world?"

"That's my idea of paradise. I get horny just thinking about a world without Democrats. Why do you think I want to go into space? The Democrats would be too chicken-livered to follow and I'd be left in the company of real people."

"What would you do out there—carve Eisenhower and Nixon and Reagan into the mountains of the moon in replications big enou   see from Earth?"

"   thing like that. Things would last up there."

"Wouldn't you let even one Democrat into your pantheon?"

"Well, maybe Truman's daughter."

"A minute ago you were decrying the building of anything—since everything gets destroyed."

"I've changed my mind. The USA isn't going to be here in five hundred years and if I don't start building the world that replaces us, I'm a dead end."

"You're being serious."

"Naw." He got up. "Let's get going. I'm just talking. I'm trying to talk myself into leaving the Air Force. My father was a military man. The Army. I never wanted a military career. I hated the life. I hated my father's discipline. And yet here I am—a military man. I rebelled against my Army father. I defied him—I joined the Air Force. Shit!"

She felt this was the right time to show him a djin. It was a block of stone, four by two by one. The Nabateans left them everywhere, some big, some little, but all in the same proportions.

"Everything you want is in there," she said.

"Even your yummy?"

"You're like a child! Your emotions change so fast! One minute you're fired up serious and the next you're a baby at the breast. And when *Ah* try to be serious you just start that teasing. Ah'm trying to educate you. God lives in that stone."

"That's serious?"

She smiled. "The Semites all had one thing in common. Their gods lived in stone. Yahweh lived in Beth El. The Semites weren't sculptors so they couldn't humanize their gods. Their gods remained abstract and powerful. Al Uzza of the Nabateans. Yahweh and Allah. Allah still lives in a stone in Mecca. It's *that stone* that a devout Moslem faces five times a day. Yahweh lived in the stone that was housed in the Ark of the Convenant, and the Jews would still be worshipping it today if it hadn't been destroyed when the Temple of Solomon was sacked. 'The God of my Rock; in Him Ah will trust,' " she said, quoting the Southern Baptist Bible.

A djin in a bottle, waiting to be released, ready with three wishes if only you'll let him out. A god imprisoned in a rock, toted about on a wheelbarrow ready to do the bidding of those who cared for him, but cantankerous and unpredictable because of the confines of his prison. *I'm a god trapped in granite*, thought Byron.

"The Greeks were wonderful artists in stone and they could make their gods look so human that the Greeks believed them to *be* human—so we have a womanizing Zeus and a stupidly jealous Hera and no one was ever really able to take the Greek pantheon seriously. Semitic gods are fearsome because they have no form. God with a beard, sitting on a throne, is a Greek corruption of a Semitic universe Western man could not understand."

They wandered along the South Walls and up along the Attuf Ridge to the Moon Shrine where Byron stopped and offered up a short prayer to the universe. His mother had been an atheist, and the Democrat in him never quite took religion seriously, but his father had taught him how to pray. His father showed him Hell so that he should know Heaven when he found it.

Amanda walked up the slope, pulling Byron to the altars of the High Place, which must have been used for sacrifice, perhaps animal, perhaps human. The gutters for the blood were still there but the blood of history's Aarons was not.

Byron was tired and thirsty and no longer really enjoying himself. Thankfully the Nabateans had made the descent down to the Outer Siq an easy one. Every obstacle on the mountainside path had been cut away. The trail took them straight through solid stone when the stone dared block them. Byron dragged his feet; Amanda was still light-footed. The sun was setting, promising a dark desert night.

"Will I ever see you again?" she asked.

"Of course. I'll look you up the day I divorce my spouse."

"No! Before that! The very day Ah divorce mine!"

"Your husband will chase me with a shotgun! You know I don't trust Texans."

"He won't know where Ah've gone. Ah'll disappear."

"I suppose I could sneak you away to Saudi Arabia and hide you in a tent with my other three wives."

"Ah just hate you!"

"Amanda, don't say that," he said tenderly, teasingly.

"Why not?" she asked defiantly.

"It's a sure sign you're falling in love."

They continued in silence until they reached the awesome Khasneh again, now in the twilight shadows, but still formidable when you were standing beneath it.

"*That's* what I want to build on the moon," he said. "I want to carve it out of Pico Peak, facing out across Mare Imbrium. It would stay out there longer than man himself could last."

"Until the sun runs out of hydrogen fuel and grows into a red giant and gobbles up the moon in the Days of Fire." Amanda's mind wasn't on monuments. It was on romance. "Will you still love me when the sun becomes a red giant? Isn't there anything about me you could love?"

"I'm madly in love with you. You don't smoke. Who else can I kiss whose breath is as sweet as summertime?" And he kissed her, a bit shyly—the way he had seen his father kiss his mother in public. The Khasneh watched over the kiss, ten stories tall and two millennia long.

"You don't kiss very well," she said petulantly, stooping to steal another one. "Don't you ever French kiss? Ah like that."

"I'm afraid of your teeth."

CHAPTER 11

You who once were rulers of many lands
  now lie on this barren earth,
  and your faces darken from decay.
O my dear brothers! O my dear warriors!
Never again shall we share joys.
Why were you extinguished?
I have not had enough joy with you!

PRINCE INGVAR INGVAREVICH OF RIAZAN
  UPON FINDING THE ROTTING BODIES OF HIS BROTHERS
  MASSACRED BY THE HORDES OF THE MONGOL BATU.

Reject my game, will he!
For days the heavy boots of Limon Barnes paced over the
stone floors of the Cathedral of Saint Marx the Benefactor. Why
was he here? He didn't need the money. Royalties on his old
games were coming out of his ears. Sam Brontz gave him a
job—and then put him down when he did it. How could a man
work for someone who had grandiose plans and no clear direction?
What the hell did Brontz want? Bastard!
Sam was playing on some larger stage. He was into reality:
that's what was frightening Limon.
In rebellion the young gamesmaster took to wearing chain
mail. *That* wasn't real. Sometimes he carried a cast iron mace,
growing more and more furious. One morning he insulted old
man Matthews, the M in SMB, and gentle Matthews, the
quintessential negotiator, took him into his office and gave
him lessons in the proper way to resign—it should announce an
end, not a failure.
"But Brontz won't accept my resignation!"

"That's right."

"I'll have to sneak off into the night like a cut-pocket."

"Be firm. Forceful."

Limon decided not to take Matthews' advice. That damn oily Matthews wanted to do him in anyway—bring peace and sanity back into the SMB he had founded. He *wanted* Limon to resign. Matthew's counsel was sound, but dull and smacked of common sense. *Of course*, Limon should resign forcefully rather than work for a megalomaniac who didn't know what he was doing! But why the hell should Limon, who had ambled down Denver's Colfax Avenue in a Superman suit while wearing a Reagan rubber mask, resign by the traditions of any normal human?

Revenge was what he wanted. Stick that righteous Brontz was what he wanted. Stick him good. Stick him clean. Expose him for the ass he was! Dump him in a trap with dragons!

Reality was far too slow to ever engage Limon's mind and whenever he was living in reality, he had a languorous way about him, the patience of a Russian waiting in line for sausages. But during a game in which a year of game-time spanned a day of real-time, he came alive. Revenge was a game. In an accelerated mode he began to check out the possible opening moves of a game which at its climax would prick Sam's composure so completely that he'd actually forget himself and in a rage *fire* Limon! Being fired was far more marvelous than a mere resignation!

The spastic gamesmaster marched through the woods with his mace, twirling the spiked head on its chain, his mutters conjuring up out of the forest's gloom the ghosts of ancient royal advisors, all of whom failed him—one after the other. They were useless, unoriginal lackeys of kings and tsars, recommending in their spectral voices the rack or quartering or flailing, simple tortures which if inflicted upon Sam would surely be endured with an equally simple nobility! In fury Limon let out a great cross-handed swing with his mace.

Calmer, he wandered into a lazy Massachusetts meadow. Five Holsteins were by the stream, a thousand of their hoofprints in the mud on the banks, trampling their own odorous manure into a wine of mud that fed the rich grass upon which they munched.

A flickering vision from hell superimposed itself upon this pastoral scene, the apparition's pale colors made even more transparent by the intensity of the sun. The vision was of a horrified Sam, in his meticulous gray suit, bent to his knees in that muck, having no choice but to kiss a country-fresh Holstein plopping.

Praise the Goddess!

Limon had the climax of his revenge. Now all he had to do was create a game so complex that Sam would be taken through it without ever understanding *until that very last moment* that its only purpose had been to lead him to a meadow muffin on his knees with puckered lips. With the joy of a nine year old, Limon relished the image. All the way back to the cathedral his mind was in a frenzy. It would be the practical joke of the century.

Didn't Sam want to get into the gestalt mind of the Russian people for some crazy scheme of his? That made a perfect hook. How better to empathize with a culture than through a simulation? But a simulation could be manipulated to make a fool of any man.

All afternoon Limon explored Russian history, picking the era of Mongol conquest as the ideal setting for his con: 1237 AD to 1395 AD. That way Limon could be a powerful khan. He would have a license to do anything. It would be easy to convince Sam that the Russian archetype had been profoundly shaped by the invasion of the Golden Horde—because it had. and thus, for the purposes of a simulation, he could ask Sam to take the role of a Russian prince.

Limon Barnes read and plotted, sometimes for thirty hours without letup. He needed magic. Only a gamesmaster who controlled magic could locally intrude upon reality.

To aid his design, he pulled down the arcane books of wizardry he kept on the High Shelf in his office, one after the other. Vogt's *World of null-A* he used for its Law of Similarity which told him how to adjust one world to be so like another that at the moment of similarity the merest touch would transport Sam willy-nilly down time's Volga. Anton J. Bitter's *The Harmony Book of Phrases* he used to create archetypical resonances that in his hands became a mixing of moods and power vectors that would overwhelm all the cultural fixations of an individual foolish enough to pass into its focus. The frenzy of his conjuring lacked only the dust of ancient Mongol law books.

He read and read until the floor of his office was layered by books. It was annoying to find books without maps, without illustrations, wholly content to describe events. Mindless books. How could he capture a Russian mind without the essence of old fingernails and priest's wool and *muzhiki* sweat? It was frustrating.

But on the day he found an illuminated Mongol manuscript, arcane with the phrases of ancient magic, Limon knew that Sam was doomed. It was pieces of *The Yassa*, written by Chinese servants who had access to Genghis Khan's lost golden records and who had been placed in charge of subjugating the Russians.

Limon called on friends from the Society for Creative Anachronism, at company expense, and set them to work. He hired an unemployed historian and a desperate summer stock theater director. He induced out of retirement an old Ukrainian witch.

Because a gamesmaster couldn't leave the creation of the sets for his play until the last minute, Limon's costumers went to work immediately. They were experienced medievalists and produced for him the garments of the Russian fourteenth century nobility and the sky-blue silks and the fine trappings of the Mongol court at Sarai. Pinning and sewing they put together peasants and boyars and beggars and priests and warriors.

Just to watch the costume tryouts honed his magic. It did not matter that in his eagerness he had temporarily lost his way in his search for the grail that held the Great Russian mind. He set deadlines and proceeded anyway. He mixed his teas and drank them, cups on top of books—teas from Tibet, from a lost valley of Ceylon, from the cellar of his Ukrainian witch. By a process of automatic writing on his computer screen, he composed scripts, subroutines, scenes, branches, story lines, plot, hints for the actors, details for the directors.

By astral projection he wandered over the face of his stage.

In 1237 AD, ten years after Genghis Khan's death, son Ogadai recommenced the Mongol conquest of the universe. Grandson Batu was recalled from the far west. There he had grown up with his sullen father, Juchi, who had retreated to the outskirts of Mongol power, having been forever scarred by being the seed of the rape of the All Powerful One's beloved wife—though his "father" had raised him like a son. Batu, nephew of the new Khan, was not sullen and Ogadai bestowed upon him an army for the conquest of the western domains, honoring the boy by placing under his command Genghis Khan's greatest general, Subotai.

The grandson swept out of Karakorum across thousands of miles of steppe, crushing the Bulgars and riding on through Russia with 150,000 horsemen of his Golden Horde—Mongols and Turks—aided by newly mastered Chinese siege weapons and Mongol experience distilled from the conquest of the powerful Chin.

Together Batu and Subotai, comrades of an earlier campaign,

shocked and terrorized the Slavicized Norman society of the Rus by entering the safe forests traditionally shunned by the steppe horsemen. The Viking warriors had become masters of Russia throughout its swampy waterways, building stockaded fortresses against the Finns and Slavs, building a commercial Kiev at the borderline of forest and grass—close enough to the Black Sea for trade in furs and slaves with Constantinople, yet close also to the wealth and protection of the dark forests.

The Slav-proof wooden stockades of the Viking-Russians led Batu to comment derisively, "See how the little pigs have gathered in their pen to be put to death!" He put them to death in all the towns of Riazan, swept into Suzdalia, burning the minor village of Moscow. Then he besieged great Vladimir. The city fell after six days of berserk resistance and the battle's survivors were slain, the city destroyed. Suzdal, Rostov, and a multitude of surrounding settlements were swept away on the northern march to Novgorod. Novgorod itself was spared only by a horsebarrier of swamplands created by an early spring thaw.

The Golden Horde retired to the southern grasslands but after a year of consolidation, returned to destroy Chernigov and Pereyaslavl and all the people of Kiev. The Russian nobles were still Normans at heart and by tradition had never dared arm the same Slavs they had raided for the wicked slave markets of Constantinople. Defenseless, undefended, the peasants were slaughtered. Such a desperate condition earned the Russians no pity in Christian Europe. Indeed the Swedes found it an opportune time to attack Novgorod.

Batu and Subotai, each with their own army, mastered a two pronged thrust through Poland and Hungary during the year 1241. The depopulation of Hungary, and the appearance of the Mongols at the gates of Vienna ended only with the death of Ogadai at the end of that same year. The kuriltay had to be called together to elect a new khan and, since Ogadai's sons were Batu's enemies, it was politically dangerous for Batu to absent himself from such decisions.

"In war be like tigers, in peace like doves," said *The Yassa* of Genghis Khan. Batu chose peace after the settling of the succession. From the imperial tent city of Sarai, which moved along the banks of the Volga with the seasons, he imposed a political philosophy on the Russians which they were never to forget. Government is no more than a machine for enforcing the collection of tribute from weaker men.

It took 3000 white mares to provide Batu's drink—and when he drank from gold cups, wild Tartar pipes shrilled and cymbals clashed. Because of his gout Batu was carried everywhere on a palanquin with a tassled canopy. Sixteen wives served him and he could not remember the names of his sons. The cowed Russian survivors paid his baskaks—the squeezers—so that he could import rugs from Persia, glassware from Egypt, silks from China, and giraffes and monkeys from Africa.

Political strategy was simple for the nomadic hordes. A town was looted and then totally destroyed, its surrounding farmers murdered to clear the land for the nomad's herds. But the Mongols were not consistent. After they became intrigued by wealth and loot, it became their policy to spare a town which capitulated without a fight or treachery, especially if that town did not command desirable grazing land. By rule of *The Yassa*, subject people were to be taxed one tenth of everything they produced, but, as long as war continued, were required to provide the suicidal shock troops of the continuing Mongol advance—to reduce Mongol casualties and to eliminate the possibility of revolt in the rear.

In the domain of the Golden Horde, imported Chinese census-takers counted all things. One out of every ten Russian males was taken into the Mongolian army to serve—perhaps as far away as China. Sometimes one tenth of everything was not enough. If something was in short supply, the Mongols took more. When Birkai, the heretical Moslem brother of Batu, assumed the Khanate after Batu's death and built a stone and brick Sarai, his men took for the Mongol cities every stone mason in the whole of Russia.

A comment by Will Durant lay open on top of the books that layered Limon's floor. ". . . it was Russia, bending under the Mongol whirlwind, that stood as a vast moat and trench protecting most of Europe from Asiatic conquest. All the fury of that human tempest spent itself upon the Slavs—Russians, Bohemians, Moravians, Poles—and Magyars; Western Europe trembled, but was hardly touched. Perhaps the rest of Europe could go forth toward political and mental freedom, toward wealth, luxury, and art, because for two centuries Russia remained beaten, humbled, stagnant, and poor."

While Limon's wizardry was building him a portal into this time zone, he found it necessary to conjure up Batu's ghoul and to enslave him temporarily so that someone else might remain on the other end to hold the fragile time gate open. Mongol souls could be controlled with blue flame.

The conjured Batu was able to hold this special time portal open, for Limon, no farther than the year of 1395 AD. Within a century-and-a-half of their initial conquest, the formidable Mongolian kuriltay, which had ranged with impunity from Hungary to Korea, was suffering a fatal disarray. During one such internal dispute Mongolian Tamberlane from Samarkand spent eight years destroying the major cities of the Mongolian Golden Horde, leveling even the stones of Sarai. By 1395 AD the heritage of Batu had been squandered and the little village of Moscow, which had grown into a cunning city, no longer had a viable enemy.

A minor town in 1238 when it was sacked by Batu, Moscow rose to power by excelling at the art of collaboration. The Moscow princes, fascinated by a horde that could overwhelm their Viking virtues, studied their masters from the educative viewpoint of the slave, smiling and hating at the same time, and learned all that the Mongols had to teach about repression, even building the Mongol words for repression into their language. But the fate of those who resist an enemy by apprenticing themselves to him, is to become that enemy, and in the end, by the laws of karma, to share the fate of their enemy.

Limon—knowing that the remnants of the Golden Horde were a despised minority in the Soviet Union, lately living on the bare Kazakh steppe where they had been deported by Stalin, denied upward mobility, governed by special KGB directives when they were in the army—sat there in his office and mused with a gout-ridden Batu about the various fates of Hated Overlords. In six hundred years would a great Polish-Afghan-Chinese civilization, spreading from the Atlantic to the Pacific, give alms to its few Russian beggars? Perhaps they would be allowed to live in peace on the ice of the island Novaya Zemlya? Batu only growled, not at all pleased to be in the thrall of a twentieth century wizard.

It took Limon Barnes less than two months, with the aid of his reluctant Mongolian slave, to open a crude trap-door above the medieval layer of the Russian mind wide enough to take a man. It remained to drop Sam Brontz through this portal into the century of the Black Death.

"We'll treat him right," he said to Batu the Merciless.

CHAPTER 12

For years she grew near city tower,
a gutter-sprouting pretty flower
soot upon her yellow petals
mischief making between nettles.
AMERICAN FOLK SONG.

At nine Diana Osborne took up archery in school. She wanted a bow of her own and timidly asked her father for one while climbing up the back of his leather chair. Sometimes if she smiled a lot and was affectionate with him he gave her what she asked for—sometimes. "I'm the Goddess of the Hunt, Daddy-pops, and I need a bow and lots of arrows so why don't you buy them for me? I'll shoot all the rats in the alley!" He bought her a bow with a quiver of multicolored plastic arrows, each a whole foot long, each with a rubber cup on the end. She traded her bicycle for a real bow and got beaten.

"I'm out of a job and you give away your bicycle!" He was always complaining about ceramic engines. How could a man earn a living if they made engines out of plastics and pottery! The engines were a crock-of-shit! How could he keep his family alive? "You don't esteem your father!" Whap! "I buy things for you when I don't have any money and you give them away!" Whap.

When she was ten she ran away from home to Fairborn to visit an aerospace museum but the police caught her trying to get into the cockpit of the X-15 and brought her back. After the police were gone her father beat her until her mother cried. She limped to her room and made paper planes, fixing Plasticine and pins in the tail so they would flip over and stick, thud, when she threw them at the photomontage of the moon on her wall. Two of her paper ships landed, one on Flammarion and the other on Mare Undarum, but mostly they bounced off onto the floor.

She stared at the huge lunar photo. She had a red thumbtack stuck in Theophilus on top of the five year old Russian moon base. And she had blue thumbtacks at all of the old abandoned Apollo sites, sacred to the memory of past greatness. On the wall crowding the Oceanus Procellarum was a painting of the orbiting lunar station as it would look when it was finished, with the great arms of its upper and lower skyhooks. At the moment it was only a framework, still being built with supplies shipped up from Earth via the leoport.

A fresh article was still on Diana's desk, *Third Millennial Man*, about her hero Byron McDougall who would be up there building the American base once the first exploration teams had found a site. Maybe he would plant a forest for her nymphs in some crater. She didn't like the buildings he had planned. They looked pretty dumpy.

At eleven she became the school champ at archery for her age group and lead her team to the regional championship, much to the disgust of the two best male archers. Diana beat up one of the boys who was teasing her teammates by painting insults on their arrows, but he got his revenge. He made a "stage" arrow and stuck it to his back and chest and with the aid of a package of ketchup saved from a hamburger purchase, staggered into the classroom, groaning. Everybody believed Diana shot him. She took him on again after school.

But when she was sitting on him and pounding his head against the cement he was wise enough to offer peace terms. He knew her secret weakness and he knew her family TV set was senile.

"Ouch. Lay off! My brains! My poor brains!"

"You want me to save your brains? How about if I break your arm instead?"

"Hey, I gotta be in shape to watch TV tonight!" That reached her—as his cunning knew it would. Tonight was the big finale of the show that had been building for a week—after almost two days of carefully descending the orbiting lunar ladder, the four men of the Mayflower were about to jump off. Diana stopped pounding his head. He didn't move a muscle.

"Yeah!" she sneered, "babies have to be in bed by nine!"

"Not tonight. I get to watch TV all night. My ma doesn't even care if I go to school tomorrow." He waited just long enough for the conflict to cloud her face, but not long enough for a new rage to power her again. "Wanna watch it with us?"

"Yaah! I'd trust you like a frog with a fly!" She really wanted to watch it. One of the crewmen was a woman.

"You can come over to my house *now*. My Dad has the TV on the back porch and we're going to have a hot dog barbecue."

She marched her enemy home with his arm as security, bound behind his back in a half-nelson. Ma was bringing out chairs to the backyard and Diana helped set up the table and chop tomatoes for the salad. The boy's fat Dad, from his hammock, kept watch over the CBS, ABC, and United Satellite Systems. It was too early for anything exciting but the networks always had filler.

CBS reran the President's short speech, made just before his limousine took him away. This annoyed fat Dad. He had seen it three times. With a portable communicator and a TV beamer both gripped in one hand—and in between potato chips as he carried on a phone conversation with his mother—this master of the reclining position zapped CBS. ABC was carrying an oration by the mayor of Detroit. Zap . . . to the silent flight of the command module of Apollo 11 gliding just above the desolate surface of the moon in the summer of 1969. He flipped again. The studio mixers at United Satellite Systems were replaying the two day old pictures of the Mayflower docking with the top of the lunar ladder that would have stretched from Seattle to Los Angeles. Zap. Now the TV crews of CBS were cutting into parties and interviewing party goers. Zap. ABC sneaked in a panorama of the celebrating VJ day crowds from the San Francisco of 1945 just as a joke.

None of this interfered with grilling hot dogs and stuffing buns with onions and mustard. Neighbors dropped by or chatted over the fence. When it grew dark they turned on the outdoor spots. The children organized a game of hide and seek but Diana used the TV table to hide under, or the tree suspending fat Dad's hammock, so she could hear the commentary.

The evening went on and on. Some of the kids brought out their sleeping bags and went to sleep on the grass. Tired, Diana had a name calling session with her tormentor, but she had to watch her mouth with his mother around. She managed to trip him once when no one was looking in a way which spiced his eighth hot dog with gravel.

Then, all at the same time, the networks went live to the cramped interior of the Mayflower as it skimmed over the lunar landscape at a leisurely 3000 kloms per hour, far too slow to stay in orbit without being held up by the floating skyhook whose center of mass was more than a thousand kloms overhead. The four man crew greeted their fellow Americans a world away. "Wave at us," said a beaming commander Allan Bydgoszcz through the solar noise. Diana waved at the moon up there above the housetops of Ohio, her heart in her mouth.

The lander released its grip on the skyhook.

"We have release," Houston announced.

The moonscape tipped. Rockets fired. The image vibrated. In the end there was nothing to see but boiling clouds.

Were they going to make it? At 1:27 AM Houston announced, "We have touch-down! All systems A-Ok!" This sober NASA announcer couldn't resist adding, "Yahoo!"

The generation of Americans who had aborted the first American space program were dead or retired. The generation who still remembered Americans reaching the moon while they were in grammar school had passed on to middle-age. The present under-thirty generation had grown up watching movies about galactic empires, yet had only learned of local lunar adventures from history books and old men. American children as young as Diana thought of the moon as Soviet territory that the Americans were invading. All celebrated the return to the moon in a national orgy.

When she was twelve Diana decided to run away from home even with her arm still in a cast, having had it broken by her father when he found her collection of newspaper stories about families who murdered their children in the night. He burned the newspaper stories and hacksawed her bow in two but didn't bother with her scrapbook of heroes so she put it in her packsack.

Her hair she carefully fixed to imitate the March cover girl of Cosmopolitan magazine and she wore one of her mother's bras, stolen, which she stuffed with an extra pair of socks. People gave her rides. From her escapade in Fairborn she knew to avoid policemen. She told everyone she was going to visit her mother in California because her father was out of work.

The best ride she got was from a truck driver whom she targeted at a diesel station in Newton, Iowa, mainly because his rig carried a Washington license plate and she knew vaguely that flying saucers were built in Washington. He wasn't supposed to take on passengers but she flaunted her spare socks and he broke down and got to like her over the steak he bought her.

He told her stories of the road. She chattered to him about a historical novel called *Diana's Temple* that she had ordered in a drug store in Cincinnatti after spending twenty minutes playing at the book-terminal while resting her legs and eating an ice cream cone. It cost her ten dollars instead of eight because the drug store didn't have the right laserdisk for the printer and they had to bring her book in over fiber. Complaining about the extra two dollars hadn't done her any good. It was just a corner drugstore and they only stocked 8000 titles. She read it between rides, sitting in the sun.

An endless journey later, through farmland and broken hills and over decaying interstate highways, they pulled into a rest stop near Elk Mountain to sleep in the cab for the night. She caught her driver typing a message to *Childsearch* into his dashboard digiphone and pulled the plug. He had a tiny dish antenna on his roof and could contact zillions of computers in a second via the *Attman* net. He was a very dangerous person. She made him swear on the cover of *Diana's Temple* that he wouldn't turn her in, inventing on the spur of the moment some cock-and-bull story to convince him.

"Promise?" She held tightly to the plug.

"I already promised. You could let me fax your ma."

"She doesn't have a phone. She's poor. If you turn me in on your digi, some social service will just pick me up—and then I'll never get to see my mother. Poor people get hassled. We're always getting hassled! I know what I'm doing. I'll bet it was a lot easier to be poor before they had phones and welfare!"

She plugged his digiphone back into its power, watching him.

For a second he looked rueful. "You got the right spirit." He lifted a big hand and squeezed her affectionately on the back of the head. Diana tried to seduce her driver then because she thought girls were supposed to reward nice men. She brushed his crotch with her good hand. When she tried to kiss him with her tongue, the cast on her arm got in the way and a sock fell out of her bra.

He laughed, restraining her by the chin in a vice-grip between thumb and fingers. "Diana was a virgin," he said with stern good humor.

"Yeah, I know. You think I don't know about Diana?" She squirmed out of his vice to a position as far from him as she could get, shoving her backbone hard on the cab door in shame.

This gentle man didn't want to hurt her feelings. He reached out and tenderly pulled her shoulders into his large arm. "Your virginity is the most valuable thing you have right now. Hang onto it. Grow up a little bit and when you throw it away make sure he's the nicest guy in the world."

"How do you tell the nice guys from the mean ones?"

"Did you ever have any trouble with that?"

"My father always beat me. For *nothing!*"

"Then you know what the bad ones are like."

"What are the good ones like?"

"Me," he laughed.

For a year Diana stayed in a small town near Seattle where the workers assembled, for the leoport, the feeder spacecraft popularly called "flying saucers," as well as the mach-seven scramjets that launched the saucers.

Diana was excited at first. The saucers were sending up supplies for the moon colony! She missed her big photo of the moon, but she had added to her collection of lunar articles one which included a map of the Sinus Medii and the Horrocks-Agrippa badlands centered on the Crater Rhaeticus. Why did Byron pick *that* place! It was one of her least favorite areas on the moon. The Imbrian Alps were much nicer!

She did housework and cared for the children of one of the foremen whose wife was recovering from an auto accident. But this sleepy town of the northwest was just as far from the moon as Ohio. She watched the freight planes fly away with the new saucers on their heads like silly hats—and mourned. If she could build a dollhouse in a payload compartment and sneak aboard she might make it to the moon. But she didn't know where to buy an oxygen mask.

CHAPTER 13

Are you a lucky little lady in the city of light?
Or just another lost angel . . .
                              City of night!

City of night, city of night, city of night.

I see your hair is burning;
Hills are filled with fire.
If they say I never loved you
You know they are a liar.
    Driving down your freeways;
    Midnight alleys roam;
    Cops in cars, the topless bars.
    Never saw a woman . . . so alone . . .
        . . . so alone . . .
            . . . so alone . . .

L. A. WOMAN, THE DOORS, APRIL '71**

Sam Brontz had flown his daughter into L.A. with him as bait. Half in his mind he was thinking to marry her off to Ray Armsiel. The best way to insure a family dynasty was to bring in good new blood. Other than that, Ray was crucial to his plans.

"That's him." Sam Brontz pointed out a gaunt young driver who was avoiding an obnoxious taxi trying to butt him out of his stopping place in the airport frenzy.

Linda grabbed their luggage and ran after her father.

"Sam the Man!" Ray was grinning while the two of them piled into his car for a quick getaway. "What a time to arrive! Why didn't you pick three in the morning! I recognize your daughter from the kid pictures you carry around in your wallet. Hi, Linda!"

He shouldn't have said that, thought Sam. She was sweet but she was only nineteen and very sensitive about being thought of as a kid.

Ray jockeyed them in and out of traffic until they found a ramp of cars where a single light dripped them, one by one, into the San Diego artery. There, six lanes of traffic moved as sedately as a lowing herd of cattle which had been promised water but had yet to smell it.

"Sam, you surprise me," chatted Ray. "I thought I put you off with conditions that were impossible to meet. You keep coming back! You know what you are trying to do is insane. What's your counteroffer?"

"Not now, son. We have to decide where to eat."

"Daddy, we just ate on the 747." It was the first words Linda had been able to speak. It was the first time he had ever seen her shy.

"That was Afternoon Tea. We're on a twenty-seven hour day today and we need four meals." Besides, he had to impress Ray.

"But it was steak!"

The exterior of Santa Monica's Kamsamal was Main Street American, from a period when the duller American architects used brick instead of flat glass, but inside it became a two story, four-sided fantasy overlooking an inner courtyard of vaguely Moorish style, arches and intricate filligree, an Arab palace as seen through the dream of a Mexican priest. The niches for Our Lady of Mercy carried azalias instead.

Graciously, Ray Armsiel helped Linda into her wrought-iron chair at their table in the courtyard. He had the grinning friendliness so characteristic of the men from the West, but he was also nervous. *He knows I've set her up as a trap*, Sam thought. *Smart man.*

Linda listened curiously to their passionate discussion about a ninety-mile-long fragile structure arrowing in orbit above the Earth. Ray explained to her politely how catching cargo pods saved energy by storing energy in the structure itself for later recycling. She smiled and Sam wondered if Ray knew that she did not understand. It wasn't easy to explain to anyone how such a system would be cheaper than using space-shuttles once the tonnage volume to space reached a critical level.

The gaunt young man ate like a horse while he argued. Linda watched him, and Sam knew she was in love—again. At the end of the long meal, over the Korbel Champagne from beyond California's Valley of the Moon, the two men signed a series of contracts, shoving aside the dirty dishes, in too much of a hurry to wait for a clear table.

"A graying man and a child happily signing their names to pieces of paper promising each other billions of dollars," she commented. "I haven't played trading games like that since I was eleven. Boys!"

"She used to buy and sell palaces from the torn-off covers of paperback romance novels," Sam teased, and got a kick under the table from his miffed daughter.

They drove her to a noisy nightclub, featuring a troupe of Mexican dancers who filled their show with stomping feathered Aztecs whose wild enthusiasm dominated the club visually and vocally for a full hour. And then it was rush-rush-rush to a party Ray didn't want to miss.

Linda put her father in the back seat. She watched Ray's face as he drove, mesmerized by the thrum of the freeway madness, the steady flashby of headlamps, until they turned off the Ventura somewhere into the hills around Topanga Canyon.

"I'm lost," she said.

He's pretending she doesn't exist, thought an amused Sam.

The party was loud rock-and-roll to the beat of quaint music twenty years out of date in a room of jerking bodies framed against a great window that overlooked the city lights.

> *. . . the day destroys the night . . .*
> *. . . night divides the day . . .*
> *. . . tried to run . . . tried to hide . . .*
> *Break on through to the other side!*

Ray dismantled his freeway face—and put on his party smile. He went straight into the arms of a blonde with slashed skirt, blue and black garter, and pickaninny hairdo.

> *. . . we chased our pleasures here . . .*
> *. . . dug our treasures there . . .*
> *. . . can you still recall the time we cried?*
> *Break on through to the other side!** wailed Jim Morrison.

A stricken Linda posted herself by the kitchen door where she could, within a sound-shadow, chat with her father. There she was cornered by a crew-cut boy in jeans who had escaped from his parent's aging hippy farm in Salinas. The strains of . . . *she gets high, she gets high, she gets high* . . . drowned out the boy's first words, but he repeated himself. She was from Boston? Linda found out that he thought Boston was in South Carolina and was still recovering from its losses to the Bluecoats in the Civil War. Eventually she broke away from this prodigy of the Californian public schools and took her father for a walk.

"I'm tired, Daddy. Let's go home." She was already calling a cab when a friendly couple, who were just leaving the party, insisted that the Brontz's come with them. Central L.A., it turned out, was only twenty miles out of their way.

The hotel had given them two large double beds. Sam was humming happily over his portable ironing board, touching up his suit for the flight home tomorrow, when Linda appeared from the bathroom in her nightdress, ready to conk out. She flopped down on the mattress angrily.

"You didn't tell me he liked Swedish pickaninnies!"

Sam warmed to the topic. "What a pair of legs. That was some dress. I haven't seen the likes of it outside of a Hong Kong cat house! She's a bit of a show-off. Last time it was her bosom."

"Daddy! You knew about *that* woman and you didn't tell me!"

"My dear child, *that* woman is the wife of one of the chief aeronautical engineers at McDonnell-Douglas. It was her party, and she is thirty-five years old. Didn't you notice that she was playing music from the late sixties in honor, I suppose, of the time when she was a teenage queen?"

"She sure didn't look like an old lady to me."

"That was the *Doors* for God's sake, right out of my second childhood. The only time I ever cheated on your mother, they were playing *L.A. Woman*," he said wistfully. "Crazy Jim Morrison."

"I wasn't born then."

"Yes you were. You were learning to walk and falling on your tushy."

"She *can't* be *that* old!"

"You must learn to be observant and see the person under the latest styles. She smokes pot and that dates her."

"Look who's talking."

"Well, I drink alcohol and that dates me."

"Daddy, I've never *once* seen you drunk. You're the most outrageously controlled man I ever met! They must have been very good at brainwashing in the fifties. Don't you have *any* sins?"

"My only sin has become totally obsolete. I know how to screw nubile chicks in the back of a car, a fine lost art."

"You look ridiculous standing there with your pants off."

"I'm not as apt to wrinkle them that way."

"He doesn't like me, does he, Daddy?"

"Ray? He will. Right now he's just afraid of you because you're the boss's daughter."

"It doesn't matter because I don't like *him*."

"Then I suppose you'll be flying with me back to Boston tomorrow?"

"Daddy, I just got here!"

He hung up his pants and coat and a fresh shirt that he had prepared, telescoped the ironing board, turned out the lights and crawled into his bed after eating the mint that the hotel staff had left him.

"Daddy?"

"I need the sleep, honey."

The only light in the room came from the haze of blatant advertisements outside. "Daddy. You'll be gone in the morning and I won't be able to pump you tomorrow. What were those things you were signing at dinner?"

"Nothing a girl would understand."

That was his way of teasing her for taking English courses at college instead of physics like he wanted her to. Silently she slipped out from under her covers and, crouching beside his bed, seized one of his wrists in both her hands and twisted the skin.

"Ouch! I'm an old man. Take it easy."

"Tell me or you get an Indian Burn!"

"You don't have a need to know. All you'll have to do is take care of him and he'll produce. Ouch! Hey, that's my right hand! I need it! All right! All right! Uncle!"

"How is he going to make a billion dollars for you, or a trillion or whatever it was? He's too young. I wasn't born yesterday. I know men your age don't trust men Ray's age to do *anything*—except maybe face machine guns for you."

"He'll be working for Joseph Synmann and gang, a group we just took under Shantech's wing. He has the aeronautical engineering skills they need for a military project Charlie and I are cooking up, and Synmann has the maturity that Ray lacks. He'll ride herd on our young man and act as a mentor."

"That baby makes guns?"

I said the wrong thing! Patiently Sam searched for a way to explain. "The deal has levels of complication." Casting about for appropriate analogies he recalled commercial nations, reluctant to spend their wealth on arms, who had failed to defend themselves—and were no more. For instance, the Etruscans. And he remembered sprawling military powers who had failed, in the end, to generate enough wealth to pay and equip their soldiers—and likewise were no more. For instance, the Sioux.

"Yes, Ray is going to be working with Synmann on defense concepts—you have to think about defending your wealth if you want to keep it—but his main job will be creating the kind of wealth that can *pay* for a defense. There's enormous wealth up there, but no cheap transportation system to bring it in. A hundred years ago Ray would have been a railroad man."

"And shooting Indians who got in his way!"

"Ray is working on a fabulous space transport scheme. You want me to explain it to you, but I can't. Think of it as magic, a magical way of getting into space, a flying Persian rug. Ray needs an electromagnetic genius at his side and Synmann is an electromagnetic physicist who has spent his life working on particle accelerators and is now working on ways to stop ICBMs. *He* needs to team up with a crack aeronautical engineer. They're made for each other." Sam gently took his daughter's hand from around his wrist. "Now go to sleep."

She wouldn't. She coaxed more details out of her father, none of which meant anything to her.

Later, Sam listened to a restless Linda. After an hour of being unable to sleep she blurted out, "The men I know don't understand science either! All those fantasy writers *lied* to me. Magic is hard! It's not just a matter of saying spells and drawing pentagons and grinding up freeze-dried newt tails!"

CHAPTER 14

And if you ever want to see her
She will never be the same
For she has flown to L.A. to live
By some invented name.
The name's
The number and the flame
Flickers fame.
And don't you ever try to tame her,
Blame her for your sorrows—
For she can never be your game
While you live lost tomorrows.

TAWN, FROM *TRANCE RAMBLINGS*

Diana stole some money and caught a bus for L.A. at the Seattle terminal. She slept through Oregon and when she woke up it was dawn in Northern California, a pale sun behind low clouds to touch the trees and meadows.

The old man was still illuminated by the little spotlight above his bus seat, reading his book. The black lady was asleep in her chair, her daughter asleep in an ample lap, the husband snoring with his feet in the aisle. Four Mexicans stared out the window. A white-haired grandmother knitted a sweater for a grandchild, having confided to Diana at the midnight rest stop that she had wasted her youth hustling sailors in San Francisco during the Second World War. An emaciated woman with a pink punk hairdo endlessly staggered to the swaying toilet room.

Diana took a day's vacation in San Francisco to see the city she had heard so much about. She had a map and she zig-zagged by foot along the hills to get the best view of San

Francisco bay. Oceans still amazed her. With her last dollars she treated herself to octopus on Fisherman's Warf.

Somebody left a gate open to their tiny garden, and she spread her sleeping bag in among the bushes. Midnight is full moon time. Tonight the moon wore a rainbow and diamond twinkly stars. The Crater Rhaeticus was right at the center, she knew, and Byron was there. If he looked straight up, he could see her sleeping in a San Francisco garden. She half exposed one breast and giggled.

Before dawn she left her haven to avoid being caught and wandered down to the beach to watch the moon set in the ocean. It was nice to do what you wanted to do and not get beaten but it wasn't so nice to be broke. On an empty stomach she wandered back to the bus station. She didn't hurry. There were always buses to L.A.

It was scary panhandling in Hollywood. She got picked up by a pimp she didn't know was a pimp and had to push her stuff through a window and crawl out after it in the middle of the night and sleep under a car like a cat. After three days alone without food she found a family of runaways and slept on their floor. They were all into stealing and hustling and the one who befriended her was into heroin, but she found a job as a waitress from which she got fired because she didn't have any papers.

Twilight was panhandling time. She dressed in stolen clothes to look older than she was. It was an actress's art. In case of danger like a police patrol car she had to project the purpose of someone who was going somewhere. And then when a mark ambled in sight, she had to pose and stand out. Different people she caught by different wiles. Some people would give her money if she looked lost and forelorn. Some people were suckers for the story that she didn't have busfare—they weren't going to leave a young girl out on the streets of L.A. alone.

Men tried to pick her up but she had the perfect line for them: "I'm collecting money to pay my doctor's bill. God, the things you catch these days! I've even got a rash between my fingers." She'd roll her eyes and they'd give her a dollar coin without touching her and hurry on.

For people she really wanted to get rid of, she had a spastic, drooling act. *She* would proposition *them* with brain damaged tongue-control centers. It was great for *destroying* men's lolita fantasies.

Once she actually saw Tawn, the reigning madman of trance, on her favorite panhandling corner. He had cutouts on his buttocks and trance music coming out of his hat, but she didn't approach him. He also had two bodyguards. L.A. was supposed to be full of famous people but she suspected they were all hiding or wearing rubber faces when they had to be out on the street.

And then one day at twilight she spotted a very famous man. He had the right build—small and wirey—and she followed him for two blocks, partly because she was too awed to speak to him, partly because she was afraid. Finally she walked up beside him and matched his pace with her skinny little legs.

"I'm hungry. Why don't you give me a dollar."

"Nope," he said and started to move faster.

She matched his pace. "Uncle Ray! Is that any way to treat a starving cousin?"

That stopped him. He looked at her. And she knew she had power over him because she knew his name and he didn't know hers. "Jog my memory," he said.

"I'm the Moon Goddess and you've been trespassing on my territory, building leoports and skyhook-ladders and things where you haven't any business being. Gimme a dollar!"

"What would you do with a dollar?"

"I could pound it into a copper arrowhead."

"Now when I was your age, I *earned* my dollars."

"You got yourself a deal, Mr. Armsiel. I'll work for you anytime. But you have to buy me my spacesuit. Gimme a dollar to start off with."

"And what's your technical expertise?"

"I'm *hungry.*"

"Hmm," he said, supporting his head on this thumb like a bronze thinker. "I won't give you a dollar, but I'll *buy* you a hamburger."

"A hamburger!" Her eyes twinkled. "You're very smart, Mr. Armsiel. You're the first person who's ever noticed that I'm really a sixty year old tubercular rummy only pretending to be a starving girl. Come on, you wouldn't deny an old man his pleasures—gimme a dollar to put on a bottle of gin!"

"Or a shot of coke."

"Yuk! Cokies are all impotent. Coke makes your penis shrivel up to the size of my little finger, did you know that?" She demonstrated. "And it gives you varicose veins," she added. "Only *ugly* lawyers who don't like women shoot coke. I'll take a McDonald's hamburger any day. There's a McDonald's six blocks from here." She pointed with a skinny finger. "You could just gimme a dollar and save yourself a long walk."

He headed in the direction she indicated and she fell into

step, putting down her right foot when he put down his right foot, and putting down her left foot when he put down his left foot.

"What are you doing out so late?" he asked by way of starting a conversation.

"It's not even my bedtime yet! And besides, I'm a runaway and I can stay up as late as I want."

"Tell me, how did you know my name?"

"Some joker pinned a big sign on your back."

He began to try to reach up his back with a hand on the end of a crooked elbow.

"Silly!" She spanked him on the bottom.

"Well?"

"You just want me to tell you that you're very famous, because you don't believe your own press. I have lots of pictures of you. You're very handsome for a pip-squeak." Flattery might get her *two* hamburgers.

"Where are you from?"

"Texas," she lied.

At McDonald's Diana sneaked in front of him at the order panel and punched the square for *Big Mac* with cunning speed. Then, with a furtive glance at Ray, also ordered a large fries.

"Just a Coke for me," he said.

"Yuk." She punched it in. "Can I have a McWine?" That was McDonald's version of grape and apple with a touch of cinnamon.

"Sure."

She smiled mischievously. "Can I have a quarter pounder, too? With cheese?"

"Sure."

Rapidly the fingers danced on the panel. "I'm hungry. I want another Big Mac."

"And don't forget the apple pie," he added sarcastically.

Before he was finished speaking, fingers stabbed again, and the light went on for apple pie and a second Big Mac. The machine asked for a deposit of $14.75. He stuck in his credit card and his thumb. Fifteen seconds later the transaction had been cleared. The machine also ate paper money but it took longer to run the tests.

Robot cooks, programmed by queing theory, had the meal delivered within another fifteen seconds.

Diana took the tray smugly and led them to a table by the fountain. "See. I told you it would cost you more than a dollar. You could have got off easy, only you have to be smart enough to listen to me."

She sat down, and after one motion in which half a hamburger disappeared into her mouth, she added, in a somewhat muffled fashion: "I once tried to steal some toilet paper in here but the damn washroom robot locked the door and called the manager. I had to bullshit my way out of that one. I told him I was very *upset* that a respectable place like McDonald's would have spies in the bathroom watching me while I sat on the flusher."

"What did he say?"

"He said it was all right because it was a female robot."

Ray Armsiel sipped his Coke.

She gobbled up the first Big Mac and started on the quarter pounder. "Where do you get your crazy ideas?"

"I steal them."

"You better watch out. Pretty soon they'll have a robot that will clean out *your* toilet bowl if you do that."

"Don't you think your father and mother are worried?"

She shrugged. "Yeah."

"L.A. is a dangerous place for a young girl."

She stood up with half an apple pie in her mouth. She undid her blouse and loosened her belt so that he could see her belly. Still standing, after finishing the pie and washing it down with McWine, she pointed to two small scars. "My father stabbed me when I was four because I stepped on his glasses." She buttoned up and sat down. "Mostly he just beats me." She shrugged.

"Oh," said Ray. "And how is your mother? Does he beat her, too?"

"No. Only when she tries to protect me. I've always known I was going to leave. I remember packing my things when I was three. I had a little cardboard suitcase. He caught me and held me up by the heels with my head in the bathwater. I used to lock the bathroom door and take baths a lot to get over my fear of water." She watched his horrified expression, remembering that she had broken her own vow never to talk about certain things. More than anything else, sympathy could get you into trouble. Getting trapped in sympathy was *worse* than being beaten. She grinned at Ray. "Don't take me so straight. Don't you know that runaways always lie about their parents?"

"Who's caring for you now?"

"The best person in the world—me."

"I could put you in touch with a good social agency. Why don't you come up to my hotel and meet my wife, Linda? She'd know exactly what to do."

A brittle fear undercut Diana's happiness, triggering a wary eye to check the position of the door, while she calculated how long it would take to bolt for freedom. She knew an alley and a stairway and a shortcut through a restaurant. "Maybe I can do you a favor too. I know this great psychiatrist. He has all these friends in starched white coats who want to help out disturbed techies." She grinned, and wolfed down the last hamburger as if she might not have time to finish it.

Just as a precaution, she disarmed her man with the hand that wasn't holding the burger. The digiphone in his coat pocket magically appeared on the table. That way he couldn't slip anything past her. It was the smallest one she'd ever seen. She was fascinated. "What's its range?"

"Planetwide."

"Let's call Poland!"

"These gismos are illegal in Poland."

"Let's call the moon!"

"That's a different problem. The antenna on the set is pointed the wrong way. It's done, but you have to go through the leoport or Big Mama."

She became very sly. "I have a picture of you with Byron McDougall."

"Yeah?" Ray was smiling.

"Are you his friend?"

"Yeah."

"Enough of a friend to have his digiphone number in memory?" She tapped the tiny box.

"Yeah."

"Call him! Can we call him even if he's on the moon?"

"He's Earthside this month."

Zip, she activated the antenna with a flick of her thumb. It opened like a flower, and she typed in *I Love You* with quick double-finger motions. "Send it!" she ordered.

"You have to sign your name," said an amused Armsiel.

She gave Ray a crafty smile. He wasn't going to get her on that old trick. She added, *Sinsirly, The Moon Goddess*, to the flowing blue display. "Send it! Please."

Ray Armsiel had children of his own and he genuinely liked them. He put in the code. The message was sent—and a satellite far above the United States acknowledged. Byron just happened to be "live" and in the mood to reply, which he did, lazily, in lower case, without punctuation.

what kind of nut are you ray

Just sitting here having hamburgers with the Moon Goddess and thought we'd say hello.

give her a kiss

"He says to give you a kiss."

"Byron McDougall said that to me?" She was wide-eyed. She didn't know how to respond. She grabbed a McDonald's napkin. "Can I have your autograph, Mr. Armsiel?"

He signed the soft paper, his first autograph.

Happily she stuffed it into her blouse. "It's right inside my bra where it belongs." She loved to make men blush.

Minutes later, on the sidewalk by the golden arches, he seemed disoriented. "You're sure you have a place to stay?"

Diana couldn't help one last tease. "Sometimes I sleep under cars." She wanted to kiss him, but even she felt shy. She took Ray's hand and shook it.

Block after block she ran along the street. It was the best day of her whole life. She danced around the sidewalk, begging. People weren't able to resist an imp so full of gaiety and, within half an hour, her pockets jingling with dollar coins, she ran home to collect her addict friend to take him to the local basement dive, the only one she could go to because it didn't check IDs. Maybe she could cure him of being depressed.

He was miserable because he hadn't made a hit yet, and he looked around the crowded room with haunted eyes, searching for Jim or maybe the Big Bear. "Hey man, you seen the Big Bear? Hey Diana, gimme a buck—I need a drink."

Cigaret smoke coiled through the dim light, choking at life. Even the brightest of the evening's clothes smelled of stale tobacco while the irritated eyes of the young girls wept mascara. Diana sat there, full of her own dreams, crazying, wondering why she suddenly hated this place. She was depressed. How could she be depressed after talking to Ray Armsiel?

She nudged the boy next to her. "Jeez, what a day!"

"Yah. Goddamn nothing ever happens."

"I got picked up by Ray Armsiel! That's something!"

"Who he?"

"That the new coke man?" asked someone at the other end of the table, brightening at the prospect.

"Oh come on Lem—sissy don't know coke from coal, do you sissy? She's straight. She's into music."

"Yeah, now I place him. That the Ray into trip-point trance? Jah, da dowie wah! Bang, bang, bang." The boy started to pound his fist into his hand.

"This Ray is a *spaceman*. He took me to dinner and wanted me to come up to his place."

"Yah. Columbia's into space-trance. Soft blue ripples! He with Columbia? God that's oochy stuffings. You hear the drum rolls Tantemount's doing in that new space-trance disk? Cept it don't hit the ear like drum rolls—been dijjed to the way-blue, like somethin outta the inside of a rocket engine."

"You seen the Big Bear? Hey Lem, lissen: he ain't laying low, fer Chris-sake? Shit, life is too hard. Diana, gimme some hit-coin—I gotta find the Big Bear. Gotta, gotta. Hey, Jossie, boy, friend-a-mine, gimme a drag-roll. Gotta have one of your cigs!" A toss and a catch. "Jesus-God I'm saved!" came the born-again cry of the addict, striking a match. Blue incense rolled out of his nose.

Suddenly Diana was darting toward the ladies' room where she knew they had a little open window where she could breathe for a minute, alone.

A large hand clamped itself to her shoulder as she went by. "Hey, little cake, you got holes in your skull, spending time with that buzzhead! How long have you known Jimmy? Jimmy the Suck. He'll take you for everything you've got."

She whirled on the scruffy young man who had the 1950's hairdo of a "laxer" and whose hand was not going to let her go. Laxers believed in hard work so long as it wasn't legal. "What have I got to take? I haven't even got a job."

"Lots of jobs around."

"I don't want to be a whore, smartass."

He smiled sardonically. "A waitress, then?"

"I got fired as a waitress because I don't have any papers."

Her assailant shook his head. "No papers! How about that!" He seemed pleased. "You need a little forging job and I'm a forger. Serendipity." He escorted her into the ladies' room and, after locking the door, climbed up on the toilet seat and hung his head through the window.

"You're not going to let me have some fresh, too?" she demanded indignantly.

He lifted her up beside him, holding her affectionately. "Can't have you fainting, little cake."

"Why is a forger better than a heroin addict?" Her voice was deliberately antagonistic.

"I make up histories for people. I give them new lives. That's different from destroying the one life they do have. What name would you like to be known by?"

"I can change my name?"

"Yeah and you get a birth certificate and an L.A. high school record and a social security number. I figure if we stretched it a bit you could pass for eighteen."

"What would you get out of me being eighteen?" she asked cynically while the arm he had around her shoulder slowly cupped its hand under her tiny breast.

"Me? Right now I need a girl to ferret around record offices who doesn't arouse suspicion. I need new faces all the time." He laughed at her fragile toughness, knowing why it was there, and tried to find a way to put her at ease. She was cute and he liked her. "I'm square." He stopped a moment to let himself be aware of the warmth under his hand. "My battle-axe—that's my lady-love to you—would kill me if I didn't give every underage cake an integrity deal. God, she's even old enough to remember woman's lib. Never puts up with man-crap—even the innocent man-crap I grunt out. You'll meet her. She'll see you get class papers."

"Could I get a job on the moon?" asked Diana with the round eyes of a thirteen year old. Then she giggled.

He dropped his hand, reminded suddenly that she was a child. "Jesus! How will you ever pass yourself off as a woman with a chortle like that? It's a dead giveaway."

"I want a job on the moon," she insisted.

"There ain't no jobs on the moon. Maybe if you were a communist and had a good record in the Komsomol."

"A lot of people are working with Byron McDougall! I talked to him today!"

"People—shit! Men, you mean."

"NASA hires women pilots!"

He shook his head. "Not on the papers you'd get from me. Hell, you want a job as a waitress, that I can get you. But you want a job jockeying a hundred million dollar spaceplane, what I've got to give ain't good enough."

"I sure could use some papers," Diana mused. "As long as I don't have to screw you to get them." She glanced up to him, out of the corner of her eyes, defiantly.

"How come all you women have lost your romantic nurturing sensibilities? What happened to the sexual revolution of your mothers? What's wrong with a little lay for services rendered?"

Diana was never cowed by repartee. "In my mother's day they didn't have food additives. It's the food additives that've killed romance. Men's hands have grown big and hairy since the multinationals started to put tetramyacin in your feed. Yuk."

"You say such grossed-out things while you and I are cheek-to-cheek sharing the night's cool air. Girl! feel the glory of your surroundings! The mellow stars are out and the sounds of laughter waft at our backs! Isn't that romantic? What better excuse for a lay?"

"Yeah and we're standing on a toilet seat!"

"Trust a woman to notice the flushers sticking out of the universal truth."

She giggled. She took his hand in hers and turned her head to kiss his stubble. She didn't feel threatened at all—mainly because she was closer to the door than he.

CHAPTER 15

Hush-a-bye, Baby, on the tree top,
When the wind blows the cradle will rock;
When the bough breaks the cradle will fall,
Down will come baby, and cradle, and all.

MOTHER GOOSE

With only the hint of the summer's slow twilight in the air, overeager crickets had already begun to call to each other for their Friday night romancing. The Bond family had arrived from Boston via Texas by Canadair Challenger 601 and were swarming over the Stonefield residence celebrating the birthday of little Charlie McDougall even though it was no longer his birthday. He was already five days old.

Junie's three sisters were in charge of the feast. From his corner, Byron watched Myra arguing with Sheila about whether they should put a candle on the cake since it was a *zeroth* birthday party, while Mary-Jane tried to make peace. Sheila insisted that *every* birthday cake had to have a candle "to grow on."

To end the dispute Sheila produced a wax aviator, six inches tall, with a wick sticking out of his bald head. The father wondered wryly how long it would take before the flame burned brightly in place of the aviator's brains.

For days, a pensive Byron had been fingering the love letter from Amanda, hot in his pocket, his mind mulling over the speed with which he had been pulled from Saudi Arabia into the Houston whirlwind. He was now working for NASA. Rumors abounded of new multi-billion dollar shuttle contracts. And he was in love with the wrong woman. Enough to set any man's brains afire.

It *must* have been old Bond who had pulled the strings. The clues added up.

He wasn't pleased. Flying the skies over the Persian Gulf, he had felt like his own man. There were difficult decisions to make but ample time in which to make them—he had known he wanted to get out of the Air Force; he had known he wanted to move in the direction of space. But he hadn't come to any conclusion, hadn't let his mind test all the alternatives, hadn't even talked to anyone except his friend Abdul Zamani. Then . . .

Like a goose flying into his engine at 5000 feet, Bond had made the decision for him. It rankled. Byron did not know why he had acquiesced without a murmur, hurrying home as meekly as any young boy bound to rules beyond his control.

He went upstairs and tip-toed into the baby's room to watch the tiny sleeping face of his toothless son. *I can't ever remember seeing one so small.* He poked his little finger into the boy's palm, and the fingers closed around it, tightly, without even waking the child. *You're going to be the best space engineer the United States has ever seen!* Across the wavering world of his mind passed elegant lunar cities built by his son.

Then Byron laughed. He was only twenty-seven, with his life ahead of him, and here he was projecting into his son those precious ambitions of his own, ambitions that awed him, that he felt too frail to accomplish for himself. *Old Charlie has me in his sights—I'll be a flyboy all my life.* And never get beyond low orbit with the speckled ball of Old Earth rolling by.

He let little Charlie hold another finger. "Son of a bitch," he muttered, "and they didn't even let me choose your name!"

He was wondering how important a stable family was to NASA's officials when Charlie Jr. opened his blue eyes.

Oh, oh! Here it comes. The only time babies ever woke up was when they were hungry or smelly. The face reddened. A high pitched wail blasted out of those lungs. Byron laughed and lifted the child to his shoulder, sniffing to see if he needed his diaper changed. "I guess it's just that you're hungry."

Junie rushed into the room, her mother screaming after her: "Don't run! You're just out of the hospital! You should still be there!" They both arrived to confront Byron, scowling. "What are you doing to my *baby!*" crooned Junie.

"He just wants a piece of his chocolate birthday cake!"

"Give-him-to-me-before-he-has-apoplexy," Junie said firmly. Mrs. Bond was even more insistent. "He's strangling. The poor baby's strangling. Can't you see!"

Byron handed the child over and went downstairs and poured

himself a drink. "I can't get used to alcohol after Saudi Arabia," he told his audience, and sighed, letting the taste of the Scotch linger on his tongue.

"All rot-gut over there, eh?" said Charlie Sr.

"Rot-gut? There wasn't *any* alcohol."

"I'm sure an old military man like you had his sources."

"Dad, some of those Saudi's drink, but I didn't want to know about it and they didn't drink in front of me. Sometimes you have to be a diplomat."

Byron felt a strange hostility to this man who had found a job for him within NASA. He couldn't attack him, but he could lecture him as if he were an ignorant American tourist.

"Do you know why the Russians horrify the Saudi's? Not only are they atheists who worship a Jew, but half of the Soviet international set are pickled alcoholics. My bosom friend, Abdul Zamani, who has got to be one of the best F-15 pilots around, was being recruited in London by a KGB type from the Embassy who was so stupid that he was trying to reach Zamani by getting him drunk! I thought only American businessmen were that dumb!"

"You've been out of the country, too long." Charlie chuckled. "I'm glad we got you back in time—that was a very unkind cut, comparing noble American businessmen with a vile KGB agent posing as a diplomat."

"If you were working in Saudi Arabia I suppose you'd find a way to smuggle in your Scotch?"

"Of course, son. No Arab screws around with *my* freedom."

"Yeah, Dad, and I'll bet you were hanging out in those speakeasies during prohibition when drinking was illegal!"

"I swear I was only old enough to drink my mother's milk when Al Capone was driving trucks. I'm innocent."

Charlie Sr. had conveniently set himself up for the kill. "You liberals are all alike," snarled Byron, diving from the sun. "If you want your likker or cocaine, you'll get it, even if you have to set your mother to drinking in old shuttered warehouses so you can take your hit mixed with mother's milk!"

Sheila guffawed nervously. "Is he drunk, Daddy?"

Byron patted his sister-in-law's bottom. "On one glass of Scotch?" He held up the amber fluid to the light, watching the ebullient coruscations of the setting sun through the ice cubes. "I'm just high because I'm a father and I'm working for NASA." *And I got a letter from Amanda.* He let his thoughts fly from that. "God damn! I was only a kid when NASA went to the moon and I've never forgotten it! And now I'll be flying one of those babies! God help me, and I have to work with gentlemen who'd besmirch America's Honor by staggering down the streets of Riyadh like some common KGB agent!"

Charlie Sr., oblivious to the insult, raised his glass for a toast. "Here's to the flying father!"

Byron raised his glass higher. "Here's to the sinful old grandfather!" He turned his attention to his mother-in-law. "And to the ribald old grandmother who kisses every young flyboy she can find behind her old man's back." And he took her in his arms and kissed her, just to see her blush. *That's for accusing me of strangling my own child.*

They all went to the table and filled their plates from the buffet style birthday feast. Byron missed the playing of Pin-The-Tail-On-The-Donkey, and the marbles, and the toy car models, and the plastic water pistols. *This must be a Boston birthday party.* They brought the child out for the cake. He stared at the candle flame in fascination and Byron wondered what he saw and what it meant to him. Junie blew out the candle for her son. *That was the Bond way—to do everything for their children so that their children would grow up crippled.*

"What did he wish?" asked Byron, concealing his sarcasm.

Junie didn't notice. "Little Charlie was wishing he'd grow up to be a great violinist."

Over my dead body.

"Don't you think he has a violinist's hands?"

"No way," growled Byron. "But I did catch him smiling. I think he's going to grow up to be Bob-Hope-Entertaining-The-Troops, what with the military on my side of the family and the jokers on his mother's side of the family." Sheila threw a bun at him, and he winked at her and poured himself another Scotch.

Later Byron went upstairs to piss. He locked himself in the bathroom and pulled the shade, then seated, reread the letter from Amanda for the fifth time. He was going to have to burn it. It was too dangerous. He'd meant to burn it in Texas, three days ago, but he was too sentimental. How could a man fall in love with a woman who was taller than he was and had buck teeth? When he was in Saudi Arabia and couldn't get her out of his mind, he thought it was the sand that had addled him, but the beautiful women of Houston hadn't made any difference.

He found it comfortable that evening to lie with Junie on an expanse of fresh sheets even if she did reek of tobacco factory. God, bodies were addictive. Junie was calmer and easier to live with here in the hills of New Hampshire among the buttercups than in the desert where cardamom seeds were mixed into her coffee.

At some awful hour he woke up and fed the baby. He didn't mind at all. He liked to have the boy to himself, watching how such a little tyke could suck with every bit of the muscle of a trombone player. How fiercely the fingers held to what they touched. Always full of surprises, this time he only gurgled when Byron changed his diaper.

McDougall wandered through the greenhouse before going back to bed. The brilliant moon blotted out the stars above the glass. It reminded him of flying at night over the clouds. *So this is to be my home?* Not a bit of it was his own choice. He had to admit that Junie had good taste, but he was still angry that she bought it first, and only afterwards asked his opinion. In the darkness he wandered into the computer room.

He was still slightly hysterical when he sat down at the console. It was an industrial 32-bit machine, no home toy, an engineer's dream, and he was an engineer—but he didn't know how to use it. When he lived away from the Bond family, he felt like a man, but when the Bonds were near him, somehow he was overwhelmed. They made a child of him—like the little kid he had been in the streets of those endless army towns.

Well, he knew how to power up the computer. That was as easy as turning on a toaster. He tried a graphics demo in the disk drive because that was all he had figured out so far. A bird-cage image of the space-shuttle popped onto the screen which could be turned and viewed from any angle. He could even fly the damn thing down into the atmosphere, watching the temperature of the tiles appear in color codes of blue and yellow and red.

But the Unix operating system baffled him. He took out Amanda's letter and reread it for the sixth time while the untended shuttle burned up on the screen in front of him. Then he laid his head on the keyboard and cried.

In the morning—while the birds were still twittering—after eggs and toast and a pleasant chat with Junie—he went down to the basement workshop, sprayed Amanda's letter with a fixative and preserver, squeezed the stiffened paper into a bottle and then, upon replacing the air with nitrogen, sealed the bottle by wrapping it in glass fiber saturated with wet epoxy.

I should burn the damn thing, he kept grumbling.

When the epoxy was dry he took his mummified letter, hidden under his coat, on a walk in the woods and there gave it a proper religious burial with full Republican honors and a military salute.

CHAPTER 16

As we find in the history of all usurping governments, time changes anomaly into system, and injury into right; examples beget custom, and custom ripens into law; and the doubtful precedent of one generation becomes the fundamental maxim of another.

HENRY HALLAM (1818)

It looked like any New England village street—sanded-oil paving, breaking at the edges, no sidewalks, one yellow fire-hydrant, a white clapboard house placed every fifty feet along the gently rising hill. The shrubbery and trees were at least thirty years old and in need of pruning. All of the lawns had been mowed within the week.

Sam Brontz grunted. He'd been sent on a treasure hunt, following little pieces of paper, and he was none too pleased. What the hell was Barnes up to? The instructions mentioned *137 West Elm,* the only salt-box on the street with a red door and red shutters bordering the second story dormer windows.

When he buzzed, a disembodied voice spoke from an invisible grill. "Please enter. The door is open."

But no one was inside. The rooms were stark—ceramic floors printed with some computer generated design, glass shelves, white plastic furniture holding rich futons, the only wood a cut and carved sea-polished bole, now sitting alone on glass.

Ah—there *was* somebody! Sam's host, whoever he was, stood at the top of the metal-railed stairs wearing a silver skullcap with spathed ears more appropriate to a lily than to a man. He wore comfortable white overalls. His face was powdered white and his lips were painted crimson like some Parisian mime artist. One of Limon Barnes' goddamn cronies!

"May I have your papers, please?"

Brontz ascended the stairs, his anger rising. Had Limon gone over the canyon? *I'll strangle that sonofabitch if I have to fire him!* thought Sam. It was enraging to find a man with the rare talents needed for a delicate task, only to discover him applying all of his genius to counting the hairs on his penis!

Who could be found to replace Barnes? Scholars were hopeless. Sam knew dozens of men who had mastered everything there was to know about Russia—yet he couldn't name a stellar *strategist* among the lot of them.

Saving The World wasn't at all as easy as Sam's overactive teenage mind had fantasized. Then he had seen his planet as a commune of co-conspirators who would stampede with him to mutual glory because mankind's path of destiny was so clear. Instead, to his horror, the maturing Sam had discovered prima donnas.

Sheepishly Sam Brontz handed over to Limon's powdered and perfumed stooge those sealed play "orders" so solemnly entrusted to his cloak's inner pocket. The agent did not let Sam pass until the papers had been painfully examined. "You've been assigned to the fourteenth century. I'm afraid you're in for a long briefing. The area is extremely dangerous. We'll have to attach to you one of our permanent agents—Iziaslav Dimitriev, ordained in the Orthodox Church, who will be your permanent companion. Listen to him closely if you value your life."

Two sober-faced women, neither of them more than five feet one or more than ninety-five pounds, each with the lily-like ear pieces and white makeup, escorted him into their bleached bathroom and stripped him. He was bathed very professionally and given a tingling antiseptic rubdown.

They dressed him in linen and wools and furs. The colors were sober—browns—only a touch of embroidery gave the garments a noble richness. The women showed him how to pull on his felt boots. They nagged him about his walk. They showed him his purse and how to use it. They sat him down and taught him to eat a Russian meal. The soup, cabbage, and cucumber, was drunk from a wooden bowl with a wooden spoon. He had honeycomb for the dark rye bread. He had to learn how to eat with his knife and enjoy raw turnips. They reminded him that on Wednesdays and Fridays all animal foods were taboo, including milk and eggs.

When he asked for a snort of vodka, grinning, they reminded

him sternly that vodka was a Tartar invention. The more delicate of the Time Agents even suggested to Sam that the Tartars
had provided the barbarian Slavs with vodka for the same
reason that Englishmen had provided Amerindians with whiskey.

The briefing room of Limon's crazies was a dim back-chamber
of scattered books and precisely laid out machines. Sam found
himself being led to a chair which might once have held dental
patients or perhaps criminals undergoing the third degree. He
protested when the three of them began to strap him down but
they bound his wrists anyway, and attached electrodes to his
head. It was necessary to monitor his learning, they said as they
powered up the computer next to him.

Sam was stunned to notice their Kensakan Kambi-1000. The
rumors were that the first of this series was not even in production yet. Had Limon's gamesplayers transported him a year or
two into the future for their convenience?

"That thing has *eight* thirty-two bit processors in it!" he
exclaimed, trying to point with his manacled hands.

Agent Whiteface looked chagrined. "That's true, but it was
the best we could do in this time zone." His voice oozed
apology. "Field agents have to live off the land. Sorry."

Live off the land! How in hell had Barnes found one! Suppos-
edly at the Kensakan's core resided four megabytes of "instinct,"
the essence of librarian—allowing it to learn the reference
needs of its operator by interaction. It could access about
ten-thousand books worth of data per laser disk drive.

Whiteface was still being apologetic as he scanned some
screens and put requests to the machine which he insisted on
referring to as a *she*. "She's only a puppy. You'll have to forgive
her naivety. There is no way you can switch on a machine like
this and have her up and running in seconds."

"The programming has bugs in it?" asked Sam.

"Possibly—but the program is so fault-tolerant that you probably wouldn't notice. That's not the problem. There is no way
she could cross reference a whole library in the single month
we've had her—she hasn't helped enough people yet. She'll be
a couple of years growing up—at least. Nevertheless she will
have to serve—you have only twenty hours to learn how to be a
Russian nobleman of the fourteenth century."

The hi-res screen lit up, a meter-square window into another
dimension. "A *real* Russian of that century wouldn't know
much of his own history—he'd just carry it in his bones and in
his stories, considering literacy as an aid to bookkeeping, no
more. You, on the other hand—being a *poseur*—will need a

quick and clear structure upon which to hang your faked personality."

"I don't even speak Slavic," said Brontz dryly.

The mime-white features grinned a ghastly grimace by the glow of the screen—while surgeon-thin hands tapped the metal electrodes on Sam's head suggestively. From across the room one of the women explained patiently to her savage, "In six hours you'll speak Slavic so fluently that you'll think it's English."

During the final eclipse of the Roman empire, while the Alans and Ostrogoths and Huns and Avars and Bulgars and Khazars fought their reverberating battles across the gold and green steppes above the Black Sea, trampling the blue corn-flowers and the fairy flutes of the white milfoil and the great grasses with their horses' hooves, while Moslem armies disrupted the commerce of the squabbling Mediterranean Christians, while Roman Law was in the final stages of its self-destruction, the non-political Slavs were moving out in all directions from the Carpathians and the Pripet Marshes, building their little stockaded villages—migrating to the east, slash burning the endless empty forests for crop land—migrating to the south, attracted by the man-tall grasslands and willing to accept the protection of the horse-mounted Bulgars and Khazars—moving to the west into land vacated by German migrations. And always breeding steadily.

The eyes of the wall-screen above Sam's dental chair flowed through a flat forest of pine and birch like a wandering woods-man breaking into a virgin land where no one could follow, the thick growth shutting out the trail behind and the daylight from above. Sometimes there was a stand of oak or ash. Moss covered the rotten detritus and the black swamps of the lowlands slowly ate all footprints with mouths of ooze. The forest was endless. A bear pawed swarming ants from a broken stump, licking and nibbling. Once, only once, the curious screen probed into a Slav's deserted pit-hut, dug on higher ground to the depth of half-a-man and roofed over by reeds from a local beaver pond.

Sam's briefing officer nodded. "We're looking at the eighth century Russian wilderness into which the heathen Slavs are being driven by suddenly warlike neighbors. They are tillers of the land and hunters. Unfortunately for them they have been pushed into terrible farmland. The soil is acid, cold, infertile, badly aerated and poorly drained. Once the land is cleared its fertility dies. They have to keep moving, clearing new land,

and they have to hunt and fish to survive. The poverty of the land will plague them for a thousand years."

He touched the console of the Kensakan Kambi-1000. The forest disappeared—to be replaced by a ninth century map of Europe centered around the Baltic Sea and showing the explosion of Norse invasions in red.

"Prince Samislav, you are not a Slav—though your name is Slavic and you speak nothing but Slavic. Your ancestors are Norman. Your princely class has retained for centuries a semi-colonial character. Generations ago your family lost contact with its Scandinavian origins—and you have personally never even seen the sea—but you still think like a Viking. Deep in your soul something yearns for the ocean. You are a sea-warrior trapped into owning Slavs. Your principle interest is not in exploiting the land but in exacting tribute."

A deft finger motion expanded the map.

"Look at the available river networks. It is ideal country for explorers who have mastered the art of boatbuilding." The map could be scaled and scrolled and overlaid. Northern Russia showed a swath of flatlands, snow-filled and bleak in winter, soggy in spring, water moving across its face in slow meandering paths, some escaping north along the Memel-Nieman, Dvina, and Volkhov river networks. Most of it flowed south.

High on the map the Baltic rivers intertwined with the source-fingers of south-seeking waterways—the Volga which fed the Caspian Sea and the Dnieper which fed the Black Sea. Portages across the meek divide lay over gentle land and never for great distances. Brontz couldn't help but notice that a minor river called the Moskva, flowing into the Oka, which flowed into the Volga, dominated this strategic transportation hub.

Whiteface stepped the map backwards in time.

Under the first starlight of the Dark Ages the Khazar city of Itil on the Caspian dominated the inland trade reaching up the Volga. Single Scandinavian traders and adventurers were attracted southward, fascinated by the luxuries that sometimes came out of the inhospitable forest, the silks and spices and glassware which had once flowed copiously from a now ruined Mediterranean commerce. These far-ranging Norse traders, too few during the eighth century to be a military threat to the Slavs, brought with them wealth and trading posts and diplomacy. They bought the local furs and honey.

The blond traders were quite willing to work with the Slavs and to accept the protection of the Khazars—but when Arab invasions and slave raids and depradations proved that Khazar might was more illusion than fact, and then when the Khazars, increasingly uneasy at Norse trading success—deliberately caused them commercial grief, they began to look north to their own people for help.

The massive Norse invasions of continental Russia during the early ninth century are hailed in Russian history as the arrival of heroic saviors—the sagas being composed by Norman conquerors, and sung only later by the confused Slavs. From their fortress base on Lake Ladoga, down the Volkhov River, the Vikings raided and looted in bands of several hundred as was their nature.

"Let me scroll forward in time." Forts and trading centers blossomed along the dark rivers. In their songs the Normans called Russia "Gardariki," the country of strongholds. One could see the rapid advance of the Norsemen down the map, following the early traders, first as pirates and then as colonial masters.

Like a plague the settlements rose on the rivers below Novgorod. Then, enticed by inland traders who needed the backing of warriors, they raided down the Dnieper and took Kiev, bypassing Itil on the Caspian, to open a route through the Black Sea to marvelous Constantinople. Brashly the Norsemen even attacked Constantinople with a great fleet of 200 ships, always willing to loot when they thought piracy more rewarding than trade. Constantinople retaliated by sending them Christian missionaries and simultaneously appeased them by making sweet deals for their furs and slaves. The heathen Normans were happy to supply Christians with slaves from the abundant Slavic villages which came with their conquered lands.

By the early eleventh century Norsemen were so plentiful in Constantinople that the emperor formed a whole regiment of them, the famed Varangian guard. Scandinavian pilgrims to the Holy Land of the Savior liked to make a round tour, coming by sea through the Mediterranean and returning overland via the rivers of Russia.

As the machine scrolled through time, Sam watched the Kievian empire grow strong enough to attack and defeat the weakened Khazars on the eastern border—an unwise decision which opened the plains to the penetration of Pechenegs and Cumans who, with practice, learned to strangle the Kievian outlets to the Black Sea. The Slavicized Normans then no longer had markets for their slaves and had to find work for them on their own northern estates. They could not ship their furs south to make a living and had to take up the demeaning life of Slavic agriculture.

Limon's agents began to drill Sam in the attitudes of a "Norman" overlord whose *vochina* included huge tracts along the Oka river, remnant of a sub-divided patrimony which had once extended from the Baltic to the Black Sea. As centuries passed this pirate family had evolved from fast-moving adventurers into landed Slavic nobility, from heathen to devout Christian—but their minds remained separated from Slavic tradition. The Norman state in Russia was a great colonial merchant enterprise. Its princes saw the land as property and its people as property to exploit for profit.

And the soul of Brontz struggled with the man whose body he was possessing, the man wearing Russian furs and wool— outraged that this primitive knew nothing of democracy and freedom. But Samislav could not hear him from his lands on the banks of the Oka, 600 years down-time: he was of the noble *rodoslovnye*—and the others were chattel. Through a single-minded devotion to Christ he resisted being taken over by this devil with his ideas about free women and flying.

Whenever Brontz emerged dominant, in brief victory, his instructors beat him senseless with questions that demanded archaic answers from Samislav. The trio tormented their student as a team—when one of them faded into exhaustion, another took over. Brontz-Samislav had to remain and endure.

The screen flickered. A world overwhelmingly alien to Sam flooded from it by unearthly light; he had to answer endless questions and when he was wrong, he was recycled through the attitudes of the fourteenth century until he could hardly remember how an American thought. Gradually, as his tormentors rotated places, the white-faced Time Agents transmogrified into ascetic monks. The room dimmed. An ikon appeared, celebrating in its stilted colors the holy world of suffering. The grilling never stopped. The Time Agents were gone but the monks kept at him and kept at him. God have mercy. Sam felt his age. He needed sleep.

Samislav sat alone in his private chapel with the monks, obsessed by his choices, resenting the Mongol curse. This scourge not only bled from him the taxes which belonged to him by right of inheritance from his fathers, but it might, if the whim struck the overlords of Sarai, even take from him the right to collect those taxes. He was tired, tired, tired—so tired since the death of his father—but he had to come to a decision. Abruptly he forced himself to his feet and left the room.

His monk followed him with a flickering bee's wax candle. For need of peace he had to confer with this man of God. "I confess I am afraid. I am so afraid I dare not speak my mind even to my own brother Sviatopolk with whom I wrestled as a child and have shared everything. The awful shame of my fear drives me like a caged wolf."

"Ah, the trip to Sarai?"

Samislav nodded. He feared what the short monsters of Sarai would do with his inheritance. He longed to revolt, to gather an army and attack them, but merely dreaming of revolt made him sick with fear. Eighty percent of his family had been killed and left to rot when the first Tartar Tsar had scythed over the land almost a hundred years ago—and among his family had been the mightiest warriors and heroes that Russia had to offer. Even the women had been slaughtered as they took refuge in the church.

And now the death of his father was a personal catastrophe. Samislav had always taken for granted the cunning with which that man handled the Tartar *baskaks* and the cruelty with which he put down the local rebellions against the Tartars, but he had not known until these responsibilities had devolved upon his own shoulders that he was a coward, and now he was too afraid even to tell his brother of the fear which knotted his stomach. Among noble families the problems of death were resolved by the law of *votchina*, by the passing of the land and property and taxation rights of the father to the sons. But under the *Bozhi Batog*, the cudgel of God, as the Russians liked to call their Tartar overlords, it was not so easy.

No Russian prince of the occupied territories collected taxes without being granted an *iarlyk* by the Tsar of the Golden Horde himself and that meant a journey of homage to Sarai. The Tartar Tsar could strip a family of their property, without a thought, and award everything to whichever grovelling snake reached Sarai first and offered to extract more taxes per head than had the former lord.

The Tartars chose their princes with care. Patriots were suspect. Men who pleaded for their people were ignored. The local princes had no rights. The only trait that the suspicious brutes liked to reward was absolute obedience. Samislav's fear filled him with indignation. *He* had to beg that heathen Tsar at Sarai for *his* own land, grovel, call *himself* a slave, promise more than his father had given, bring elaborate gifts—and somehow sell the new taxes to his people who were always on the edge of revolt, all just to keep what had been granted to him by the God of his ancestors. God was merciless in punishing the sinners of Russia for past transgressions. When would the purification be done? When would they finish atoning for those monstrous sins which had brought the Tartars upon them! God have mercy!

But his thoughts wandered from God and back to the Tsar of all Asia. What if, without intending to, he offended that stinking child born of a horse's anus? Some sons had never returned from Sarai.

He was terrified—but he had to go.

CHAPTER 17

O for a Muse of fire, that would ascend
The brightest heaven of invention!

SHAKESPEARE, *HENRY V*

Byron McDougall called it his Houston Palace, with just a touch of irony in his voice, because he thought of himself as some kind of pampered consort of Princess Junie. Though still fascinated by the NASA job that "King Charles Bond" had found appropriate for his son-in-law's station in life, he was already planning to parachute out—into another job, into another world, anywhere, just so long as he landed upon a distant kingdom he could call his own.

The slanted wooden windows opened north upon suburban gardens to avoid the Texas sun. On the far wall hung a dozen crisp images of stellar miracles, broadcast to Earth by the Space Telescope and decoded by computers, framed in wood and glass—among them a bizarre, knotty jet of gas spewing from the galactic core of M-87 in the first photographic confirmation of the mythical black hole. Below it was Byron's favorite, a ragged nebula caught in a slow motion explosion. The largest frame was filled with a pensive portrait of his wife.

The room might have been a designer's showpiece; no one would have thought of it as a workplace for there were no papers in sight and the books on the shelves were modest in number and sorted by size rather than by content as if by a decorator who valued the balance of line and form above reading. The science fiction collection was modestly hidden beside the desk, out of sight from the doorway. The jungle plants from Brazil had air and space.

Even the flat screen computer did not seem to be used. Its table was bare. His disks were all in neat pseudo-Harvard Classic's leather cases above the computer, their program manuals next to them, all in order. The single object which had no place was a thumbnail-sized square of silicon, opalescent and legless because it was not mounted, an oddity, a failed prototype.

Byron hated to return to a messy desk after his long astronaut training sessions. He filed everything in its special place with the effortlessness of a man who has always enjoyed finishing every one of life's small cycles before starting a new one. His father and his grandfather were military men, and he never remembered a time when he had not been neat. He had yet to decide what to do with the chip.

Near it, one whole folder of clippings and notes was devoted to monitoring his alternatives. Religiously he took out that folder every other night for updating. So far he had developed eight different paths that might lead him to an escape from Charlie Bond. The possible routes were tenuous. Not many people besides NASA needed an engineer whose only experience was as a fighter pilot.

Sometimes, when he was out of fresh ideas for his own folder, he opened the folder he had begun to build for his son and made entries in it instead. He had his son organized by age—when Charlie Jr. would walk, when he would talk, what toys he should be playing with at two and a half, when he should learn to read, what books were appropriate for which age, and when he should start camping.

At seven Byron had his son down for learning to clean, assemble, and fire a rifle. At eight he had him down for building his first electric motors. To the task-sheet for the ninth year was attached a construction project from Popular Science. Ten was marked off as the age to be introduced to his first Robert Heinlein novel and it was also the age they would begin to hike together. How he had hated those hikes with his own father, but it had forged a tough man out of a resentful boy, taught him to hold in the tears and walk on the blisters. It took a while to understand fathers. Byron remembered the old bastard saying with chilling calmness, "I don't give a damn if you like me; I'm going to make a man out of you!"

Byron planned for his son when he despaired over his plans for himself. Sometimes he thought that all of his meticulous scheming to conquer his own kingdom, which so far consisted largely of paper lists and diagrams, was merely procrastination to keep him away from a decision. He wasn't sure he could survive on his own. He wasn't sure he even wanted to.

Bond, who fawned on his daughter, had bought Byron his own Cessna. How could a poor kid, who had loved airplanes since he was five, resist a lifestyle like that? Yet . . . since leaving the Air Force he had been *driven*—the idea of living as some woman's "prince consort" appalled him to the core of his soul.

He picked up the darkly opalescent chip. It was defective, a piece from an experimental run, too expensive to be of any use to anyone even if it had been perfect. It was a curiosity—but there were billions of dollars in that little patch of silicon for the men who learned to make them cheaply. Strange things floated around the labs, this one picked up by a NASA scientist in Concord who swore that it was a micro-rectenna array carved by an electron beam from metal deposited on a transparent substrate, its wires a hundredth of a micron in diameter, the grid spacings approximately a third of a micron across, each square holding its own diodes.

Byron still stared at the chip with amazement, but he was getting used to the idea. After all, light *was* electromagnetic in nature and there wasn't any reason it couldn't be converted directly into electricity in the same way that radio waves were picked up and sent to a receiver—providing one knew how to fabricate antennae with lengths half as small as the wave lengths of the light. The micro-rectennae were potentially far more efficient than photo-voltaic cells.

In pondering the potential of this proto-device Byron was, of course, dreaming about the moon—not about African villages which needed compact power sources or about portable coffee pots that could be taken on a California picnic. Radiant energy arrived at the equator of the moon's surface with a flux of 1400 watts per square meter. If one assumed that micro-rectennae could operate with an efficiency of seventy percent, then one square meter would generate about 1000 watts of electrical power, and one square kilometer, a thousand megawatts—about the electrical output of the average nuclear plant.

Byron thought of land area in terms of the 150 acres that Lincoln had granted the Civil War veterans and so he computed the power for that area at the moon's equator. The number came out to be 600 megawatts. He whistled through his teeth—that was sixty times as much power per unit area as they were getting out of that 150 acre photo-voltaic power plant that had recently gone on line in the California desert. Beautiful! His mind flicked through pleasant images of heavy lunar industry thriving on that kind of power.

The long lunar night was a problem but there was no reason that enormous quantities of surplus daytime electricity couldn't be stored as magnetic energy in a giant superconducting torus. He had once thought of storing the energy in molten sodium tanks and taking it out via a steam turbine at night, but worried about heavy, imported machinery with moving parts that broke down. The torus was simpler, its heaviest component being the conducting buffer needed to absorb the rapid dump of electrical energy if the supercooling failed. The moon could supply plenty of aluminum for that.

Still staring at the bluish flame of the dark chip, Byron took a sudden turn of pessimism, the cautious engineer in him talking the enthusiast down to a safe landing. The price might never be right. Electron beam machining was expensive. Even if the moon was the ideal place for that kind of manufacturing, the process might still be too expensive.

His mind began to sort through alternate ways of fabricating micro-rectennae. He remembered a private tour through a Corning Glass factory and recalled marvels like glass that bent as if it were metal sheeting and spiders that spun optical fiber. You could put holes in glass and extrude the glass to the point where the holes were so fine that they couldn't be seen though they still retained their original proportions. Wires in the glass could be extruded in the same way. If the thermal expansion properties of both wires and glass were identical, the extrusion process could be continued almost indefinitely and all that happened was that the wire got thinner.

Would it be possible for a ribbon of glass with embedded parallel wires to be drawn out to the point where the wire diameters were reduced in thickness to a few percent of the wavelength of visible light and spaced half-a-wavelength apart? A sandwich of ribbons, the top layer at right angles to the lower layer, would form a grid. But how might one add the invisible diodes? Byron didn't know.

But he did know a glass physicist. The next time he flew back to New Hampshire to visit his wife he'd have to stop over in New York's boondocks and ask. He might even get in some gliding at Elmira.

Byron's message light went on. He touched the display, read the liquid crystal's flowing note—and called the secretary, already in a better mood remembering how he had soared in a flimsy glider on a summer's day hundreds of miles over the farms and forested mountains of New York State.

"Isn't Colonel Brown early?"

"Your appointment is for four."

"It's sixteen hundred already?"

"You've been dreaming again, Byron. What would you do without me?"

"Send him up."

Byron went to the window, a wry sense of humor overtaking him. It was harder to avoid the military than it was to escape Charlie Bond's clutches! He remembered his boyhood dreams of fleeing from the constant punishment and regimentation of the military life. He lived in the clouds. His secret passion was to fly a *Farman* biplane (1912) or to blast Prussia from the bowels of a giant four engined Sikorsky *Ilya Mourometz* bomber (1916). He was still so dumb when he was eighteen that he had thought joining the Air Force would liberate him. He had identified military life with the Army.

And now, as a civilian, the military still claimed him.

Colonel Brown knocked on the door lightly.

"Come in."

The Air Force officer was just neat enough to pass inspection, but not a bit more. His sky-blue uniform should have been pressed two days ago. "How do you like the training around here?"

"It's pretty rigorous. They don't leave anything out. Sometimes it's all right. Sometimes I'm exhausted."

"Anxious to fly up there?"

"It'll come."

"We have a recon mission we'd like to talk to you about. I'm blunt. I'll get to the point right away. We want to have you orbiting in *leo* six months earlier than your NASA training schedule calls for. The Soviets seem to have a small five-ton payload craft being readied at Tyuratam for operational testing. She goes up on a booster but comes down on wings."

"Is she military or civilian?"

"Put it this way—Snowfox is a civilian with features that a non-military craft wouldn't need. Basically she's got the capacity to visit our satellites. With a stopover at the Soviet Mirograd complex she can even be outfitted for a trip to *geo*, right where we keep some of our major spy stuff. She doesn't violate any treaty—but in a crisis we think a group of Snowfoxes could take out all of our crucial satellites in a matter of hours. We don't know enough about her."

"So?"

"We'd like you to volunteer for a special mission."

CHAPTER 18

Love will never take you where you expect to go.
A BUM WORKING THE STREETS OF CENTRAL L.A.

The iron gates of Ray Armsiel's stucco-walled apartment building in Van Nuys were manned by a Secretary of Defense, a Mexican bandito, who did not trust girls. "One meenit." He raised his finger and disappeared.

Ray lay under the shade of an umbrella at the swimming pool, tanning only his toes in the sun, ignoring the housewives who were nagging their children not to bother him.

"Is girl for you," said the bandito disapprovingly. "Beeg eyes. You know? I let her in?"

"Yeah, sure." Ray didn't get up but he scanned through his memory. None of the women he knew had big eyes.

"Hey!" he exclaimed when he saw Linda Brontz. "What are you doing here? I thought you were running away from me?"

"I got tired of teasing you over the phone," she grinned contritely. "How come you're not at work like the rest of the men? You've got a tan! And my father is paying you!"

"I'm between jobs, remember? Actually I'm not but my boss doesn't mind if I goof off. I've put in more than my share of sixteen hour days. The clean-up men are still working over my stuff and won't call me in until they hit a snag, which they will, so I haven't been able to start with Shantech. That's all right; Sam the Man know's he's lucky to get me at all." Ray wondered why he was babbling. "Of course, I'm lucky to get Sam and am pretty eager to work for him. Going for a swim?"

"I don't have a bathing suit. We don't swim in Boston."

"I'll lend you mine."

"Does it come with suspenders?"

113

"Hey, aren't you supposed to be working yourself?"

She sank into the deck chair beside him. "I was fired this morning." The afternoon sun made further talk seem unnecessary. Eventually one of the four year olds came over with her mother's nail polish kit and began to paint Ray's toes while watching him studiously to see when he would get mad.

"Jody!" screamed the mother.

"S'awright Mrs. Stern. Red toenails are the least of my problems. Let me handle her. Jody," he said to the little girl, "if you keep taking care of me like this, I'll marry you and then you'll be in a real pickle. You'll have to make me a sandwich *every day* even when you have a headache. You know what a hard life wives have."

"Don't worry, Jody," said Linda. "He's already spoken for. My father has already made arrangements for him."

Ray stared at the underside plaid of the umbrella, but he was speaking to Linda. "So he told you his plans? Is that why you've been running away?"

"Of course. How much did he tell *you?*" She was smiling.

"He ordered me to marry you."

She sat up. "Oh, he didn't!"

"Well, he didn't order me to go to work for him either, but it amounts to the same thing. I refused five times, but I signed his contract anyway. What are we going to do about your old man? Can *you* handle him?"

"I promise not to propose to you, if you promise not to propose to me. That should make the beginning of a truce."

"Won't do any good," said Ray glumly.

"Do you do *everything* he says?"

"He breathes excitement. He knows which worlds are possible. I can't resist him."

"And, of course, you do cocaine, too?" she asked scornfully.

"There's a difference. Cocaine is the rush of losers. Winners have their own special rush. You have to be a winner to know what I mean. Sam the Man sells that rush, and when you've known him for a while, you can't give it up."

"Did he convince you that being stuck with me would be exciting?"

"Damn right! You should hear his stories about you!"

"His stories about me," she said evenly, "aren't true." She tried to be amused, well aware of her father's sly insinuations. "I come in late from parties so he imagines things. He always wanted a boy so he expects me to play around. I'm really just a quiet virgin who's afraid of my own shadow."

Ray grinned at the sun. "He says you lie very well."

"You may think what you wish," she said with irritation. "Why is my father so interested in a jerk like you?"

Ray wiggled his grotesquely painted toes. "Sam the Man is a fighting frontiersman and so am I."

"You don't really believe that crap, do you? That's just jargon you learned in grammar school."

"Don't you ever get restless? It's an American tradition. Go up, young man!" He was pointing to the sky.

"Up you, young man," she smiled. "My father says he can't explain to me what you are doing because I'm a *girl*."

"It's really because you're an English major. It helps if you know some physics."

"That goddamn word again!" she grumbled.

"If you are very patient with me, I could try explaining to you how the leoport works without mentioning physics. Leo stands for low-earth-orbit."

"Hmmm," she muttered.

"But it won't mean anything unless you let me show you my blueprints."

"Blueprints? What an old fashioned word. Aren't all your drawings done by computer these days?"

"All right. Come up to my room and let me spread my CAD designs out on the bed for you."

She liked his apartment. The main window overlooked the patio. The rooms were spacious, open, with little reliance on doors, but with enough corners and breakwalls to give a sense of privacy. While he brought out his drawings, she examined the cupboard shelves and refrigerator to see what he ate. Eggs and ham and pancakes for breakfast. A coffee maker, its grounds still in the filter. "You're a very conventional man," she said while she put the dishes in the dishwasher, turned it on, and tidied up.

In the bedroom the drawings were now everywhere, on the bed, on the floor, stacked up against the dresser mirror. He really was going to explain to her what he was doing! That annoyed Linda and she thought of telling him to put the damn things away and not take her complaints about the inaccessability of the male world so seriously—but she didn't.

The careful sketches were dominated by a central component— two nested hula-hoops, one outer, one inner, attached together by radial spokes. The interior of the smaller hoop was empty. In the sketch a tiny drawing of a spacesuited man indicated scale. The hoops were large: the exterior hoop about twelve man lengths in diameter and the inside hoop about ten.

"A Papa bicycle tire and a Mama bicycle tire skewered together by lengths of coat hanger," she mused. "What's it for?"

"By itself, nothing. We need about fifteen thousand of them working in unison."

"You stack them?"

"No, no," he laughed. "You can't stack them. We string them out in a necklace a hundred and fifty kilometers long. Each pair has to be separated from its neighbors by about ten meters of vacuum. They don't drift apart because the hoops contain superconducting magnetic coils."

She looked at the relevant drawings. "So tell me, why is your leoport thing so long?"

"I have to answer that?"

"Not if you don't know how."

He paused, thinking furiously. No physics. "You're an English major, right? Do you know what gravity is?"

"Yes-I-know-what-gravity-is!"

"Good. Do you know what I mean by five gravities?"

"Which planet?"

"You're smarter than I thought. Five *Earth* gravities."

"I'd be very heavy. I think I'd be confined to bed and my cheeks would be running off my skull."

"Excellent! Have you ever noticed how gravity changes when you go up and down in a fast elevator?"

"My stomach in my mouth or in my shoes."

"Excellent! Have you ever noticed how gravity changes when you goose the car's accelerator, or when you slam on the brakes?"

She was puzzled. "Is that gravity? I thought that was force or something."

"Einstein showed that gravity and acceleration are locally indistinguishable, but let's not get into that. That's physics. Just think of gravity and goosing as the same thing. Now, do you know the difference between driving your car at a hundred miles an hour into a brick wall and into a haystack?"

"The haystack wouldn't kill me."

"You're right. Why?"

"Well, it's *softer*."

"What does soft mean?"

"Cuddley. I don't know. You tell me."

"If it is soft, it gives. The impact, the momentum change, is extended over a longer distance—and it is the *rate* of change of momentum that we feel as force."

"Momentum is a physics word," she said sternly. "You promised."

"Shit," he said—and paused. "The brick wall stops you suddenly but smashes your head. It uses lots of force and very little distance to do its work. The haystack stops you just as well but uses up lots of distance and very little force. It is force that bends your head out of shape—so when one has a lot of stopping to do, prudence suggests a recipe long on distance and light on force."

"Is that physics? So far it's easy."

"Yeah. Now do you remember your original question?"

"No."

Ray showed her one of his drawings, a perspective of the leoport in space, an endless queue of those double concentric coils, each floating free of all the others, fifteen thousand rings dwindling off to a point among the stars. "You asked me why it was so long."

"All right. Why is it so long?"

"Because it has to be a haystack instead of a brick wall."

"Oh," she said.

"We shoot up a little freighter from Earth. The leoport is in orbit and moving in the same direction. When our freighter reaches the top of its orbit it is travelling at 9,000 miles per hour, about half orbital velocity. The leoport overtakes the rocket at 18,000 miles per hour—like a fast car bumping into a slow one from behind.

"If the leoport acted like a brick wall, everything would be torn apart just like you'd be torn apart if you were travelling along at 50 mph and were hit from behind by a car doing 100 mph. We don't want that. That's a couple of billion dollars shredded. But if the huge leoport acts like a haywagon, the cargo carrier gets embedded deep in the hay and captured intact."

He showed her a picture of a flying saucer. "That's our freighter. It has coils in its rim and goes zipping down the axis of our leoport—belly first. If the saucer is braked at five gravities—all done with electromagnetic interaction between the hoops of the leoport and the rim of the saucer—we need a cushion with ninety miles of give."

"My father is hiring you to design flying saucers?" She looked at Ray askance.

Ray caught one of his drawings that had suddenly buckled

and was falling off the dresser. "One saves fuel. In fact if you build your system right you can extract more energy out of it than you put in."

"My father is hiring you to tap perpetual motion?"

He shrugged. "A shell game doesn't violate the laws of physics. It just doesn't *look* reasonable."

"I don't really understand."

"I'll give you a rain-check."

"You don't think I'm capable of understanding!" She knew she wasn't but she was miffed anyway.

"I'm ready to call it a day."

"It's hardly past twelve yet!"

"Never study physics in the afternoon. Let's hit the beach. I'm anxious to see you in my bathing suit plus suspenders."

She was disappointed. He didn't think she was a good student. "I'll make you a sandwich. I'm better at that than boring you by making you teach me kindergarten physics."

He cut onions for her in the kitchen alcove. "One of these days if you learn as well as you did today, I'll be showing you how to work out the diffusion equations for onion smells."

"I can't wait," she replied sarcastically. "I think engineers run off at the mouth with shop talk worse than lawyers or doctors or *businessmen*. Do you want salami or corned beef? You have a lousy selection of meats."

"Hey, wait a minute," he said, backtracking. "*You* asked for the shop talk!"

"Don't confuse me with the facts. How do you know I wasn't just bolstering your male ego?" she snapped.

"You're in a bitch of a mood today."

"I was snarled at all morning, and I blew up and quit my job. I'm panicking because I don't know how I'll pay my rent."

"Oh, my poor darling. Where does it hurt?"

"Right on your kisser—which I'm about to punch."

"I have a better idea than the beach. You've opened up a couple of days for yourself. I'll show you California. I'll give you the grand tour."

She was slightly less miffed now. If she didn't tease him so much, he wouldn't tease her. She poured him milk and set his sandwich on a plate with a proper knife and fork, and when he didn't take a napkin, impulsively tucked one under his chin. A tour of California! They might even find the village where Lana Turner met the Postman.

Ray munched through his onions and tomatoes and corned beef. He stood up. "Let's go!"

"Right now?"

"Right now."

"I'll have to pick up some luggage at the apartment."

"Naw. We'll only be gone three or four days."

"My car!"

"It's parked okay. Not to worry."

She didn't know quite what to say to that. He took her down the back stairs into the underground garage. "My *pills* aren't in my purse," she said meekly and a little bit desperately.

"You're the boss's daughter. You think I'm crazy?"

Linda changed the subject. "Which one is your car?"

He went over and patted a gigantic Honda 850, purple and black, two huge wheels straddling a rocket engine of chrome tubing. She paled when he handed her a helmet and put one on his own head.

"I'm not getting on that motorcycle!"

"The first thing we do is buy you some leather. Don't want the flesh scraped off your beautiful bones. Don't worry. I won't take you far the first day. Don't want you to get saddlesore. We'll head north up to the coast road. Get on."

"I haven't got any handlebars to hang onto," she wailed.

"Some things you don't need."

They roared up out of the garage but gently rolled along the street to the first red light. "Don't hang on so hard," he said gently. "I have to breathe and you'll only tucker yourself out." At the next red light he spoke again over his shoulder. "The first thing you have to learn about motorcycles is that every maniac behind the wheel of a car is a murderer-at-heart out to get you. They'll never give you an inch. They'll run you off the road—and then back up at full reverse to get you again."

"That doesn't make me feel very safe!"

"We're more maneuverable." And off he zoomed.

She had never been so terrified in all her life. Fifty-five miles an hour, weaving in and out of L.A. traffic on two wheels, faster even than the cars could go, and with her legs hanging out the windows!

What had her crazy father gotten her into!

CHAPTER 19

*In 1242, after his father's death, [Alexander Nevsky] jour-
neyed to Sarai to pay homage to the conqueror and most likely
to request from him an iarlyk for Vladimir. [Instead] the Mongols
entrusted Vladimir to Nevsky's younger brother. But Nevsky
did not give up . . . and ten years later succeeded in persuad-
ing the Khan to reverse himself. With a Mongol force placed at
his disposal he captured Vladimir, unseated his brother, and
assumed the title of Great Prince. His subsequent behavior
fully justified the Mongol confidence in him. In 1257-9 he
stamped out popular uprisings against Mongol census-takers
which had broken out in Novgorod, and a few years later did
so again in several other rebellious cities, all of which must
have pleased his masters.*

RICHARD PIPES, *RUSSIA UNDER THE OLD REGIME* (1974)

The dawn played with leaves yellowed by autumn's chill, its
tubercular light dimmed by the fog drifting through the birches.
Their top branches were invisible. Horses snorted gray vapor,
impatient to be off along the narrow trail, but having to wait
while the estate slaves finished loading the pack animals. Prince
Samislav's entourage of priests and boyars was starting early,
hoping to reach the Rzhevolo piers on the Oka by dusk, the
first leg of a journey which would take them down the distant
Volga to Sarai where, to keep his father's commission, the dead
prince's son would have to beg before the Tartar tsar.

A priest, Iziaslav Dimitriev, was to be his constant companion and teacher, knowing as he did the savage's court etiquette.
Samislav watched him curiously. Wrapped in his great *podry-
asniki*, the bearded cleric wheeled his horse, calming the impa-

tient beast, and they began their trek through medieval New England wilderness, swampland, deserted woods, abandoned farms.

Once while the prince's horse was making passage through a collapsing fieldstone fence that divided a new stand of birch from an old stand of gloomy trees, a subdued Sam Brontz, reduced to passivity by his giddy drop through time, pondered a rusting car and telephone pole from his own century, and beyond, an old road that lead to a glimpse of asphalt—but the prince he had become hardly noticed the large red boulder and the tree, dead and stripped of its bark by beetles, rising alone on an abandoned cut-and-burn field in his beloved Oka countryside.

Their day was filled with inspiring chatter. When the old trail, grassy and sometimes mud-rutted, was wide enough for two to ride abreast, the garrulous Dimitriev whispered the old tale of Fedor of Riazan who, when sent on a diplomatic mission to the Mongols, refused to give his wife to the grandson of Genghis Khan and was fed to the animals and birds with all of his retinue.

Later, while they were dismounted to water their horses, the priest picked his teeth and told the tale of a Mongol victory feast held on a platform built on top of suffocating Russian warriors. He did a good imitation of the screaming and moaning and the soup slurping.

Endlessly, Dimitriev could weave his cautionary stories: He told of princes rerouted from Sarai across a year's journey of eastern plains to chastise themselves before the tsar's Tsar at Karakorum, and of the painful seven-day martyrdom in Sarai of a prince who had dared to impale, by the anus, an over-zealous Chinese "squeezer." He relished the story of the martydom of Prince Mikhail who, by refusing to pass between the Devil's Two Fires and by refusing to bow toward the rising sun in obeisance to the Khakhan at Karakorum, earned death by rib-crushing—the Tartars did not believe in spilling a nobleman's blood even if they fed him to the animals afterwards.

"They won't shed a drop of your blood," he cackled through his beard at Samislav's paleness.

Around their mid-day campfire, while dipping into the turnip and rabbit stew with one set of fingers and holding bread in the others, Dimitriev mused informatively about the sin of greed. There was always some traitor prince ready to outbid a rightful *gosudar* by promising the Tartars more *vyhod* in the hopes of being awarded administration of the coveted estates. While sucking rabbit bones he suggested which of Prince Samislav's rivals should be murdered.

Full of laughter and sauce in his beard he gossiped about the squeezings of the collaborator Ivan Moneybags of Moscow who would not hesitate to rush to Sarai and lead a Mongol army back with him in a devastating raid against his own Russian brethren when such cynicism served Ivan's private interests. Skinning Russians for Mongol profit was a Nevsky family tradition when there was enough graft in it. With a childlike smile Dimitriev implied that Ivan would bugger a priest for a copper *puto*.

A quiet boyar, who had up until then said nothing, took out his knife and absently tossed it at a stump, where sometimes it stuck and sometimes bounced off. In a monotonous voice of hatred he told of the sacking of Tver, of the rape of women and the murder of boys and the looting of the noble homes in an act which had enriched Ivan and ingratiated him with the Tartars. "Those Muscovites will roast in hell. Traitors. Whores of Babylon, God curse them with boils!"

"And did they tell you of the Vlatsyn?" The gossip between the five companions of the prince became animated. Many peasants of the Vlatsyn region had fled because of taxes but they were still on the roles. Those remaining had to provide taxes for themselves, the dead, and the deserters. Every Russian knew how the Mongols responded to revolt, but sometimes the sole recourse to oppression was riot.

A *baskak*, come to collect his quota of boys for the Mongol army, of which few were left, had been beaten by a father and barely escaped with his life. Ten days later a Mongol hundred rode through the village, slaughtering. Instantly, neighboring inhabitants fled in terror but an old man, too arthritic to run, was tied to a post and used as a target—a lesson among the flames. Others were caught in a field and deliberately trampled to death under the horses hooves.

Prince Samislav was listening, full of revulsion and hatred—and fear. But the captured soul of Brontz was also listening and remembering the story of the peasant villages in the Panjsher Valley of Afghanistan being bombed to rubble by the children of the survivors of Vlatsyn. He had flashing images of Russian pilots diving their SU25s to take out a farmhouse or mosque or flour mill . . . Slavic infantry finding two blind brothers in a village vacated by terrorized peasants, strapping dynamite to their backs to blow them up . . . soldiers casually herding peasant women into a mosque, locking the door, and tossing in grenades through the window . . . a Red Army tank commander, defending National Socialist principles, ordering his sergeant to drive over a bound Afghan man, laughing. Brontz saw the Socialist *baskaks* rounding up children, forceably taking them away from their Afghan parents, to be sent back to Russia for indoctrination in how to become superior Mongol soldiers.

"What can we do?" asked the sullen boyar, who then answered himself rhetorically. "We can revolt every decade, be crushed by the newest traitor, and wait and gather our strength to revolt again. Such is the fate of every Russian forever and ever. What God wills we must endure for the sake of our souls." He grinned the grin of the helpless and burst out laughing.

It was a phrase that echoed . . . *be crushed by the newest traitor, and wait and gather our strength to revolt again.* Each word echoed across a canyon of six centuries from the ears of Brontz to the ears of Samislav, back and forth, across and back.

Prince Samislav was glooming cynically, but also with the admiration of a trapped man: *The heathen riders of the steppe teach us how to rule . . . and if we learn?* . . .

. . .while Brontz's mind was seeing General Wojciech Jaruzelski, agent of the Great Russians, inheritors of the domain of Genghis Khan, truncheoning his own Polish people with his Zomo thugs so that they might be convinced to work harder for their Russian masters and thus avoid a savage Russian invasion that would slaughter their leaders and, with Tartar pity, bury them in another Katyn Forest where the father of Jaruzelski had died a generation earlier, shot by the officers of Stalin.

How would it feel to be a man who *had* to betray his people in order to save them? thought Brontz. But the morose Samislav, worried about his reception in Sarai, not understanding Brontz, shut out the strange thoughts of the cunning devil who had possessed him on the day his father died. There were rewards in being a tribute collector for the Tartars—a cut of the tribute. But how much wealthier he would be if the Tartars would oblige him by slitting each other's throats!

The horses didn't reach the river by nightfall, but the fog had lifted, allowing an autumn moon to cast enough ghostly shadows so that a serious observer could tell the trees from the bears. It was the moonlight which encouraged Samislav's impatient companions to continue. In a meadow with the dark hills beyond, the prince remembered children's stories his mother had told him at bedtime of how the gods had created the boy Moon to roam the night, and of the wolves which pursued him across the sky. He prayed, as much for himself as for the moon.

God watch over Moon and keep the wolves from devouring him at least until they might return from Sarai!

Their river barge was waiting for them at the Rzhevolo pier. The gruff boatman was none too pleased to have his sleep interrupted but nevertheless rushed about to get a giant samovar boiling so that the prince might have tea with his honey. The slaves began to load the barge, and Samislav took time off from his tea to see that his gifts were put aboard gently. The fine fox fur and ermine he was bringing did not worry him but for special effect he had purchased a delicate piece of carved clockwork that had come in through Novgorod and he was afraid to have it crushed or shaken. What a catastrophe if he should present the geegaw to the tsar and it refused to perform!

Dimitriev had suddenly weakened at the end of their journey and, while they were establishing themselves below deck with the ropes and tar and cargo, began to complain jovially of pains visited on him by God to slow down his interest in sin. Before the night was out, he was deathly sick with fever. He cried and would not let Samislav leave his side, holding his lord's hand in delirium, sometimes quietly, sometimes raving about the heavenly hosts which he saw plainly as the angels hovered about ready to take his soul away to peace.

The priest was obviously terrified of death and terrified that he would die without the proper rites being performed. Wide-eyed, the fever-sweat running off his face in rivers, he instructed his prince in exactly the correct ritual. When Samislav gently reminded him that a prince was not a priest, Dimitriev, in a rage, ordained him right there with a short lecture on the mission of the church.

Samislav managed to feed the miserable man tea, laced with the juice of rare southern lemons, but could get him to eat nothing else. The priest, finally resigned to his death or else sensing recovery, returned to the purpose of his mission, the instruction of Samislav so that he might pass the grueling test of loyalty to the Moslem tsar and save the fortune of his family and them all.

He was taught to crawl along the bottom of the barge and to kiss the mouldering boards while he abused himself verbally. A feverish priest corrected all mistakes with groans and curses. The prince had to learn to refer to himself as a worm and as an old woman and as "less worthy than the dirt under the tsar's feet." He had to learn to use, for the first time in his life, that special form of speech that a *kholopy* employed when speaking to his masters. He had to find a way to carry himself as if he were nothing, and to treat his life as worth nothing.

Samislav grew sick himself one night, plagued by the priest's snores and the smell of tar and that special smell of green rot and rat droppings. The barge rolled and the boat slaves sang their monotonous dirge out of tune. Somewhere from deep inside the prince's aches and misery the whining Brontz-devil pleaded, cursing him for his folly, tempting him with the soft warmth of Holidayinnmotel which he insisted that Satan would grant him had he but the basic courage to rise up, to climb to the deck and jump overboard. It was a clever trick to drown him and steal him off to the black netherworld. He crossed himself when he heard the oily voice and quoted from psalms he knew by heart to quell his anguish.

One morning the prince's boyar friends gave him relief from the relentless teachings of the raving Dimitriev. They took him up to watch the river meadow and the cattle herds grazing there. They dined on a fine *zavtrak* of eggs and cheese and roast squirrel legs, and then he went below for more lessons.

The barge landed at dusk and was met by an escort of Mongol warriors on horseback who surrounded Prince Samislav to shield him—mainly from the shadow evidence of a New England town whose mayor had been cajoled into turning off critical street lamps at a critical time. One teenage boy came out to heckle the costumed freaks, to find himself facing two murderous Mongols with bone bows at the ready—who knew exactly how to frighten him away.

"Don't mess up the filming, kid!" they whispered in an off-the-microphone aside, symbolically making the gesture of cutting their throats, meaning his. The boy disappeared instantly, horrified that he might have offended the American God of Film Making. He'd be crucified if they had to reshoot!

Water channels ran along the terraces, splashing onto the blades of great wheels. They passed courtyards of tiled walls with glimpses of carpeted gardens. Beyond was a reddish glow of smoke from ceramic furnaces and the flickering lights of the bazaar. An ox cart laden with cloth from the garment makers creaked along the road and their horse guard pushed it aside roughly to let them past.

Limon sat on the throne in the great room of the Cathedral, Khan of the Golden Horde, Tsar of all the Russias, gray wolfskin over his Chinese silks. Behind him were the tapestries of a lord's tent. Surrounding him were guards and nobles and generals and the court mullah to oversee their prayers and, conspicuously, swinging in a wicker cage, a mad Russian dissident who had been foolish enough to sponsor the revolt of a-town-which-no-longer-existed. Two shamanic flames from a nomad past consumed the air above their brass bowls. Prince Samislav approached in stages, crossing himself as he passed through the Flames of Satan, then crawling, professing his unworthiness.

Limon Barnes twiddled one braid of his black Mongol hair as he watched Sam Brontz kiss the grubby floor, the scene giving him a curious feeling of absolute power. The fastidious capitalist was in pain, but he was actually *doing* it, bringing his lips in contact with the greasy dirt—he crawled forward on hands and knees, head bowed. The wizard who had taken Khan Batu in thrall to create this very moment was at the same time over-joyed and incredulous. Had he actually *broken* Brontz?

No, no, never.

In the next ten seconds this Russian prince would rise to his full height and an angry American businessman would burst through the fabric of the fantasy, confused and out of place, demanding the instant resignation of the Great Khan, effective immediately—don't even bother to clean out your desk!

Limon wasn't sure that a khan, intent on humiliating a Russian, would have rubbed fresh cow manure into the hem of his robe's skirt—but a khan intent on humiliating an American could have found no finer way to insult him. An American's life was served by swift water and porcelain robots which whisked his shit instantly into another dimension; even the foul traces could only be approached with silken tissue behind one's back.

The courtiers of the mad khan from Brooklyn watched in fascination as one of America's most powerful executives approached the throne like a trained animal trying his best to be an authentic Russian prince doing what he had to do to stay alive. The mullah was transfixed. The crazy Russian dissident stopped his gibbering. They all knew of the cow dung and they had all heard Limon's mocking stories about Sam's spotless gray suits and the socks he changed twice a day. None of them had ever seen it, but they all knew about the marble shower room Sam Brontz kept in his office in Boston.

Prince Samislav touched his forehead to the ground, twice, and then rose to kiss the hem—and froze.

The smell of the barn had reached the nose of Sam, that devil who fought for the possession of the body of Samislav.

Waiting on a knife's edge was Limon's *Ming the Merciless* laugh. With one gesture of his hand he was ready to summon the guards to slaughter this foolish supplicant who refused, as form required, to kiss the skirt of the Tsar of all the Russias.

But the sober prince of the Great Russians took in his fingers the silken fabric of the robe of the world's master which had dragged over the ground he walked on. Samislav's fear was under control—his fingers barely shook—but nevertheless fear drove him. Reverently, almost in relief, he kissed the tainted hem, proud that his hate did not show. This was his Tsar, and he was a slave, the most useless of the Tsar's *kholopy*.

The astonished Khan had no choice but to ask him to rise to his knees. The pleading began. There was no bargaining. The Khan belittled the abilities of the man before him. And Samislav, admitting his worthlessness, promised him that there was no other prince in all of Russia who could run the rat-infested principality along the Oka with more firmness.

He would make up for his known weaknesses by depending upon the Khan's advisors. There would be no revolts. The taxes would be paid on time. There would be special gifts. The census takers would be escorted and fed. The Russian boys raised for the Khan's armies would be the strongest and the healthiest. He pledged with his life that this was true. He even hinted that if Riazan, for instance, was not prompt with its taxes he might intercede—with a little help from a small Mongol regiment.

The Khan also made a promise. He promised to think over the proposition.

The merriment began. Acrobats amused and amazed. Bufooning jugglers would even fall all over each other and still catch their balls and batons. Fierce Mongol warriors danced, shaking the Cathedral with their vigor. The women brought on the feast. Gradually the Khan put out the signal to relax . . . bits of America began to show through.

"Man, what a gas!" said one panting Mongol warrior, throwing his arms about another.

"Where are the hamburgers!"

"Get Debbie! She's supposed to take some photos of me!"

Limon watched Sam unwind, still astonished that the man had proved unpredictable, unsure of what had happened to Brontz. The game was over and yet Sam was still behaving as cautiously as a lark who thought he saw a peregrine. Perhaps Russian paranoia was contagious, perhaps it would take hours to fall away and only then, when he had recovered, would Limon's boss explode in anger. Yet Sam began to smile. There really was no peregrine. Brontz smiled and smiled. He posed for Debbie and strutted a bit. He came over to Limon and slapped him on his back.

"You could get killed for that," said the Khan jovially.

"Excellent job, Ghengis! I'm always right about people." And he dragged Limon to the kitchen where he mixed salt and water for an emergency gargle. Yes, the boss-man had fully recovered—he even tried a light swab of iodine on his lips from the emergency medical kit. "The whole thing has stunned me. I've never had so many insights tumbling over each other! My God, I want you to get all of it. Capture it! Distill it! I'm going to send my key people here!"

"Too expensive," said Limon.

The executive officer of Shantech became an executive officer. "The first run through is always expensive. It's called the design phase. The first hand-tooled Chevrolet cost a million dollars. You may be a medievalist, Barnes, but you're not stuck with medieval technology."

"We could use a new blackboard," the Khan said wryly.

"If I ever catch you writing on a blackboard, I'll fire you so fast you'll think you were scalped by Tamberlane! When I went to Princeton," he exclaimed incredulously, "I even had a psych professor who taught me *learning theory* by writing it on the blackboard. The sonofabitch was waiting around for the printing presses to improve. Stick to simulations, Limon."

"Mr. Brontz, you are very wealthy but simulating Russia for the last thousand years is a big budget movie."

"Do they train airline pilots in 747s? They train them on the ground in a flight simulator, and a pilot gets more experience in an hour in one of those things than he'd get in a hundred hours of the real thing. That's exactly what I want—a simulation of Russia for the last thousand years!"

Limon laughed, a somewhat subdued Ming the Merciless. "I can see why my board game didn't impress you."

Sam pulled aside one of the Mongol warriors to examine his helmet. "Did you steal this out of a museum?"

"No, I make them in my basement," said the warrior shyly. "They sell pretty well at Boskone."

After borrowing the helmet for his head, the Russian prince took the Khan of the Golden Horde and retreated to an upper study of the Cathedral. Someone brought them soup and Debbie took their pictures, forcing them to pose in ways which interested her before the party spread elsewhere. When they were alone, Limon continued to needle his boss. All was not lost—perhaps he could still get Brontz to fire him. He was beginning to think that Sam was a madman who could afford to play meaningless games to entertain himself. He said as much.

Prince Samislav the Morose paused for a long moment. "No. This is the most serious game of my life. And I assure you that if it doesn't work, I'm getting the hell off this planet. I have plans for a spacefleet in the works." He paused again, placing the iron helmet on the table between himself and the Lord of the Steppes. "I'm trying to work out a riddle. Haven't you ever wondered why the greatest military minds of the United States and the Soviet Union have been unable to come up with a strategy that protects their civilians?"

CHAPTER 20

"Trust me!"

ADAM, POOH BEAR, JESUS CHRIST, JIMMIE DURANTE,
ELIZABETH I, S. FREUD, JOSEPH GOEBBELS, HANNIBAL,
POPE INNOCENT III, JEZEBEL, MARTIN LUTHER KING,
V.I. LENIN, MOTHER, RICHARD NIXON, OCTAVIA, PYRRHUS,
DON QUIXOTE, THE ROLLING STONES,
THE SNAKE IN THE GARDEN OF EDEN, MAO TSE-TUNG,
UNITED AIRLINES, THE VIRGIN MARY, GEORGE WASHINGTON,
XENOPHON, BRIGHAM YOUNG, EMILE ZOLA.

"I hear Joe Synmann's in town . . ."

Byron McDougall, who was sitting at the same cafeteria table
as the gossipers, perked up his ears. Before the lunch was
over he had established Synmann's purpose in Houston—lobbying
for space weaponry. That was puzzling because the rumor mill
had him involved with a large space project that was *non-
military*. It was these rumors which had intrigued Byron.

After putting his tray on the conveyor belt, it took only a
moment on the public telephone to establish that the physicist
was staying in the Rosal Hotel.

Fifteen minutes later the pilot reconnoitered his target area,
finding ample time to set up his ambush. He hid himself in a
cafe, his back to the sun, and when the Shantech man arrived
by cab an hour later he had a story well worked out. They had
never met before but Byron was not bothered by minor details.

He crossed the street to the Rosal and at an appropriate
moment popped out from behind a pillar beside the elevators
to make eye contact. He let a surprised look of pleasure cross
his face, then broke into a grin and extended his hand. "Joseph
Synmann! What are you doing in Houston?"

"Doing the turkey dance." Infected by the contact, Synmann smiled, too, and shook Byron's hand warmly. All the while he was searching his memory and drawing a blank.

"Byron McDougall. I married Charlie Bond's daughter. We belong to the same Mafia. I can't remember where we met, but I do remember that you tell good stories." That was a safe lie. "I left the Air Force and am working for NASA now."

Synmann showed new interest. "God, you've got a red tape machine down here."

"So has Charlie—or haven't you noticed?"

Synmann shook his long hair back over his shoulder. "I rue the day I ever left the university."

"Need help? I've done the party circuit down here and I know all the right secretaries."

"Can't talk about what I'm here for. Classified." He shrugged. "It's not important. You remember the bill the House passed two days ago? I just wish to hell somebody would run for Congress who wasn't a lawyer."

Byron tried to recall the latest Washington stories. "The amendment that put the rider on the space defense bill?"

"Yeah, the 'we'll-be-a-good-boy-to-encourage-you-poor-insecure-Russians' clause."

"It won't last."

"I know—but in the meantime my ass is frozen. I'm not allowed to run until the Soviets catch up."

"You won't have long to wait. Have you seen the latest recon photos of the new additions to the Mir complex?"

"Mirograd?" He chuckled. "No."

"Come have a drink with me at the Top."

Synmann nodded and they entered the elevator. The physicist pressed the special button for the Rosal's Top Hat Restaurant.

"I'm an Air Force pilot," continued Byron, "so I have this special eye for recon photos. But I'm an engineer, too. With that double edge I see things other people don't. Of course, I can't tell you about it." He smiled. "It's classified."

Synmann grunted.

"How did you ever get involved with defense work?" asked Byron as they stood waiting for a table.

"Game theory was a hobby of mine. I even simulated some very fancy stuff on a Cray. Ever do any game theory?"

"With women."

Synmann smiled in his slightly cynical way. "So I can assume you have a sixth grader's background. Actually game theory boils down to a triplet of simple rules.

"One: your best possible strategy is to cooperate; you win maximally.

"Two: a poor, but serviceable, strategy is to treat your partner as a potential enemy—assume that he might do you in and so take countermeasures.

"Three: your worst possible strategy is to cooperate; you get wiped out."

"Say that again?" queried Byron. "Didn't you put a catch-22 in there somewhere?"

"You're so young to be so smart. Yeah, it's a catch-22. Cooperation is the riskiest strategy there is—it's double-or-nothing. You win big or you lose big. And who wants to lose big? So we stay in the middle and choose caution and smaller winnings. But treat a friend as a potential enemy—just to be safe—and it isn't long before he is one. The Russian mind is one of the most cautious minds that cultural evolution has ever produced—and it breeds enemies like warm meat breeds flies."

A young woman in a top hat and tails, but no visible cover for her legs or hips, doffed her hat and took them to a table.

"How goes it tonight, sweetheart," said Byron. "Busy?"

"I'm always busy."

"How about at three o'clock?"

"I'll have a brandy and ice," said Synmann.

Byron wasn't ready to order yet. He was looking at the dark eyebrows of their waitress and her half-smiling eyes. Once he ordered she would have an excuse to leave. He spoke to Synmann.

"Let me see if I've got you straight. One: if she *is* my friend"—he glanced warmly at their serving wench— "and I assume that she's my friend and encourage her, then we have a wonderful night together. Two: on the other hand if she's my friend and I suspect that her smile might be a cunning way to trap me, and thus decide to handle her with extreme caution, then I'll only succeed in convincing her to handle *me* with suspicion, and we'll both lose a little. And finally, three: if she *isn't* my friend and in my naivety I trust all this sparkling good nature, then I could wake up in the morning without my wallet."

"Oh, I'm not *that* mean. I'd leave you your picture of your wife and your credit cards." It was fast repartee but the woman gave Synmann a puzzled look nevertheless.

"You just walked into the middle of a philosophical discussion," explained Synmann. "Mad McDougall here is working out all the implications of mathematical game theory at the sixth grade level."

"He's cute for a sixth grader." She grinned.

Byron took her manicured hand, kissing it. "You're my friend and I believe in the promise in your eyes. I love you and we must run away together and live happily ever after."

Slowly she withdrew her hand. "The bartender doesn't carry that."

Synmann had been watching the exchange with fascination. "You don't trust him do you?"

"Of course not." She leaned over and kissed Byron's forehead.

"Ah, trust!" said Byron. "Bring me a scotch on the rocks."

While they watched her leave for the bar, Synmann commented. "There's your catch-22. If the Soviets and the States trusted each other, *and were worthy of trust*, they could cooperate. The cooperation would produce miracles on Earth and an incredibly rapid exploration of the solar system. But the trust isn't there—and perhaps not even the integrity."

Byron was watching their waitress. She had a saucy way of moving and she was flirting with the bartender. "Lovely. Think of the wonder-filled time you and I could have tonight if she trusted us."

"Are you trustworthy?"

"No."

"Would you bullshit her?"

"Yes. Poetry is already fluttering through my mind."

Synmann sighed while he twiddled with his long graying hair. "I'm recalling my old hippy farm . . . the profound discussions about trust around the old Franklin stove while we were stealing each other's women. A wretched lot. They'd pilfer dope in the name of sharing. I remember when we had a phone and some jerk was always calling up Germany—for sixty bucks, sometimes more, sixty bucks that none of us had to spare." A flicker passed across his face. "We'd borrow tools and leave them in the grass to rust. It seems long ago. It wasn't so long ago. I was a pacifist and an idealist. And a damn good applied mathematician. I used to set up large pay-off matrices on the computer and play games with myself to try to understand trust."

"Did you make progress?"

"Yeah, better than in any philosophy class. Mathematics is an amazing tool. You can demonstrate conclusively that you can't have a viable cooperative game without mutual trust. But unilateral trust gets you killed. Like what those congressmen are trying this week."

"Muddy-headed *Democrats!*" grumbled Byron.

"When I was doing all that game theory back then, I figured that trust had to start somewhere. I had the Soviet-American conflict in mind. I was thinking about H-bombs and ICBMs which were new in those days. A lot of us who grew up with the H-bomb developed this obsession with saving mankind.

"I wanted to model games that began with both sides trapped in the if-you-win-I-lose mentality, and show that if one side *unilaterally* started to trust the other, then their deadly game could be converted into a mutual effort. I was stunned to find out that I was wrong. Trusting someone because it is virtuous to trust is a quick way to get your family locked up in Warsaw and shipped off to Treblinka body by body."

The drinks arrived. Their wench delivered the brandy, bowed and doffed her hat, as did all the Top Hat waitresses, but before she could serve Byron, he was at her again.

"How do I get her to trust me?" he said to Synmann. "What does mathematics have to say about that?"

Synmann glumly shook his head and swirled the ice in his brandy, watching the play of crystal blue and amber. "Can't be done. You can't do *anything* that will *make* her trust you."

"He's that bad, is he?" she smiled.

"Joe! That's despair! You can't mean that." He looked up at the girl. "Symbolically you're the Soviet Union. And here I am, a nice American. We'd have a wonderful time in bed together. How do I convince you that we'd both benefit?"

She had been holding his double scotch on her tray, watching him. She set it on the table. "You could start by not pointing your ICBM at me."

"Jesus!" said Byron.

"Then you could open a joint checking account with me."

"Good God!" said Byron.

"And if you signed a contract promising to be my slave for life and, let's see, gave me a leash to a ring in your nose and did everything I asked you to do, perhaps I might trust you."

"Karl Marx! Get me another scotch!"

She left laughing.

"See," said Synmann, "it's hopeless. You can earn trust by being trustworthy, but *earning it* and *getting paid* are different things. That was one of my most amazing math discoveries— trust is something you can't impose. Trust is an act of faith."

"Bullshit! It has something to do with probabilities. If I always do what I say I'll do, then you start to trust me."

Synmann grimaced: "Yes, of course." And his voice became ruthless. "And that's the way every *con person* operates. She borrows a dollar, and pays it back. She borrows two dollars and pays it back. She gives candy to children. She helps little old gentlemen cross the street. Her behavior is *indistinguishable* from the behavior of a solid citizen. She fails you only once— the time she flies to Brazil with your hundred million dollars. So trust is *not* a matter of probabilities. Statistics can't handle a sample of one. Trust is an act of faith. Trust is the gateway to either heaven or hell—and the gate is unmarked."

"Damn few have gone through."

"How come I trust you, Byron? I just met you."

"I dunno."

"Do you trust me?"

Byron raised his glass, and they touched brandy to scotch.

"Do you trust the Soviets?" asked Synmann.

"No. They're almost as evil as the Democrats."

"So here we are, two strangers who trust each other. We trust a lot of people. That's the foundation of American wealth because it means that we can keep a lot of cooperative games going together. But we don't trust the Soviets and that means an enormous tax burden and a lot of time wasted building weapons we wouldn't need in a world of trust."

"I guess we have to tough it out," said Byron, quoting his father.

Synmann's face took on a faraway look. "Do you know why I'm working for Sam Brontz? Have you met him?"

"No," said Byron. "Bond talks about him a lot. My wife loves him but thinks he is stiff and pompous."

"I sure didn't like him when I met him. I knew he was there to take over the company. I was ready to go down in flames first. But Sam is the first man I ever met who plans ahead."

"I've heard rumors," said McDougall.

"He has this crazy Cathedral and he's invited me on staff to do games theory when I get time off from everything else he has for me. God, he's working me! I'm on the front line knocking out ICBMs and he has this hairy space transportation project going. Got to get back to Boston by morning. We need five hundred engineers and there's only five of us."

"That keeps the red tape down. It makes for speed."

"It does."

"If you need any free engineering, give me a problem. I've

been flying too much. Have to keep my hand in. All I'm going to be doing with NASA is more flying."

"If you get out east, look me up."

"I'm thinking of flying out to New Hampshire tonight . . . have my own plane . . . see the wife and kid. Why don't you fly back with me? A more exciting trip than American Airlines. It'll give us a chance to chat some more. Another drink?"

"Sure."

"Not that I need another scotch, but I can't resist talking to that broad again. Have you noticed, she hasn't smoked a cigaret all evening? God, that makes me horny. Once a long time ago I got up enough nerve to kiss a woman who smoked Marlboros. She tasted like a horse. Never trust a woman who smokes."

CHAPTER 21

You say yes, and I say no.
You say stop and I say go, go, go.
Oh no!
You say goodbye and I say hello, hello, hello.

JOHN LENNON AND PAUL MCCARTNEY**

Ray Armsiel had a cot in Shantech's Westlake Complex near Boston. For days on end he didn't go back to his apartment which was still a shambles from the moving even after all these months. This morning he was up at six. When he peeked inside the vestibule fridge he found only some overage yogurt and three slices of dried salami. That meant eating out.

Shantech's isolation required a long drive through patches of morning fog to find an all night restaurant. Grumbling, his ill humor was abated somewhat by an autumn carnival of celebrating trees whose costumes of red and orange bathed in the neon splendor of a diffuse dawn. He ordered eggs and pancakes at the counter, enough to last him as many hours as possible before the next fill-up. The buxom waitress was full of chatter about her daughter. He was glad that someone had a nice daughter. Why hadn't the good Lord protected him from a brat like Linda?

By seven Ray was back at work, programming on the VAX some design speculation that had hit him in the middle of shovelling the pancakes into his mouth. Sam the Man, who was forever catching him doing such menial jobs, kept insisting that

---

** (c) 1967 Northern Songs Limited, Maclen Music Inc., c/o ATV Music Corp 6255 Sunset Blvd., L.A., CA 90028

he delegate more tasks to lesser men but the youth in Ray often rebelled—delegating authority was like letting subordinates discover the beetles under all the choice rocks.

The pleasure of working at night was in being *without* help. He could pace down the enormous halls of this converted factory and not meet a soul. No one reprimanded him for playing janitor or technician or god. He could spot-check the figures of some engineer fresh out of college. He could have audible debates with himself. He could nap on his office floor without shocking a receptionist. Still, keeping a finger in every project was impossible: without the handymen which Sam sparingly provided, the work would be going very much slower.

Before eight Ray changed out of his coveralls into a fresh striped suit with matching velvet vest and pale blue tie. His daytime persona was pleasantly normal. He was a ready listener who cut-in only at the moment some engineer paused to begin a repetition. He asked precise questions when a man waffled. He almost never ended a conversation without making a summary and a decision. No meeting he chaired lasted longer than half an hour.

But for *bull* sessions Ray ordered sloppy food that could be eaten with fingers, like pizza, and he encouraged irrelevant speculation, beer drinking, illogical trains of thought so weird that they provoked only laughter, dirty jokes, outrageous slips of consistency, gossip and creative complaining. That kind of foolery he let continue for hours, coat-off and tie loosened, a hospitable but patient spider waiting for his fly. The moment that fly touched his web he became instant sting, wrapping it up with his eyes ablaze, cutting through the speculation, leaving only a conclusion bound in silk.

Except when he caught a bumblebee like Linda.

This morning a courtier arrived with the first study of the equatorial bases that the leoport would need to feed its immense appetite. Ray paused over the spectacular photos of Namala. He thought of Linda. Shantech's potential Pacific base was an exotic haven any romantic man would be delighted to show to either mistress or bride. Why did *Linda* keep popping into his mind? *What an ass I was to let her sneak into my bed!* He wasn't about to blame himself for what had happened—he was totally innocent—but Sam would kill him anyway.

Later in the morning Joseph Synmann arrived with a NASA pilot in tow who had conveniently flown him up from Houston. The physicist was expected. Already by last week Sam had informed Ray that the Great Man was being assigned to Armsiel's staff for an indefinite period—though, Ray thought wryly, perhaps it was the other way around and *he* was being put under Synmann's wing. Thank god he got along with the crazy old hippy!

Ray took both men down to the lower lab for a visit. Synmann knew what it was all about but the pilot didn't and Ray felt obliged to explain to him what they were doing. He didn't get away with short explanations.

This was no pilot. This was a goddamned NASA spy.

"Well, we've been thinking about it for a long time. Roger Arnold originally proposed three basic designs for the leoport: two horizontal versions and one rotating one. We're working with the magnetically coupled double coils strung out along 150 kloms with ten meters spacings between them."

"They don't float away on you?" asked Byron.

Ray smiled thinly. "Each hoop can be individually controlled by adjusting the strength of the magnetic field in the concentric coils and in the eddy-coils through the connecting spokes. The hoop interacts with adjacent hoops." He showed Byron a mock-up of the design.

"We can move any hoop in a direction perpendicular to the leoport's axis to keep the whole leoport ramrod straight. Laser beams parallel to the axis tell us when a hoop moves out of line and the appropriate feedback signal is sent."

"What about pitch?"

"No problem." Ray explained how the eddy-coils were used to keep the plane of each hoop perpendicular to the axis of the leoport.

"And motion *along* the main axis?"

"She plays like an accordion. We can move the hoops closer together or push them apart. We can send compressive waves up and down the leoport. The control center could play Dixie on her if they wanted to. That solves a lot of problems. A leoport has to take huge compressive stresses while capturing a load. Shock waves propagate along the leoport's axis. The control center anticipates a load coming in through the hoops and predicts its shock wave and plays the exact countertune so that while the freighter is being captured the two wave-fronts exactly cancel each other. It's sweet. I owe Roger Arnold a beer."

"You've got fifteen thousand loose hoops up there. Right? How do you keep the axis of the leoport horizontal as it orbits around Earth?"

"Conservation of angular momentum. If we compress the whole leoport, the axis starts to spin faster. If we stretch it out, she starts to spin slower. We have perfect control over the inclination of the axis. I owe Roger Arnold two beers."

They took Byron into a room where some technicians were building a cryogenic refrigerator, a scale-up of a NASA design to liquify helium in satellites. It was an elegant machine with one moving part that rotated on magnetic bearings.

"The leoport coils will be superconducting," explained Synmann. "Superconducting requires supercooling."

"What if one of the hoops fails?"

"We just pop it out, close up, and tow the defective ring to the repair station. If the whole leoport fails and has to be shut down, it's no big disaster. We just have fifteen thousand hoops in the same orbit. Then Houston sends us cowboys."

"That's a lot of hoops," whistled Byron. "How much do they weigh? You'll never get them up there with the shuttle!"

Ray smiled. "Now we're on *my* home ground. Have you ever seen the work Jack Bell's group at Rockwell did with modified shuttles? The hoops have a hole in them fourteen meters in diameter. We stack a hundred hoops on top of each other, shove a propellant tank up the hole and add an engine compartment using the shuttle's main engines. No crew, no life support system. The tank stays in orbit, and the engine compartment comes back on a heat shield. A hundred trips gives you a leoport."

"How are you going to sell it!" groaned Byron.

It was Synmann's turn to laugh. "Wait till you see Ray's flying saucer."

"Flying saucers?"

"Once the leoport is operational we need a circular supply ship," said Ray sheepishly. "What good is a leoport if it doesn't capture freighters? The hoop geometry dictates the shape of the supply ship—it has to be circular with a coil in the rim. The saucers go through the hoops belly first—with a clearance of about two meters."

"Good God!" exclaimed Byron, not so much horrified by the two meter clearance as by the thought of piloting a saucer.

"I think its great," said Synmann. "Everybody in America believes in flying saucers. How could they *not* sell!"

Byron grimaced. "How in God's name would you make it fly! It will have to get up there and come back down. I mean, there must be more to this than shooting the hoops!"

The aerospace engineer shrugged. "Give me any shape—and I'll make it fly—my specialty. We put control surfaces on a frisbee, that's all. I'll let you have the honor of test-flying our first capture," Ray joked.

"Like hell you will! That's a job for little green men."

Synmann was examining some prototype section of coil with the eye of a man who has built linear accelerators. "We'll hook the conductor supports here. Like this." And he waved his arms in some kind of code that Armsiel understood.

Byron had a thought. "Jesus! To accelerate a captured payload to orbital velocity takes *power*, even if your saucer arrives at half-orbital velocity. You've got a first class power problem!"

Ray smiled again.

Synmann tapped Byron on the back. "You just made a gaff, Byron. You go to the bottom of the class. The leoport is a linear *generator*. It *generates* a godawful amount of power when the saucer is captured. What do we *do* with all that electricity!"

Byron frowned in momentary puzzlement.

"Look," Synmann explained carefully, "when the saucer is captured by the leoport, there is a momentum exchange. The saucer speeds up and the leoport slows down. Since the leoport slows down it has to drop into a lower orbit. That liberates energy. Some of the energy appears in the added velocity of the saucer and some appears as electricity in the coils."

"Ah," said Byron, embarrassed. "So how do you keep it up?"

"An age old question," pondered Synmann.

"The leoport, I mean!"

Ray ventured a more serious answer. "Eventually we intend to keep it up by importing mass from the moon. Moon mass, any kind of moon mass, contains about six times as much potential energy as you can get by burning the same mass of oil. If Earth imports more mass than it exports, we end up with a power surplus—but that's for the future. Right now we plan to keep the leoport up by ejecting the empty saucers at a higher speed than their arrival velocity. They emerge at rest relative to the atmosphere and don't need heat shielding."

"Ah, then the *ejection* is going to take power."

"Yeah."

"What are you going to use?"

"The re-cycled power generated by the incoming saucers, augmented by solar power."

"Photovoltaic cells?"

"Yeah—in orbit, beaming power to the leoport. Each of the hoops will have its own rectennae."

"Photovoltaics aren't very efficient," commented Byron.

"We use what we have."

"Suppose," said Byron, "I could get you a solar power source that was one fourth as massive per watt as the best photovoltaic cell array?"

Ray looked questioningly at the long-haired physicist. "Who is this guy? I thought you told me he was a pilot."

Synmann smiled. "He *is* a pilot. He drinks beer and picks up all the pretty waitresses. I'll bet he even watches the Superbowl. NASA has him training to fly Rockwells."

"You bastard!" Byron complained. "I'm an *engineer*. I keep telling people I'm an engineer. I want a piece of the action."

"We don't have any money," Ray said to put him off. "Sam the Man is bankrolling us, and for a heavy sum. It's a big shoestring but for this kind of game it is still a shoestring. We're lean and I'm hiring only workaholics."

Byron McDougall was suddenly adamant. "NASA is paying my salary, and my wife buys the extras. I'm not interested in the money. I want a hobby to keep my engineering brain alive."

"A super photovoltaic cell?" Ray asked suspiciously.

"It's not a photovoltaic cell. I know the people who are doing the micro-rectenna research. I have a prototype chip in my office in Houston. And I think I know what they have to do to manufacture it cheaply."

"Okay. You're on for a dollar a year." Ray grinned. "Henry Ford once defined an idealist as a man who helps somebody else make a profit. When we make our first billion, I'll strike a medal for you."

"Thanks," said Byron sarcastically.

"Sticking around for lunch?" asked Synmann.

"Can't. Have to get back to New Hampshire. I've got a kid to raise. Can't let the wife make a sissy out of him." He turned to Ray. "Just give me a page of specs on your power system, and whatever work anybody has done on it and you'll hear from me again in a week. I'll give you a report. It'll be bullshit—but it'll be a good first swipe at the problem by a Texas greenhorn."

Synmann took Byron away to drive him back to the local grass patch airport, and Ray Armsiel was left alone for a while. He handled a couple of short meetings. Then exactly at twelve—nine o'clock Los Angeles time—he phoned Linda Brontz. For the first time in weeks she was home to answer the phone.

"Hello-whoever-it-is," she answered sweetly.

"It's me, Ray."

"Oh, you." Frosty pause.

He wasn't expecting her to answer—she hadn't answered his

last eleven phone calls—and just to hear her flustered him. "I've figured out how to fix everything up. You come out here and we'll get married."

"Now you've done it! You broke our contract! You promised never to mention that word!" And she slammed down the phone.

Ray sat in his swivel chair, consumed with fury. A man had to be an absolute fool to get himself involved with a nineteen year old! They didn't mature until they were twenty-two!

He picked up the reports on the equatorial bases again. That was the weak political link in the whole launch system. The equatorial countries had a stranglehold on the good launch sites, and none of them were very stable.

Banana republics and spoiled girls!

He might use scram-jets as launching platforms to reduce the number of launching sites. That solved the problem of bananas but it didn't solve the problem of nineteen-year-old *children*.

CHAPTER 22

Queen and huntress, chaste and fair,
Now the sun is laid to sleep.
Seated in thy silver chair
High and stately manner keep;
Evening Star entreats thy light,
Goddess excellently bright.

BEN JOHNSON

It was a nice name. *Diana Grove*. She had picked it when
she had taken an illustrated children's book out of the L.A.
Public Library about classical mythology. It didn't please her
that the book was for children but she couldn't resist the
pictures. One of them showed sunbeams through a grove of
trees in ancient Italy dedicated to Diana, so peaceful—with a
mossy shrine and a deer.

She could go anywhere and do anything with her new name.
Her birth certificate said she was eighteen. She even had a high
school diploma. Boy, did that save a lot of work! John said her
name was in the school's computer with all her grades and
everything. She even had good marks in algebra and geometry.
That made her panic a little.

"What if someone wants me to do an algebra problem!"

But John assured her that *everybody* forgot the stuff. He told
her to remember that she had taken it years ago. She stayed
with John the Forger and his Lady-love for weeks, living out of
a little back room that looked over into somebody else's azalea
garden. Lady-love was raw-boned and congenial. She liked to
fight and bash people around, but forgave them easily, in five
minutes usually.

The first time Diana heard Lady-love screaming and beating on this guy, she had been so terrified that she locked her door and was planning to climb out the window and run away, but John coaxed her out.

"She only breaks *men's* bones, little cake. She likes you. She would never touch a girl."

That wasn't true. Once Lady-love slapped around a young Mexican girl who was on heroin and nearly broke her head against the kitchen cupboards. But the girl stayed for supper and didn't seem offended.

Mostly thirteen year old Diana went to Texas and Arizona because John the Forger's main business was manufacturing new identities for Mexicans. She slept in the back of his half-ton pick-up with his computer and wiretapping gear, and ran all sorts of errands in graveyards and backwater courthouses. After six months of indentured service with John she became too well known and he crafted more special papers for her and let her go. She became a waitress.

Rooming with older girls taught Diana how to imitate adult behavior. She read voraciously to educate herself, spending time in student haunts around Westwood to test the ideas she found in books. Her manners became flirtatious. She was a sassy summertime flower to the bees, little caring whether the men she attracted were young or old or handsome or married—but she never dated the same man twice. It wasn't smart for a young girl pretending she was a woman to trust men. She had a perfect excuse when a man wanted a second date.

"But that's the day I'm seeing Larry."

"How about Saturday then?"

"I always go out with George on Saturday."

Once she recognized an astronaut from the moon-run and trailed him all over L.A., biting her nails in the front seat of a taxi when she thought they had lost him, and finally, when she could see him getting into another car and she knew she wasn't going to be able to follow him again she brazenly went over and asked him for a light. He was glad to oblige, but she didn't have a cigaret. Smiling, he "lent" her one and lit it for her. She never smoked it, because she didn't smoke, and when he was gone she dropped the butt into the gutter. It had cost her twenty-seven dollars in cab fare to get that cigaret. She was furious at herself for being so shy that she was unable to ask him to say hello to Byron McDougall for her.

When too many people wanted her, she changed jobs or roommates. Eventually she began to move up the coast, carefully picking employment in only the most expensive and popular restaurants. Once in Coos Bay, Oregon, a drunk whacked her around and that so frightened her she flew to San Francisco the very next day.

Not having a job was unimportant. At the airport she went to the public terminal and called up the classified ads, coding for *waitress*, and sorting by restaurant type. Her scrolling stopped at an ad that called for an exceptionally attractive and experienced waitress to work at Namala in the Pacific. Diana was a long time space buff and knew very well that Namala was one of the equatorial stations that supplied the orbiting leoport. In only a moment the terminal had connected her to the employment office. She passed the verbal screening, then answered the brief questionnaire which appeared on the terminal and was given an appointment.

Diana was calm during the bus ride downtown. Then the underground world of BART left her wide-eyed and she forgot about jobs while she rode up and down the rundown subway to see the stations and the tramp musicians who camped there, one with a real trombone. But she had to face the interview. She developed a bad case of sinking heart in the elevator of San Francisco's most elegant earthquake resistant monument. After all, she was only fifteen years old even if her birth certificate said twenty. It was her first job interview in a *skyscraper*. The elevator was too quick. She found herself in the corridor on the 37th floor taking deep breaths and adjusting her hair in the polished marble.

Hey feet! Don't just stand there.

The secretary of Ling Enterprises smiled and Diana reciprocated. It helped her nervousness that the secretary was sitting down and she was standing. She could pretend that she was just earning a five dollar tip. All she had to do was be very attractive and do whatever was asked of her, quickly and efficiently.

The speaker beside the video camera spoke in a gentle voice. "Send her in. She's expected."

Diana instantly turned her smile to the camera—and received her first shock. It was President Ling speaking. That was *very* suspicious. Presidents of restaurant chains did *not* interview waitresses. She knew she should just leave. There were too many traps for fifteen year old girls that she didn't know about. But there was something exciting about a trap.

When she peered around Mr. Ling's door she found him to be Chinese and ancient. His office was contemporary American except for the paintings—one a battle between Earthmen and beastoid in a jungle under a large red sun, the other a desolate landscape somewhere in the galaxy near a star cluster. The fear went out of her.

"You're another space cookie," she said, relieved, all her poise returning.

"It's a comfortable disease."

"Do you remember when they first landed on the moon?" she asked.

He laughed. "I'm so old I remember when they thought landing on the moon was impossible."

"Do you own a restaurant on the moon?"

"No but when they build one, I'll be running it."

Diana loved him already. She was his slave. She'd eat the bait in a trap like this any day. She sat down on the couch and couldn't take her eyes off his face, lined and old and frail and the most fascinating face she'd ever seen.

He moved closer, sitting on the desk top. "Are you wondering why a president is interviewing waitresses?"

"Yeah," she grinned. "I'm ready to run out the door screaming."

"I have six space-related restaurants and I take a personal interest in them. The frustrated astronaut in me."

"What's Namala like?"

"Hard work for you. Too many men. The women we hire for Namala have to be adept at turning away men without offending."

"I'm a good girl and very self-reliant."

"Sometimes you'll need advice. Madam Lilly, who runs our Namala franchise, has large skirts for hiding behind when it is necessary."

"I never need help," said Diana defiantly.

"An unwise consideration."

"It is better to give help than to receive help."

"So women have told me. That's why we men run the world."

"I think you like being in command. Are you used to having people help you?" Her eyes sparkled.

He sighed. "Good help is hard to come by these days."

"So *that's* why men are doing such a poor job of running the world!" She couldn't stop grinning.

He returned a parchment smile. They talked. He found out all he needed to know and she found out all she needed to know. He offered her the job. She accepted. There was nothing more to say but she didn't want to leave just yet.

Ling watched her silence as she moved her fingers and

played with a ring. "Ah," he said, "I've finally caught you when you are not beaming like a mouse with stolen cheese."

"I'm hungry and I want to invite you out for lunch to share my cheese," she croaked with frog's legs in her throat and cheese in her paws.

He smiled a thousand wrinkles.

Then she asked even more awkwardly, "Would your wife mind?"

"I'm a widower."

"We could go to the Calchas. I've worked there. It's beautiful and I miss their food."

She made him talk about himself over too much wine. He was the rebel in his family. His father wanted him to take over the restaurant business and he wanted to be an engineer. He had edited a science fiction fanzine called *Betelgeuse* which went to fourteen issues but when he became engaged to his illustrator, who was a Caucasian, his family disowned him. He didn't do well enough in school to get a scholarship and ended up as a city bureaucrat, married, with three lovely mongrel children while he tried to write at night.

Finally his father died and his brothers expanded and took the family fortune into a close brush with disaster and he made a pact with his mother to run the family business. He was good at it. Later he made his breakthrough by discovering how to franchise variety in a world of McDonalds, Johnsons and Colonels.

Diana had fun. They ran up quite a bill at Mr. Ling's insistence (he thought he was paying) and she had the best fight of her life taking the bill away from him. To make up for it he bought her beautiful luggage. She sighed and told him she had nothing to put in it, so he bought her clothes. She sighed and told him she had no place to take them because she hadn't rented a room yet, so he gave her the key to his place.

Ling went back to work and she went window shopping. At first she was just another sophisticated San Franciscan woman out for a stroll, but the happiness seeped into her little girl's heart. She tried skipping. She saw a brick hill and ran up the sidewalk counting which cars had their wheels turned to the curb.

"Hey," said a man, "you're not allowed to be that happy!" She puckered her nose at him. "Arrest me!" With her last dollars she bought a dozen roses from an ancient freak who wore his dirty hair to his waist and kept the roses in a can by his box while his quaking fingers rolled a joint of Mexican Gold. She was so happy that even he gave her a toothless grin. In the park she passed out a rose to every derelict she met. One of them tried to sell it back to her for beer money.

She cooked Mr. Ling a gourmet dinner in his kitchen after making many phone calls to his office to find out what he liked and when he would be in. They spent the whole meal and three liquors discussing the history of Jerusalem. She discovered his wicked sense of humor. He convinced her that there had been a whole order of Chinese Knights who fought in the crusades.

"Don't laugh so hard!" she complained. "You're just lucky I didn't find a lemon meringue pie for supper or you'd have a pie plate for a new beret!"

Ten o'clock was his bedtime. He excused himself gracefully and escorted her all the way to the guest room where he put an arm around her shoulder and thanked her for a lovely evening before he left her.

Diana peeked. She waited until the light went out under his door and then, dressed only in a candle flame, entered his room. "I've come to kiss you goodnight." It was easy to pretend you were twenty years old when you were nude.

His smile in the candlelight was wistful. "Goddess Diana, I am much too old for such escapades."

"That makes us even. I'm much too young for such escapades." She blew out the candle and slipped under the sheets with him. "Don't die of a heart attack just yet. I want my job on the moon." She snuggled up beside him, deciding that she liked to sleep with men. Her fingers grazed on his chest, exploring, nibbling. "I didn't know that Chinamen had fur on their chests." She left her lips on his shoulder. It was a sleep of innocence.

Two mornings later a gale was blowing in from the Pacific, and she could smell the sea and rotting kelp all the way across the peninsula as far as the Bayshore express. Mr. Ling was driving her, carrying her ticket, playing hooky from his important job, pretending that it was his function to take care of his waitress on her first day. She clung to his black leather greatcoat feeling oddly at peace with herself, at home, as if she had a home, even though she was going away. They had driven down at dawn to avoid some of the traffic and had time to walk around and play the fool with each other.

Part of her wanted the gale to be so strong that the airplanes would have to hide in their hangers and she could have another few hours with her lover, but the wind just blew her hair awry and chased pieces of San Francisco Chronical printout down the highway in summersaults. The wind raged but nothing stopped the great wasps from buzzing in and out of their monstrous South San Francisco hive.

She saw them lined up for take-off and saw them rolling in along the runways almost every minute but, when it was time to leave, everything was done through tunnels and she never saw the outside of the carbon black Boeing that lifted her out across the Pacific, then up and high above a whiter ocean of clouds to the world of the equator where the flying saucers homed.

CHAPTER 23

Look carefully, and you will see that each important fact in our history is a fact that was forced upon us.

PETER CHAADAEV, *APOLOGY OF A MADMAN*, WRITTEN IN 1837, AFTER BEING DECLARED INSANE BY ORDER OF TSAR NICHOLAS I FOR WRITING THE ESSAY *A PHILOSOPHICAL LETTER* WHICH CAUSED THE MOSCOW *TELESCOPE* TO BE SUPPRESSED, ITS EDITOR N.I. NADEZHDIN TO BE EXILED AND THE CENSOR WHO PASSED IT TO BE DISMISSED.

Joe Synmann arrived at the Cathedral of Saint Marx hours earlier than called for by his appointment with Sam Brontz. Frankly he was curious. If he was going to work with this Limon Barnes character on game theory—and he had almost decided, just on Sam's say so, that he would—he needed a better feel for the place. People told such strange stories about Limon that the only possible way of judging him was in person.

Without making a fuss he sneaked into the lecture hall while Limon was speaking to some of his trainees. The visual picture did not fit the stories. Limon was wearing a business suit of dark blue with a pale blue shirt and tie, not something that could ever be called costume. He was standing at a podium and lecturing to his trainees like any professor.

Synmann watched Limon cross-reference and lay trails through seemingly unrelated materials and bring them instantly to the huge screen. He was chatting about the Mongol impact on Russia, not so much to give his students a history lesson, as to instruct them in the power of the Kensakan Kambi. He was calling up (and editing) text from the cathedral library, even illustrations. What he wrote in script at the lectern miracu-

151

lously appeared as *print* on a large screen. The "professor" was
a showman.

For a training exercise Limon was tracing out the influence of
one particular Mongol practice on all subsequent Russian regimes.
The Mongols collected taxes and they did not care who paid
them as long as the tribute was forthcoming and unrest was
minimal. In order to squeeze wealth out of such a dispersed
and poor country their administrators developed the concept of
collective responsibility for tribute—*you* were privileged to
pay your neighbor's taxes if he couldn't, or died, or didn't.

After the Mongols had destroyed themselves in fratricidal
war, collective obligation tended to persist. Muscovy neither
repealed the Mongol tribute laws nor changed the nature of the
tribute collection machinery which had oppressed them. Two-
hundred fifty years after the twilight of Horde power, Mongol
assumptions about accountability were formalized into *Russian*
law. A *dvorianin* forwarded the taxes of his serfs, and had to
pay the (Mongol) head tax whether the serf had produced it or
not, whether the serf had died or run away. Indeed, when a
dvorianin went bankrupt in any enterprise, his debt became a
liability to be paid off by his serfs.

Slowly, carefully, Limon showed the evolution and diffusion
of collective responsibility like a paleontologist following the
fossil evidence which traced the history of the horse. What had
originally appeared as a simplified administrative procedure for
Mongol *baskaks* had, by the Soviet Era, evolved into such
things as factory quotas. With his trails of evidence Limon laid
out the picture of Soviet factory hanging on the same skeleton
as a fourteen century Russian estate.

The Soviet planning apparatus was originally organized by
men whose only prior experience was in setting tax quotas for
the tsar—men so ignorant of Marx as to be unaware that Marx
himself describes factory quotas as a kind of tribute laid on the
working class by greedy capitalists. A Soviet factory manager,
like a conquered Russian prince, hides as much wealth as he
can from the Moscow *baskaks* but religiously meets the quotas
imposed from above no matter how little likeness they bear to
real need and real ability to pay. Only an accounting practice
which has, for centuries, been raising wealth to meet the demands
of a colonial exploiter could run the incredible double and
triple set of books which are second nature to any bureaucracy-
wise Soviet citizen.

With a flourish, Limon called to the screen a sheet from a
tsarist landowner's records which involved the buying and

selling of dead serfs to balance the estate's tax accounts. And with another magician's wave, displayed the books of a Soviet factory which, in collusion with other factories, had been logging the shipment and receipt of non-existent goods so that each could appear to the Moscow apparatus as a factory meeting its quotas.

When the show was over Synmann avoided the cluster of trainees who converged on the podium by taking a walk through the cathedral grounds. There were signs of all kinds of new construction—a bulldozer, raw earth, forms, a construction shack. Sam Brontz was certainly serious about something.

Later, at the appointed hour, Synmann felt slightly foolish in his pullover sweater and jeans and long hair when he met the meticulous Brontz and the blue-suited Limon in the little office, but Sam ignored his clothes and went out and found a chair for him so that they could all sit down.

"I've been telling you about Dr. Synmann whose hobby is game theory and the numerical simulation of conflict," Sam said.

Limon nodded to the physicist. "He thinks two freaks are better than one."

Sam spent the required amount of time on small talk. Then he explained to Limon that he had seen Synmann strip the best strategic defense papers of the United States and Russia down to playable axioms. "He's going to show you and me why the most competent American and Soviet defense planners can only come up with ideas like atomic terrorism for technological peoples and 'bomb them back to the stone age' for the peasant civilians of Vietnam and Afghanistan." It was clear Sam wanted alternatives.

"All right," said Limon. "So we sit in our little fairyland and revise east-west defense strategy. Why simulated Russians? Why don't we use real Russians?"

Sam Brontz grunted. "Have you ever tried to talk to a Russian from the Soviet power elite? His negotiating skills are essentially nil. He is paralysed by something. What, I don't know. Give me a *simulated* Russian any day. I want a quick American, someone I can talk to, but not one trapped in our cultural biases. I want an American who can think like a Bear only twenty times as fast."

Limon answered with his straightest face. "We could get a *simulated* peace treaty done and signed with a hundred *simulated* signatures within the month—long before a real Russian could decide on the first agenda item."

"That's right," said Sam Brontz, approvingly.

"You're serious!" Limon was incredulous. "How could you impose a simulated peace treaty?"

"If you had to impose it, Limon, it wouldn't be a *peace treaty*. It would be a Bill of Reparations, or Terms of Surrender. Note that New York and California hate each other's guts, and they are both armed to the teeth with nuclear weapons, but they have a very carefully worked out peace treaty between them, the Constitution. No Californian ever signed it. People *simulating* Californians wrote it and signed it."

Synmann was saying nothing but he was listening to the exchange intently.

Limon scoffed. "A Soviet apparatchik would never shake hands on a deal he didn't make."

"A peace treaty isn't just shaking hands or telling an enemy what he wants to hear so that you gain a temporary truce. It is an elaborate structure, like the American Constitution, worked out very carefully by geniuses with foresight, who aren't trying to sneak in a special benefit for themselves or a time-bomb for their favorite enemy. I'm not going to ask anyone to sign it. A workable peace treaty has *market value*. It will take over the market like Kleenex in a world of handkerchiefs."

"People make very strange assumptions about what is good for them," injected Synmann.

Brontz brightened. "That's exactly why I won't deal with real Russians. I'd be willing to deal with a man like Sakharov—but sane Russians like Sakharov have always been locked up in psychiatric hospitals or sent off to bust rocks in Siberia."

"You're suggesting that Americans can make better guesses about Russian welfare than a Russian?" Synmann doubted.

"No, I am not! Americans are half-blind and useless as benevolists! That's why I want a *simulated* Russian to do the Soviet half of my thinking. Americans will always peer *into* Russia. I want a man who is looking *out* from the true center of the universe which is the stone mound in the Kremlin known as the Lobnoye Mesto, the Place of the Skull. Lend me your eyes for a moment. Stand on the Lobnoye Mesto.

"In the southern distances are the bottled inland seas coveted by Tsar Peter. To the northeast lie the bottled shores of the Baltic which the Russian spirit has been forced to conquer to break the exploitation of Russia by European navies. To the east is an ocean guarded by Japan and to the southeast lies the ancient Chinese enemy. There are rich and barrierless steppes to the west through which hostile armies can, and have, struck like lightning at every opportunity. To the north are the dread skies open to the swift hellfire and brimstone of American arrows."

Synmann smiled ruefully. "It isn't possible to train an American to think like that!"

Brontz blazed. "Damn it, Joe! That's not your job! It is *Limon's* job to soak an American in acid, strip his skin off, and graft bear fur in its place!"

"I forgot," said Synmann with mock contrition. He nodded obeisance to Limon.

Brontz was enjoying himself as his eyes targetted the physicist. "*Your* job is to analyze content-free conflict at a deep enough level to pin-point the basic strategic mistakes made by the United States and the Soviet Union in the last fifty years. You can do that?"

"Perhaps."

"All right. Once you have your pure distilled strategy then you and Limon can get together and add the content and play a real game. And mark my words. I want it very clear what our objective is. I'm not interested in a defensive strategy that works for the West alone. We've had enough of that—*no one in Washington or the Pentagon has ever taken any measures to assure the survival of Russia in case of war*. Nor am I interested in a defensive strategy that works for Russia alone. What we need is a defensive strategy that works at both ends of the stick and can be implemented by two peoples who do not trust each other."

Synmann leaned forward. "Any simulation is inevitably going to be imperfect in some of its aspects. What we get might not be acceptable to the *real* Russians for genuinely valid reasons."

But Brontz was looking at the long end of the lever, content to generate strategic concepts—the *real* Russians would be left to forge the tactical apparatus. "See? If we make the mistake of trying to sell them a biased American trap, someone in their defense military will spot it. It won't sell."

Limon played his mock-astonishment. "Other than me, Mr. Sam, you are the most arrogant man I know. You're telling us that Russians are so slow-witted that *Americans* have to figure out a viable defense for them."

"They *are* slow. And they *haven't* figured out a defense against the United States—we can totally destroy the Soviet Union within 24 hours."

"By that token, Americans are pretty dull-witted, too," Limon commented sourly.

Sam Brontz grinned. *"Exactly."*

CHAPTER 24

A wet sheet and a flowing sea,
  A wind that follows fast
And fills the white and rustling sail
  And bends the gallant mast;
And bends the gallant mast, my boys,
  While like the eagle free
Away the good ship flies and leaves
  Old England on the lee.

ALLAN CUNNINGHAM

During a year of training and rehearsal Byron McDougall learned to respect Colonel Brown's ability to plan, but it was the climactic week of mission execution which convinced him that Brown was a master intelligence officer. Nothing at all went wrong from the moment of lift-off until touchdown. The Colonel merely talked to them several times a day and grunted his approval from an operations desk far away on the globe below.

They didn't have to shoot anybody. The object of their curiosity, the Soviet Snowfox, didn't swoop down on them and deliver a boarding team of provocateurs to foil their mission. They didn't have to suit up to chase a mad Soviet agent through the shuttle's cargo bay with the panorama of the Earth's awesome sphere above their heads. Or flee for their lives to the shelter of the OMS engine nozzle while enemy agents, having captured the flight deck, tried to dislodge them from their haven with blasts of monomethyl hydrazine and nitrogen tetroxide.

Byron fell in love with space. He often thought about it when he was drifting off to sleep in the bunk cage, or changing the lithium hydride canister in the floor, or being "cook" for the crew at the tiny nose galley of the Atlantis. There weren't going to be enough shuttles to get him up here as often as he might care to come! Damn, but that would have to change! In the few private moments he had, Byron pondered obsessively upon the merits of Armsiel's leoport. Sometimes, peering outside the spaceplane, he forgot to work.

> Each star incredulous . . . a teeming city . . .
>   . . . pinned, riveted on black eternity.
>   . . . gibbous moon unmoving goes,
>   frozen in astonished pose;
>   now four billion years in thrall
>   witness to the sunrise birth of Sol.

He was the only rookie on the flight and had to take a lot of ribbing from Commander Mueller's persistent sense of earthy humor. Although third generation German American, the commander still played with an endless repertoire of latrine jokes. Byron sometimes felt out of place at the pilot's controls of a plane big enough to *carry* a latrine. By all his fighting-aircraft standards the Atlantis was unflyable—she had the gliding angle of a brick and either far too much power, or when you needed it most, no power at all. Nevertheless she flew like a dream, even backwards when she wanted to. And she was a *spaceship!*

Under the yin-yang bowls of heaven and earth, during the critical transfer maneuvers to an orbit which would cause the Soviet's Mirograd to pass beneath them, commander and pilot chatted small talk about their wives. Byron made the mistake of proudly mentioning that his son had learned to walk. This reminded Commander Mueller of the age of toilet training and he launched into several of his favorite stories. He was quite willing to speculate on how each of the great men of NASA had managed their first potty. Byron discretely checked to see that radio contact with Houston was down.

"Thar she blows!" exclaimed an excited voice.

The sight of the growing Mirograd structure majestically crossing their orbit silenced them into the terse officialese of mission business. Mueller did make one unofficial comment. "Goddamn! If they'd've gold-plated it, they'd have the Kremlin up here!" The spheres did somewhat resemble cupolas, but not much. Byron saw in the filigree a lot of the genes of the Eiffel Tower and the genius of some unsung architect. In full imperial splendor the Russian city floated across the visibly rotating underprison of Lord Earth's bondsmen.

The rookie pilot of Atlantis, dwarfed as a camel might have been by Babylon, thought of Amanda and her buried and mutated cities. Who would glide through Mirograd's corridors eight centuries from now? What language would its inhabitants speak? What would they be buying and selling? Within a welded crust of new habitats would there be an Old City section with flavorful remnants of Borscht soup and Uzbek humor? Would there still be traces of Slavic in the computerese? Would Martian clothing be the rage? Or would Mirograd be a tomb like Petra, open and empty to space, stripped by scavengers, signed in its bowels by the graffiti of the curious?

During the shuttle's very carefully timed maneuvers they had three significant glimpses of the Snowfox clan, and took some beautiful photos of two Snowfoxes in docking mode. They monitored calls and probed through subtle attempts at camouflage.

As the glorious week slipped by, the pilot in Byron gradually ceased to think of the Atlantis as an aircraft. She was a horse. She would take a hint from a nudge or a pat, and passively go where you wanted her to go—within reason—but she insisted on doing all the thinking about where to put her feet. She was no dumb machine. If you wanted her to jump off a cliff she got stubborn. If you went to sleep at the "reins" she didn't trot you into a telephone pole.

Then, in his final hours as pilot, Byron felt the full force of her willfulness. Once he had her nose pointed at the Cape, her systems snorted alive as she flawlessly galloped home to the stable, forcing her "passengers" to hang on to the pommel for the ride. But what a ride!

After a weather perfect landing, rain hit Florida and storms crossed the South. The crew spent an unscheduled two hours holing up from the downpour in a truck that wouldn't start, and were delayed fourteen hours in catching their flight out.

Mission debriefing was thorough. The Colonel pulled it all together, probing, evaluating, allowing speculation but never fancy. Computer enhanced photos posed beside chalk scrawlings on medieval blackboards. Special agents with special data gave their talks and flew away again. Printers spewed paper which got lost in safes or shredded before its useful life was over—sending clerks scurrying to the printers for more copy. Brown was a careful man who neither averaged data nor took the road of highest probability. He established lower bounds and upper bounds for everything and built himself an impregnable territory of possibility.

In this whole process Byron was only a cog left over from the mission but, because he had been there, he became a constant source for the analysis process, watching with fascination as the conclusions formed out of the data. He couldn't resist aiding the synthesis team with the insights his effortless mind seemed to be able to generate at will.

The report said it all. The Soviet's were exploiting a vast flaw in the American military space systems.

The Snowfox had *seemed* like such a trivial flea, nothing that could even begin to rival NASA's Cross Continental Trailer Truck. Intelligence sources had known about the puny Snowfox for a long time. They *perceived* it as a modest spaceplane built along the lines of the outdated US Air Force dynasoar of the 1960s. They *perceived* it as the best that a fumbling technology could produce—it had to be launched atop an expendable booster; it had no more than a five-ton payload capacity, and could not possibly carry more than a crew of three. Dismissed.

Mirograd now carried six berths for the Snowfox. At the interminable disarmament conference, in which the Soviets relentlessly pressed for the military neutralization of space, the Snowfox was represented, quite accurately, as a shuttle vehicle to transport people to and from Mirograd. In fact, its use wasn't so limited. Nor was its use intended to be that limited. Mirograd was already being supplied with special booster modules that could take its Snowfoxes on many missions, even missions as high as geostationary orbit.

Commander Mueller put it his own way. "Them foxes is gonna eat our chickens," he lamented.

The integrated bits of intelligence added up to a significant story. Within the next few months a Mirograd-based squadron, manned by crack Soviet fighter pilots, would have the capability to penetrate to *geo*, to drift right through the main communications system that linked the American defense network. Their Snowfoxes were to be equipped to destroy, within hours, every major American satellite and then to remain in orbit in order to prevent the deployment of replacements. Piloted ships gave flexibility to any Soviet mission. For instance, after boosting up to *geo*, instead of acting as destroyers, they could retrieve, *unopposed*, the most secret American satellite.

Within the same leisurely time span that the Allied armies of World War II had rolled across German-occupied Europe, Moscow was taking de facto claim over the whole of the space above Earth to a height of thirty-six thousand kloms. They would have a full half-decade to consolidate their position before *anyone* had a chance to challenge them. Tsar Peter would be proud. His people had found their long sought access to the *open* seas. What are land barriers to an aerospace power?

It was a brilliant end run, an obvious if unforeseen one, and the defense analysts Byron talked to were stunned that America had been so easily outfoxed. The American Space Truck might be technologically superior in every way—but, *whatever* she was, she couldn't reach geostationary orbit. NASA's Orbiter was about as useful against the Snowfox as a Jordanian tank against Israel's Air Force in 1967. The same Americans who had once picnicked on the moon in their dune buggies no longer even had a raft to take their heroes up to meet the Snowfoxes.

Commander Mueller was always the optimist. He was the wit with special words of encouragement for his fellow Air Force officers. "We're the ones with a sanitary space toilet that freeze-dries shit. How can they beat that?"

CHAPTER 25

Four of us sat with the old man around the wooden basin, spooning our soup with voracious appetite. I talked with him, asking questions about the life of the workers while listening to his tales of the past. It was a cruel story. The peasants, moved from their homes against their wills and placed by their landlords in a position of hopeless slavery, had rebelled several times, demanding to be returned, balking at the assigned work in the sugar factory. Every fifth or tenth man was flogged. Squads of soldiers were brought in to keep order. Like grasshoppers these soldiers devoured everything, leaving not a crust of bread for the inhabitants. The fate of the serf leaders was terrible.

KATERINA BRESHKOVSKAIA,
SOCIALIST AGITATOR IN TSARIST RUSSIA, 1874,
FROM *GOING TO THE PEOPLE.*

A stone wall and a medieval city gate now blocked out the parking lot of the Cathedral of Saint Marx the Benefactor. American dress was not permitted beyond the gate, and if one appeared at its oaken and iron facade improperly attired, one was stopped by the Strelsky or KGB, whoever happened to be on duty, and politely directed through an arch down into a dungeon tunnel inside the wall. The gloomy tunnel led to the basement lockers of a rotund tower where one might choose a proper costume.

This watchtower, and one other, fat and cylindrical and copper-roofed with a witch's peeked hat, had been completed in the style of the Pskov fortifications of the fifteenth century, though not constructed of a thickness to repel determined Swedes and

161

Poles. One was a theater-in-the-round, the other the shell of a dormitory for monks. It was in the bowels of the theater that the costumes were kept.

Dressed in proud police uniform, an *ispravnik* was chatting with his *stanovoi* about the quality of boots when Joseph Synmann arrived in jeans and sport jacket. Joseph took an odd comfort in the early nineteenth century dress that he affected on the cathedral grounds: a linen shirt that seemed impossible to press, a soft brown coat without collar, a silken scarf of deep lilac tones wrapped and tied about his neck to keep him cosy, baggy pants, boots—all copied from a portrait of Alexander Pushkin.

Such theatrics gave the Cathedral grounds a peculiarly warped flavor. It wasn't Russian to meet Russians from a thousand different years of Russian history all in the same spot, it was more like a Grand Central Station of the timelines, Moscow Sector. But this flavor was the mix Limon wanted, bringing to life the discordantly layered depths of history, breaking myths.

It was, after all, only a myth that God had created the Russian enigma out of Lenin's rib on the night of the twenty-third of October 1917. Soviet Russia was a hastily cobbled facade over a very old being. Here, on the Cathedral's acreage, when one saw a revolutionary party worker of the 1920's eating at the inn with Archpriest Avvakum of the 1650s, both of them heroic, passionate and fanatical, the whole structure of the communist facade dissolved into a deeper history.

Limon was quite certain that if a man identified with his clothes, he was stuck in a rigid viewpoint and would never be able to shift back and forth between different cultural premises. If he couldn't bustle about in the livery of a landmaster, if he was, God forbid, embarrassed to wear the apron of a Russian blacksmith, how could he ever learn to think like a Russian?

If a young American girl couldn't be Katerina Breshkovskaia, reading her leaflets and telling her tales surreptitiously to the "liberated" serfs at a factory, living on bread with apples and lard, and cast by the tsarist police into jail where peasants searched her shabby, almost beggarly clothes—then how could this American girl comprehend the Russian passion for justice which endlessly rose up among the people and was endlessly repressed?

If, demanded Limon, one of the SMB's military strategists couldn't see himself as Pyotr Yakir, abandoned as a child by the State, left to wander through the Gulag's labor camps for orphans, brooding on his father's murder by the Stalinstate, vowing to grow up to fight injustice no matter what the odds, and doing just that, accepting persecution by the KGB hoodlums, struggling for human dignity, struggling until the police, with the whole power of the Brezhnevstate behind them, broke him first in body and afterwards in mind—if an American boy couldn't be Pyotr Yakir then how could he ever understand the fanatical Russian need for a defense against the enemies of mankind?

"We have to learn to represent all Russians, not just the power elite," said Limon.

Out of sight, around the hill, a new section of wall was being laid, rising from bedrock and already waist high. Joseph Synmann wasn't sure where such industrious masons came from but he had been seeing them on their scaffolding for months as he commuted between Shantech and the Cathedral grounds.

Limon insisted that the workers he employed were a mere rabble of history students on leave from a dozen scattered universities, aided and abetted by an old Russian mason and a local contractor. While they were finishing the interior of their round dorm, Limon had them housed in an abandoned high school in town where they also held seminars built upon the nourishment of the SMB's growing library.

The Wall was supposed to be a "bonding" project to break down interpersonal barriers and supply a sense of group identity to demoralized American students who had been raised in forced isolation from each other, bound by vows of silence as day after day they faced a blackboard and the one person in the room who counted. Deep in Joseph's cynical heart, however, the physicist suspected that Limon had been playing communist tsar-khan for so long now that he intuitively understood the ploys that made slave labor possible. How else would one get a feudal wall built around an estate in the heart of Massachusetts?

In any event it was quite amazing what these mason-scholars were doing to the SMB's research library when they weren't hauling stones or rehearsing Chekhov in their theater. They were modern monks transcribing books onto laser disk via optical reader—food for the mind of an uncanny robot librarian.

The SMB's present limited Russian database was already on the market over the phone network to high demand customers in enough volume to make the project a modest financial success. Synmann knew that Limon was trying to expand his market by arranging to pay use-royalties for copyrighted material—but was caught in a legal nightmare because libraries had *never* paid royalties and there was no legal machinery by which they could do so. How do you pay an author for his part in a pamphlet you have cut-and-pasted together out of a dozen books by a dozen authors, then formatted electronically in seven microseconds, and worse, transmitted over glass to a distant place, there illegally "printing" it via a technology unknown to legislators?

Synmann came down to the SMB as often as he could make it from his defense work and the leoport design marathons which Ray was always arranging. In some ways it was a fantasy escape from his real work. Every week Limon had new surprises and the place was feeling less like a think-tank all the time. Synmann's group had been assigned to one of Limon's more bizarre creations—the Marching Society of the Soviet General Staff and Waterworks.

He went around by the side, over unlandscaped dirt.

They now had a couple of rooms for his mathematics students in the half-finished new Cathedral which was already known as Saint Sakharov the Good though never officially christened. The core of the building had been put up in months but the domes and the facing were yet to come. A studio of local artists, old Polish hippies who had revolted from their father's life in the Ohio steel mills, were working with a leisurely, feudal speed on the building's facade.

The new Cathedral's decorative details, to be executed in stone and ceramic, were still only drawings and wooden models of the carvings to come. Fragments already finished were reminiscent of the Vladimir-Suzdal masters, folk images of birds, beasts, and plants, illustrated fairy tales, done with Slavic simplicity and force, somehow modified by a third generation American nostalgia that had passed through a fascination with Japanese brush work and a stint with African wood carvers and an attempt at reading Mayan.

Synmann had let his taste for antique rolltop desks decorate his small office. There was an ikon of Saint Sakharov atop the corner chapel, and, on the wall, a framed reproduction of Vasily Surikov's brooding *Menshikov in Beriozovo*, a man deposed, sitting in melancholy contemplation of his frozen exile, at a table with his daughters, the sad-eyed Maria wrapped in black furs, the family a reminder of the ancient Russian predisposition to destroy one another.

A young mathematician stood at the window watching Limon Barnes cross the square to meet some appointment. Peter Kaissel nodded to Synmann and made a face. Peter didn't like

Limon and Limon didn't like him. "He's wearing his Stalin uniform today. What does *that* mean?" he asked sarcastically.

Last summer Synmann had rescued Kaissel from Florida State but it had been a bit like taking an eighteen year old Mormon girl along with a busload of freaks down to the dam for a skinny-dipping party. Peter only doffed his regular clothes at the gate because he was too embarrassed to be conspicuous. He conformed even when it made him uncomfortable.

Synmann chuckled. "Maybe it's time for a purge?"

"I saw some very suspicious Armenian/Tartar/Jews loafing around the inn," groused Kaissel, sarcastically trying to imitate Russian paranoia.

"When we learn more about games we'll study the dynamics of this madhouse. In the meantime . . ."

Synmann's game team at SMB consisted mostly of Peter Kaissel and Hans Dorfman. When you stripped off the positions and dogma and the justifications built into a conflict until you couldn't tell which side was which, you were left with a stylized conflict structure ruled by mappings which transformed every move into a new set of potential moves.

During play a player either increased his freedom of action, maintained his status, or lost options. When he ran out of moves he was dead. These multiple-player, multiple-state, multiple-reward, content-free games were so complicated that they were impossible to study except by numerical simulation.

". . . what's been happening?" asked Synmann.

"We're making progress. When were you last here? A week ago? Were you here for any of the Version 4 runs?"

"No. You were just starting up. I got whisked off to Washington before you got the bugs out."

"The battle-station idea is hot again?"

"Yeah. I don't know why. But I'll find out. They want to build it without telling me what I'm up against. Desk men! I've suddenly fallen behind on my leoport work. Ray got his whole team syphoned off by my battle-station crew and he's screaming. So brief me and I'll comment. I have to be back in Boston by five."

Kaissel went to the terminal and powered up. "It turns out that *cooperative* behavior between game players isn't the optimal way to maximize group-payoff."

"Oh? That's counterintuitive."

"Yeah; it's something we never thought of, but it is pretty obvious when you see the details of the simulated play that makes use of the cooperation axioms." He keyed-in some games and the action flickered across the screen, ghost players dancing in a silicon universe.

Synmann stared intently at the phosphorescent flow for ten minutes without comment, sometimes freezing the action for a closer look. "They're cooperating all right—but they are converging on pretty strange solutions. Peculiar. They aren't coming anywhere near the top group-payoff."

"They're Luddites. Once they've found a way of cooperation that works, they don't want to change."

"Amazing," said Synmann unhappily.

"I think my players just aren't smart enough. The situation is too complicated for them. If a player doesn't understand the possibility of a better way, he won't go for it."

Swift fingers cycled the screen back through the results. The physicist took rapid notes with a pencil, or pulled at a strand of his long hair. "Ha. Our players aren't willing to lose, they can't take risks, and they are fanatically unwilling for any of their co-players to lose, either."

"Yeah, they're moral little buggers," said Kaissel.

"Okay. Here's your assignment for next week. Program some gambling. I don't mean zero-sum gambling and I don't want a house that always wins—that's the Las Vegas game of accountants versus suckers—I mean true gambling. My intuition says that a *little* gambling will drastically improve the group-payoff and that a *lot* of gambling will kill the group."

"What do you mean by gambling?"

"Doing something you've never tried before. A mutation. You should be able to program that into our players. Don't let the probability of any single move remain constant."

"Will a willingness to risk their arse make better capitalists out of them?" grinned Dorfman.

"How should I know?" Synmann always liked to be the devil's advocate. He scowled properly. "If they are willing to take risks, might they not organize labor unions and go out on strike for more payoff?"

CHAPTER 26

The impression [Marx] made on me was that of someone who possessed a rare intellectual superiority, and he was evidently a man of oustanding personality. If his heart had matched his intellect, and if he had possessed as much love as hate, I would have gone through fire for him.

LIEUTENANT TECHOW, REMEMBERING KARL MARX (1859)

The more outstanding a man is, the more dangerous he is and the less deserving he is of "forgiveness."

V. I. LENIN, (1 NOV 1917)

An outstanding man who has used his talents destructively will immediately perceive a danger as great as himself in another outstanding man's abilities. He will distrust able men, even destroy them, and seek to surround himself with inferior men like Stalin and Dzerzhinsky whom he will not perceive as dangerous at all—until it is too late.

DR. WRIGHT OF THE HOLY SOCIALIST ZAZEN CHURCH OF L.A.

His Californian Zen master, fraud that he was, had, at least, taught him how to deal with surprise.

Without notice or preamble, two unobtrusive KGB *sotrudniki* had picked him up at the special school and were driving him north. Both wore Czechoslovakian suits and that meant that they were middle rank officers. One drove. One sat beside Bijad ibn Jamal in the rear.

His escorts did not talk and thus he had their silence in which to remember the story of an elderly Romanian he had met who had been the chauffeur of Ana Pauker after the war, once

167

driving Ana and the leaders of the Agrarian Reform Party out to the country for a conference. Only Ana and her bodyguards had returned to Bucharest in the morning after the murders.

Bijad's natural Saudi Arabian *hadhar* caution was examining his situation while he still had the time. Leisurely the Chaika rolled past the Khimki Reservoir where he watched, briefly, the summer sculling of Komsomol youth. The water disappeared behind trees. They rode onward over a bumpy road under repair, far beyond the outskirts of Moscow, much farther than he really wanted to go. If the KGB had discovered that during his prison term as a Marxist agitator he had actively cooperated with Saudi counterintelligence to save his own skin, then he was a dead man.

But Bijad ibn Jamal was sure that Saudi counterintelligence had not been penetrated. Unpurified Marxism was, after all, a Jewish conspiracy; Israel was full of Jewish KGB agents and no member of the House of Saud would be tempted to feed information to such a devil. Only pig-shit eaters like Syrians would shave their beards in Russian piss. How then had he, so cautious, so meticulous in his planning, how could he have let precious water leak out of his goatskin while on this deadly journey into the Soviet's own Rub Al Khali?

Surely, the persona he had constructed to deceive his Soviet hosts was flawless. He had not wasted those prison years of befriending and betraying his Marxist comrades. He had used every moment and every agent of the Front for the Liberation of Saudi Arabia who had been thrown into his bugged cell, and used them well to teach himself how the KGB recruited agents, and what kind of men the KGB trusted. No, he would not have made his mistake in choosing a persona. The KGB was unable to see through a man who "feared" them and whose motives appeared to be those of wealth and power, decently hidden under a chador of socialist piety. He had a prison record and the reputation of a man whose Marxist beliefs were unshakeable.

For a moment he glanced at the grim faces of his companions, and estimated how long he would live if he bolted from their car.

Then was it a theoretical error which had betrayed him? Certainly miscalculation was a possibility five years ago, but today? Impossible! Zen had liberated him from the materialistic flaws which lay like Jewish booby-traps throughout Das Kapital, waiting for the unwary. Hundreds of days of meditation in prison had perfected the Zen skills he had first been taught so crudely in San Fernando Valley by sincere California teachers. His mind was too clear to make errors.

Prison gave a serious student time to separate the sand from the flour, grain by grain. Marx had not been able to purify his Marxism of its Jewish wealth-lust and for that he could not be faulted; all Zionists were trapped in their illusions. Wasn't it natural that the revelations of historical progress came in painful jerks, centuries apart? California-Zen, applied by a dedicated man, was a sun that vaporized all materialistic bias, boiled away the remaining Jewish money-lust that was so evident in these KGB agents corrupted by a Zionist need to better themselves by wearing Czech suits instead of Moscow suits.

Bijad still remembered his despair in prison as he watched his Marxism boil under the focus of meditation. So much impure socialism was based on the squalid struggle to grasp a greater share of the wealth. How horrified he had been by this discovery that he was himself a Zionist dupe! He had considered suicide. It was as if his whole being had smoked away while he sat in the lotus position on the floor of his wretched cell.

The final pure Zen distillate of Marxism contained not an atom of the mundane, neither gold nor silver—the socialist heaven was gone and the Jewish houris were gone. He had been devastated in his loneliness. But it is under such conditions that one reaches satori.

A man is not his ego and he cannot see himself until he has stripped away the beliefs of his ego. Through the clarity of despair Bijad discovered justice and mercy and the nobility of the working man and compassion and the necessity of revenge— all of which are not sculpted of atoms and cannot be bought by oil money or KGB gold or American engineering know-how.

Surely, Bijad told himself, his hard won Zen-Marxism was as clean as the desert air under a star brilliant sky. The KGB could know nothing of his intentions because he was too centered to show any intentions at all beyond those of his lie. No flaw in his thinking could have betrayed him to these insensitive KGB thugs who tortured Moslem children in Afghanistan.

Conclusion: *he had made no error*.

He paused, his eyes focused on a distant place.

With such clarity of spirit he should be looking right at the answer to his puzzle, yet it eluded him. The Chaika wound among the trees, its engine knocking as they crawled up a grade.

If he had made no mistake, then they must be suspecting him without cause! It was unjust! To have made the perfect plan and yet still to be taken in by Russian paranoia! . . . but his mind had not even completed the thought before it triggered a blinding satori. . . .

Shoof! he exclaimed to himself in Arabic.

Ze! he said to himself in Zen, feeling an immense relief.

This was a camel he could lead by the nose! *The KGB had nothing on him* but they suspected him just the same and, of course, *now* he knew exactly how his interrogator would behave: hadn't his KGB instructors spent the last six months teaching him everything they knew about the rules of paranoia—how to make a man feel guilty for sins he did not know he had committed, how to make a recruit afraid that the KGB knew what the KGB did not, in fact, know?

Assume that the man you are recruiting is guilty, hint that you have seen the secret reports of *stukachi*—then carefully observe his reaction. *Insinuate* from trivia that you have *all* the facts and are just playing with him to test his reliability.

If you do not immediately tell me what you cannot know I don't already know, I may find it necessary to send you to a labor camp or crush your family or take away your wealth.

Never smile until *after* your recruit smells of fear.

His escorts hadn't told him where they were taking him or why—and they had yet to smile. They had been forbidden to smile. He was dealing with apparatchiks who were following instructions in a tradition passed down from ancient masters whose fearsomeness still ruled the Russian soul. Even when these undermen pulled into the asphalt driveway of a modest dacha hidden by pines, they could not smile.

Bijad ibn Jamal knew by the Persian rugs and the Danish furniture and the Japanese stereo that he had risen above the class of the Czechoslovakian clad flunkies and was now dealing with the Soviet aristocracy. He was left to wait—to increase his suspense, to hone his fear.

There were some inlaid brass pieces on the table and on the walls, probably from the southern states of the USSR, but perhaps stolen from Afghanistan. A rare cut-steel urn from the Tsarina's Tula State Arsenal sat on the mantelpiece, a perfumer which had once dispelled the odor of unwashed Russian nobles. He had seen nothing like it outside of the museums of London.

Such splendor was meant to impress. But one cannot awe a Zen Marxist Master with Leninist Imperial Materialism! They were bringing him here to cut his throat or to offer him the rewards of heaven—and thought themselves cleverly cruel by not telling him which, as if there was a difference between life and death.

The rest of the furnishings were antiques, none from the same period. The cabinet wore a vaguely French nineteenth century look from the Classical Revival, but with peculiarities of craftsmanship that no French cabinetmaker had ever used to Bijad's knowledge. The Karelian birch inlays were definitely Russian. Three simple Biedermeier chairs spoke of a common Central European ancestry and though they showed the wear of more than a hundred years they also showed the care of a recent restoration.

Bijad knew, as his unknown host probably did not, that the best of the Russian cabinetmakers had not been free craftsmen as in the Moslem states, but had been serfs bound to a particular nobleman's property much as modern Soviet workers were bound to their factories by the modern lords of Great Russia. Imperialism was no faint-hearted foe. Chop off its head and, like a worm, it grew a new head with the same memories which collected the same antiques and used the same police methods.

The portly Russian who emerged from the study matched his house. He had a slightly Uzbek face, indicating impure Moslem blood by Great Russia's racist standards. He wore a London made business suit and, *Wallahi!* was offering a friendly hug— which meant that he belonged to the school that believed in putting you at ease before they took you by surprise.

He offered Bijad vodka from a cut glass decanter. Was he a chauvinist who knew nothing about Arabs? Did he hold the customs of Arabia in contempt? Perhaps he was also an alcoholic who slept under tables at parties? Bijad accepted the drink: it was part of his persona to "be above" conventional Arabic values.

The Russian had spoken to him in English. He raised his glass and replied in English, "To the victory of socialism!" then repeated himself in his still crude Russian. This was all part of the charade that Soviet officials liked to go through in the presence of their third world inferiors. He nearly choked while he drank, not because he despised vodka, but because he was trying not to laugh. *To the victory of California-Zen!* would not have been an appropriate toast.

"To the future President of Saudia Arabia!" The vodka disappeared in one gulp, much to Bijad's amazement while the KGB colonel's face broke into a broad smile. "Yes. We think you are right for that job. Perfect."

"So do I," said Bijad quietly, with complete sincerity.

They moved to the office overlooking the colonel's rose garden. "I have your report here—your plans for a subversive organization. Very detailed. Very competent. I have staff who will help you modify them. It won't be easy. If you begin to succeed the Americans will do all in their power to use military force to erase you." The colonel grinned, showing golden molars.

Unimpressed, Bijad nodded agreement. This man would be a textbook strategist, slow and unoriginal. The Americans were irrelevant. Their Arabic specialists were slow and unoriginal. It was the sons of Abdul Aziz themselves who would crush a poorly conceived revolution.

In less than a single second, the whole mood of the room changed—the colonel was no longer smiling. He pushed aside Bijad's report. He opened a drawer and took out a file. He opened the file. He pretended to read parts of it, but Bijad, now totally alert, knew that this very dangerous man had already prepared everything that he was about to say.

"You were in prison in Saudi Arabia."

So the ritual began. The robot had been wound up and now he was whirring through Standard Operating Procedure. Bijad was tempted to slip in one of the more deadly Zen *koan* to derail the machinery, but he did not. "Yes, I was in prison as a Marxist."

"During this same period of time an unfortunately large number of our comrades from the Saudi Arabian Front were also picked up by the Saudi police."

"Prince Turki al Faisal is a very efficient man."

The winter tundra in the Russian's eyes told Bijad that they knew all about betrayal and had a special treatment for men who betrayed the cause. "You were the only survivor."

"I was not a member of the Front for the Liberation of Saudi Arabia. I was merely a simple Marxist who believed in a better life for my people."

"It would be interesting to know how you survived when the others did not. Perhaps you could enlighten me?"

Bijad was remembering a California girl. His Los Angeles Zen master used as his studio a room with white walls and sparce furniture, a walk-up above a drycleaning emporium where he taught Zen and Marxism. That evening there had been only five students and the girl had been wonderful at baiting them all. She had enraged Bijad into attacking her. And only in cold afterthought had he realized that *she had never once asked the questions which he had felt compelled to answer so defensively*.

Such was his first encounter with satori, the feeblest flash of sanity—but an event never to be forgotten. Here, facing a professional KGB officer, he had not the slightest need to trip all over himself to answer questions which had not been asked.

He created, instead, his own ritual question with a ritual answer designed to flow like honey down the throat of this Russian excuse for a Marxist. "I survived because I have a passionate concern for the working man of Saudi Arabia who has been so ruthlessly exploited by American imperialism. My passion gave me inner strength. It is good for me that one so competent has been assigned to guide me. By myself I am as naive as the camel cows of the Murrah. Your less outstanding predecessors, while recruiting the men of the ill-fated Front, unfortunately trusted the movement to those who were ruled by fear and greed. Prince Turki breaks such women apart in his hands like dried camel dung. He has no fear. He is a man of God. His men have no fear and are also men of God. Does the KGB send easily recruited cowards against the House of Saud and expect them to live?" Jamal's voice was poisoned with sarcasm. "Were these cowards not destroyed? For this you expect Saudi respect? Turki's men could not break me, and so learned to respect me. That is why I survived and the others did not."

How easy it was for a Zen master to deceive a man who, out of caution, insists on seeing lies everywhere—just to be safe— and therefore cannot see the truth. A shadow moves invisibly at night.

The ritual was almost over. The KGB wanted a man who was not afraid of the Saudis but not one so strong that they could not manipulate him. Bijad used Zen control to bring sweat to his hands, and Zen control to let the fingers tremble. He stared at this Russian, who would never reveal his true name, and pleaded with a slave's eyes. "Sir, it was a terrible experience. I could not have survived without knowing that beyond my walls there was a great socialist country willing to help. I need your help. My single terrible fear is that I might fail you. They tortured me." Tears rolled down his cheeks.

The colonel reached out a hand to comfort him.

Allah! thought Bijad, *I've overdone it!*

But he was amused. The old Front for the Liberation of Saudi Arabia had been destroyed. The sons of Abdul Aziz were too efficient. And now the KGB was desperate for replacement players for their nineteenth century imperialist game of colonization. They had their back to the wind while stalking a coffee bean. They prodded the bean for weapons while the wind threw knives.

Those who fear betrayal are doomed to be betrayed—but, in this case, not until the victory feast! In the meantime, Bijad ibn Jamal and the KGB would work together on the elimination of the House of Saud and the humiliation of the Americans.

CHAPTER 27

He met us at the platform on the train station. It was getting toward evening, and the sun, big and red, was already dipping under the horizon. "That sun," said Andrei Dmitriyevich, "reminds me of the explosion of the hydrogen bomb. . . ."

Now a red setting sun always fills me with a feeling of alarm: I see it indifferently hanging above our lifeless planet. The longer the people holding the fate of mankind in their hands avoid solving the problems identified by Sakharov, the more unswervingly will we slide down into the abyss into which he has already peered.

VLADIMIR VOINOVICH (FROM EXILE IN GERMANY)

Snow was falling in blobs, settling like little caps on the hydra-headed cupolas of the Cathedral. It was the season of the New Year. A squat Christmas tree in the Pioneer's Palace held gaudy paper and painted wooden dolls, dried fruit on strings, and little cellophane packages of candy. For days there had been a party atmosphere. This evening was the big celebration, but minor eruptions of party had been happening since morning.

After grumbling about the waste of an hour decorating a hall, Peter Kaissel had retreated back to the math offices and was re-programming Synmann's basic game universe while Hans Dorfman, still with artificial snow in his hair, was engrossed in the finicky problem of adding subroutines to the algorithm of their best cooperative player.

"Limon's been stealing all the candy canes off the tree," complained Kaissel.

At his desk, Joseph Synmann wrestled with the stability problems posed by their preliminary forays into a new computer simulation, *BalanceOfTerror*, which had first been

175

suggested—and initially programmed—by a curious twenty-one year old Marshall of the Society of the Soviet General Staff and Waterworks. The simulation used familiar players whose algorithmic attributes were now so well known that they could not be blamed for the extreme instability of the game. It was the game itself which was unstable.

The Cathedral kitchen had been busy all morning. A matron in kerchief appeared at Synmann's door and offered stuffed mushrooms to the three mathematicians. Later a troika of women arrived in long, flowing bright-colored *sarafans* embroidered with golden and silver and red threads, billowing sleeves restrained at the wrists by bracelets. They carried trays heaped with Russian *bliny* and insisted on interrupting all work. After batting their eyes and kissing the tops of embarrassed heads, they fed the two young men their pancakes, drowned in egg and butter sauce and capped with smoked filet of sturgeon.

The bravest of the braided girls hesitated in front of Joseph Synmann for he was the fiercest looking of the three mathematicians. After cautious preliminary flirting she sat on his lap to pull his long hair and tweek his nose while he ate. Synmann, in turn, poured these welcome invaders small glasses of a Georgian brandy which he had spotted on the shelf of an uptown Manhattan liquor store.

Joseph glowed, remembering the foolery of his hippy-farm days. The Cathedral village was always a pleasant change from designing battlestations whose major use might be to shred Soviet cosmonauts into freeze-dryable pieces of meat. Games offered a different kind of hope than weaponry.

After due thought and scribbling, still nibbling on pancake and smoked sturgeon, Synmann called up the code of the *Terror* universe and, god-like, changed a few parameters and added several necessary constraints to its basic laws. It wasn't easy to program game rules which:

(1) gave alliances of players the collective power to reduce (permanently) the payoff of all other players to zero, without:

(2) creating a game in which *all* the players eventually destroyed themselves.

Initially everything went well for the first alliance, but inevitably a second deadly alliance formed, and even a third. (The United States was the first member of the Nuclear Club. Then there were two. Then there were three, etc.) The stability of such games degenerated in a complicated way.

"When will you get the new universe running?" asked Synmann.

"Not today—unless I skip the party," said Kaissel.

"It's okay. No hurry." Synmann compiled his code and ran a test game in universe-four, without spy and betrayer algorithms. It ran too fast for him to follow—but the payoff graphs on the screen kept his attention. Even they jumped around almost too swiftly for his eyes. "Kapowie!" exclaimed the physicist.

"Another atomic war?" asked Dorfman without looking up.

"Yeah. They blew themselves to smithereens. But I got them to go past the thousand move mark before they did themselves in."

"A thousand moves to maneuver yourself into a corner is shit for a game that's supposed to stabilize," commented Kaissel.

"I'm beginning to suspect that we have an intractable stability problem on our hands," said Synmann morosely.

Dorfman was so compulsively good natured that he would have maintained his good cheer even in the event of a real war. "Keep smiling. You weren't the one who invented the strategy of nuclear deterrence."

Kaissel was now pointing at one of Synmann's symbols. "You know, the theta coefficient is causing you a lot of trouble. If you could fatten it to the point where subroutine XnoPan returned negative roots, your region of stability would be infinite."

"Kaissel! Always keep track of what your symbols mean. Sure I could kill the problem by causing theta to be sufficiently large. I could end the nuclear threat to humanity tomorrow, too. All I have to do is increase the price of an H-bomb to a cool trillion dollars a throw. Do you know how to do that?"

Kaissel went back to his seat. "I keep forgetting I'm a mathematician!"

"How the hell do mathematicians survive?" grumbled Synmann.

"We have physicists to remind us when to wear our rubbers."

"A lot of good that would do," retorted Synmann. "You'd just start to wander out in the snow with condoms on your feet."

"Hey, I'm sorry," said Kaissel, smiling.

"*Can* you stabilize *BalanceOfTerror?*" asked Dorfman.

"I doubt it. I *suspect* that the problem isn't model specific. I'm afraid our dance with the Soviets has built-in seeking-wobble with randomly alternating p-n feedback. A kind of Brownian motion-powered Parkinson's disease. Neither we nor the Soviets will even be able to predict, more than five minutes in advance, *when* our defense will fail, only the probability of failure. MAD seems to have the nature of a radium atom—stable right up to that unpredictable moment of violent disintegration."

Dorfman couldn't resist a teasing jibe. "We die tomorrow?"

"Ask Murphy."

"All Murphy *ever* says is that anything that can go wrong, will go wrong."

"Yeah. I'm going down to the Inn for a cup of coffee."

At the Inn, Joseph Synmann sat by himself in a corner, sipping, staring out over an infinite valley with eyes that turned through some crooked dimension, wondering if there was a modification to *BalanceOfTerror* that might make its outcome less lethal. The season's friendly people passed around him like doves around a mountain.

Soon he wasn't even sipping. The coffee was cold and his hand didn't move. His consciousness had gone to that nether region where only a scholar who has long studied the arcane incantations of applied math can ever hope to conjure his mind. It fascinated Synmann to explore this sunless universe of inner vision where all men are blind and only the most gifted can grope their way around the bones of older expeditions.

There was purpose in his probing, bodiless search. Nuclear deterrence as a strategic policy had always displeased Synmann— it was a subtle marijuana high—but he was just getting used to viewing this illusion-of-well-being from inside a symbol-wizard's space where feel has no hands and vision no lens.

His numerical model of the strategy of deterrence by nuclear threat showed it to be a fatally flawed strategy, but that might be an artifact of the model. Wrong assumptions give erroneous conclusions. So—strip down the model dispassionately—check it, check it, check it. In his symbolic world he sought out flaws in his shadow creation the way he always did—by measuring fine art against the real world.

California and New York both had nuclear technology but were not involved in an arms race. That implied the possibility of a safe nuclear world. Well, his program could handle that nicely but to build into a model the same level of communication and trust as existed between California and New York could not be justified if the model was designed to provide insight into the American/Soviet impasse. Soviet borders equipped with robot machine guns to kill trespassers were nowhere close to trust.

Willingness to trust is a function of the stakes. A man can afford to trust a stranger if the worst that might happen is that his feelings will get hurt. But if betrayal means the death of civilization, then the level of caution is high. Trust must be earned with great integrity if it is to influence deals. The stakes in *BalanceOfTerror* were very high. It was quite natural for the model to be insensitive to minor increases in trust.

A fascinating—and counterintuitive—facet of Synmann's game was that if both sides were committed to nuclear deterrence, then nuclear war *always* erupted *even* under the extreme assumption that both sides were desperate for peace and that neither side was planning to attack the other. Nitroglycerine will certainly explode if someone detonates it—but nitroglycerine will also explode "by accident" while just sitting on the shelf.

What else?

In Synmann's model the central driving force that led to a runaway arms race and eventual collapse into war was the search for "parity." To a mathematically unsophisticated mind "parity" looks like a good idea. What is more reasonable than both sides being equally armed and equally strong? But math is no respecter of common sense.

Bernard Brodie, the creator of the strategy of nuclear deterrence, thought that there was a balance point, like balancing salt against brass in a high school chemistry class, but in the real world there is no *unique* balance point—a gram against a gram is no different than a kiloton against a kiloton. If you are terrified, the costs don't matter—you keep seeking the security you never feel and slowly climb up through all the balance points from zero to the balance point where the scales crack into rubble. In Synmann's model the numbers went the same way as they had been going in the real world.

Nuclear deterrence generates fear—as it is supposed to. Fear *requires* one to exaggerate the strength of a potential enemy. A Russian may or may not perceive Americans as a military threat but his fear demands that he *plan* as if they were. An American may or may not take Leninist bombast seriously, but in a nuclear world he damn well better *assume* that when the Russians say they intend to conquer the world, they mean it. Neither nation is powerful enough to achieve military superiority over the other—so they seek "parity."

But what is "parity"? The Russian feels that, because his electronic guidance is inferior, he needs to aim three times as much nuclear kilotonnage at the US as the US has aimed at him so that in the event of hostilities there will be a "parity" of strategic hits. The American freaks out and increases arms production in the name of throw-weight "parity." Since "parity" *cannot* be defined, Russians and Americans persist in perceiving their weapon-making as "catching up." Thus a very rough parity *is* maintained—but at growing levels of deadliness.

It was a classical case of runaway feedback. Cost can be the only ceiling on such an arms build-up. But the cost-per-kill by H-bomb is so low that cost itself is incapable of controlling parity-inflation. Synmann scanned through every axiom of his game searching for a place where he could introduce some kind of damping feedback that would give an advantage to the side which had *fewer* H-bombs. He could not find it.

How could it be that bad? His awareness was sending him those first alarms of lethal wrongness—a rat sniffing the faintest sweet aroma of spring steel from the cheese; the guest in the haunted house testing the front door from the inside to find it locked.

Escape. There had to be an escape.

In the awesome sunless elsewhen of his mathematics, Synmann felt through the inner dynamics of reasoned terror with neuronal tentacles. Here an H-bomb was only a black flash and a cold searing that rumbled soundlessly through algebras where death/life was not a question. He slithered off the silvery convolutions of abstract dimensions, now tasting the hidden rapacity of numerical cancers, now following the silent musical hymn of a differential equation, straining with slug-white eyeballs to find a way around the nuclear etiology. He saw, in his numerical mirror, seven generals of Moscow and Washington staring in enraptured captivity at the gorgon of *peace-by-terror*.

Gaze upon nuclear deterrence directly and it seems to be a snake's nest of rocketfang ready to to swarm after an enemy; it is a technological marvel powered by the fear of death; it is that mythical devil-whore with the heart of gold who has kept us from fighting with our wife for the last half-century at the price of our soul. On the surface the shape of peace through nuclear deterrence is as rock solid as the tranquil hills of San Francisco under the March sun of 1906.

But in Synmann's mirror of equations, stripped and x-rayed to its mathematical bones, nuclear deterrence was only a strategy for avoiding earthquakes by building houses vulnerable to them. Insanity. The warning was clear: gaze upon Medusa's face and become shattered stone.

The message went in circles.

Fear creates parity-inflation. Parity-inflation leads to holocaust. Conclusion: eliminate the fear. But if there is no fear there is no strategy of nuclear deterrence. The concept appeared to be *hopelessly* flawed. It exchanged safety today for suicide tomorrow. The serpent in the Garden of Eden was speaking his cunning wisdom. Stay alive by eating your children.

. . . and one of the doves did not fly around the granite mountain but settled on Synmann's head, as gently as a woman's hand. "Do you want more coffee? Your coffee is cold."

. . . and Synmann's eyes looked out from his sunless world. "How about a crash passage to Alpha Centaurus instead?"

"Is that a new kind of bagel?"

"What's a nice New Yorker like you doing here in Kiev?"

"You look like you need some loving."

"I'm just thinking."

"A penny for your thoughts," she asked.

Synmann smiled and, on impulse, made up a story for this pleasant woman. "Back on Earth, in the real world of 1945 when madness was not yet fatal, a university educated politician in a business suit, advising the government on post-war defense, took from his embossed purse a newly minted penny that flashed in the sun when he threw it into a great plaza's wishing well. He asked from the water nymphs only that they grant mankind peace. No more war. A peace based on *eternal fear*. He was a MAD man."

"I should have offered you a dime!" She kissed him awkwardly because he was so much older than she was. "Merry Christmas and Happy Lenin!"

Synmann sighed. Time to shower and change. The hour of the party was upon the village and the gifts had yet to be wrapped. He wandered back to the Cathedral of Saint Sakharov, no longer wondering *if* there would be a Third World War, but curious about how it would start.

Gorbachev wouldn't *deliberately* start it. He was a man of peace who was trying to convince the world's people to cut back to only one ton of nitroglycerine in their basement from two tons, and for years his propagandists had been warning the world of how dangerous it was to mix nitroglycerine with clay. Nor would the Americans *deliberately* start it. To fight a major war they'd have to give up hot dogs.

But could you trust Murphy? It was Murphy who snuffed out the Challenger. It was Murphy who melted the Chernobyl reactors. It was Murphy who blew himself up while priming a Belfast bomb. There are only two defenses against Murphy.

You can concentrate on building machines which have non-lethal failure modes—such as an ICBM killer that burns up harmlessly in the atmosphere if launched by accident against a radar spook.

Or you can build a *perfect* machine.

And who thinks that the best Soviet and American engineers

can build Murphy-proof ICBMs that will never be launched from their silos by accident?

Even as I walk across the snow, thought Synmann, *the agents of Murphy are out there, closing in.*

CHAPTER 28

*An astonished historian might well ask why the extended
period of wars between the Second World War and the Great
Accidental War was popularly known as the Nuclear Peace.
During the Nuclear Peace more people died in war than during
all of mankind's previous wars. The major ideologies of the
twentieth century made no grand attempt to end war. They so
feared each other and were so confident of their overwhelming
might that they never even noticed the military geniuses being
bred in the violent shadows of their conflict. It was a fatal
mistake. No ideology can survive an error of that magnitude.*

PROFESSOR J.H. NEVARAKO,
HARVARD UNIVERSITY, NEW CAMBRIDGE, LUNA, 2049

The child saw his first Russian airplane when he was out
tending the goats. He watched the winged shape with a naive
pleasure because it was flying so low. Never had such a
machine . . .

The blast lifted him off his feet.

When he regained consciousness his family's house was half
gone. The goats were scattered. He ran to the shambles in a
panic, blood pouring from his nose—to see: a quiet mother torn
out of her clothes in the yard among a wild bundle of bloody, but
once clean, bedding. He stared in terrified horror at this first
gift of the Red Angel who had arrived so suddenly to free him
from his feudal life.

It is a Russian folk saying that to free a man one must first
break the mother's umbilical cord. The boy Yahya wailed,
gasping, thrown from the medieval century of Peter the Great
into the century of the rule of the Soviet working class. Dazed,

he tried to find his sisters under the ruins of the flat roof. He found a head. He found three bodies. His four year old sister, who had been playing away from the house, was still alive but grieviously wounded by fragments of house. He tended her as best he could, her fingers tight on his sleeve with shock. She would not let go. But then, no Soviet apparatchik had ever promised that the road to socialism was easy.

At the twilight setting of the sun, a frantic father found his shattered home. He comforted his son as best he could with tears in his eyes. He would not say it was Allah's will but he talked about the peace of paradise. He buried his family hastily under the rubble of their home and told his son they would be back but now they had to flee because the Russian tanks were pouring up the valley.

They carried his sister two days without medical attention before she died high on a mountain looking out over the awesome hills and the smoke haze of the pillaging Soviet troops. The medical facilities of a feudal state are inadequate.

"In Allah's good time we will kill them all," muttered his father.

Yahya was still bewildered by the catastrophic appearance of these people about whom he had never heard. "Where do they come from?"

"The Kremlin," said his father who smiled affectionately when he saw that the word meant nothing to this young man. He drew a picture in the dirt and pointed north-west. He pissed on the picture and Yahya dutifully pissed on it too. That scribble in the dirt, half washed away by urine, became the core of all that he later learned about Russians. He never made a vow to destroy the Kremlin—but Allah gave him that dream often enough, vivid and dark and ominous.

Later, son and father returned to the valley. The man was mullah and would be in charge of rebuilding the village. But mainly this bereaved husband was drawn home because he could not bear the thought of his family lying in the rubble without a proper burial. Few others came back. "More will come when they grow less afraid," said Yahya's father but it was a Russian patrol which swept through the village and took what men they could find and shot them. They were merciful and did not kill the wailing women. The boy survived by hiding. He had no reason to believe that these men would spare a child who had pissed on the Kremlin towers.

With the women's help he buried his father. He spent another morning burying Abdul Dar, the village carpenter he adored because the man had once built Yahya his own little table. Firmly he remembered to ask for Allah's justice to be done in Allah's own way.

If you want a young man to ride out of feudalism and embrace you as his savior, do not kill his mother and father, nor tell him later with a sly smile how innocent you are, that the CIA did it. There are consequences for every action—some immediate, some delayed. A generation later when you think you have finally pacified an ungrateful nation, such a man as Yahya Karargah has the power to step out of some fourth dimension and slit your throat. He has been motivated.

For a while Yahya lived with relatives but they were killed also. He was adopted by a motley band of mujahideen who spent their time hiding from the helicopters, sometimes attacking two mud-walled forts maintained by the Afghan army and, on occasion, blowing up a supply truck. They got mines by stealing Russian mines that had been deployed around the mud forts. Their munitions expert was a deserter from the Afghan army who had been trained in Russia. Yahya became his apprentice.

They lost two men digging up mines and Yahya rashly took on that dangerous task himself. He became so good at it that he was the band's main source of ammunition. He learned about all the wonderful things one could do with an anti-personnel mine, from making bullets for Lee-Enfields to assembling a package powerful enough to blow up a truck. That was before they were equipped with Chinese made AK-47s.

One day he salvaged a radio from a Russian truck. It didn't work but the electronic innards of it entranced him and he took it apart and put it back together endlessly. There was little military activity then. It was winter and they were starving in the mountains. In desperation the least sick of the band came out of the mountains and ambushed a truck trying to reach one of the forts. They got flour and a second identical radio that didn't work which they brought back for Yahya because they loved him.

He made one good radio out of the two. By so doing he impressed himself. He impressed the other mujahideen. They came one by one to listen to his radio and smile and nod their approval. It was a single solitary victory, nothing like it ever happened again, but the event so sustained Yahya's sense of power that years later when he was given the chance to go to university in Lyon, he chose to study electronics without knowing anything at all about what it meant.

Upon such small events, the history of mankind hinges. How could the comfortable architects of nuclear deterrence have known that the success of one illiterate child in piecing together two battle scarred radios would lead, in due time, to the structural failure and collapse of their whole grand edifice of locking and interlocking safety features?

In the annual summer offensive of the Soviet army versus the villages of Afghanistan, Yahya's band was destroyed in a single hour's engagement among the mulberries. He was one of the four survivors, not because he was clever or brave, but because he was young. The band was fond of him. He was their Allah-blessed sapper and they never risked him when there were no mines to defuse.

The three other survivors walked him to Pakistan, up steep red hillsides that looked out over rust and green mountainscape and then down over the rocks that jarred and dusted his feet. They had tea and sugar, no other rations, except the odd stolen apple or tiny apricot. Once, in a silent valley, they walked through ominously deserted fields along an irrigation channel, its water bubbling in the heat. They could hear the hum of a Russian jet, higher than the eye could see.

In Pakistan he was too young for the commando training camps but he would not be put with the women. The men laughed and kept him as a mascot. The camp commander, a soldier loyal to the old king, was not pleased, but relented gruffly after questioning Yahya and finding that he knew more than a child should about mines. He put the boy to serving food. Mujahideen, twice his age, were not ashamed to have him teach them what he knew.

One of the trainers was a Frenchman. He was the first European Yahya had ever seen, strange of face, and strange in the way he spoke the language.

"You speak like a goat," Yahya said impishly one day when he had lost his awe of this man.

"Ah oui, my accent. I learn your language late. I cannot get the francais off my tongue."

Yahya demanded that he make more goat noises and when Claude obliged, the boy whooped and tried to imitate him. Thus began a friendship. Claude, at last, had someone to talk to who would listen to the golden language.

For two years Claude and the mujahideen kept their boy out of the fighting. But in the summer of 1985 he disappeared across the frontier to return to his trade of "killing Russians." When the casualty reports of that vicious battle came in Claude

thought he had lost Yahya forever, but no, *l'enfant* came strag-
gling back across the border in August, smiling, with a T72 tank
and crew to his credit, real Russians, he grinned, not Afghan
mercenaries dragooned to fight for the Soviets. He had pissed
on the Kremlin and he was proud. Claude sent him away to
Lyon to live with Claude's sister for his own good.

He loved Europe. There was so much to see! There were so
many machines! He taught himself fluent French by memoriza-
tion—and one of the stories he memorized was the tale of
Lenin's hero, Stephan Khalturin, who had smuggled dynamite
into his small room in the cellar of the Tsar's Winter Palace,
underneath the main guard room, which was underneath the
Tsar's dining room. Yahya never tired of rattling off, in French,
how Khalturin had blown up *dix soldats russes* and almost
assassiné le Tsar.

At a kiosk in Lyon he found a picture postcard of the Kremlin
and kept it for years in his Koran, curious about whether it had
a cellar. He read French military trade magazines, and kept a
sketchbook of weapons. He also wondered where Frenchmen
kept their goats—Claude's sister said in Paris, but he wasn't
always sure he could believe her.

If it hadn't been for the Russian invasion of Afghanistan in
1979 Yahya Karargah would have lived out his life as a farmer
raising wheat and goats on terraced mountainsides. He would
have known the harshness of an ancient lifestyle, perhaps been
unhappy, perhaps died at a young age. He would have helped
to marry off his sisters. He would have learned to be a mullah
as crafty as his father. But progress, in the form of socialism
dedicated to saving him from Koranic feudalism, intervened to
educate his young mind in the ways of the twentieth century.
Methodically, year after year, during the eighties it taught him
the primary skill of great socialists like Stalin—how to be an
efficient murderer of Russians.

He spent his winters in school and his summer vacations
harrassing military convoys. In Lyon the French school masters
were polite but firm with their students. In Afghanistan the
Russians killed the students who flunked their course. The
survivors became very, very good. Thus was born one of the
true geniuses of modern electronic warfare.

By the time he was twenty Yahya Karargah made better
mines than anything that was coming out of the American or
Soviet arsenals. When he was twenty-two he engineered an
attack on a Soviet military convoy that took out 80 vehicles in a

multiple synchronized blast using microprocessor mines that talked to sensors and pooled strategic decisions with one another.

He often thought about heavier weapons. It annoyed him to be dependent on outside suppliers who had their own motives for supporting the mujahideen. But at the time it never occurred to him that light weapons were the wave of the future. It never occurred to him that by the end of the century Russian heavy weapons would be obsolete, even in Afghanistan.

CHAPTER   29

What are the critical factors determining the size of the leoport's power plant? The main function of the power plant is to counteract the tendency of the leoport to sink back to Earth in a slow downward spiral as it captures saucers and loses momentum to them. All other uses are trivial by comparison. Momentum is always conserved, and when a leoport captures a low momentum saucer and accelerates it, lending it momentum, the leoport itself has to lose *momentum. To prevent eventual disaster, the lost momentum must be restored.*

Momentum is mass times velocity.

Energy is half of the mass times velocity squared.

Momentum may be restored to the leoport in either of two ways:

(1) We can eject little mass at a very high velocity. This is our alternative if mass is expensive and energy is cheap. Ion beam thrustors mounted on the leoport would be an example of such a strategy. But we must be aware that for every HALVING *of the reaction mass used, the energy price* QUADRUPLES. *Such huge energy needs imply heavy in-place energy generators. And every ton of the power plant has to be carried into orbit from Earth. What one gains by using high specific impulse thrustors that require little reaction mass, one loses in massive power plant.*

(2) We can restore leoport momentum by ejecting a lot of mass at a low velocity. This is our alternative if mass is cheap and energy is expensive. Is there such a thing as cheap mass in space? We can eject the emptied saucers (free mass) at a modest velocity. That consumes more electricity than the fully loaded saucers generate when they arrive, but since the empty saucers are still massive, the energy-price of using their mass to restore

189

leoport altitude is much smaller than that of using ion beams. It is cheaper still if the saucers are returned to Earth carrying finished products or wastes.

There are other combinations of mass and energy use. If the leoport imports material from the moon we both generate electricity and cause the leoport to rise in orbit. This can be used to balance mass imports from Earth which also generate electricity. If the net flow of mass is in the moon-to-Earth direction, we can run a leoport space transportation system which will generate surplus electricity as a by-product.

RAY ARMSIEL, *REPORT 12/879/AT*

Byron had his baby boy out on a field trip. Little Charlie didn't like it. He was very upset that the ground wasn't flat like a proper hardwood floor. He sat down on the crunchy autumn leaves and went on strike. Byron watched him, damned if he was going to be sympathetic. Junie spoiled the little bastard to death and it was time he shaped up.

Of course, Byron wasn't going to be as tough on Charlie as his father had been on him. That was too much. He had grown up with nails for a father! Byron waited patiently, smiling. The baby looked up coyly, then picked a stick and began to play with it, poking the earth with rapid little jabs. And Byron waited exactly one minute longer than his father would have waited before walking away, deeper into the New Hampshire woods.

Charlie watched him go in alarm. He dropped the stick. Very carefully he stood up. Watch that floor with the brittle rug and the bumps! It was a very strange place, wind howling, tall dark trees, things falling from the ceiling, smells, and a father who was disappearing into the gloom. He ran, he fell, he got up and ran and *ran* and stumbled over a rock and fell and cried his heart out, alone and lost. He was fifteen months old.

The father returned and stood over him, patiently, but unmoved. *God, Junie's spoiled him rotten.* A *man* didn't expect to be picked up every time he tripped. It was a McDougall family saying that a soldier only cries when his best buddy is killed, and then when the battle is over. Byron had heard that bit of old sergeant's drivel from his grandfather as well as from his father. He wasn't having anything to do with such nonsense.

Babies were allowed to cry when they were really hurt or hungry—but you had to watch them. They tried to fool you. They pretended to be hurt when they were merely tired. He remembered all the tricks he had used on *his* father. How could the rascal be hurt by just falling down on a pile of soft leaves!

Byron turned the boy over with his foot. "Come on. Let's go. Enough yammering." He said it gently, if severely, and Charlie saw the smile. He was ready to howl some more but his father was moving away. Struggling, he followed for another ten steps and his father waited for him and let him hold on to a finger to help him. They went up funny stairs without any railings or ledges to rest on, vast in expanse, big-big with fallen logs and moss and ferns until Charlie was ready to whimper but something kept him silent. Then he saw the most marvelous sight, and stopped to make excited noises.

"That's a cave in the rocks. You want to go in? You'll have to go in alone. It's too small for me."

Byron sat down and let the boy explore. It was amazing what intrigued a little kid. He came out with some rocks and threw them down with great force, his tiredness forgotten. He went back inside and found a big black beetle that had lived under the rock. It half-frightened, half-fascinated him the way it scrambled across the leaves and climbed up the rock and fell off.

"Bug," said Byron, touching it with a stick.

"Brgle," said Charlie touching it with a stick.

Only when Byron rose to go home did the boy remember how hard it had been to get there and began to wail in protest.

"Horsey," said Byron, putting on a horse-face and neighing.

Charlie smiled. He raised his little arms.

The midget Mongol Warrior clung to the hair of his pony-father with fierce fingers, yelling his high pitched war cry and skewering Russian Knights as his horse galloped back down through the woods. It was Da-Da's second night home and he wasn't to be feared anymore, only watched and cajoled.

Byron could see from the meadow, long before they reached the house, that Ray's car was in the driveway. His offer to fly them up had been accepted—and then later refused by Ray after he had consulted Linda who was afraid of flying. She had scared her family half to death by disappearing for a week while she *drove* home from L.A. One of the *landbound!*

The boy was asleep—and slung over Byron's shoulder like a sack of onions—when he strode through the front door. "You mudfaces made it. Great!"

"Oh, he's exhausted!" said Junie, rushing over. She took the baby tenderly. "My poor little baby! You've kept him all of *three hours!* She rushed Charlie off to the Throne Room with its shelf of animals and two-meter tall stuffed giraffe. Immediately her head reappeared at the door. "Byron! He's bleeding!"

Byron grinned. "Yeah. We were up in this tree trying to corner a porcupine and I dropped him on his head. Sorry about that." He winked at Ray.

Linda vanished into the Throne Room, attracted to the baby like a bee to wildflowers, while Byron watched her graceful flight in the way a frog might be mesmerized by a mysteriously buzzing "fly" who was, perhaps, too dangerous to swallow. It was hard to imagine that old Brontz had produced *that* wench.

"Your directions were very good," said Ray. "Except it's a *right* turn after the Amoco station."

Byron thought for a moment. "Yeah, but you're left-handed. You're bi-symmetrically inverted to the normal. Your right is my left. Can't you remember that? And my left is your right. It's a shame what they do to left-handed people in school! Guys like you get so confused. Teachers should just leave leftys alone."

"If you have a bottle of wine, I have a left-handed corkscrew."

"How about a beer? You have to ask Junie for the wine. While they're spoiling my baby why don't you come and look over Junie's computer? I can't get used to it. I love toys." But Byron headed into the kitchen, not the computer room.

"If you need some help with the dinner, I'm very handy," said Ray.

"If you go near the kitchen, I'll kill you. I have a spoiled child on my hands; I don't need a spoiled wife." He pulled two beers from the fridge, popped the tops, handed Ray a crystal glass and they clinked cans at Byron's raised command. "Here's to the leoport."

"It's not going fast these days. Synmann pulled his whole team off on an emergency."

"The battlestations?"

"Jesus H. Christ! What is this?" Ray was pouring his beer and it was red.

"That's raspberry-grape beer. Don't look so stunned. I've seen you drink Coke. If you can drink Coke you can drink this. I phoned up Junie from Houston and asked her to lay in ten cases of beer." He shrugged and laughed. "It's got alcohol in it. Hobos use it to heat their beans."

In the magnificent office, Ray relaxed and stretched out on Byron's puffy swivel chair. He made loud settling groans.

"Rough trip?"

"It's been a hectic life since Linda arrived on my doorstep. Changing the history of mankind and pleasing a woman at the same time is a tall order. I've been busy. Mostly moving boxes."

Byron was smiling. "You're being organized."

"You can bet your ass on that!"

"The old Brontz talent for hustling men is hereditary, eh?"

"You don't sound like you have an ounce of pity in you."

"You have rosy cheeks."

"It's called burn-out fever."

"It's good that Synmann is off the job for a while. You'll get a vacation."

"Yeah I will; my workload has doubled." Ray was staring quizzically at a model of a solar power system that Byron had suspended from his ceiling. "What's that?"

"I've been talking to Dubrovsky here at Silicon Factory in Concord and gave him my wires-embedded-in-glass idea. He didn't believe it so I flew him out to the Glassworks and took him into the plant and a few of my friends showed him how to draw, in glass, micro-wire with diameters of less than a hundred angstrom units." Byron produced a cross-section of solar powerpanel out of a box. "Dubrovsky thought about it and said he couldn't use the stuff, but a month later he got a brainstorm."

"It's light as a feather," said Ray, hefting the panel.

"It wouldn't stand up in the wind on Earth but its fine for space. The silver-black stuff is the micro-rectenna array, the rest mirrors to concentrate the light. The rectennae can handle a lot more power than the thousand-plus watts per square meter that the sun puts out—and the mirrors are cheaper than antennae. But don't get excited yet. The rectennae ribbons Dubrovsky makes are shit. A lot of production problems. He uses chip technology to make them, but they are far cheaper than chips because you don't need the same kind of reliability."

Ray was still staring at the prototype. "The boy who assembled this frame knew his materials tech."

"He's a NASA boy," said Byron proudly.

"It gives me dreams."

"I've been having some wild dreams myself."

"I'm listening."

"Wait till after dinner and after we've finished the serious business. Then we can break out another case of raspberry-grape beer and treat ourselves to one of your famous bull sessions."

"You're threatening me with more of this swill?"

"Ray, you've got to help me drink it. Junie stashed *ten cases* of it in our cellar."

They spent the next hour running through Byron's designs. His basic power system was set up on the highly flexible Tinker Toy CAD program that worked like a graphics spreadsheet— you could draw pictures and then assign equations to the pieces of the picture, and see what happened as you varied the parameters and the initial conditions. They spent their hour harassing various mass-sensitive components and came up with a four percent mass saving before they were called to dinner.

Ray found the salt and pepper shakers. Byron did his part by carrying in the hot food from the kitchen and helping Linda into her chair.

"Where's my little brat? Isn't he going to eat with us?"

"He's asleep and a siren couldn't wake him up," said Junie accusingly. She admired her spread. "What I love about the country is the fresh vegetables. We're having pumpkin-potatoes."

"Well," said Byron, smiling, "that's a change from raspberry-grape potatoes."

"No cracks from you, you ungrateful pig. Just sit down at your trough and eat." She slipped out a box of red matches, each with its individual gold stripe, and lit up a well deserved Virginia Thins, the very picture of an emancipated American woman defying death by cancer. Beside her salad plate she kept an elegant Chinese ashtray from some ancient opium den.

Byron opened the window eight inches and, before sitting, stooped over and whispered something into Linda's ear so that he could smell her hair. One of the small pleasures of life was nuzzling the hair of a woman who didn't smoke.

Linda laughed at Byron's wit, then was caught by surprise when Junie bowed her head and began to say grace. Ray nudged his startled girlfriend back to her senses and she lowered her lashes.

"May God bless this meal and bring His hope to those of us who partake in His bounty. Amen."

"Amen," said Byron.

A sneaky glance told Linda it was safe to lift her head. Byron was already rising. He motioned for his wife to stay seated while he went for the heated soup bowls and a bottle of wine from the cooler. "Ray. For your left-handed corkscrew!" The soup bowls he set in front of himself and the salad bowl he gave to Linda. He began to ladle out the clam chowder.

"He's pretending he's the chef," said Junie. "Wouldn't he make a good Manor Lord?"

Linda whispered to Ray, "Do married people always snipe at each other? Do your mother and father snipe? Mine do. I'm *never* getting married especially to a grouch like you." She turned back to her soup, careful to tip the bowl correctly.

The two women began an animated conversation about Bostonian social life. Ray listened like a Pacific tuna in Boston harbor, and Byron used the time to fill his stomach. It always fascinated him to listen to Junie talk. He loved her accent. She was one of the earth's very good people and nothing pleased him more than eating her special meals.

Byron helped Linda fix up the guest room and then went downstairs and helped Junie stack dishes before heading back to the computer room. Ray was already there, fiddling with the Tinker Toy graphics and trying out a few of his own hunches.

Eventually, with a little more ersatz beer in their bellies, they got into a raging cock-and-bull session. They whumped up a leoport for Mars as a warm-up—and then, closer to home, carved out an electromagnetic spaceport built right on the moon's surface so that incoming moonships would generate electricity, instead of wasting propellant, and outgoing moonships wouldn't have to use any of the precious lunar carbon or hydrogen.

With these problems "solved" they spent an hour arguing about the design of a powerplant in Earth orbit that could generate electricity from the "waterfall" of moonrock. For some reason that lead to a discussion of life on the far side of the moon and from there it was no great deviation to examine the scientific prowess of an intelligent species of spider able to travel between the stars on webs accelerated by microwave beams.

Of course, after such a wild insanity, sobriety returned.

"You know something," said Byron casually. "How in hell are we going to bring the stuff in to build that electromagnetic track on the moon? That's a lot of track."

"We build it out of moon beams."

"After importing the geologists and the mining machinery and the machine tools?" complained Byron.

"We could buy our mass from the Russians. They're certainly planning to be there first according to you."

"Piss on that! How about a skyhook?"

"All the way to L-One? That's 56,000 kloms above the moon." Ray turned up his nose. "Forget it!"

In retaliation Byron handed him another raspberry-grape beer. "The grass that makes your cheese starts out as bullshit. An old Wisconsin saying. I was thinking of an *orbiting* skyhook."

"One of Moravec's rotating skyhooks?"

"No. An orbiting skyhook that's always vertical."

"I can see why you're a pilot instead of an engineer," chided Ray.

"Hey, you're starting to sound like my wife."

They opened a new Tinker Toy file on the computer after consulting Byron's skyhook scrapbook. He already had a subfile on disk for the moon and its gravitic field. They added a vertical line with mass-center and shape determined by tensile strength and density.

"Good God!" said Ray after the first couple of runs. "You could build it out of steel!" Steel is not known for its high tensile strength.

They tried better materials and, even with a safety factor of eight, found that each ten tons of cable could lift a ton of load. For one of their skyhooks the center of mass was in orbit 1130 kloms above the moon's surface—the lower tip, skimming 30 kloms above the surface, travelled at 805 meters per second, while the upper tip, 1876 kloms above the surface, travelled at escape velocity for its altitude.

That meant that a one ton ship which needed three tons of propellant to land on and leave the moon, needed only half a ton of propellant to do the same job when it climbed the skyhook.

All sorts of configurations bloomed on the phosphor screen and grew and shape-changed. It was half serious fun and half a kind of arcane arcade-zapping. A mesmerized Byron and Ray competed to shoot down the CAD images while conjuring up new horrors to harass each other. To find a physical principle which the current screen model violated, and thus to shatter it, was to score.

In the middle of their game, a wide-awake infant appeared at the door, silent, watching, ready to run away (with laughter) in case he was chased, but betting that he wouldn't be. Byron called him in and set his son on his knee. It was time Charlie got used to a man's tools—otherwise he might turn into a musician. The father watched him reach for the keyboard . . .

. . . to hit seven keys at a time with the flat of the hand like the big people did.

Swiftly Byron grabbed his arm and guided the tiny index finger to a special key. On the screen the phosphor skyhook began to oscillate jerkily under the stress of a descending load.

Charlie frowned. He didn't want to be told what to do. His unrestrained hand cleverly reached around all obstacles, smashing at the keys, blanking the image and creating an eruption of symbols. Byron resettled the boy in his lap with a firmer grip, painfully resurrecting old images with four careful keystrokes. The skyhook shattered and its pieces began to fall.

"Interesting," said Ray. He reached over the baby's hands with his fingers, tapping out a command to zoom in on the load. They watched in detail as the vibration built up destructively. "Yeah. I know what's going on."

They tried cures. Ray inserted sections that could be contracted or relaxed at will to control waves. That implied signalling and power systems on the cable. They had to control torsional flex. They tossed around elevator concepts.

Ray won most of the designs rounds and Charlie went to sleep again in a nest of computer paper and Byron kept contributing new angles but in the end, around three in the morning, they both admitted that they were tired and stumped. "We'll have to bring in Synmann. He's our electromagnetic expert. You can fly them, and I can build them but I think electricity is out of our line."

"I think we've made *marvelous* progress," said Byron, waving his hands around drunkenly.

"You call that progress?"

"Damn right! We've demolished half a case of that bloody beer!"

Ray looked at Byron rather woozily. "Man, you sound desperate. You need a little help." He took Byron out into the wild blackness of the country night and located a pipe in the shed. "Bring me a case!"

Byron hurried indoors to the basement and came back with a full carton of cans. Somehow they jury-rigged a mortar that worked on compressed air supplied by a red bicycle pump and a judicious shaking of the can before it was dropped into the cast iron pipe they had found for the barrel.

They labored by the light of a waning crescent moon, half hidden by branches, and by the time the moon was gone and the sky was hinting that it was time for dawn, they had improved their design so that the raspberry-grape beer was being lobbed a full fifteen feet over the backyard fence, a can at a time.

CHAPTER 30

The new moon is Diana's bow
But when she lets her arrows go
To thunk into some starry hearts
This virgin stares upon the sight
Of mortal, wounded men in fright—
And waning, from the sky departs.

FROM THE DIARY OF JACK A.

To Diana's airborne eyes a billowy clouded terrain gave way to an underworld of ocean. Then, as the airliner banked, the Namalas appeared on the horizon of the tropical sea, distant green islands sleeping in the vast moat of the Pacific like the backbones and snout of a drowsy crocodile. Such was the aircraft's distance that the beast never seemed to grow closer. The blue water had already deepened into the purples of a sunset before they began their gliding approach to the airfield.

This was her first real adventure as a pretend-woman, the high point of her life and she felt exhilarated. She was here—part of a base that was shipping supplies to the moon! She had an introduction to a Grand Lady and reservations at a very high sounding hotel called *The Third Millennium*!

While she worried about her luggage on the airfield terrace, waiting for Mr. Ling's Madam Lilly, the drowsy crocodile woke. Its thunder was too reverberating to be a storm and the sudden brilliance too constant to be lightning. Her eyes turned to the fire. A delta-winged scram-jet freighter began to lift from the launch area on its rocket boosters, roaring flame, carrying its load of saucers into the sky, to be flung along spaced trajectories that would disperse them so that, one by one, they could

198

be swallowed into the maw of the leoport's rings. The rocket blast faded—but another freighter thundered to life with a glow that created a new sunset—and another.

Awed, her luggage forgotten, Diana stood there until the last of the squadron of rocket-boosted scram-jets were lost in the dark sky. Into the peace, the silver thread of the leoport rose majestically out of the ocean. At first it was only a small thread, a wavering glimmer. On the horizon its 210 klom length was foreshortened to hardly more than a degree of sky, but perceptibly it grew to stretch its gossamer strand over almost a sixth of the heavens—before vanishing into the shadow of the Earth, leaving only stars.

She remembered seeing in her telescope the building of the leoport, its construction shack a tiny spider riding a filament of sunlit web over the cornfields of Ohio, reappearing every day until the first 100 kloms of hoops were in place. Then McDougall had towed it away into equatorial orbit.

The show wasn't over. Soon a fleet of down-bound saucers, electromagnetically ejected from the leoport to balance its momentum losses, began a screaming drop from the blackness, swooping into the floodlamps of the lagoon to be received with the efficiency of a flight returning to the deck of its aircraft carrier. Some of the winged saucers were laden with goods made in the factories that had attached themselves to the leoport like factories had once sprung up next to a railway spur line. Some of the saucers came down empty.

Across the bay, ground crews ran a standard maintenance check on each vehicle, inserting a new payload module, pumping propellant into the maneuvering tanks, recooling the saucer's rim coils, reprogramming the silicon pilot. The saucers didn't need heavy heat shielding like the shuttle because the leoport ejected them back into the atmosphere at substantially less than orbital velocity. However they didn't really look like they could fly, with their canards and retractable delta wings.

Finally the freshly readied saucers were rolled to the launch site and loaded into the bay of a scram-jet freighter, there to await the return of the leoport. Thus passed the "down-time" of a flying saucer's grueling life.

Every ninety-six minutes, day and night, this same cycle repeated at all of the equatorial stations.

Madam Lilly was standing behind Diana Grove, unwilling to intrude on the girl's rapture. "Do you want to wait for the scram-jets from Sahili to come in? Ours don't come back—they hop around the world before we see them again."

"I think I've had enough for one night! You're Madam Lilly? I'm so pleased to meet you!"

Madam Lilly turned out to be a hard taskmaster. Her restaurant carried the Ling symbol but, like all of Ling's restaurants, it supported its own name, the *Kaleidoscope*, a reference to Madam Lilly's devotion to a constantly changing atmosphere. Madam Lilly was a theater person. She could do miracles with a few props and backdrops and screens, but her main focus was on the girls whom she adored. She costumed them perfectly and taught them gesture and emotion and expression and dialog.

The week that Diana arrived they were all doing World War II at the *Kaleidoscope*. There was a Rosie the Riveter in slacks and Sultry Pinup in black negligee. Diana was given "shorts" and set to serving the veranda with a tray over her head. She wore the persona of a Hep Carhop. Sometimes she chewed gum and she always said "swell" to the customers. On off hours she did her homework by looking at *Life* and reading *The Saturday Evening Post* and early Mailer. The juke box music ran to "Deep in the Heart of Texas . . ." or "Kiss me once and kiss me twice and kiss me once again, it's been a long long time . . ."

From there they sank into the Great Depression. The backdrops became WPA courthouse paintings of stiff workers which the girls slavishly reproduced themselves with considerable success. Diana watched movie clips of Claudette Colbert until she could talk and move in the curiously limited way of the pre-television Americans. She ran the "soup kitchen" and learned to chat knowledgeably about *swing*. She fell in love with Artie Shaw and played his fast spinning platters with a passion on an obscenely large machine that used *needles*.

Namala was a paradise for a girl scared of men. The ratio of single men to women was three to one and she had so many dates that she could easily play one against the other for safety. If that failed, Diana pleaded work. She had to rehearse the movements of a Burmese dancer, or walk like a Persian lady, or catch the subtle way a geisha presented a plate of raw fish. You could find her laughing with her arms around two men . . .

. . . or alone on the beach in the moonlight watching the fireworks shoot up into the night sky with macho splendor. There she had time for the secret thoughts she never shared.

The beach was more gregarious by sunlight. During the *Kaleidoscope*'s Twenties' stint Madam Lilly strictly forbade her girls to wear their monokinis and had them splashing about in daring flapper bathing suits that exposed the knees. It caused a riot and that was good for business—and tips.

Time and the smallness of the Namala community was her enemy. She met a boy named Jack in her martial arts class. He always spoke to her; she constantly ignored him. Their Japanese instructor repeated that the greatest perfection was to defeat an opponent with the minimum of force. Diana was having none of that. She was there to learn how to *demolish* rude men with the thrust of her heel or the back of her hand. She believed in a safety factor of ten. Break their skulls and then ask questions. She willingly practiced on Jack, he willingly let her. Still, she allowed no other communication.

But Jack survived. Smitten, he arranged a surprise birthday party. There were twenty-one candles on the cake even though she was only turning sixteen. She had a fabulous old time hugging everyone for their crazy gifts and singing and fooling around and pretending. It was delightful to tell mysterious lies about her past, especially about places she had been before she was born! For three hours she successfully avoided Jack, never forgetting how dangerous a man in love can be.

Her fatal mistake was to need a Kleenex. Jack kept some in his study which had remained off limits to the party because of the delicate model of the lunar base he kept there. She caught a glimpse of its detail while blowing her nose and fell heels over head. Long after the revelry had died she was still in the study, her arms wrapped around Jack, kissing his nose and asking him questions about the lunar electromagnetic landing tracks and why they were so much more powerful than the leoport's track. She had him explain the workings of the lunar spacehook elevator which hung, appropriately, from the ceiling.

The affair lasted two weeks, a miracle of involvement for Diana. She went everywhere with him. She haunted the launch site when he was at work and she wasn't. He, in turn, spent all his money at the *Kaleidoscope*. They went surfing together and kissed at every opportunity. He hinted that he wanted to sleep with her. She hinted that she wanted to wait but in an internal debate with herself decided that he was the nicest guy in the world and she was going to throw her virginity away on him and live happily ever after.

In time they found themselves alone. Unhurriedly, gently, he began to undress her. That didn't bother her. Diana was only noticing that he was between her and the door. Since she had been a small girl she had learned to keep herself always between her father and a door. It was a Very Important Rule.

For a while she tried to suppress her silly need—she knew very well that Jack wasn't going to knife her or knock a joint out of its socket—but the anxiety didn't go away: it became worse. It became imperative. Smiling at her insanity she took Jack in her arms, hoping to roll him away from the door, a little closer to the wall. It was important that she not have to say anything. He chose the moment to be assertive—holding her rigidly so that he could look at her disheveled beauty.

Suddenly panicking, Diana threw him off the bed. When he looked up in anger, still commanding the doorway, she was so terrified that she struck him with a reflex karate kick to the head, and ran, not remembering that she ran. The next day he apologized when he found her. She turned away without speaking.

He flew in flowers from the States. He sent her letters. He papered love declarations on the corridor walls of her apartment. He slept on her steps. His intensity frightened her. The more she avoided him, the more he pursued her. She stayed awake with images of him murdering her. When he came to the *Kaleidoscope*, the other girls waited on him. Madam Lilly soothed her and told her that it was normal for men to go crazy, that it was nothing to worry about, but Diana worried. Jack persisted. He even sent one of the female mechanics he worked with to talk to her. Diana became so upset that she typed a letter into her phone and sent it via the Attman net to Mr. Ling's personal electronic mailbox pleading for a transfer.

The reply bounced back via satellite later that afternoon and when she called up the message with shaking fingers it read, "Spend a week with me. Ling." She regretted her impulse. She thought his message very cold and did not reply, but by evening he had transferred to her account a thousand dollars. Having a man who loved her was very reassuring.

CHAPTER 31

Never underestimate the power of a woman.

THE LADIES' HOME JOURNAL

Junie McDougall took her son down to Florida to watch his Daddy's second shuttle flight. She had chatted to him a lot about aircraft but she wasn't really sure if he understood because he didn't like to talk much. But he had ridden co-pilot with his father in their Cessna and his favorite toy was a wooden airplane made in Sweden that he could assemble and disassemble by himself. She was afraid that the awesome light and sound of the blast off would frighten him—it had frightened *her* the first time—so she held him very closely to her body while she listened to the countdown over her earphones.

Little Charlie was patient at first but he got restless. Watching Florida from a high balcony wasn't as interesting as sticking his fingers into the humming air conditioner. Junie let him go to play by himself for a while and thought he didn't understand, but he kept running back and asking, "Ready yet?"

"Don't go away. They're ready."

But he knew that when she said "ready" he had whole minutes left so he ran off and came back with his model orbiter before he asked to sit again in his mother's lap.

"They're on internal power now," she said.

"Boom! Boom!" he said impatiently.

"They've swiveled the main engines to launch position."

"Daddy ready?"

"Daddy's ready. They've just closed the oxygen vents."

"Roger, out. Boom! Boom!"

"The hydrogen pressurization is up." Her heart pounded.

Suddenly the light and the sound began, a thundering firefall upon the blossoming billows. She felt Charlie's tiny fingers grip her ring finger in total surprise. He said nothing. She said nothing during the seven seconds of roaring build-up. The fragile moth, clinging fiercely to its booster cylinders and its brown cocoon, began a graceful rise through blazing clouds, climbing up a tower of vapor.

"Daddy all gone. Roger." Charlie looked up at his mother for reassurance.

Junie was smiling. She was wondering how she ever came to marry a man like Byron. When she had dragged him home from Saudi Arabia she thought she was getting him a safe job in an office. It was only getting worse. He had told her that if this mission was successful he was in line to be commander on the maiden flight of the *Constitution*, the first of the second genera-tion of shuttles to come off the Rockwell lines.

After an hour of hyperactive play in the strange Florida apartment with the chintz curtains, Charlie confronted his mother very firmly. "Daddy back?"

"No, but he's in orbit. And he's safe. And everything is fine. I wish we could stay until he returns, but you're going to be flying away with your mommy."

"Orbit?"

"No silly. Just home to Stonefield."

During the past summer Junie had soloed in a light plane, and qualified herself as an instrument and night pilot. It wasn't really new to her—she had been informally airborne since she was sixteen—and though her father hadn't allowed her to solo or land she had been an instrument navigator since the ninth grade. She would never have the devil-may-care reflexes of her father, and she couldn't yet duplicate the smooth precision of Byron who anticipated everything in advance, but she was proud of the fact that Byron didn't mind flying with her.

This time up, Byron was pilot on the mission to deploy a one-sixth scale mock-up of an eight unit leoport section which was to be left in orbit. It was something that fitted the two-minute attention span of the television newsmakers and so, back in New Hampshire, Charlie got to watch the cameras inside the orbiter's bay watching the release. The eight hoops, each with an inner and outer coil, were almost as wide in diameter as the shuttle cargo bay. They moved out together, magically springing apart, unconnected, but remaining bound by the invisible tug of electromagnetic forces.

Charlie sat on the New York Times which was spread over

the floor of their Stonefield home. He was smudging the ink on his father's picture with an agitated palm. "Daddy in orbit. Daddy not back." He shook his head.

It was a mad race for Junie to keep up with her husband. She hardly had time to talk with him. Sometimes he had to catch an airplane right in the middle of one of their arguments and she had to wait two weeks until he climbed out of another airplane before she could finish saying what was on her mind. So when she hopped down to Florida to pick him up after his second mission she fully intended to hammer at him all the way back home.

She hit her stride while winging through a pass in a bumpy mountain range of clouds. The engine noise made her scream at him, but if she didn't get in her licks now she might never get another chance. She *insisted* that he quit NASA and settle down with a big company—it didn't have to be Shantech. While she pleaded, the air current under a disintegrating avalanche of white mist snatched her breath away for a moment and her husband took over the conversation. She had to listen to him prattle on about the serene pleasures of floating two-hundred miles above the turbulence while she was fighting to turn the Cessna out of the downdraft.

At home she thought he seemed tired. *Poor boy.* Then when he came back from his obligatory trip to Concord he seemed to be painfully depressed about the progress Dubrovsky was making with the micro-rectenna assembly. Silicon Factory was up to its ears in financial trouble. He bitched and bitched.

Once she found him lying on the couch while Charlie tried to play with him. Byron just lay there and let the little boy beat him up, almost without lifting a finger to defend himself. She was going to have to *force* him to change jobs! Immediately after Byron dragged himself back to Houston she called up Dad. What was happening to the leoport idea? Was it going anywhere? Was it falling apart?

"Doesn't Byron tell you anything? We're putting together a construction consortium." He was very gentle in telling her that his chief engineer at Shantech didn't take Byron seriously.

That made her pause. Was Byron worried because he was being cut out? Worry could make anyone tired. Was he going to lose his chance to be something else besides a pilot? An uneasy suspicion set her alarms and her energy into overdrive.

She called up Ray. He was very diplomatic but he confirmed that Silicon Factory was in trouble and that they were going to have to go to a different power system than Byron's, which was unfortunate because a conservative design was dicey and, worse, would both cost more and weigh more.

Junie's expertise was in the financial world but her PhD was in music. She watched Charlie dance while she played some Bohemian folk airs to calm her nerves. Her darling boy was so beautiful pirouetting and stomping around the Persian carpet of her living room. As the misty melodies flowed from her fingers she dreamed that they might have a real artist in the family. She was the boring financial wizard and Byron was the all-around jock. Baby Charlie was the artist!

At his nap time she returned to her scheming. She called one of Brontz's accountant types. She had met him at a party and had been impressed by the savvy of the man—enough to make a point of cultivating him. The telephone call lasted an hour.

Then she called Dubrovsky. His hoarse voice sounded muddled and had the vagueness she immediately identified as evasive action. Only after patient and gentle pressing did he admit to problems. It was just that Silicon Factory "needed refinancing for expansion." She asked him ten very carefully designed questions and very carefully listened to the answers for clues about the health of his company.

He doesn't know what he's doing.

Dubrovsky was talking to her partly because she was Byron's wife but mostly because she was Charlie Bond's daughter and he was desperate for help. It was all in his voice. Self-deception is always the last layer of vanity's armor to crack. She eased past Dubrovsky's central fear without confronting his pride.

"I may be able to get you some money. I'll be down with a man tomorrow."

That was all she had to say. Money was the bait on the hook. If Dubrovsky had actually seen what was on her mind, he would not have let her near his Silicon Factory—but a macho warlord *will* let his drawbridge down for a woman, not being able to conceive of a female warrior. She had in mind a controlling directorship for Byron, a good solid ground job.

She knew that the Soviet Snowfox was making discrete visits to American military satellites beyond the reach of the shuttle. The sober Washington mood was an ingredient that she added into her own private think-tank soup. And her father was telling her that the top level of military planners were panicking over projections which showed that, even with the new shuttles, the American ability to deliver mass to orbit was going to fall well behind demand. The assembly of the full space station would have to be postponed, perhaps five years, and *even the delivery*

*of the defensive battlestations to protect American military
satellites might be retarded.*

She studied many reports. The generals were pleading on
their knees with Congress—but the lack of orbital delivery
capacity seemed to be worrying the congressmen for a reason
the generals would not have understood: what if the development of space was slowed to a rate where even this fastest of
growth areas was unable to generate the tax dollars that the
government *had* to have to meet its massive debt payments?
Congress was waking to the horror that without super-rapid
economic expansion it just might be *forced* to make drastic cuts
in its aid program to the middle class.

Piety and fear and anger were the kind of things that told her
where the dollars were going to go. It all added up. It was the
right time to invest in space.

Seven weeks after taking an interest in Silicon Factory, using
her inside knowledge that the upcoming leoport contract was
certain to be signed, Junie found new money—pulled in from
secret sources Dad didn't even know she had. To convince the
new money, she maneuvered a potent re-organization virus
into place along the spine of Dubrovsky's organization—*that*
particular hit-team being borrowed temporarily from Brontz.
Long ago a naive music student had learned that skillful manipulation of money wasn't enough—you had to be decisive and
you had to have the right people hiding in your closet when
your victim went to put his coat away.

She didn't covet power for herself. She did it all for Byron.
Yes, she loved the thrill of the hundred yard dash but she hated
all marathons. She believed in delegating, to men, the responsibility for full time nose-grinding. What was the use of knowing all about money if you couldn't forget it and tease your feet
in the sands of Biarritz? Silicon Factory interested her only
because she knew she was going to be able to hand it over to
Byron.

Dubrovsky was so pleased by Junie that he bought her a
bottle of champagne and took her to Concord's best restaurant.
She talked all night about her new love, stunt flying. Her
instructor was showing her how to do rolls. Dubrovsky didn't
see any danger at all in this helpful girl. All he saw was the new
money. *Poor baby*, she thought. He was a nice man, really, and
she decided to make sure that he kept his illusions and, when
he came to retire, a good pension. Perhaps more important to
him, she would see to it that he always had a good lab to putter

around in. But mostly she was thinking about how the blood slopped around in one's head during a tight roll.

On the day when the leoport contract was signed—news phoned hush-hush to her by her father—Junie was making pies for the church supper. She mused to herself about how easy it had been to sell Silicon Factory piggybacked on top of the leoport. But what amazed Junie was that Sam Brontz had *long ago* seen the crunch in space delivery capacity. Because of his foresight Ray Armsiel's lightweight, low cost, mass delivery system was sitting in the anteroom at precisely the right stage of development, at the exact moment of crisis, ready to soak up the money that such crises always generated.

His vision was mysterious but not unprecedented. She had heard similar stories from Brontz himself, the man who knew them all. The whole Boeing empire had been built on the foresight of Claire Egtvedt who had the Flying Fortress ready for a world war no one thought was going to happen. She remembered Sam's cluttered office when he was just one of her father's hot assistants—the painting of the B-17 on the wall and the green glow of VisiCalc on his Apple when no one else she knew had even heard of personal computers.

She rolled out the pie dough, flipping it over onto the mincemeat filling in one easy motion while she applauded Sam in her mind for his beautiful intuition, proud of her old time friend and sometimes mentor. The leoport was too big for any one company to develop and too big for a government which had been crippled financially by its obese growth during the Reagan administration. Her father and Brontz had had to bring together the largest consortium of private and government capital that had ever been assembled for one purpose if you didn't count anomalies like the Second World War.

She noted the time. Hubby would be in his office in Texas. Still with flour on her hands she picked up the phone. "Byron," she said, and the machine dialed Houston from memory.

"McDougall here."

"Byron, you've got to be in Boston on the twenty-first."

"Can't. The Cessna's in for overhaul."

"I'll buy you a ticket on American. You can relax."

"Can't it wait?"

"It's a party." She paused. "The leoport contract has been signed," she said, dead-pan.

"What! Already? A party?"

"A fatted calf party."

"What year is this?"

"Same year as yesterday. And you, wonderman-of-my-life, have something special to celebrate. I've reorganized Silicon Factory for you."

"What! What's going on?"

At the Boston festivities Byron McDougall remembered all the old movies he had watched on the family's GE TV in the living rooms of their various cramped Army camp bungalows. Bond owned the kind of mansion that hard-working poor girls always seemed to inherit in those old American Dream movies. It had high ceilings and a crystal chandelier and a ballustraded stairway to the second floor that would have served the New York Public Library. There were more than seventy guests and Byron half expected them to form up and race down the stairs kicking up their heels and doffing their hats in true musical style while Benny Goodman and his boys played *I'm In Love With You* down in the basement. That's what this party lacked— Fred Astaire!

Byron was always happy when he visited the mansion—it was like being given the run of a carnival fun house. He found himself shaking his head and smiling, trying to dream what it would have been like to grow up here. What war games he could have had—like darting down the hallways and tossing imaginary grenades into every room to flush out the Nazi snipers who were holed up in Antwerp's most prestigious pre-war hotel.

Junie took it all for granted. He had never seen her looking so sultry. She had on a light silk dress hand-dyed by some ancient craftsman from a lost civilization. He could sense her body moving under the silk, he could almost feel the touch of her breasts against the silk and he was sure that he could see through it. And yet after it had induced a randy warmth, forcing him to stare a little more attentively to catch that glimpse of body line under the silk—the dress taunted him with an innocent respectability.

Byron knew he was going to have a good time in the later hours of the morning. Junie loved nothing better than to make love to a man in the room where she had grown up as a child. To Byron it was like a visit to a slightly gaudy whorehouse and he wasn't going to knock it.

Junie caught up with him in some butler's nook and reserved a moment to neck with him on the wooden bench.

"You're going to be the director of my company now! It'll be you're first big job and you're not even an old man yet! I love you!" Moving from pilot to powerful corporate executive did not strike Junie as anything unusual—that's what her father had done. If a girl wanted to reach the corporate stratosphere, marrying a pilot was the most natural thing in the world to do.

"Hey, watch those ears. That's the only right ear I've got." At first he hadn't understood how she had resurrected Silicon Factory. He was still bewildered. He *knew* Junie. He couldn't imagine her walking out of the kitchen and taking over an ailing corporation to please her husband and then demurely going back to her cooking and harpsicords—but that is exactly what she had done. It was a bit terrifying to find himself married to a closet executive. Of course, it wasn't the first time she had surprised him.

"I have your office in Concord all picked out. That old warehouse that Dubrovksy has been using for Silicon Factory offices just won't do. I get to decorate it. You can't refuse me after all I've done for you."

The old panic started in Byron. "It's about time I'm due for a new job, isn't it?"

"It certainly is. Piloting is a young man's job."

"I'm pretty lucky that this leoport thing came along."

"You can't believe how smart you are! How did you see where Dubrovsky fitted in? You'll make millions! I never would have picked Silicon Factory off the heap. And in my own backyard, too! It's nice to have such a smart husband. What title do you want? I can arrange anything." She nudged him.

"I'm thinking of Chief Construction Engineer." He grinned.

"What are you talking about? You're not thinking what I'm thinking you're thinking, I hope!"

"But they're going to need me," he said. "Who else is qualified? How many engineers have experience in space?"

"You rat! You cross me at every turn! Don't tell me you don't! I saw you buying a toy handsaw for little Charlie. I even know where you hid it. You think I don't know anything. I'm not going to let you make an engineer out of him. One in the family is enough!"

The next day she went shopping along Boston's elegant back streets for artist's supplies. She got the very best and she started Charlie on his lessons that same day. He couldn't hold a brush but he could certainly finger-paint. She was distracted by a phone call and when she came back she found that Charlie had become bored with the artistic challenge of the playroom. He was in another room and, after pouring his water paints on one of Charlie Sr.'s most expensive rugs, was adding great sweeps of yellow and red and dayglow orange to its intricate design with a careful imitation of his mother's finger-painting flourishes.

"God! Oh my God!" she screamed. "You and your father!"

Little Charlie instantly sensed that he had done something wrong. He stood up, yellow to one elbow, dayglow orange and green down his front, and announced, "Bad! Bad!"

CHAPTER 32

The man who drives the wedge, splits the wood.

NEW ENGLAND SAYING

With his usual single-mindedness Byron McDougall readied himself to lead an American return to the moon. Nobody was paying any attention, all raised eyes were focused on space stations and low Earth orbit factories and leoports and an ICBM defense—but that didn't matter. Byron had taken lessons from Sam Brontz on how to plan in advance.

He used his frequent commuting flights from Houston to New Hampshire to schedule detours around the country. His favorite ploy was to give talks to undergraduates at engineering schools. Then he would have dinner with a few of the more aggressive engineering professors who were into teaching and convince them to use the moon base as a design problem for their students.

Where would your power come from for the 340 hours of night? One team researched a small atomic reactor. A Stanford class looked at the feasibility of beaming microwaves to the lunar surface. A Cal Tech professor gave his thermodynamics class the problem of a steam turbine powered by hot sodium which had been solar-heated during the day. Three boys in Utah tackled the storing of energy in the magnetic field of a giant superconducting toroid.

One time during a lecture to a physics class in the new Texas Technical High School the kids smuggled up a lunch of cafeteria bean sandwiches. Later, while making jokes to explain away a loud fart, Byron recalled the lack of hydrogen on the moon.

Would the fuel needed to land upon and leave the moon's surface have to be brought in from Earth?

This challenged a tiny slip of a girl hiding at the back of the physics lab. She asked if hydrogen fuel could be replaced somehow by solar electricity. An energy source was an energy source, she insisted stubbornly—after apologizing for being stubborn. She was razzed by the boys because electricity can't be turned into hydrogen. The joker in the class said she was probably dumb enough to think that electricity could be used to atom-smash oxygen into protons.

"It could!" she retorted hotly.

Byron disagreed on the economics of that, but he defended the besieged girl. Electricity might not be able to provide the colony with hydrogen but electrical shuttles could certainly replace rockets and thus obviate the major need for hydrogen.

"What's your name?" he asked.

"Mary," she said meekly.

"Mary was quite correct," he told the class. "It's the energy that is basic and not the rocket fuel itself."

He connected up an old electric motor and showed them that when they sweated to turn the crank, they were pumping electricity through the machine—flicking the needle on the galvanometer. The machine was converting mechanical energy into electricity, like the generators at the local power plant. But if, instead, they connected the machine across a voltage, the induced flow of electricity reversed the action and forced the crank to turn. The machine was then converting electricity into mechanical motion like a motor.

He told the class about the electromagnetic landing track concept. A lunar lander, built like the armature of an electric motor, coming in horizontally over a track that acted like a winding, would generate enormous amounts of electricity as it braked. Instead of using power, a landing ship would generate power! To those who looked puzzled he compared a descending ship with the water coursing through a hydroelectric station.

For two weeks after his enthusiastic reception Byron commuted in and out of Texas Technical leading a whole class of bright teenagers through the problem of a linear generator-motor, patterned after the leoport, but capable of handling heavier loads because it was anchored to the moon. He showed them how to use high school physics to get a handle on some of the fundamental problems.

How did you store the huge amounts of electricity produced during a coupled landing? And how did you feed electricity into those ships as they were being accelerated along the same track for orbital launch? His kids came up with a "first stage" platform that stayed on the moon like a railway car, gulped energy from a power torus, reached lunar orbital velocity, launched its freighter, then decelerated along a continuation track, perhaps after capturing an incoming freighter. It might not work, but it was their idea and they certainly learned a semester's worth of physics tackling the problem.

That slip of a girl, Mary, was always the iconoclast who found a design flaw in everything. At the end of the project she waited to catch Byron. Nervously, but also defiantly, she gave him a folder with her estimates of the mass of the track. He sat down on the floor by the water cooler to read it. Massive amounts of stuff which had to be imported to the moon could kill a lunar project. She didn't care for the implications.

Byron liked this girl. She was the best of the lot. Her mother ran a cleaning business and her father was a painter. No one in her world understood her capabilities. Defiant as she was, even she had her doubts. Byron took her out to dinner to fatten up her bony frame and gave her a first lecture on lunar skyhooks and how they could be combined with electromagnetic tracks to dramatically reduce the initial mass requirements of a colony. He also gave her his card and wrote down on the back of it, "To be redeemed for one job after university training."

"What does that mean?"

"It means you're good. And by the time you're out of college, maybe I'll be building the damn thing. I'll certainly be up there building the leoport."

"You wouldn't want a *girl* engineer!"

"I'm not prejudiced against women—only women who smoke."

"Does smoking cornhusks count?"

"Good God, child!"

In one moment of madness Byron landed his Cessna in a Texas field and visited Amanda in her home territory. He caught her in a cowboy hat and jeans. She still had buck teeth and even though she was bowled over, she was pleased to see him. Her husband was a very affable rancher, a good rancher, but a very opinionated man. He had a theory that it was friction with the Earth's atmosphere which kept the moon in orbit. Byron cringed.

Amanda met him in Houston a week later. She didn't want to come but Byron insisted and they checked into a bridal suite together. She refused to take off her clothes.

"Ah'm not pleased. You never answered my letter!"

"How could I? I'm married!"

"Ah'm married, too! What difference does that make?"

They quarreled. Byron hadn't felt so comfortable with a woman in years. Finally he said, "Enough, enough," and grinning, went over to the ornate desk and took out hotel stationary and, with a complimentary hotel pen, began to write her a love letter. She read over his shoulders and bopped him on the head whenever he scribbled *I love you*.

After softening her up he began to take her clothes off. She protested. "Ah won't let you do what you want to do!" But her voice was muffled by her skirt coming over her head. "And watch my hairdo!"

She let him kiss her for a while, looking over his head sadly. Then she pushed him away gently and grabbed her clothes. She fled to the bathroom.

"Hey, what are you doing in there?" He tested the doorlock.

"Ah'm dressing, you oaf!"

She came out wearing her cowboy hat over combed hair. And a lacey garter of the kind that courtesans wore to hold the money after they had been paid. She went to the bed, inspecting it. "Damn hotels!" she muttered. "Even in their *suites* the beds aren't long enough! Ah always get cold feet when Ah make love in a hotel. Maybe we'll have to do it on the floor like we did in Petra. Ah liked that."

"We can do it diagonally. The diagonal of a rectangle is longer than the sum of its sides."

"Ah always liked intelligent men." She crawled onto the bed and pulled the covers down and crawled inside. The pillow pushed the brim of her hat down over her eyes and all he could see was her bucktoothed grin. "Don't forget to take your boots off."

In a hurried minute he joined her. They hugged and sighed and both of them began to cry at the same time.

"You have such sweet breath," he said deliriously.

"You don't smell like a horse, yourself."

They cried about rancher husbands—boring—and Boston wives who nagged all the time. The warmth of their bodies inflamed their passionate need to bitch. For an hour they raked their respective spouses over the coals.

"Joe doesn't want me to dig anywhere some Arab might rape me and booby trap my coffin with plastic explosives. But Ah don't know where else Ah could go to find so many dead cities!"

Byron, who had been able to match marital horror for horror, was ready with a retort. Junie was even worse than that. "She's *driven* to have a cigaret after sex."

Amanda began to giggle. "Isn't that a funny habit? Joe is like a cuckoo clock. Ah wind him up with sex and he pops out to the edge of the bed and puffs away, chiming all the while, 'great, great, great.' He means the cigaret."

In graphic detail, they imagined Junie and Joe having a sordid affair together. When they got to the great cigaret climax, Amanda was blinded by tears of laughter.

"Oh, Ah'm a cruel woman!"

"What do you mean, cruel? Junie's a great lay and *he'd* never notice her bad breath. It was mean of me to put her to bed with such a boor."

Amanda rose up indignantly, and flicked her Stetson back. "Joe's a very good businessman! She'd like him. *You* try to raise cattle and make money sometime! Joe's a genius!"

"Well, maybe he does have good taste in cows and women."

"Aw Byron." Amanda snuggled to his arms.

In the afterlove, conversation was slow and full of pauses.

She was possessive—and curious. "Have you ever made love to another woman since Petra?"

"Yeah. My wife."

"Ah mean with wenches!"

"Yeah, sometimes with wenches. And you?"

"Sometimes with horses," she said, piqued.

Silence. Byron was holding her hand. "You ever going to dig that mound of yours in Jordan?"

"Ah don't know. Being a rancher and an archaeologist don't seem to mix so great. It takes money and Ah'm a woman and Ah'm stuck here in Texas. We dream a lot in our twenties and then we get to be thirty," she sighed. She squeezed his hand. "You ever going to carve out your Petra on the moon?"

"Yeah," he said.

"You're lucky to be a man. Sometimes Ah wish Ah was a man."

"You'd make a great coalminer."

She bopped him on the head. For a long time she remained quiet. "We don't have much in common. Ah dig up old cities and hate Texas—and you're going to a desert where it's worse than Texas and there are no buried cities."

"Yeah, but with me you'd get to dig out the city for the first time. No secondhand thrills."

Byron was so pleased with the long afternoon that he ordered up a sauteed fresh salmon dinner with champagne and all the little side luxuries he could think of. When it arrived Amanda eyed the feast. "That's a Republican spread," she said disapprovingly. From then on there was no more small talk. They discussed politics passionately. She picked a fight with him as the evening lights of the city came on, and in the end drove away in her pick-up truck, burning rubber. Republicans drove her crazy!

Byron dashed off his first letter to her before midnight.

The drive to the moon continued.

He attended ceramic conferences and noted: (1) the main thing holding back the use of ceramics was a lack of energy needed to manufacture them; (2) the moon had energy in abundance. During the next few years he acquired a formidable knowledge of ceramic manufacturing and machining. Once, while he was building his own high temperature lab, he wrote Amanda a letter about the kinds of ceramic objects that archaeologists would find on the moon in a thousand years.

In his lab his son helped him weigh out powders. They fired and machined toys together. Sometimes Byron took Charlie on long expeditions to collect different rock samples which they ground and analyzed and purified to make their own powders.

The shuttle flights kept Byron's enthusiasm honed. NASA was aware of his interest in lunar bases but they knew him as a space construction expert as well as one of their best pilots and when they began the assembly of the American space station they left him up there for a full month, floating above Earth, just to give him the experience of working with the construction crews.

Junie was glad to get him back after that long absence. She threw an elaborate party in Boston where he met a Harvard professor of economics. He relaxed in bed with Junie all the next morning, eating eggs Benedict and catching up on the Stonefield small town gossip about dogs and potatoes and the arson attack on the university chapel. In midsentence, Byron looked at his watch, shot out of bed, and rushed over to Harvard. He was always busy.

The Business School had a new method to minimize costs that Byron wanted to adapt. He needed a quick system of inputting parameters that would let him decide whether something should be manufactured on the moon or imported. After that he meant to get back to Junie and the kid—but Synmann collared him instead for dinner and spent the time wondering out loud how easy it would be to build a lunar anti-matter factory.

"Why?"

"Never mind why!"

Rumors began to race through the space community that the Russians were assembling the logistics for a full scale attack on the moon—a colony! They had the boosters. They had the staging facilities. They had everything. Byron was counting on a ponderous *apparat* to slow them down.

All the while the leoport design teams were busy. Rockwell was putting together the giant automatic freighter that would lift 120 leoport hoops in one shot. Shuttle-like external boosters pushed the behemoth to scramjet speed, and then the scramjets took over, gulping atmospheric oxygen to combine with hydrogen from the huge tank that filled the hole in the hoops. Boeing was designing the flying saucers.

For Byron it was one rodeo after another. L.A. Seattle. Houston. Utah. Stonefield. A kiss and a goodbye. In the evenings at a strange hotel, when he seemed all alone in the world, he would again write to Amanda.

Periodically he chucked it all to spend time with Charlie Jr. It was terrible how the years flew. Byron looked away and when he looked back, Charlie was an inch taller. All his plans for Charlie's life were in a shambles. He laughed when Charlie got kicked out of all of those sissy music schools for being oversexed with the young ladies. The pleasure of that was worth the hours it took to calm Junie!

He cancelled plans to attend an important symposium so that he could be in New Hampshire when the Titan probe reached the largest moon of Saturn. Gotta be with your son when the really important things happen! He let his son have a beer since it was his birthday. And they sat there in the rumpus room eating potato chips and guzzling Molsons while the Magellan-probe, fighting its way through unknown Saturnian straights, sent back pictures of the yin/yang face of Iapetus. Four sacks of potato chips and a six-pack later—a fair amount of that stowed away by Charlie—saw the probe going down on Titan, gliding on its wings. The colored pictures began to come in, one every two seconds.

"That's where we build our summer palace," said Byron.

"Yeachh!"

The familiar TV screen framed an alien landscape of brown-orange and purple—mountains, billowing clouds of methane, haze, rivers of methane running through methane ice flows.

"Best planet in the solar system besides Earth."

"Yellow snow! Yeachh."

CHAPTER 33

H-bombs, plus their delivery systems, are an economic liability to a country trying to defend itself. They cost enormous sums of money to deploy, weakening the economy that buys them, and destroying any economy which dares to use them in self defense. H-bombs pay for themselves only by creating intangible fear. Their effectiveness as weapons is irrelevant; only their perceived effectiveness counts. In such a situation, strategic advantage goes, not to the team with the greatest ability to destroy, but to the adversary who can buy a cheaper fear.

PETER KAISSEL, *REPORT 19-0-345A*

Ascetic Peter Kaissel, as usual, was in a complaining mood and no sooner had the beer been set up in front of him than he was launched into a witty attack upon the strange colleagues with whom he had been forced to associate for so many years. At least in the tavern here there were real people: hardware salesmen and carpenters and bartenders and his drinking friend Glenn.

His girlfriend had been ruined, he lamented, once a cheerful graduate of Iowa State who had a way with stuffed chicken. She wasn't like those "have a nice day" California girls who were infected by the L.A. disease and came down with every fad around. She had corn silk for hair and knew how to bully a bull and could run a 2000 acre farm with her father's Apple computer. But even she had been transmogrified into a Russian peasant by the SMB.

It wasn't that he didn't like Russians. It was that the people at the SMB weren't really Russians at all. They were neither fish nor fowl. He had once had reason to intrude into a meeting of the Marching Society of the Soviet General Staff and Waterworks. Peter the Great was there, haranguing his generals. M. N. Tukhachevskii was there complete with Stalin's bullet hole in his head. There was a general in the Russian uniform of the Napoleonic Wars, eating a McDonald's hamburger.

It was all a delusion in the head of that power madman, Limon Barnes.

"Why do you stay?" asked Glenn.

"Synmann." Kaissel sighed. Even Synmann didn't turn up much any more. He had become a raving hawk, the kind of man he himself had derided in the sixties. He was obsessed with the defense of America. "I'm working for a genius," explained Kaissel, and stopped—as if that said everything. He neglected to mention that the universities were full, their faculties aging, and all of them stingy with new appointments.

By closing hour Kaissel was talking very volubly and since Glenn was so sympathetic they both somehow agreed that Kaissel's current problem could use a little midnight oil. And besides, the young mathematician wanted to *show* Glenn the madhouse where he worked. Together they drove out to the Cathedral of Saint Marx the Benefactor. And what harm could there be in that? In the costume room Kaissel suggested Red Army uniforms because of their simple comfort, but Glenn rather fancied the outfit of a KGB colonel.

Kaissel demonstrated the SMB's latest computer proudly. He wasn't sure how Synmann had picked up a unit, suggesting that his boss was connected with SDI research and that the computer was one of DOD's answers to the programming bottleneck posed by an ICBM missile defense. It had a Von Neumann brain that talked to a holographic brain—leading edge stuff. The multi-processor holographic brain "learned" the serially executed programs being run in its VN hemisphere, compacting them into a distributed procedure which ran 100 times as fast as the original.

"But the best part," said Kaissel, "is that it's an autodebugger. All I have to do is *find* the bugs, describe them, and it proceeds to dilute them until they vanish—I'm told the bugs get squeezed out by the compacting routines. Anyway I'm always reprogramming my games; it saves me an ungodly amount of time and grief not to have to debug them, too."

"It can debug an Ada program?"

"Hell, it rewrote my Ada compiler."

Glenn was as curious about the game simulations as Kaissel

was eager to explain them. "It's really neat." He called up the latest version of the old game of *BalanceOfTerror*, set the initial conditions and let the game roll on to Doomsday, freezing the action from time to time to illustrate a point.

"What was it you were saying about a weapon that could control the arms race?" asked Glenn.

Kaissel frowned. "You don't understand. We don't have a weapon. We just have a conditional demonstration. In math such a result is called an existence proof. *If* we could build a certain kind of weapon and *if* we applied it in the context of a specific strategy, *then* the nuclear arms race would wind down. Here, I'll show you."

Peter Kaissel restarted the game he had just played after calling up a new set of initial conditions. The players jockeyed for position, hurrying to outclass each other in the electronic corridors of the machine. But the advantage always went with the alliance which had slightly *less* nuclear weapons than the opposition. Doomsday never happened.

Glenn was skeptical. "*More* bombs should give a nation strategic advantage."

"Not so. Bombs use resources that might better be applied elsewhere. Sometimes *less* gives you more. For example, a lean runner can beat a fat runner. What if the defensive imperatives could be juggled so that it was always possible to outclass 100 H-bombs by deploying only ninety of your own? And what if both sides were primarily interested in defense?"

"Obviously they would compete to reduce their nuclear arsenal. I'll buy that." Glenn was taking photos with a hidden mini-camera. "So Synmann has invented the specifications of a superweapon?"

Kaissel grinned. "The game invented the weapon. We just varied the parameters until the game played like we wanted it to. Synmann is a terrible cheat at games. Unscrupulous."

They poured over the results. The defusing weapon had to be non-nuclear and useless against people. It had to be able to find and destroy nuclear weapons within minutes. And it had to be able to destroy five to ten times its own value in H-bombs.

Glenn's sharp eyes picked over the output critically. "I don't think your generals are realistic," he said, twiddling with the camera in the lapel of his KGB uniform. He was referring to the generals who lived in the computer program.

"How can you say that? *I* designed the generals!"

"Look." Glenn pointed to the graphs. "They aren't deploying

enough of your superweapons to protect their own cities. Real generals wouldn't do that."

"You don't understand strategy. A cub reporter for the New York Times thinks that the object of an anti-ICBM robot is to protect New York and all the rest of the cities of the United States, including Philadelphia. But that is an *offensive* consideration. Only if you are preparing a first strike against your enemy do you *need* to protect *all* of your cities.

"If you are merely *defending* yourself, your main objective is quite different. You attempt to cause your enemy to disarm so that you can disarm, too, and spend your money on something else. If you deploy only enough weapons to zap, say, half of your enemy's H-bombs, you force him to double the cost of his strike force. But if he goes that route, you can counter his deployment for *a fifth to a tenth* of what it costs him to counter you. He has to spend his money on arms he can't use—and you get to spend your money strengthening your economy. With a weapon like that you can ruin your enemy economically without lifting a finger. The safest way for him to meet your new strategic advantage is to *reduce* his stock of nuclear weapons and spend his money building up a similar anti-H-bomb capability of his own."

"It sounds pat." Without saying so, Glenn was hinting that he'd like to get a look at that mythical weapon.

"Sure it's pat. It's all shit. It's only numbers in a machine. Don't remind me. Synmann reminded me. I once boldly calculated the exact proportion of ICBM's we should be prepared to shoot down to start arms deflation. I was jumping up and down when I got those results. I was ecstatic and called Synmann up at three in the morning. And then he reminded me that the weapon our game had designed was just specifications in a machine—and a very tough problem for a team of physicists and engineers to tool into a real weapon." Kaissel smiled ruefully. "He also reminded me that the Soviet economy is so badly run that it might not be very sensitive to weapon costs."

"But Synmann *is* on a team which is designing just such ICBM killers."

"Yeah, but he never talks about it."

Gently Glenn shifted the subject. "How did Synmann ever come to be connected with a Russian research institute?"

"The guys who run America all know each other. They scratch each other's backs." '

Glenn groaned. Peter spouted stupidities as soon as he left the subject of mathematics!

Kaissel sensed reproof and shifted his focus to please his friend. "You like electronics. Have you ever played with a holographic computer?"

And so, while the mathematician worked, the man in the KGB uniform sat at Joseph Synmann's terminal and explored the memory of the SMB. He was cut off from Peter's view and when he found some hidden files, he played with encryption tricks he knew.

The CIA blocked coding research in the United States because they were afraid unbreakable codes would fall into the hands of the Soviets—but that just made getting into the files of Americans easier than it should have been. Glenn couldn't find any weapons files, but he found Synmann's leoport studies. He was unable to copy them. Still, he had no trouble calling the drawings to the screen and photographing what he saw.

At two in the morning Kaissel's curiosity brought him to lean over Glenn's shoulder. "God, I'm bored!" said the mathematician. The leoport files had been quickly returned to the innards of the machine in time to avoid detection.

Glenn looked up warily. "Ready for a nightcap?"

"I feel more like a lark. I've figured out a way to break into Limon's office."

Glenn was now alarmed. "Man," he said, "I'm not interested in you getting me into trouble." But he was intrigued. "You wouldn't dare!"

"I've got to show you something. Come with me."

They found themselves crawling along a dark ledge and through a window. On tip-toes, and with his hand masking the flashlight beam, Kaissel led Glenn into a great closet to view the wardrobe of Limon Barnes. He closed the lightproof door. He switched on the lights, laughing. He donned the outfit of a rich boyar and dressed Glenn as an Admiral of the Russian Navy of Peter the Great—while Glenn struggled ineffectively, not knowing whether he was a fool to be here or whether to enjoy the joke.

"Where did you learn burglary?" the spy asked with approval.

"I used to steal exams. I always hated studying the wrong thing. It did marvels for my grade-point average. How else do you think I got this job?"

CHAPTER 34

The peaceful moon
Rises in the western chamber;
A breeze creaks the door
Stirring the flower-shadows.
Does my earthly love come with heaven's brightness?

LING TI
SUNG MASTERPIECES
FRIENDSHIP BLOSSOMS PRESS
BEIJING 2005

Every civilization contains eddies of its past, sometimes within walking distance of its major centers. An eddy of a bygone era lies tucked away between two rotund mountains of the California Coast Range, below the grasslands where the topography traps enough ocean fog to water a redwood stand. For a century a Chinese family has owned a log cabin in that canyon beside a dammed stream where they took refuge after the great San Francisco earthquake. There is no electricity. The road is dirt. Legend has it that every time a logger or a land developer comes this way, the wood nymphs call up a fog from the sea to sift through the redwood forest until it is cloaked in invisibility.

When Diana was with her Chinese friend she was all woman. At night she lay cozy with him under heavy blankets, sometimes wondering at the rutting chemistry which took her body and curious about the shy way she arranged to be touched. By day she cooked over wood for her sage—flapjacks with sweet fried tomato syrup, and eggs and beans and bacon, even bread from flour and yeast. She kissed him and swam with him behind the dam and massaged him and flattered him. She was twenty-one.

But when she was by herself she reverted to girl. Being sixteen was a secret and one had to be alone to enjoy a secret. Deep in the forest she built a shrine out of stone to the goddess of moon and glade so that Diana might properly be worshipped. She used flat sedimentary rocks and fitted them together with sand and flakes. Nothing wobbled when she stood on it. She tracked animals but they got away. For hours she shot target with a compound bow supplied by Ling, the lightest, most powerful bow she had ever held. Once she saw a deer and they both froze, staring at each other in awe in that cathedral of trees.

She was very happy.

He told her stories about the cabin. When it was raining and the water dribbled in through some torn hole he recalled that long ago he had rebuilt the roof and the exact details of the family argument concerning tarpaper versus shingles. Once when the sun was shining through the forest's lace in midafternoon after the fog was gone and they were sitting on the porch stairs, eating lunch with their fingers, he traced with a waving finger the exact path his brothers had taken when they dragged the entrance stone down from the mountain.

"How come there's a stairway cut in the redwood?" She meant the huge tree that lay where it had fallen against the hill.

He smiled his tao wrinkles. "That one crashed down upon us during the terrible winter storm in 1943 when I was a teenager and my brothers were away in the Navy. We knew that my oldest brother's ship had been sunk by the Japanese and we thought he was dead. None of us could talk about it. I needed something to do. Why not? A stairway to heaven. We all need to build one once in a lifetime." He ruffled her hair.

"Could your brother swim?"

"He certainly knew how to hang onto flotsam."

"Were all of your brothers in the Navy?"

"That's where I would have been, too. But the war ended."

"I can't imagine a Chinaman driving a boat."

"Ho now. I could tell you some stories."

But he fell silent instead. She smiled, remembering his story about the army of Chinese Crusader Knights liberating Jerusalem, and chewed a stalk of wild oats to mark her happiness.

That evening she tried to seduce him. She undressed by the Coleman lamp, turned down to its lowest, then extinguished the flame before she crawled into bed so that in the blackness there would be no universe but her touch. For a while he let her fondle him, and once, almost responding, he giggled like a sixteen year old boy, but finally he took her hand in both of his, and held it against his bony breast, caressing the soft flesh with his bony fingers. She had never made love to a man before and she wondered if she had been clumsy.

"It's all right if you do it to me," she whispered. She was not sure that she should be saying such things.

"You've only found the ghost of me."

She pinched him, annoyed at his rejection. "You don't feel like a ghost to me."

"Ah, but I'm half into the world of my ancestors."

"Are you half-in-love with me?" she teased.

"Half-in-love yes, and the other half infatuated."

"If you're half with your ancestors, do you see ghosts?"

It seemed that her question startled him. He had never looked, and for a moment his fingers ceased to caress her fingers and only held on affectionately while he looked. "Ah, my family has powerful ancestors! I can see them all!"

It wasn't really what she wanted to hear.

"I'll tell you a story," he said.

She sighed.

"Shang yeu t'ien t'ang, hia yeu Su Hang," he said.

"I didn't know you could speak Chinese?"

"Once I knew a lot, but I remember little of it—mostly the poems I memorized when I was young. The ditty I recited translates as: 'There's Paradise above, it's true, but here below we've Hang and Su.' That's a reference to Hangchow and Suchow, known in the days of the Sung as Kinsai and Sugui, about three days journey away from each other by the Grand Canal. In all of Medieval Earth there did not exist two more beautiful cities."

"I can tell you're Chinese."

"Do not interrupt my story. Hangchow was the greatest port in the world at the time, thirty miles in diameter, bigger than a dozen Venices. If your Europe had silk, likely as not it was originally shipped from Hangchow and picked up by the Arabs in India. The city was built upon what had been lagoons and swampland so that it was crisscrossed by canals and teeming with ships. All the produce of China passed through its warehouses and markets, bales of silk and cotton, porcelain and cast iron, rice and spice wine, pearls, jade, and every sort of manufactured article. The quays were lined with junks as far as the eye could see. From Indo-China and the Indies came spices and aloes and sandlewood, nutmegs, spikenard and ebony. The junks sailed as far as India and Celon and Japan."

"And what made Hangchow so beautiful? New Yorkers think *New York* is beautiful and they look down their noses at Cleveland."

"Well, it was a rich city."

"Rich isn't beautiful."

"But there were twelve thousand stone bridges spanning its waterways. Lords and merchants moved down its streets clad in silk. The most elegant ladies in the world were carried by in embroidered litters, with jade pins in their black hair. From pleasure barges on the lake-of-many-islands one could view the city, its palaces, temples, convents, and gardens, and listen to the tinkling instruments of the barge's revellers."

"So tell me your story."

"The first ancestor of which I have knowledge was an old lord of Hangchow."

"As old as you?"

"Old but not as old as I. Richer, I suspect. And I suspect he was as displeased with his wife as I was pleased with mine. One day when he had travelled up the Grand Canal to Suchow on business and was inspecting the silk made by one of his silk weaving suppliers, he found a young indentured slave at the looms who took his fancy and he bought her as his concubine."

"Did he love her? He doesn't sound very romantic."

"Well, they had a son and that pleased him."

"That's not love. I want to know if he loved her."

Ling kissed her gently and then touched her lips with his fingers. He held her and his hand caressed her and for a moment she was frightened because he didn't seem as helpless as she had come to expect, but he made no mistakes in arousing her and she remembered that he had been happily married for fifty years before his wife had died and that he had loved her and that he had raised three children. Half of him might be a ghost but his hands were certainly still in this world. Wow.

"Tell me how he loved her. It's important."

"Tao tells us to keep our mouths shut and just do it."

"Oh."

"But he wrote poems about her," conceded Ling. "Five of them made one of the greatest of the Sung poetry collections. That's how we know about him."

"Did they live happily ever after?"

"No. He died when she was only seventeen but on his deathbed he sold her to a nephew to keep her away from the clutches of his wife."

"I'll bet the nephew beat her."

"No, but he lost his fortune and saved only one ship and took to the sea to try to restore himself in the graces of the gods. That's how we Ling's came to be sailors, and how my great-grandfather was in Canton when an American ship was short of hands. Half of California was once Chinese."

"They didn't let Chinks bring in their women so how come *you're* here?"

"Baah! We were sailors! A Chinese sailor knows everything there is to know about smuggling."

She snuggled up close to her ancient mariner. "Am I your concubine?"

"Wait until I find a nephew to sell you to. I have nephews and a grandson just about the right age."

"But I'm in love with *you*. What kind of poem does an old man make for his concubine?"

So Ling sang for her five Chinese poems—in what he thought was the dialect of the southern Sung.

The next morning she nearly broke her leg getting out of bed because her foot went through a rotten floorboard. Ling was horrified. He apologized. He was old, and it was harder for him to make repairs. His family was scattered, and his grandsons, he had to admit sadly, were incompetent with their hands.

Diana just smiled and took him for a ride in his Chrysler. While he drove she inserted the Central Coast laser disk and punched up for lumber outlets by order of proximity. The best bet was only eleven kloms away. He said he knew a good place eighteen miles back toward Frisco but she overruled him and called up MapDraw, minimal option. Slowly, amber lines etched themselves out along the dashboard screen, indicating just the crossroads and the signposts they would need. Finally she punched for Zoom so that the screen distance between car and destination was always ten centimeters. After winding up grassy hills and past the ocean down into another mountain valley, they discovered the weatherbeaten lumber yard, as promised— *Founded In 1923*, said the peeling sign, ancient for California.

"I'll need some tools."

"I have tools."

"A saw and a hammer."

"Yeah."

"And nails!"

"Yes, yes, yes."

Back at the cabin he took her down into an almost hidden concrete structure that she had mistaken for part of the well, dry inside and still solid but musty and obviously never used—

except as a storehouse for the odd junk that a summer house collects, a flaking wheelbarrow, cots, hose, parts for a dam slipway that had rusted out and been replaced but never thrown away. The tools were in good shape and there was a set of five bows and hundreds of arrows, and a place for the missing compound bow that Ling had lent her, to her delight.

"It's an old bomb shelter," said Ling, laughing. "I forget when we built it—but it was before Kennedy was assassinated. Sometime in 1962? It used to be airtight with filters, all done without electricity. People were afraid of the bomb then. We kept it well stocked for five years."

"People are still afraid of the bomb," she said.

"But they don't build bomb shelters. We have the battlestations to protect us."

"What a lot of crap," snorted Diana. "I've heard they wouldn't stop anything. We'd all fry. Sometimes I'd like to go back to 1962 when weapons were simple and everybody was safe."

In the year Diana was born in Ohio, the first of the anti-ICBM battlestations were deployed, the Titan probe was launched, the Soviets returned in triumph from the first manned landing on an asteroid, the Americans put the Advanced X-ray Astrophysics Facility into orbit, and the Africans spent the year killing each other in the Zambali Massacres.

As she grew up the number of nuclear weapons was gracefully declining while mankind somehow managed to survive to celebrate the sixtieth anniversary of a nuclear peace in which not a single year had passed without war—or without the communist/capitalist arms profiteers each claiming moral superiority over the other in the blood of some small country. Socialist/capitalist economic morality has only one commandment: Do not sell atomic weaponry to minor kingdoms and local despots.

Diana smiled, nostalgic for innocent times. "I know everything about those old rockets. The Atlas. And Heinkel bombers, too. You guys had it soft! Imagine being able to defend a city against buzzing subsonic planes by hoisting balloons on cables!"

"It wasn't all that easy," Ling grumped.

"Ha. It would take a thousand B-17s making a raid a day on a city every day for a year to equal one H-bomb. Don't tell me you didn't have it soft! It was easytime, like the Civil War."

"We didn't have penicillin."

"Oh, poor you." She hugged him. "It must have been terribly hard to fight wars without choppers, and supersonic fighters, and digiphones, and tank assault robots, and beam guns, and satellite eyes to see for you, and ASAT missiles to poke out the eyes of the enemy, and radar ovens to cook your C-rations. We're all so thankful to your generation for having the foresight to make war easy for us!"

Diana spent a happy afternoon ripping out the old floor planks, then sawing, fitting, and painting the new planks with help from her mentor. The radio alternately blared out Trance music and announced the assassination of the Argentine president, the strike of the Santa Clara police force, and possible delays in the opening of the lunar electromagnetic track.

On the last day of her vacation she splashed in the cold pool behind the dam and toweled herself sassily in front of her boss because she knew he liked to look at her body even if he couldn't do much with it. A wondrous evening light sneaked through the filigree of the redwood canopy.

"I have a job for you," he said, lighting the coals for a barbecue.

"You just sit down," she smiled. "I'll take care of everything. What do you want me to cook?"

He smiled. "I mean a job *opening*. Work—as in nine-to-five. One of my places needs a new girl."

"Are you ever nice to me. You don't have to be. I think I have courage enough to go back to Namala. Where?"

"You might not want it. It's a costume place. It involves playing up to some crazy men."

"What other kind are there?"

"Put this on," he said, giving her a shining package.

She held it out. "Brass bras!" she hooted. "*Mr. Ling*, I didn't know you ran a skin dive."

"Try it on."

Modestly she held it to her body. "I'll show through."

"You'll look beautiful, if slightly kinky."

So she stepped into what there was of it. Her hair spilled out of the helmet, a simple brass band around her forehead that supported oval headpieces which might or might not have been earphones. Her breasts spilled out of their immodest cups and her hips spilled out of their hardly adequate metallic banding.

"Where do you get your outrageous ideas?"

He took her by the hand into the cabin and pulled out his old copies of *Planet Stories* from a shelf, each one sealed in its plastic bag. "Treat them like gold. They are from the forties and early fifties and fragile."

Diana shrieked at the cover of an issue he handed her.

"That's me! Brass bras and all! And if that *monster* goes with the job, I'm quitting yesterday! Where is this restaurant?"

"On the leoport."

Her heart jumped. "How high is that thing?"

"Three hundred and ten miles."

"In kloms! I didn't go to school in the dark ages like you."

"Five hundred kloms."

"And how high is the moon?"

"Too high for the restaurant business at the moment. They have to make do with a cafeteria."

"Damn," she said. "Don't forget me when you get your first lunar franchise. I'm going to send you vitamin pills every week. I want to make sure you'll live that long."

"You haven't said yes to my leoport proposition yet."

She squeezed his hand. "When have I ever said no to you? I'm so thrilled, I'm speechless. What's the name of your restaurant?"

"Planet Stories."

CHAPTER 35

The zeal of Patriarch Nikon finally drove even a pious Tsar to contain ecclesiastical power. After the restructuring, Russia no longer had a church: it had a pacified state religion which slowly, over centuries, absorbed all morals, dutifully reforging them to the needs of the state, dutifully rejecting Christ the Savior as the tsars became less and less willing to tolerate authority greater than their own—even, in the end, re-tailoring the teachings of Saint Marx the Benefactor to better serve the worship of the Godtsars who, by doctrinal evolution, now no longer go to heaven but live on as mummies in the Kremlin wall.

LIMON BARNES
LECTURES ON THE FOUNDATIONS OF THE SOVIET STATE

Peter Kaissel walked through the floating dandelion fuzz to the old Cathedral. There was something nice about spring and Christ. He wasn't in any particular hurry to see Limon, and stopped for a game of blind-man's-bluff with some of the actors who were doing Gogol's *Inspector General* at the theater that evening. But there came a time when he could delay no longer.

In the grand offices of the Cathedral of Saint Marx, Limon was wearing the robes of the Patriarch of Moscow, and he scowled from his corner through a bushy beard—intense, alien.

Holy Christ! thought Kaissel. For just a moment he saw Patriarch Nikon, headstrong, difficult, tactless, with a brooding fanatic brutality, very ready to draw up rules for the most minor details of the life of every man he touched, source of the great Schism which wracked the Russian Orthodox Church for centuries.

232

"Ah, my heretic," said the holy man.

"At your service, my Great Sovereign," replied Kaissel mockingly. Nikon was the last of the Patriarchs to command that title, losing it to his tsar's ire. Little wooden eggs lay on the Patriarch's desk, the kind that fit into each other endlessly with the promise of a tiny wooden chicken at the center. He had been wrapping them for the children. Easter. The endlessly necessary resurrection of Christ.

Limon spoiled his imposing image by hanging up the sacred cap and authoritarian beard on the coat rack.

"You're a strange man," he said to the mathematician. "You play games but you don't live them."

"And that's bad?"

"Yes," said Limon. "There *is* content and meaning to life's struggle. It's not just numbers."

Kaissel laughed uncomfortably. "It's not just costumes," he riposted.

"Let me put it this way." Limon began to moralize. "You think like a typical member of the Russian elite. A modern Russian is a master of socialist thought, good at detailed abstractions and the finer points of Marxist analysis. But in real life he beats Polish workers with rubber hoses and murders Afghan peasants to extend his borders. He is not even aware of the contradictions. Mr. Kaissel, the abstract morality that is coming out of your computer games is very good—but you don't seem to be able to *apply* it to the struggle facing the SMB."

Kaissel's lips curled sarcastically. "Are you daring me to simulate the great capitalist/socialist drama?"

"*That* is hardly our struggle." Limon took an egg apart, and examined the egg within, and took that egg apart. "The greater struggle is less clear-cut; it's the ancient conflict between the iron tower of the ethics we all build and the hypocrisy we use to paint over the creeping rust."

"Ah; the one true struggle."

"I could use a little help," mused Limon.

"At your service, Great Sovereign!" Kaissel replied with suppressed scorn. "I shall immediately simulate the war of good against evil . . . by next week I'll have figured out a winning strategy for the forces of good. We shall call the program *ParadiseLost*. If it works, God can retire in our favor."

Limon ignored the taunt and continued to dismantle the egg until he reached the pea-sized chicken. "Don't be in such a rush. Our *immediate* task is to fire Peter Kaissel because of his lack of personal ethics."

What was this? Kaissel could sense a deep rancor and, suddenly, a very delicate situation which called for silver-tongued smoothness. But all he managed was indignation. "I have a very strong sense of personal ethics! I don't have to dress up like a messenger of God."

"You are referring to my Patriarch getup? An interesting man, Nikon. Hardly my idea of morality, but a man every student of Russia cannot ignore. Nikon's arrogance created a popular dissent movement so strong that it marked forever the way in which Russian people choose to oppose interference in their lives from above. Entire communities of Old Believers fled into the forests. Dissidents locked themselves in coffins. They set themselves on fire. They moved to Siberia. They endured exile and constant government harassment, defying torture and persecution designed to break them. They were the source of the Christian anarchists who were the source of . . . but I deviate. We were talking about *your* morality."

The wigless, beardless Patriarch transfixed Kaissel. "I should have you knouted in public!"

Oh, oh. He's found out about my larks! Kaissel was put on the defensive and it annoyed him to be there. He was defiant, but images of teaching undergraduates at Florida State tempered his resolve. "Are you sure I'm replaceable? Ask Synmann."

"Stalin killed those at the top, so as not to frustrate the ambitions of the upwardly mobile. We are all expendable."

Kaissel's eyes narrowed, remembering Limon's black sense of humor. *Play it cool.* He said nothing.

"I have evidence that you are an enemy of the people!"

A chill went down Kaissel's spine. That was Stalin's phrase. Did the very books about Russia contain the virus of Russian paranoia, ready to attack the reader? He laughed. "I play in your coat closet, and for that I'm shot at dawn?"

Limon smiled dangerously. "So that was you? By all means, dream in my closet. Dreams I tolerate; sabotage, I cannot."

Sabotage was Stalin's favored crime. "This place is a freak show," yelled Kaissel, "but I do my job! Sabotage, I don't."

"You are not a dedicated man. You are not an ethical man. I see our purpose at the SMB as a highly ethical one. It has to be if we are to achieve our goal. We have to be rigorous. We have to be strict. After all, I have very poor raw material to work with. Americans. If you don't watch an American like he was some damn curious three year old, he's off on some crusade like bombing Vietnamese peasants to defend them against having opinions forced down their throats."

This lunatic is after my ass! thought Kaissel.

"Hmmm. You have a look of innocence upon your face. The Catholics insist that we are born sinners while the Unitarians insist that we are born innocent. It's all the same. Innocence is the primeval American sin." Limon's soul seemed to harbor a vast reservoir of malice. "Ah, my innocent Kaissel, let me tell you about yourself since you seem to know nothing. In recent weeks I've begun to notice small strange events. The intrusions into my office have been the least of these. How long this has been going on I don't know. I put some traps in the computer's call-up routines which confirmed unauthorized penetration of the files. Peter, it seems, has a friend. He gives him the run of the library."

"Limon! We're also hooked into the phone network."

Limon dismissed Kaissel's dismissal with a quick repartee. "Your friend has been searching Synmann's *leoport* files, not knowing he was being logged."

"Synmann has a code on those," said Kaissel, startled.

"Well, his damn code is shit. Only the copyright routines have kept our guest from making copies. He's been interested in breaking our copy-protect. He doesn't seem to know that he has to have a royalty contract with us!"

Kaissel was now alarmed. "He's just curious."

There was a spastic fury in Limon's tilted head. "You know less than nothing about your friend. He's probably in the pay of the KGB. Do you think that *they* aren't interested in the architecture of that holographic computer you drool over?"

"Be reasonable, Barnes!" But Kaissel was panicking. Not only could this madman throw him out of his job, he could bar him from *any* university.

"You have never believed a thing I say." Limon was furious. "Ever since you've been here you've mocked me. I swear you go around at night planting mines in the sidewalks! I hear what you say. I hear your stories. Let me tell you right now: I know what I'm doing!" Vigorously, Limon slapped his Kensakan Kambi and shook the networking cables that crawled out of it: "You wouldn't believe what these machines are doing. I can trace things I wouldn't have believed possible. It's an intelligence amplifier! I have an IQ of a thousand! You guys with your stupid little symmetrical computer games think that Soviet fears are a mirror image of our own. All right. I like what you're doing. But I know what *I'm* doing and I get pissed when someone runs around and knocks me every chance he gets!"

"Has Glenn been able to do much damage?"

"Of course, you fool!"

"I'll resign."

"I don't want your resignation! I want you in prison!"

Kaissel was very sober by now. "Are you going to press charges?"

Limon became cunning. "Sit down. I have you over a barrel. We're bargaining."

Kaissel sat down sullenly.

Limon did not. "This is a free country—a helluva way to do business but that's the way it is. You can walk out the door a free man. But if you want to stay, you go to prison."

"That's a tough choice," grumbled Kaissel. "I get to choose between a tap on the wrist and blowing my brains out."

Limon smiled ingraciatingly. "You're one of my best men. You do very good work. But you're not *involved* in our great design. I've been thinking that prison might change that."

Kaissel stared. "I can't work in a madhouse! This is a madhouse! I'm working for a madman!"

"Prison would be good for you."

"I'm supposed to work for you in prison?"

"Of course. It's been done before. The greatest of the Soviet Union's rocket engineers worked out of prison. He built the rocket that launched Sputnik I while he was in a slave labor camp. He was one of Stalin's slaves. Did that interfere with the quality of his work?"

"I don't believe you." The story of Sergi Korolev was true; it was Limon who was beyond Kaissel's belief.

"Shall I change into my Stalin uniform to convince you?"

"You want to send me to the Massachusetts State Penn?"

"Much worse. A *Russian* prison."

"I think I'll choose freedom."

"You see, that's your trouble, Kaissel. You think like an American. You want the soft way out. You avoid being a Russian. They've suffered too much and you don't want to be part of their suffering. It is easier to think of Russians as brutes who torture and repress everyone within the boundaries of their empire than to understand the other side of the coin—those brave Russians who have fought the brutes among them for centuries and suffered for their bravery. For a thousand years Russia has produced heroes. You too can be a hero. I have a fine prison cell prepared for you."

"Tsarist dungeon or one of Stalin's Hotels?"

"Moscow, 1937. With all the refinements."

"Shit! And I'm just supposed to sit here and wait for the NKVD to come and arrest me?"

"That would be very un-American, wouldn't it?"

What could be worse than prison under Stalin? Teaching calculus to Florida State undergraduates. *He's got me.* "A lot of Russians did that, didn't they?" wailed an anguished Kaissel. "They knew the NKVD was going to come for them, and they just waited. Jesus Christ, I don't understand that kind of person!"

"Wait, and you will."

CHAPTER 36

Comrades, we are not discovering conspiracies, we are man-
ufacturing them. We should tell our party the truth—that we
are persecuting and destroying people on the basis of slander-
ous and untrue accusations. I know what is in store for me, but
I cannot remain silent about what is going on in the NKVD.

V. Drovianikov, speech at the Leningrad NKVD, 1936,
(shot that same evening as a traitor by chairman of
the Leningrad Soviet, I. Kodatskii, who was in turn
executed as an enemy of the people.)

Peter Kaissel eventually came to think of his confrontation
with Limon Barnes, and the threats made then, as just another
example of Limon's black sense of humor. Still, it had been
a cautionary message and he had taken it to heart by conducting his work with unusual dedication. And so, one evening,
while working late, he was stunned when special agents of
the NKVD visited him with an arrest warrant, confiscated
his papers, and escorted him forcefully under Mongol guard
to the Cathedral dungeon, for aiding spies and slandering the
State.

Dinner was foul smelling soup which he refused to eat. His
instructions were to face the cell door at all times and to keep
his hands always in view. The bastards even refused to switch
off the light! When he tried to defy them by turning his head to
the wall, he was kicked awake. It was a miserable night, and
only his fury made it bearable.

The guard grinned when Kaissel pleaded to know the charges.
They had been so busy arresting their monthly quota of "enemies of the people" that they hadn't made up the charges yet.

238

In due time. Patience. The guard cheerfully ordered him to stand up. Prisoners weren't allowed to rest.

Kaissel was almost hysterical with relief when the quick footsteps of authority, reverberating down the hidden hallway, materialized as Sam Brontz. The guard opened the cell door and closed it behind the visitor. But the clean uniform with the high collar rattled Kaissel. Before he could stop himself he was demanding his rights and threatening a legal suit.

Sam waited icily until the tirade was finished.

Then he delivered a tongue-lashing about loyalty to the Communist Party, to the People's State, to the principles of Marxist-Leninism. "Comrade Kaissel, since when have the Bolsheviks decided to treat enemies of the people in a liberal fashion?" He excoriated Kaissel through to the blood of his raw guilt, ripping away his facade in strips. "Enemies of the people are shot. There is no forgiveness. Make sure you find the correct loyalties."

"Look, Mr. Brontz. I don't think I'm up to this kind of game. I pick oranges. I'm an average American. I don't like pain. I love my mother and my father. I want a nice little niche in the world to do my thing. I want out of here!"

A chill moment of silence before: "Comrade Limon commented on your lack of enthusiasm for correct socialist goals. Your trivial tirade forces me to agree with his perception."

"I want out of this cage! This is not my game, Mr. Brontz!"

"Your game, then, is that of a wrecker and saboteur of socialism? You confess to being a counterrevolutionary?"

"I'm just a mathematician, a lousy mathematician!"

"Quiet! Do you think that's enough? Let me speak seriously and frankly to you for your own good. Comrade Synmann is advancing mathematical game theory in the required dialectic direction. Though I'm not myself a mathematician I understand clearly what he is doing. Our work at the institute requires extreme dedication and self-sacrifice from us all. Soon we will be applying Synmann game theory to the real imperialist world. Our decisions will decisively affect human destiny. To serve the interests of the working class correctly we will be expected, in the future, to find correspondences between the problems of the workers and the solved problems of the Synmann games.

"We have doubts that an unrepentant bourgeois diversionist such as yourself can make that transition from abstraction to concrete action. We doubt that you desire that transition. You seem to have no empathy with the sufferings and aspirations of the Russian working class. Isn't that the bent of a dangerous and criminal mind? Can we afford to trust a man who will be thinking of flesh and blood Russians as cardboard targets?"

"Bravo! You've learned your part well! Let me tell you Mr. Brontz, the minute I get out of this cell, I'm taking you to court and suing you and the SMB for one million dollars!"

"I see. A million dollars for a night of mild discomfort on a hard bench. You are thinking like a sulking American—without considering all the implications." The eyes glittered. "Is it that you expect the capitalist police to help you?"

"You're damn right!"

"I see. You wish to be placed in the hands of the imperialist FBI along with the data linking you to a Soviet spy who has been searching the SMB files for critical space defense secrets?" Sam snickered.

"You'd frame me?" exclaimed Kaissel, aghast.

Kaissel had other unpleasant visitors. And slowly, once he was cut off from all outside information, once the sleeplessness of the constant interrogation began to get to him, he began to brood on his guilt. He had foolishly given a casual friend free access to Cathedral computer files. Synmann wouldn't even speak to him anymore! To a man alone, the universe is a cell with a light bulb and a cold floor.

Kaissel was visited round-the-clock by agents of Ivan IVs "private court," the *Oprichina*, by Mongol torturers from the "authority for the extermination of rebellion," by investigators from *Cheka*, "the extraordinary commission for the suppression of counterrevolution," by the agents of Peter the Great's *Preobrazhenskii Prikaz* with their hints of breaking him on the wheel, by secret police teams from the tsar's *Okhrana*, and, of course, by Brezhnev's thugs from the KGB. It was all part of the same tradition. They never let him sleep.

Kaissel found himself charged with the crime of *claiming to be ignorant* of Russian law. He tried to reason with his interrogators—the charge was absurd—but theirs was a coldly deliberate madness that would have puzzled even a Russian! They explained themselves patiently. A knowledgeable man who professed ignorance, who lied, must be planning sabotage. They *had evidence* that he was hiding his thoughts about the law. But an honest man wouldn't hide thoughts of praise, so his thoughts must be slanderous. It was a crime to slander a Socialist State.

The klieg lights glared. Why, pressed the interrogators, was he withholding knowledge of the law, pretending ignorance to protect the other members of the conspiracy when there was no escape for any of them? His silence was useless. It would all come out. They grilled the young mathematician repetitively, picking up inconsistencies, insinuating, cajoling, demanding, threatening. They wanted everything. They wanted the names of the other conspirators. They could suggest some if his mind was blank. All he'd have to do was sign a paper implicating them.

Kaissel glared at these stupid impostors.

"Ah, he wants to be tough," said one of the "brigade" members to another, lighting two cigarets.

My God, they're going to put out their cigarets on my skin! Kaissel knew that much about Russian police.

The man inhaled. "Let us refresh your memory. And stand straight if you want water."

The other interrogator took over. Didn't they already have documents in their hands to *prove* that he knew the full reading of Chapters Three and Four of the Russian Criminal code of 1845. Recite it!

What kind of nonsense was that? Kaissel couldn't understand what was going on, to be accused wrongly by a team of torturers who would not take no for an answer! None of this fitted his world-view of how people behaved in Massachusetts.

They left him papers to "refresh his memory" and grilled him cruelly on every detail he forgot. Eventually they left a data terminal in his cell. Now if he forgot, they would know he was lying!

The computer library of the Cathedral of Saint Marx the Benefactor had absorbed so much data—by hand and through its Kurzweil readers—and had worked with so many curious scholars, that it had acquired a personality of its own, not human, but not inhuman either. In many ways it had become like a doddering great-grandmother who mixed her memories in senile ways. The staff had long been calling the library computer by the name of Holy Mother Russia. She might answer your questions directly, but if you were the least bit vague or unsure of what you wanted she quickly took you off on some reminiscence that had nothing to do with your question but was too fascinating to interrupt. Kaissel trusted the sources of the Holy Mother—they bulked too large to be faked and the contradictions within those sources were the stuff of the very disorder of the human soul itself.

The mad Holy Mother became the only friend he had. She connived with him to survive. She taught him just enough about Russian law to satisfy his "brigade" that he did indeed know what they were accusing him of knowing. In this way he was able to confess more and more every day—and still his tormentors always found some aspect of Russian law that they insisted he was criminally withholding. And so, in a kind of desperate cunning, he began to plot how to keep ahead of them.

At first, Kaissel started with the assumption that Marxist-Leninist law had swept away the cruel tsarist past and that Limon's simulated version of its atrocities was a warped travesty based on American folklore. His fervor was short-lived. When he began a methodical search for the Marxist dogma buried in Soviet Revolutionary law he couldn't find it—as if the writers of Soviet law had received their Marxism from the failed students of Hegel, who had all bought crib notes from a Parisian fortune teller, who had obtained her wisdom from the palms of an ignorant Siberian priest.

And yet when he turned his attention to the arcane logic of *tsarist law* the relationship to Soviet law was startling. It was as if the revolutionaries, finding themselves inarticulate, had turned to old tsarist lawyers to write up the new order and, finally, finding the courts bewildering, had bribed old tsarist judges to run the proceedings for them from some back room.

How different was the trial (1981) of gentle Tatyana Osipova, a woman who helped anyone in trouble, a real socialist, from the trial (1877) of Katerina Breshkovskaia, a woman with whom Karl Marx would gladly have shared his home and bread?

Soviet Code of 1960, Article 70:
". . . circulating . . . slanderous fabrications which defame the Soviet state and social system, or circulating or preparing or keeping . . . literature of such content shall be punished by the deprivation of freedom for a term of six months to seven years . . ."
Where was Marx in that?

Tsarist Code of 1845, Article 267:
"Persons guilty of writing and spreading written works or representations intended to arouse disrespect for tsarist authority, or for the personal qualities of the tsar, or for his government are on conviction sentenced . . . to the deprivation of all rights of property and exile for hard labor in fortified places for from ten to twelve years . . ."

When Kaissel spent time in conversation with the Holy Mother trying to trace the law against slandering authority back through time . . . through wisps of paper . . . and diaries . . . and

scandal and exile and murder . . . and back . . . and back . . .
he came to the splendor of the court at Sarai and a Russian
martyr who would not be quiet, swinging in a cage with his
tongue cut out and his nose cut off because he had defamed the
Mongol Tsar of the Golden Horde.

Pain drives you mad.

The Russians had been driven eternally mad by the cruelty of
the Mongol invasion. So to escape their suffering . . . when it
becomes unbearable . . . they transmogrify into Mongols by
the light of the full moon, true slant-eyed vassals of Ghengis
Khan.

How the Khan would have approved of kleig lights!

Kaissel dreamed on his feet, while he recited facts for his
torturers into the glare, dreaming he could sleep while he was
awake so that he could enjoy his rest, but it was a false dream;
the hours passed, drugged, and it seemed that almost as soon as
he dozed off into a heap the NKVD was pulling him to his feet
again. It was hard to care. He just stared at them and wobbled.

The Bolsheviks had often been tortured by the tsarist police,
even though torture under late tsarist law was illegal. It was
illegal after the October Revolution, too. The Bolsheviks who
had survived torture were adamant about that.

And yet . . . under Stalin torture reached degrees of refine-
ment and mass use unequaled in mankind's cruel history. The
prototype death machine tested by Stalin against the helpless
countryside, once trained, was unleashed like the backlash of a
bullwhip to consume the old Bolsheviks. Stout-hearted Russians, who had been encouraged for seven hundred years by
the overclass to inform on each other for a reward, were told
to be merciless in rooting out the "enemies of the people."
They denounced themselves and expected reward.

Kaissel stared, hallucinating.

A Russian woman in a Soviet gold mine, thin, starving, shows
him leg scars from a tsarist interrogation where she was tortured to reveal the names of the men in her Bolshevik cell.
Proudly she says she gave the *Okhrana* nothing and was sentenced to ten years in prison. But the broken nose and the
crippled hands, she admits, come from the NKVD. She smiles
the toothless smile of a black joke. During her torture by the
socialist police she had no names to give—this time being
innocent—and she is too good a socialist to bear false witness
against any man.

While he was being tortured it amazed Kaissel to discover
that millions of Russians had never broken under Stalin's whip.

Better to die. Better to dig gold for the Motherland. They were heroes to him. When one is being tortured one needs heroes.

His interrogators presented Peter with other names and urged him to implicate them in his guilt, to sign dispositions against them, but Kaissel—holding fast to the memory of the Bolshevik woman who refused to betray her friends, who refused to break—was himself inspired to abstain from falsehood.

His cell began to fill with Red Army officers, martyrs of 1937, singing songs of revolution.

CHAPTER 37

In 1953 one young Soviet army officer collected the records of his class of 1934. Eighty-seven classmates were shot as "enemies of the people" before the war, 8 of his colleagues fought in the war and survived, 40 fought in the war and were killed, 7 survived the German prisoner of war camps and were sent to the Gulags in 1945 as traitors for surrendering, 487 died uselessly in the Gulags between 1937 and 1945 (an unknown number of them being shot in 1942 when Stalin feared an army uprising), and 34 survived their prison terms.

During the dark days of the late 1930s, Joseph Stalin prepared the Soviet Union for the Great Patriotic War against German Imperialism by purging 40,000 military officers. He shot his best strategists in '37–'38. He destroyed as "enemies of the people" the heroes of the Civil War, all of them. He decimated the socialist staff colleges, the socialist army, the socialist air force, and the socialist navy.

Hitler, in rejecting the advice of those generals who told him it was dangerous to attack the USSR, was strongly influenced by the execution of the brilliant Marshal M.N. Tukhachevskii and his entire senior staff. He is reported to have said, "The Soviet's first-class high-ranking officers were wiped out by Stalin in 1937, and the new generation cannot replace them."

Hitler wasn't altogether right. Some of the brilliant Soviet military leaders survived until 1939. There was Marshal Bliukher, Civil War hero. In the summer of 1938 he smashed the Japanese Army at Lake Khasan. In November Stalin had him shot without a trial for being too popular. He was replaced in the east by G.M. Shtern, who, after the victory against the Japanese at the Khalka River in 1939, was recalled to Moscow and shot.

Before the main German army struck, Stalin's heroic ad-

245

vance panzer company had single-handedly destroyed eight
divisions *of Soviet officers, enough to staff an army corps—
priceless men on the eve of 1941. Not having those trained
leaders at the front during the original German blitzkrieg cost
the Russians perhaps six million unnecessary casualties during
the Great Patriotic War, and probably a fourth of the Soviet
capital investment in industry. The setback was so great that it
left the Soviet Union's army of liberation too weak to overrun
Western Europe ahead of the capitalist armies of Britain and
North America.*

FROM *THE FORGE OF WAR*

Colonel Pavel Tikonovich Savichev of the Soviet Air Force
had a fourteen-year-old son and young daughter. He never
confided in his wife but he loved her very much. He didn't
approve of the way she often left the children alone, but he
never scolded her. And so when his son Pyotr called him up at
the office and asked him a question about the Unix operating
system of their four-month-old Bogatyr computer, he immediately sensed that his children were alone. It was his wife who
was the computer specialist.

The boy could take care of himself but the father wasn't sure
about five-year-old Lida, not when Pyotr was engrossed by a
machine which enthralled him, and so Pavel took the car back
home. It was a good excuse to leave the office. He found *both*
of his children at the Bogatyr, playing a game on the screen.
Lida didn't know what she was doing but Pyotr tolerantly gave
her intructions about which keys to press when it was her
"turn."

"Where did you get that!" exclaimed Pavel affectionately.
Good programs were still scarce in Moscow.

His son was evasive. "I got it," was all he would say, with a
slight exasperation in his voice. He belonged to a Komsomol
computer club and they exchanged programs and advice, and
that was probably where it came from. Maybe not.

"We're Nazi-busting!" said Lida.

War games. Pavel wasn't sure he approved of war games for
children. "Have you eaten?"

"Not hungry," said Pyotr, annoyed at the distraction.

Pavel recognized the computer disease when he saw it. He
had forgotten to eat for three days when he first brought the
machine home and his wife, in her excitement, had been too
involved to remember to feed him. Their Bogatyr was more
powerful than the huge machine she used in the ministry. It

had a military-grade Soviet copy of a Motorola 32-bit processor and a megabyte of Japanese memory, but otherwise it was an all-Russian make, even the auxiliary laser disk drive with its Russian language version of Unix. Most Bogatyrs were going to industry, but at least a quarter of the production was being shipped to the schools. Trusted members of the apparatus could also get them, and Pavel, who was trouble-shooter for the commission upgrading Soviet defense communications, easily qualified.

He went into the kitchen and prepared chicken livers on bread with sour beets and milk, and brought a plate for each of them. "Now eat! Or I'll turn off the Bogatyr! And don't spill anything on the keyboard! Or the rug!"

He watched. When the maps came on, it was Europe—but the fighting was like no campaign he had ever studied at the Academy. His son was making a deep thrust up the Danube toward Austria. He looked closely at the dates. August 1942.

"What's this game called?"

"Socialist Victory."

Rumania by 1942, eh? Indeed! Some idiot at Novosti Press was mind-shaping the children again, feeding them fantasies about Soviet might. Certainly Pyotr had picked up this game at one of the Komsomol meetings. "Well, now. You're overextending our armies, aren't you?" He was gentle about correcting people.

"No." Pyotr flipped to one of the strategic planning arrays and allocated some resources he might need that winter. "I'm being too cautious. I'll never even get to France by 1944."

Pavel laughed; he had no intention of putting down the Soviet triumphs of the Patriotic War but children should learn the bounds of reason. Very carefully he asked, "And what is the object of this game?"

"To overrun Germany and France before the English and Americans make their landing at Normandy. If you're fast you get Italy and Greece, too."

Leninist fantasies! thought the compartment of Savichev's mind which never spoke to anyone. "I see. And is it easy to invade France?" He was trying to lead his son into a trap.

"I almost got as far as Paris once. I'm not going to make it this time, though. You have to get rid of Stalin by 1936 if you want to get to the English Channel by 1944. He killed all our officers. Dumb." Pyotr went back to the game.

Eh? What was that? Pavel went into shock. No, this was *not* a Novosti game and *not* something from the Komsomol library!

His interest went up a notch. It touched on raw ground and family skeletons, stirring ambivalent feelings.

Pavel had been raised to worship the memory of his wild grandfather, an air force ace who had flown his stubby I-16 against the superior Japanese Mitsubishi 96s in China at the battle of Nanking. Until a discipline-conscious (malicious) political officer brought it to his attention, Pavel had not known that his grandfather had been executed in late 1938 as an enemy of the people. Outraged at being deceived by his own family, he had bitterly accused his father of lying.

The man broke down and wept. "Lying, am I!" He had only one memory of his father: a smiling face giving tiny hands a sweater at New Years. He hardly even remembered his mother who had died in 1943 from tuberculosis contracted in a prison factory, where she had been sent for stealing state property to keep her son, Pavel's father, alive.

He brought out letters Pavel had never seen, written to his grandmother from China, forcing the grandson to read them. They were simple letters, scrawled by a giant who loved his woman—the daily missions against the Japanese only a frame around his love. Astonished, moved to tears himself, Pavel had asked his father why he had kept such secrets from his only son? His father didn't know—but Pavel knew because he was himself a closed man who shared his doubts with no one . . .

. . . not even with his own son. Silently he watched the Soviet armies roll across Europe as the hands of Pyotr used the fingers of his sister. She tired. Pavel lifted up Lida in his arms—"Off to bed!"—and read her a story with the quilt about her chin. When he came back, it was February 1944.

"Pyotr, time to go to bed!"

"Aw, let me take Berlin. I'm almost there. Maybe I can catch Hitler this time before he commits suicide."

"The game interests me. I'd like to play myself."

Pyotr looked up in alarm. Quickly he began to do some magic with the disks. "I'll make you your own copy." It was done. He took his disk and put it in its package.

Pavel was amused. "You don't trust me? You think I'll wipe the disk if I don't like it?"

"It's very precious. You could have an accident. I can trade with it." His son was almost blushing. He wouldn't look at his father but he started the game for him.

"I'm a combat officer. But I'm going to ask your advice. How do I win at this game of yours?"

The boy grinned. "With or without Stalin?"

"What do you mean by that?"

"Tukhachevskii is your best general. He better not be dead if you want to reach the English Channel by June of '44."

Colonel Savichev waited until his son was gone—and then he tackled the program with a vengeance. He first looked at the code. But he did not find the English residues of an American program that had been converted. Nothing gave it away—but still it smelled of an American hand.

He played part of a demonstration game. It had field maps to show the battles. There were strategic planning screens. There were the battle array management screens. There were resource planning screens. The game had everything. In the Beginner's Mode it started on June 22, 1941 and began with the disastrous initial conditions set up by Stalin himself—the strategist in Savichev spotted that immediately. In that mode a player was certain to lose three million men in the first month.

He began the game three times. It was a disaster. Only once was he able to save Moscow. No, this wasn't a fantasy that gave impossible odds to the Soviet side. Then what was it?

The more advanced modes allowed the player to *prepare* for the German attack. That was interesting—but it certainly wasn't easy. There were levels within levels. One had to manage the political and economic battles that set the stage for the field battles. Three days later Colonel Savichev was still playing the game, but he wasn't playing it at home, he was playing it with his military colleagues.

Savichev did not tell them it was an American fraud. He was curious if they could discover that for themselves. They did not. They were deceived by the constraints. The political and economic battles had to be solved within a socialist context. There was no room for capitalism. The object of the game was the conquest and socialization of Europe by 1945. Why would an American create a program like that?

In the 1936 starting mode, the player got to go into the war with all of the purge victims alive—if he avoided the traps and ran a clean NKVD. *The old Stalinists will scream bloody murder if they find out about this game, but they are not likely to go near a computer.* Pavel's simple-minded colleagues loved it because it allowed them to beat the pants off the Allies if they were good socialists and fast thinkers. It allowed them to save millions—sometimes more than ten million—Russian lives.

The more Savichev played the game the more enraged he became at Stalin. The ghost of his grandfather haunted him— but it was more than that. The game forced a man to ask questions. What if those military officers murdered during the purge had been treated as patriots? What if thousands of defense industry managers and engineers hadn't been denounced? What if Oshchepkov had been allowed to continue the development of radar instead of languishing in prison? What if rocket expert Korolev and other aeronautical people had escaped prison? What if Stalin hadn't shot some of his major tank designers? What if the three million soldiers lost in the first weeks of the German offensive had been deployed in a reasonable defense configuration instead of by the amateur orders of incompetent Commander in Chief Stalin?

Whoever had designed the game had been impressed by the murdered Marshal M.N. Tukhachevskii. (The Germans were so impressed by Tukhachevskii that the Gestapo forged documents compromising him and let them fall into Stalin's hands.) More than once, with the Marshal in command, Savichev managed to lead a victorious Red Army to the English channel by the fall of 1943, the major pieces of Soviet pre-war industry still intact behind him. He found himself asking the question: Who could have stopped such a socialist army from installing a communist government in Paris? Germany? Austria? Greece?

If Stalin had not repressed Russia's heroes, what nation could have stopped Soviet might from defeating the Japanese Kwantung Army in 1944 and moving down the entire Korean peninsula? Who could have stopped them from taking over Indochina with the French communists, and making a solid alliance with the Chinese communists? They would have had the A-bomb by 1946 and, with the whole of the German rocket industry in their hands, been on the moon by 1962, and Mars by 1975.

The industrial leaders killed by Stalin could have outproduced America by 1970. The artists he destroyed and the students they never had might have created a socialist renaissance that would have filled the streets of Moscow with Third World people seeking the sun.

And at the height of his rage Colonel Savichev suddenly understood the design of the game. It was holding out the goals of the Russian soul—the strong and moral socialist world that *might* have been—and saying: You followed Stalin instead. It said: See how easy it is to make decisions that thwart such men as Stalin; why did you choose to worship him?

Savichev's rage was at Stalin, but he took it out on the programmer of *Socialist Victory*. He did not know whether this fiend was an American or a traitorous Russian circumventing censorship, but whoever it was Savichev felt manipulated. He would report this to the authorities so that they might track down the perpetrator.

And then he laughed as he approached Mayakovskii Square. When you played the game that way, the Germans always reached the gates of Moscow. On both sides of him, the buildings seemed like decaying Roman monuments ornamented for a film set. Why tell anyone of his suspicion? It was his secret. Why not find out, himself, who programmed such cunning traps for the Russian mind?

CHAPTER 38

The original Norman state in Russia resembled the great colonial merchant enterprises which were to be a European trademark only in later centuries. Having culturally descended from these colonizing Normans, who were themselves conquered and trained by the Mongols, the ruling classes of Russia have always behaved as colonials living off the land and have always had the mentality and morality of invaders.

THE SMB'S HOLY MOTHER RUSSIA, *FILE RUS-GEN-SEARCH-AX*

By the (twentieth?) day of hell, Peter Kaissel had learned that as long as he was torturing himself at the Kensakan Kambi, his interrogators would leave him alone for long periods of time. But his mind had been working too hard. It had been sending poisons to his body, now screaming in its fatigue to give up.

To the princes of Russia, both the land and its people were property to exploit and sell for profit. The institutions developed to administer this grand corporation, though never efficient, though often assaulted and sometimes destroyed, have proved their phoenix-like viability. After a thousand years the Russian leadership—whatever its social origin—still sees the state as a vast commercial enterprise dedicated to the wealth and well-being of the upper class.

Ibid.

If he rebelled Kaissel knew he would be interrogated again—for hours. Savagely he picked another item from his screen search and began to trace it, half of him cunningly planning escape. He knew the story of one Soviet hero who had escaped

252

from an overcrowded NKVD detention center in 1937 and had lived on in the Soviet world as a non-person until 1955.

Under the Moscow laws of 1649 a merchant who somehow managed to get abroad through the hermetically sealed borders of Russia suffered the loss of his property and his relatives were subject to torture and exile in Siberia. This ancient tsarist law, governing unauthorized travel to foreign lands, is still enforced, in almost unmodified form, by the modern Soviet State.

Ibid.-AX-413

The subject of passports intrigued Kaissel, zonked as he was. Having a police passport meant that one could move around the country freely. *God in heaven, why am I studying passports?* Why didn't they just shove a deposition in front of him and let him sign it? Anything for sleep!

Kaissel's hands moved over the keyboard slowly. Where did it come from, the internal passport by which a member of the Soviet underclass is tied to his land or place of work in the modern Soviet Union? He drove himself to follow the machine's indexed hints, desperate not to have to stand at attention . . . ah, there he had it . . . derived from the Tsarist Code of 1649, based on the census of 1592.

In the sixteenth century, peasants began abandoning their tax-burdened and worked-out fields around Moscow, and the peasant artisans their posody, to take up farming and craftsmanship in the rich Ukrainian prairie being vacated by the waning nomadic horsemen. Seeing their income bleeding away, the colonial Muscovite overclass passed draconian laws to bring them back, to make it a crime to move, to change.

Ibid.-AR-211

Passports. He was chasing after the history of internal passports. Keep going. Or the NKVD would come into the cell. And make him stand. Check the index. Who was tied to the land *before* 1650? Ah—cross-code: census. Check census.

It was the Mongols who introduced the census to Russia, prior to the rise of Moscow, so they could pin down the mobile slash-and-burn peasants long enough to collect taxes from them. Wild Slavs who appeared and disappeared from the forest might be caught and sold as slaves or drafted into the army, but they didn't produce the steady income of domesticated

Slavs. The Mongols taught the indiginous Norman/Slav ruling class how to administer the system, how to pen in the Slavs, and gave their collaborators enough of a cut from the tribute to make the annual Slav-fleecing worth their while.

Ibid.-AC-2f8

Today Peter's guard was a Mongol savage, a new recruit to the NKVD staff. "What year is this?" Kaissel asked facetiously. Around the SMB, the year, even the century, was problematic.

"1937," said the grinning guard, handing him his gruel.

"Still 1937!" exclaimed Kaissel with mock horror. "I thought I'd been here for fifty years!" The slop smelled terrible. Another day of nauseating food! He felt an enormous hostility to this Mongol who had taught his Russian subjects the art of empire. But then cunning brought sanity to Peter's mind. This was no Mongol warrior. This was just a soft American kid, brainwashed by Limon, living in a fantasy world.

In one fit of violence, Miami-schooled Kaissel dazed his guard and left him on the floor of the cell and went rushing down the hall.

When a runaway muzhiki was recaptured he was locked up and beaten and shipped back to his owner in chains. Under tsarist law he could be charged with the expense of the search and, perhaps, spend the rest of his life paying for it.

Ibid-AS-12g

Peter Kaissel hadn't planned his escape, but he was planning now, his freedom on the line. He met astonished people before he reached the door—but no NKVD toad carrying a submachine gun—further evidence of Limon's incompetence. It was raining furiously. That would keep those sissy American fakes inside. There was only one way out. Go through the incomplete section of the wall to the north, into the forest.

He was running through the woods, over the wet fallen leaves, his breath deep and foggy, his clothes soaked. It was glorious. He was free. He was on his way to the Ukraine to live like a God-fearing human being! It didn't matter that he was lost and wet. Some Russian peasant, full of God's mercy, would help him along his way. He slowed to a walk and watched a bird sitting cockily under a leaf.

Damn, but he was hungry! It didn't matter. He could go for days just on the taste of freedom. Maybe he could circle around and come down to that farmhouse for some Borscht soup. The rain seemed to stop but the wind lashed through the trees and doused him with leaf-cupfuls of water. He thought the road was over the hill but he only found another wooded hill. It didn't matter. Yet if he was to avoid being chilled to death he'd have to find shelter from the rain. He sat down under an old protruding rock that gave him a thin strip of dryness and looked through the foggy greenery. Russia wasn't at all like the symmetrical orange orchards of home. And it was too cold, but it had its own strange beauty.

He tried to sleep. The dry bench in the Cathedral dungeon with its staring light bulb was a much more comfortable place to be—but he was happy to be here and on the ground. There was no NKVD to remind him that life was serious. He didn't really sleep—he was too cold for that—but he dozed and dreamed stories of the steppe.

It was the sound of a horse's hooves on matted leaves that woke Peter, who found himself already surrounded by four Russian warriors. When he tried to flee, they tripped him with a pole and pounced on him, tying his hands behind his back. Their leader on horseback arrived. He gazed down like Ivan the Terrible, and reined in his horse.

"So. We've caught the miscreant." It was Limon.

Kaissel had not seen the head of the SMB since his arrest. "You!" he screamed. "You've never even told me the charges!"

"Do you think it's not serious to steal into a boyar's house and mock him by wearing his clothes?"

They marched him back to the walls, bound by a rope tied to the horse. When he resisted, the horse stepped up his pace and he had to trot or be dragged.

"Try me! Try me!" implored the prisoner.

The mounted nobleman only laughed.

As Peter stumbled behind the horse he began to comprehend. There never had been any solid Russian law beyond the superficial facade of penmanship on fine paper: the peasant's fate lay in the hands of his landlord and the law changed when the landlord changed; Peter the Great ruled by edict, not by law, and when Lenin took power, Lenin ruled by edict, for there was no legal framework to guide him. Marx gave moral principles on which someone *might* have built their laws, but when he *spoke* about law he meant only the laws of determinism, like gravity—the river that sometimes watered crops and sometimes, flooding, ravaged a village on its way to the sea. Stalin took over a Soviet Union without laws to constrain him, all the land accepting rule by arbitrary edict, never having known anything else for a thousand years.

CHAPTER 39

Lenin warned his countrymen against the evils of counter-revolution, but not forcefully enough. Startling evidence has recently been smuggled into the United States, in microprint on the back of old tsarist stamps, documenting the full extent of reactionary intrigue in post World War I Russia.

FROM *THE SECRET PRISON DIARY* OF PETER KAISSEL

They threw him back into his old cell. The new guard was kind and gave him warm clothes and hot food. He cried, but in the morning it was the same. He had a new, grimmer brigade.

"How did you find me?" he asked sullenly.

"An informer," leered his inquisitor.

Where did Russia's overclass acquire this *obsessive* need for informers? The words hissed like a snake selling apples—*stukach, shpik, seksot* . . . more words than an Eskimo has for snow, many of them with Tartar roots: words to terrify, words to awe, words that couldn't be spoken except in a shaking voice.

Between grillings, Kaissel undertook clandestine research into the Russian police. He huddled over KGB manuals used to teach student agents how to recruit finks, learning ways to coerce compliance from farm and factory workers, writers and soldiers, even Soviet diplomats.

From another file Kaissel pulled the orders of a KGB lieutenant newly attached to a battalion group of the army occupying East Germany who was assigned to recruit as informers three officers, two regular service men, one private, two officers' wives, and two German nationals within two months.

Kaissel slowly established bonds between the Soviet police and the tsar's *Okhrana,* then made a sly request of the library.

The face of the Holy Mother paused while she searched gigabytes, for a moment leaving Kaissel with only a blinking cursor.

She found his link.

When Genghis Khan had been hammering disparate Mongol and Tartar tribes into a mighty war machine he developed a means of control loosely based on informers. In Russia, a country too poor to support a corps of detectives, the Mongols continued to use informers. Carefully they trained Russians to spy on each other, to denounce tax violations—giving suitable rewards for covert intelligence. After 160 years of Mongol tutelage . . .

The screen flickered . . . each generation of *stukachi* training the next.

In all recorded Russian law it has been illegal for a Russian serf to complain about his master, yet the same laws offer a serf freedom if he *informs* the ruling class of his master's tax lapses, a Mongol custom.

Kaissel watched the screen jump.

By the time of Peter the Great's Secret Office, run by the ruthless Romodanovsky, a pervasive network of eavesdropping and denunciation was in place to back up laws which never made a distinction between word and deed. The Christians say thinking a bad thought is a sin. Romodanovsky might have executed you for such thoughts.

Kaissel was beginning to understand what had caused the "great extinction" of Russia's socialists. The next day, furious after his interrogation, his eyes glazed upon the Holy Mother's screen, he traced, questioned, cross checked, asked for names. Covertly he began his *Prison Diary*. A man who is suffering dies if he does not retain within himself a secret laughing place.

The communist revolution, Peter wrote, *seems to have burnt itself out in two long decades of flaming arson masterminded by disguised* Okhrana *survivors and low level tsarist functionaries of the old service* apparat *operating out of closet Moscow rooms and communicating through secret drops in public trash cans.*

Early in 1921 reactionary plotters devised their master plan while accidentally reading The Collected Works of V.I. Lenin *which was in use as their secret code book for the trash can messages. Lenin's major theme was a vituperative insistance upon the one correct line—his. This, the plotters deduced correctly, would lead to squabbles upon Lenin's death which could be cleverly exploited in the revanchist cause.*

The critical Okhrana *files on the Bolsheviks had been saved during the disastrous October days and were hidden away in*

*the mattress of an ex-Moscow prison guard. After hushed dis-
cussions behind black-shaded windows and the delivery of many
messages on non-garbage collection days inside hollowed-out
sausages, it was recommended that Joseph Dzhugashvili (Stalin) be set up as the plot's principle dupe.*

*He was seen as an opportunist with no tolerance at all for
men superior to himself which meant that with careful provocation he could be used as a deadly tool to destroy all Bolsheviks
more able than himself. Thus the entire socialist organization
could be liquidated. For the purposes of the plot Stalin was
assessed to be lacking only in intelligence and organizational
ability, but these necessary commodities could be supplied by
infiltrators who would do his thinking and organizing for him.
Such a man was very dependent upon help.*

*It must be remembered that the tsarists were decimated at
this time. Their entire first rank of leadership had been wiped
out, they were badly organized, disunited, and thousands of
them were acting independently, unaware even that there were
others of the same sympathy. They sat home and drank vodka
and complained about the price of food. This gave them time to
plot while the socialists were busy rebuilding the nation.*

*It was slow work at first but the restorationists used divisive
technology effectively enough to fragment the socialists into
isolated cadres. By promoting different "correct lines" and
using Stalin as a tiebreaker they lifted their dupe to power. The
reactionaries weren't able to place any of their own in high
places but by being the actual physical people who controlled
Stalin's files they were able to bring to his attention a sufficient
number of scoundrels whom they knew would appeal to him,
Stalin being Stalin.*

The Bolsheviks classified rich peasants as *kulaki;* medium
peasants as *seredniaki;* and poor peasants as *bedniaki.* Under
Lenin, authority in village affairs was delegated to the poor
peasants who were recruited to inform the government when
the *kulaki* and *seredniaki* hid grain from the Bolshevik tax men.
To destroy peasant resistance to the revolution's taxes Lenin
turned class shadings into class war.

"Attack rich peasants!" was a slogan that Stalin preached. By
then, on the say-so of informers, peasants were being arrested
wholesale by OGPU agents with large *kulak* quotas. Meanwhile
the Bolshevik *baskaks* of 1930–31 were confiscating food for
export (to be sold on foreign markets at below-cost depression
prices), leaving next to nothing in the countryside. What did it

matter if those who objected to working for nothing were tortured for withholding grain they had never dared grow, were shot, were sent to the Gulags to build socialism with their free labor? Their neighbors had denounced them. That was enough. A peasant's rights had never been guaranteed by tsarist law— why change?

The Bolsheviks made their first fatal doctrinal mistake by disavowing socialist comradship with the peasants. The Bolsheviks needed the surplus value that the peasants could supply if properly milked, but didn't relish the dirty work of collecting it, especially since it meant that to do so they would be forced to face the peasant families they were robbing. Thus The Bolshevik City Workers hired tax collectors. Hundreds of counterrevolutionaries, most of them acting independently, seized upon this opportunity like starving wolves at a fawn. The tsarists, as unorganized and demoralized as they were, had plenty of people who knew how to squeeze taxes out of the countryside.

By 1935 the counterrevolutionaries who had started out in Ivan jobs murdering peasants for the OGPU, now had respectable jobs in the NKVD, plenty of vodka, enough money for girls, and each one of them had his own room in Moscow. It was decided after much trash can searching that the time was ripe for the great offensive.

Letter writing squads, patterned after the congressional letter writing clubs of the United States, began to complain about wrecking and sabotage, named names, and demanded action. Writers from the Washington Post *were imported to write articles for* Pravda *about dishonesty and hypocricy in high places. A few arbitrary arrests were made to satisfy "the outrage of the masses" and some torture begun to prime the restoration fuse.*

There was no danger of backlash. The NKVD's victims were carefully picked to appeal to Stalin—they were in every way superior to him. At first only journalists true to the masses were executed. Socialists connected to a free press were very dangerous to the counterrevolution and so all honest voices had to be destroyed during the first strike. Then came the big offensive. In NKVD backrooms, hordes of counterrevolutionary troops began to fabricate false testimony and forward it on to the vain Stalin-tool for approval.

Here was one of the strangest things that Kaissel was learning about the Russian culture during his prison studies. Russian villains had long mastered group solidarity, while the legions of brave Russian heroes, hordes of them, continued to fight on as *individuals,* with no understanding at all of the power of union. Working Americans read Marx avidly while that shaker of men was alive. Presto, powerful American labor unions sprang up. Yet in a hundred years no Russian had ever organized a successful labor movement. Why?

Perhaps in a sea of informers it was impossible.

Squabbles are like images in a house of mirrors and can be distorted and multiplied by a provocateur who knows how to add a clever innuendo here and a little falsehood there. You destroy people through their egos and their fears. Many old tsarists, knowing certain tricks of treachery perfected by Muscovites over seven hundred years, divided their foe in the manner of hidden forward agents of a new Ghengis, spreading rumors that turned compassionate socialists upon each other like hysterical sharks.

The morale of the socialist enemy disintegrated. Soon it took only thumbscrews and hot irons to convince devout Marxists to betray each other to the Gulags, where they were starved and murdered and broken by other underlings of the tsar's Okhrana who, being the only men who knew how to run the prisons, never lost control of them, consuming their enemies, one by one, with amused sadism—even the communist prison commissars set over them—consuming all the socialists sent to them like so many Russian prisoners of war for the ovens of Bergen-Belsen.

Confined to his prison cell, Kaissel had time for the stories of hundreds of Russian heroes. Who were these amazing people who could build a modern industrial nation while they were being murdered by their leaders? They were always taken alone. A centralized command line that lacks alternate routes and bypass channels and back roads can be deadly to *the very people who wield the power* once the central line becomes infected. Marxists have never understood the strength of redundant systems.

For some reason it was the story of the wife of Nestor Lakoba that inflamed Kaissel. Policeman Beria arranged a false attempt on Stalin's life—shooting his accomplices when they turned up for their reward. This deception had been a set-up to cast a shadow over Beria's implacable enemy, Lakoba, Chairman of the Central Executive Committee of Abkhazia. A poisoning was arranged with Stalin's consent. In a typical Stalinist touch, the body of "heart attack" victim Lakoba was sent from Tbilisi to Sukhumi with great funeral ceremony. The Chairman's corpse was then posthumously declared to be an "enemy of the people."

But Soviet law does not function without denunciations and informers to give it legitimacy. To facilitate his *legal* attacks, Beria needed a deposition against Lakoba from his wife. She refused. He had this young woman thrown into the Tbilisi prison.

Kaissel followed the story helplessly. How can one go back fifty years in time and save a quiet heroine who is past help?

Beria had her tortured by night and thrown back into her cell, mangled and bleeding, by day. Because she was beautiful, he encouraged her to betray her already murdered husband by beating her about the face. She remained unmoved. Beria brought her fourteen year old son to the torture chambers and told her that he would be killed if she didn't make the deposition. She refused. Night after night she was beaten, burned, humiliated.

While Kaissel was immersed in her story, he was himself half mad from exhaustion. He was in that strange nether world beyond tiredness where his mind seemed calm and awake but sometimes fell into strange dreams. Ghosts came to the cell to talk to him.

In a dark dawning, a starved beam of light clawed into the dungeon through a window slit. Lakoba's Georgian wife lay on the cell floor, unconscious, her face bashed and blue with old swollen bruises after a night in Beria's hands. Peter tried to talk to her, to revive her, to be kind to her.

"Little sweetheart," he said. He wished he had some water. He began to cry, sobbing, and that was water. Maybe he could wet her mouth with his tears. The heaving sobs took him apart. If only he could have held her head off the floor, but she was a ghost. Maybe she was here in America because all the Russian *apparatchiki* were afraid of their ghosts and she needed love.

Beria had murdered her son, with three of his friends, because they knew too much—but through it all she had never done what Beria asked, her cellmate living to tell the story. Such were the men Stalin chose to rule with him, torturers of women, killers of children, assassins of Lenin's associates. Kaissel looked up, the tears streaming down his cheeks, to see Lenin in the corner. He wasn't saying anything. He looked disturbed.

*   *   *

As each socialist hero was shot or shipped east a trained tsarist stepped into his place. There was a big basement factory in Moscow forging lower class papers for ex-noblemen.

It was a brilliantly diffuse counterrevolution, executed by disciplined individualists of the lower tsarist echelons who had known instinctively what to do even after their officers had been killed. They had correctly assessed their dupe. Stalin did order the execution of millions of devoted socialists under the banner "destroy the counterrevolutionaries" while the tsarists wrote the denunciations that Stalin was so eager to believe.

Before the armies of Hitler rolled eastward, tsarist apparatchiki were again the undisputed rulers of the old empire of the Ghengis Tsar. It hadn't been easy. The cost had been high in heroic martyrs; the counterrevolution had taken grievous losses and their leaders had been forced to humiliate themselves by pretending to be Marxists, even to publicly worship the despised Lenin. But they had won.

Who but counterrevolutionary dogs would bomb peasant villages from the skies of the Hindu Kush, ride over defenseless farmers with T-72 armor, herd women and children into the rivers of Afghanistan to drown, pour kerosene on old men and boys hiding in a sewer and set them afire—and dare to call it socialism?

Who but petty officers of the Okhrana would club Polish workers, and disperse them with water cannon, and be stupid enough to think that the world would then honor them as great leaders of socialism?

Who but a tsarist nobleman would accept the expensive dachas and special luxury commissaries of a capitalist? Who but the clerks of some gray tsarist apparat would sign an order forcing a scientist to do his work in prison and think that Moscow's disguise as a Marxist city was impenetrable? Who but a tsarist lawyer would have the effrontery to rewrite Imperial Law with only a sarcastic bow to Marx?

And who but a counterrevolutionary fascist would write dull propaganda without a sense of humor?

"Hey, face the door!" The guard came in and whacked Kaissel across the back with a rubber hose.

The next day, after his torture session, Kaissel felt like he had been stretched on one of Peter the Great's wheels. Too much pain. Too many people had died. Madness consumed them all, and one groped even to remember those central heroic struggles that made life sweet. Survive. Live. Be noble.

Value integrity! Never make a false deposition, no matter what the price. Yet it was too easy to break, to breathe the mud and die. *I've got to get out of here. I'm going crazy.* He looked at his scratchings on the wall. Forty-three days. Only forty-three. Then it was still 1937. It seemed like forever.

The cell door moved. *The sons-of-bitches are here again. All right. Another day. I refuse to break. I can pray to Saint Sakharov before I faint.*

But it was only a smiling American soldier wearing a rusting World War One helmet with putties wrapped around his lower legs. *What the hell?* thought Kaissel. The doughboy held out a paper American flag on a stick, the kind you waved in parades.

"The US Army to the rescue," said Limon Barnes.

"Where did you come from?" Kaissel asked blankly, unable to believe his sudden good fortune. *A cruel trick?*

"Herbert Hoover sent me."

"Oh thank God!" Peter dropped onto his bench.

Limon wouldn't let him rest. He took his arm. "Come on. Back to the salt mines. The Third World War is hot on our heels."

CHAPTER 40

*WASHINGTON DC (INS) A sharp exchange of messages be-
tween the United States and the Soviet Union followed the
confused fighting in Saudi Arabia last night with the United
States claiming to have evidence that the Soviets have been
training members of Bijad ibn Jamal's JASAP (Jihad of Awak-
ened Saudi Arabian Peoples). The Soviet Ambassador to the
United States denounced the claim as outrageous slander and
warned the United States against sending its mobile troops to
the Arabian peninsula. Widespread violence . . .*

*MOSCOW (INS) A decade of experience on the moon is paying
off for the Soviets. While the United States frantically tries to
catch up by rushing completion of their own moon colony, the
Soviets are moving out to Mars. With the final supply launch
today, the Soviet Martian fleet has now been fully assembled
and will begin the final checkout before leaving on the long
voyage next month.*

How peacefully the transfer vehicle moved between the Space
Operations Center and the factory modules of the leoport. It
drifted above the shore of Earth, staying within sight of that
immense landspread like a fragile coastal ship of ancient Rome
hugging the night beaches of the Mediterranean by starlight.
There were eighteen on the cramped benches—to Diana's whim-
sical fancy, enslaved oarsmen. Her seatmate was a battlestation
construction worker, too far from the shore for his own liking,
counting the days until he could walk upon the ground again.

Diana kept to herself her slight contempt for this tiny coastal
bireme. Her mind was on the farther ranging ships which plied
the routes beyond this Gibraltar of a later Roman Empire to the
mysteries beyond: the lunar colony. God, the moon was bright!

Almost full. The stars reminded her of the magical stars above the Wyoming mountains on that evening at the rest stop long ago when she was running away from home. But the porthole was too small. If only she could walk on deck and have the whole of the sky! But they didn't allow "slaves" topside.

Already she was impatient to go to work. She had been bumped from a direct saucer flight to the leoport and routed by shuttle through Big Mama where she had spent the last three days introducing herself to free fall and waiting for a berth on the transfer vehicle.

"You got a job at the port?" asked her companion.

"Yeah."

"Pharmaceuticals, I'll bet. Wenches are always in pharmaceuticals."

"No."

"Nursing?"

"No. The oldest profession."

He blushed but placed a friendly hand on her knee and was about to say something when . . .

She interrupted him. "Not that. The military. I'm an Air Force Major General on an inspection tour."

Quickly he took his hand away. "Aw, you're too young."

"In the Space Wing we get promoted fast." She paused. "Well, not that fast: I'm already thirty-seven."

"Thirty-seven!" he croaked.

"Slow-aging runs in the family, boy. We're immortal." And she squeezed his knee. "Flabby. You've been in space too long."

"You're pulling my leg."

"I can do that, too. What are *you* in for?"

"I'm being transferred to hot-shot factory construction. Pharmaceuticals."

Suddenly, as their "bireme" rolled, she forgot everything she was thinking. They began a slow approach to the leoport. Two hundred and ten kilometers of this tunnel-in-the-sky ran parallel to the planet below, an endlessly repetitive array of huge golden disks that looked solid when you stared along the dwindling length of the leoport, but transparent, like a venetian blind, when you looked straight at it. The netting of rectennae shimmered. Attached to the far side, like boats harbored by some three dimensional marina, were eyries for industrial use and eyries for living.

It was awesome.

A man behind Diana was explaining leoport stability. She

heard words like "tidal forces." The tides on the leoport tried to pull it into a vertical position. That caught her curiosity; how did something without oceans have tides? ". . . counteract the drift toward the vertical . . . with an axial field that controls its length." She peered over her shoulder. The man was demonstrating with hands that pretend-played an accordion. "Shortening the leoport increases its spin; lengthening decreases the spin. Conservation of angular momentum. You apply a spin-torque that opposes any tidal-torque."

"Yeah but I always worry about the power it takes," said the companion, "They're always correcting for buckle or spin. And absorbing the punches of those saucers!"

". . . supercooling . . ."

". . . twenty-thousand refrigerators. Think of it. Something's got to go wrong!"

"Ah, come on. They have one moving part and that rotates on magnetic bearings . . . here, I'll draw you a picture."

Diana couldn't see the picture so she lost interest in the conversation. Anyway, they were drifting up to the dock. This wasn't anything like the zip-bang-bounce of an airline landing!

She was met by Susan Foibbs who used her magnificent smile like a salesman might use a handshake. She was to be Diana's roommate. When she wasn't smiling Diana noticed that she had gauntly chiseled features of great beauty with the faintly mischievous look of a princess who has just turned her father's favorite prince into a frog. Just the kind of woman Mr. Ling would adore. Diana was instantly jealous.

"Do you have your sea legs, or do you need some help?" asked Susan when Diana seemed bewildered.

"I'm just disoriented because nothing looks like Ohio. I can swim. Just lead the way and I'll hang onto your toes. I'm not the type who gets sick so you can move as fast as you want."

"Ah, a natural."

They took a maglev car about four kloms up the line to their eyrie and emerged into what looked like a beehive. Susan drifted to one of the honeycomb cells and pulled the hatch on their home which everyone called a "can." "It's small but we're on disjoint shifts. If you don't like the decoration, just tell me."

"I brought my mother's leather couch."

Susan laughed and Diana found herself emitting her sixteen year old giggle and instantly choked it off.

"I have to give you an emergency drill. The rules. You'll be checked out on it next week—and you'd better pass!"

Diana had to learn where to find her rescue ball and how to

get into it instantly. Her ground-training had already made her proficient at that and she demonstrated. The ball was like an amoeba with one arm and a handle. Jump into it, slip your right arm into the sleeve, put on the oxygen mask, pull the fabric over your head, and use the arm to zip it up.

Spacemen wryly called the apparatus a "snowball's chance." It was meant to be carried around by someone wearing a spacesuit, but if you were in the ball and all alone you could use the one hand to travel, and you could use it to plug yourself into various emergency oxygen and communications outlets.

When Diana popped her head out again, like a newly born chick, she looked at Susan and asked the burning question. "Did Mr. Ling hire you?"

"Did he hire *you*?" Susan replied with wide eyes.

"I'm a friend of his."

"I've heard stories about him. He's bigger than life." The mischievous look came back to Susan's fine features. "Do you really know him? We have lots of gossiping to do!"

"How did you get your job at *Planet Stories*?"

"I was in pharmaceuticals and I couldn't *stand* it."

"Have you ever met Byron McDougall?"

"Sure. The old lecher is in love with me. He gives me a hug and a kiss and a proposition every time I meet him."

"Oh boy, do we have a lot to gossip about!"

Susan showed her how their "can" metamorphosed. With everything stowed away it became a basic space for hanging out. A couple of quick motions turned it into a hammocked bedroom. For work, one of the walls pulled down into a compudesk for word processing or bill paying, or gaming, or TV watching, or library calls. A twist on another wall turned the can into a gym. But the washroom was elsewhere and they had to eat at *Planet Stories* or in one of the cafeterias.

A customer of *Planet Stories*, after leaving the maglev car and floating down the central corridor of Eyrie-43 to the hatch of his favorite bar & eatery, faced a two meter tall reproduction of the cover of a mid-century science fiction pulp magazine. Underneath the greenhouse of an alien control room, a blond and wild-eyed woman, her back arced, was struggling to remove from her breasts the green tentacles of a monster with big lips who gazed back at her with ten loving eyes. In the background, jet packs ablaze, a handsome Swede with a cylindrical glass helmet was leaping through space to the rescue.

The logo of *Planet Stories* zoomed across the top of the reproduction cover, slowly changing colors. And if the customer paid close attention he could see the desperate woman breathing and hear her moans against the almost subsonic thump of the monster's heartbeat. Headline copy and credits filled every available spot between the action, blinking for attention or shifting colors or sparkling.

CONQUERORS FROM CALLISTO
by Janice Mannely

The WITCHES OF SATURN'S METAL WORLD
a new Green Eyes saga
by Susan Foibbs

ON THE TORTURED SHORES OF THE RED SUN
the man from the atom takes his princess to the end of time!
George Allan Gardener's latest adventure of the far future.

Passing through the entrance hatch the customer found the control room of a 1940s class rocketship battle cruiser. The busy "Captain" could be seen in free fall, perhaps with his hand on the Pressor Beam Rheostat mixing a whisky sour. Beyond him was a porthole and a magnificent view of Earth filling the sky.

Beside the porthole sat a surly Bug Eyed Monster deep in his cups. He was so lifelike that the unwary frequently approached him to see if they couldn't detect a flaw left by the artist and got the shock of their lives. The BEM turned with a cat's suppleness, bared his teeth and snarled at people who came too close. His electronic innards were, of course, made in one of the leoport's factories.

On her third day of work, Diana popped through the hatch—a real emergency airlock—whispered hurried words to the Captain in his Tri-Planet Rocketforce uniform and scooted to the ladies' room where she slipped into her brass scanties and emerged ready to serve. Serving in free fall was freaky but she already knew how to do it with grace.

That wasn't half the problem that the men were going to be. Here she was, not a week into the job, and an engineer from the micro-electronics lab a couple of eyries up the line was already in love with her. She was conscientiously working on five others. Having a lot of men in love with you was much less dangerous than being stuck with only one dumb lovesick male.

While she picked up her first meal from the cook and drinks from the bar she chatted with the Captain. "When are you putting my name on the cover of *Planet Stories*?"

"You have to write a story."

"A *whole* sci-fi story?"

"At least give me a title."

She grinned. "It has to have the word *moon* in it."

Diana was very ebullient this evening. She had heard rumors that two engineers had arrived at the leoport and were on their way to the moon and would probably be stopping by for a meal at *Planet Stories*. She wanted to slip them a mash note for McDougall, but wasn't sure that she dared.

In the meantime, she flirted with a group of metallurgists who were all excited about plastic-metal alloys—or something. After they got carried away by their enthusiasm and weren't paying much attention to her anymore she turned to courting their companion, a shy boy in electronics who was morose about some new high frequency substrate—at least he kept muttering the words "indium phosphide" as if they were his nemesis. At first she had been uncomfortable about spending so much time at the "tables" because in California they would have *fired* her for sitting down with the clients, but the Captain kept reassuring her that such mingling was definitely part of the job.

And so Diana was taking her shy customer by the scruff of the neck and forcing him to turn his head to look at her, all to make him laugh—when the Nuclear Peace interrupted them by failing, an event most people would remember to their dying day.

The music cut off.

The loudspeakers came on at twice normal volume.

"Emergency! Emergency! Leoport shutdown! This is not a drill! Repeat: Leoport shutdown. Please take Priority One precautions! Priority One. A flight of missiles has been detected rising from Soviet soil. There may be an alternate explanation but the current assessment is war. Anticipate attack within ten minutes. You will be kept informed through your ball phones. Repeat: Priority One."

Waitress and engineer floated, frozen in a strange position, forced by her hold on his hair to stare into each other's eyes. Impulsively Diana kissed the boy she knew only as a substrate man. Then she shoved off to the emergency lockers of the Tri-Planetary battle cruiser, flicked them open with one motion of her hand, and began tossing the balls to her customers. She gave orders like a battle sergeant.

She noticed the boy was weeping and got him into his ball first. Another man was protesting incredulously. "There will never be a war! Nobody is that crazy! Hitler is dead! The Russians are nice people! I've been to Moscow!" "Shut up!" she snapped. "Get in!" The men crawled into their wombs and zipped up. She shoved them to the wall, clamping them down, making sure each was plugged into the house oxygen . . . and then in a rapid set of motions stowed herself away, into a masked, one-armed blackness.

She was thinking of Ling and his bomb shelter. If only he were there now! Damn him—it hadn't been stocked with supplies for years and the roof leaked. It would rain fallout on him! He was probably in San Francisco anyway. The tears collected in her eyes in the darkness and she had to shake her head to throw them off; what a silly idea to want to save an eighty year old man when the world was coming to an end!

"Situation report," twanged the tinny speaker in the ball. "Leoport radar says immediate region clear. Our condition: fully functional. Confirmation on flock of Soviet SS-78s. Situation should be clarified within minutes. Stand by. Do not panic."

CHAPTER 41

The philosophers have only interpreted the world in various ways; the point, however, is to change it.

KARL MARX, *THESES ON FEUERBACH*, 1845

Prudence, indeed, will dictate that governments long established should not be changed for light and transient Causes; and accordingly all Experience hath shewn that Humans are more disposed to suffer, while Evils are sufferable, than to right themselves by abolishing the Forms to which they are accustomed. But when a long Train of Abuses and Usurpations, pursuing invariably the same Object, evinces a Design to reduce them under absolute Despotism, it is their Right, it is their Duty, to throw off such Government, and to provide new Guards for their future Security.

THE INSURRECTIONISTS FROM
THE DECLARATION OF INDEPENDENCE, 1776

A somewhat dazed Peter Kaissel was given a boistrous coming-home-from-prison-party in a corner of the Cathedral that was made up like a Moscow flat. He was already becoming wise in the ways of the SMB. He recognized the party as being patterned after a joyous Russian family reunion once described by Smeliakov in his charming piece, "The Zek's Return." Eighteen sons and daughters and uncles and grandchildren and brothers could be wild in the welcome of a man, gone to an Orthodox hell for twelve years and miraculously resurrected. If the government betrays your trust, there is always a family's love. The Kaissel-as-Russian was moved with tears of happiness. He joined in a dance as old as the forests of Smolensk.

But when his inquisitors arrived, the Kaissel-as-American

271

reacted differently. "You!" he accosted the one who liked to use the rubber hose, "what are you doing at my party!"

The boy grinned a California smile. "I'm your friendly local *Stukach*," he said ingenuously.

Kaissel, already too full of vodka, shook his fist. "You're next, you fascist deviationist! The NKVD eats its own!" Over which balcony should he toss this man?

"Easy comrade. That was yesterday. Today we've been reorganized as the KGB. We've been allowed to keep our jobs because we *promised* not to torture any more good socialists or make up lies about workers. So you're safe. Now we're only allowed to invent lies about Jews and human rights activists."

Laurie, the love of Kaissel's life, who had been avoiding him for months because he was so straight, intervened with slices of cheese stolen from a Commissariat For The Socialist Nobility and someone was telling a Polish version of a Polish joke (a Russian joke). Later Laurie sneaked her Peter out of the party and drove him away in Limon's Cadillac to a country hotel where Limon had rented a suite for them. It was a large saltbox four miles off the Boston Post Road with rolling grass lawns and maple trees and had a famous New England dining room that attracted patrons even from the city. Laurie took her man straight upstairs, especially since he had consumed too much vodka and was bowing and doffing a non-existant hat to the ladies.

"I've changed my mind about marrying you," she shoved.

He tried to crawl in bed, a mahogany four-poster with canopy, but she wouldn't let him. She pulled off his pants and gently steered him into the bathroom where she soaped him in a hot bathtub with iron lion's legs, and foamed his hair, and caressed him, and sometimes kissed him on his wet lips.

"Are you happy?"

"I'm in Old Bolshevik's heaven!"

But the bed was a luxury he couldn't believe. Such softness took every ache away, pampering him. Pillows of goose down! If this was what a bed was like after 43 days on a hard bench, he was willing to try the NKVD again. And the satin sheets and the fluffy quilt that gentle hands had tucked around his neck! When she was nude under the covers with him, her fingers holding his ears, he wondered if Omar Khayyam had ever written a poem about the fragrance of one's beloved.

"Still love me?" she asked of his eyes. "I've been mean."

"I'm six men right now and they all love you."

"A Yankee and five Reds? I don't think I can handle that!"

His voice was blurred. She let him sleep—there was plenty of time in the morning for lovemaking.

Limon Barnes very carefully did not appear at the hotel before noon the next day. Accompanied by a young man, he waited for the lovers in the dining room. It was a marvelous room full of the antiques of the old Boston cabinetmakers. Every table had its lace doilies, and flowers set in delicate Chinese vases imported long ago by Clipper ship.

Limon rose when they came down, bowing to Laurie in his slightly stiff, spastic way, and shaking Kaissel's hand. "Meet Larry Spaceki, who is Dorfman's replacement. He's our resident Marxist scholar and Synmann tells me that he's a pretty hot mathematician. You'll be working together. He's a good man—saved our asses. You think you had a rough time—you should have seen me and Synmann trying to do your work while you were in the hoosegow. Couldn't have done it without Larry. By the way, Synmann sends his regards. He's off on some conference about wild-eyed ways of manufacturing anti-protons."

"Send him my V for victory sign with one finger," grumbled Kaissel. "My best friend, and he let me rot in prison!"

"You still want to sue us for a million dollars?"

"How could I sue the man who led a whole expeditionary force into the depths of Massachusetts to rescue me from the NKVD?"

"I'm glad you appreciate me," grinned Limon.

"Just don't turn your back."

"I've got to grill you. I have a few questions."

"So early in the morning?"

"It's noon," reminded Limon.

"High noon?" suggested Kaissel.

"Nah. Just a business lunch. I'm thinking of promoting you and I want you to confirm my hunch."

"What kind of promotion?"

"Never mind. How does the idea of aiming two gigatons of explosives at the Soviet peoples seem to you now? That's called a defense policy."

Kaissel thought it over. He didn't trust his old opinions any more—they had all changed. Strangely his mind converted the numbers into "Stalins." Two gigatons of H-bombing could do the same damage to Russia as *forty* Stalins. That was forty Stalins worth of arbitrary cruelty and destruction. What a shit defense for the United States! "It doesn't make democracy sound very humane." He visualized a dark factory in the Nevada desert manufacturing Stalins. *Buy a Stalin to protect your kids!* He tried to multiply, by forty, the number of Gulags, the frozen work crews, the awful soup, and the concentration camps built to house the children of parents who had been shot. *Why am I so sympathetic to the Russians?* "It doesn't say much for American ingenuity that the best we can do is parrot Stalin's slogan: *Vigilance through terror."*

"All right. Anything else?"

"What did you do to me?"

"I didn't do anything to you. I played around with your environment, but who was in control of *you?* You always had choices to make. Show me a man who says he has no choice, and I'll show you a man who has *chosen* not to be responsible. How could it be otherwise? One man can be shown Stalin's crimes and choose to see Russians as brutal savages, another can be shown the same thing and choose to see the Russians as victims, another will see self-deception or bravery or stoicism or God knows what. I provided the view, you provided the eyes. What did you see?"

"I saw stronger and more intelligent people than I expected. And some very brave ones."

They ordered from a white-capped young lass dressed as an eighteenth century New England farmer's wife. After his prison food, Kaissel had a hard time deciding what he wanted. He took the leek soup, the clam pie, the spare ribs with maple syrup, and a side of Sandra's String Beans with Mint.

Limon waited patiently, ready for more shop talk. "Let me ask you another question. The ABM treaty makes it a crime to shoot down a missile on take-off, in flight, and during re-entry on the theory that we are safer if we make ourselves vulnerable to the Russians. How does that strike you this morning?"

Kaissel knew his old views—they were there right on the tip of his tongue—but he was *thinking* something else. The inner voice said: *insane.* "That's an extremely dangerous position." It scared him. How secure could a man ever be after choosing to make his family vulnerable to a Lavrenti Beria? "One thing hit me: the bravest of Russians are naive to a truly awesome extent."

"Explain yourself."

"Stalin taught them *nothing.* They didn't tear his machine apart and rebuild it with checks and balances. They left his whole machine intact. Sure a superior Russian can move to the top under the present regime. He can be loved by the people and deserve it and bring prosperity for twenty or thirty years—

but what of the next man? There is absolutely *no* machinery in place in the Soviet Union to stop the top man from becoming a tyrant. Millions of Russians adopted Stalin as a father and based their security on being vulnerable to him. They haven't changed. They accept the tsar that God gives them. Should we? If our lives are hostage to him?"

"That's not the way you talked before you went to prison," said Laurie, startled by his passion.

"I feel odd today. All kinds of strange emotions are roiling around in me."

Limon had the intense look of a man moving in for the kill. He held that in check while the drinks were served and Kaissel was brought his steaming bowl of leeks. The gamesmaster didn't touch his drink and he waited until Kaissel had his spoon in his mouth. "Suppose a military defense against ICBMs *was* impossible. Suppose one of the tsars went bad on us and we were at his mercy. Suppose this tsar was as willing as Stalin to see *his own people suffer* and die by the hundreds of millions. An interesting game. How would you defend all of us against him?"

"That includes the Soviet peoples?"

"Of course."

"Do you want a military solution?"

Limon waited, without replying, his hand on his drink. Spaceki seemed to be in on the game, too, and was waiting just as expectantly.

"It's very bad military strategy to attack an enemy's strong point." Kaissel said that only to gain time. His mind raced. That bastard Limon never let up! "Don't fight the last war." These cliches weren't helping. *The last war ended with the use of A-bombs*. The military mind had since then been fixated on nuclear weapon threats. The Soviets were *expecting* to defend themselves against a nuclear attack by another Hitler.

"H-bombs are useless as a defense. Too obvious. I'd attack the Soviet legal system. If they had honest courts, outside the authority of any tsar, we'd be safe—and so would they."

Limon smiled. "You're on. You start at the Waterworks tomorrow." He meant the SMB's mysterious Marching Society of the Soviet General Staff and Waterworks.

Kaissel was puzzled. "What would I be doing over there?"

"Professional revolutionary."

Spaceki, who had said nothing, ate the olive in his martini. "Have you ever read Marx on Russia?"

Laurie volunteered an answer. "Marx thought Russia would

be the last place to have a communist revolution and America the first, I remember that."

"He was quite correct," continued Spaceki. "The October revolution was an anomaly quickly suppressed by historical forces while the American workers broke their capitalist bosses without breaking the goose that lays the golden egg. They went on to become the richest working class in the world." Sadly he stirred the oliveless martini with the toothpick of wayward dreams. "Unfortunately they lost their way. When they became rich they got confused and thought they were capitalists."

"Spaceki comes from a family that has been Marxist for four generations," commented Limon.

"I ran away from home when I was sixteen to escape it all. You wouldn't believe my grandfather. He ran a paper in New York back in the Depression. It was called *Solidarity*—that's before the word was banned by the communists as counterrevolutionary. He was very fast on the dogma switches but sometimes he didn't make it fast enough. He was unlucky. He put out a pro-German issue the day before Hitler broke the Non-Aggression Pact with Russia. That got him kicked out of the Party. I have vague memories of him teaching me to read *Das Kapital* when all I wanted to do was be normal and fill in the dots like the other kids."

Limon raised his glass. "To the misfits of the world." Larry Spaceki clinked. Laurie, who was the black sheep of her family, raised her glass. Kaissel raised his soup bowl. "No, not you," said Limon, "you're a mundane."

"Mine is a tragic story," continued a rueful Spaceki. "I escaped my mad family. I put myself through college. I got a degree in computer science. I freelanced as a programmer—made money, lost it all. And there I was, starving. I was asking everybody for a job. I asked Limon for a job, knowing he was in the pay of a rich capitalist. That impressed me. I begged him. I told him the story of my life. So he hired me as a Marxist revolutionary. What could I say? I was starving."

"I'm supposed to work with this man?" asked Kaissel.

"You won't have any trouble with me," said Spaceki. "It is Limon you'll have trouble with. I'm just a capitalist pig waiting for the next paycheck and glad to get it. Limon here is the Marxist revolutionary."

"Let's just say I'm a revolutionary who is willing to use the Marxist-Leninist language to talk to . . . well . . . *clients* who have been brought up in that language."

Kaissel was working on his spareribs. "So what am I getting myself in for, smuggling guns to Ukrainians?"

"Absurd!" snorted Limon. "Would a good rebel prepare to fight the last revolution? What if *armed* revolt was obsolete?"

"We have the models to prove it," Spaceki grinned.

"We have been busy for a month," Limon added.

Spaceki cut back in. "Your modeling language is very good, Kaissel. I was impressed. Synmann gave up on *BalanceOfTerror* for a while and decided to model revolutions. We had the whole thing up and running in two weeks. Our rebel leaders were given the task of converting society-A into society-B in minimal time. The player we called a 'converter' *always* beat the guys who used force and insurrection. It was very interesting. In fact if we used 'guns' to smash society-A and then tried to build a B out of the wreckage we usually only got some damned form of A back again. Communism overthrew Tsar Nicolas II but gave birth to Tsar Stalin, that sort of thing."

"And what *does* a 'converter' use?" Kaissel hated guns.

"He can use a lot of things, but we're looking at computers," said Limon.

Laurie brightened. "What a nifty plan. We turn all the Russians into mathematicians. They'll be so incapacitated, they won't even be able to tie their own shoes." She sneaked a look up at Kaissel's sour expression and took his arm in her hands. "I'm only teasing you, honey bun," she teased.

CHAPTER 42

The early craze in the United States for railroad building, as well as for turnpikes and canals, cannot be understood if it is thought of only in terms of eager investors seeking large direct returns. . . . It is the peculiarity of any great improvement in transportation that it may bring tremendous indirect benefits, that the multiplier effect of a relatively small investment in a railroad may have the result of greatly increasing the productivity of a whole area . . . farmers, manufacturers, and mine owners receive higher prices, consumers get more for their money, real estate values mount, favorably located middlemen and bankers augment their profits, and government revenues rise.

FROM *THE TRANSPORTATION REVOLUTION*, BY G.R. TAYLOR

It flew, six months late, but without a hitch. The first modified shuttle, specifically designed to carry the leoport's hoops into space, did not look like its parent at all. It was chubbier because its freight was carried around the "external" tank. There were four boosters instead of two, and nowhere any wings. A squat, manless module carried the same shuttle main engines that had made the parent famous, but it was the engine module that dropped back to Australia and the tank which went into orbit.

After all these years of preparation Shantech had finally begun to assemble the leoport. Byron insisted on being up there with the orbital crew. Although he didn't trust himself to lead the construction team—he was spread too thin to know all of the detail work he should have known—he insisted that he was a qualified second in command.

The "starting" shack was designed to fit into the old shuttle's cargo bay and so it was cramped. NASA flew the assembly team up in the *Constitution* and four days later the aging *Columbia* brought them their "factory." Already psychological pressures were mounting to hurry the job. The demand for cargo space to *leo* was outstripping the supply—the three original shuttles and the new shuttle fleet and the shuttle derivatives just weren't enough. People who had reason to be in orbit were impatient to double their freight thruput and halve their costs.

The crew lost a week getting the factory together. Nothing serious. Just routine delays. First a hose clamp refused to connect and they couldn't just call out for a replacement. When they finally got it on, it leaked. Take it off. Byron figured out a way to re-machine the fittings. Then they proceeded to the next snafu. Nothing went right, but when they were finished, no one would have known that there had ever been any trouble.

In the end, it didn't matter that they were late in assembling the factory. Their first supply shuttle lost an engine just prior to launch and had to be refitted, reaching them only after a ten day delay. In the meantime the Soviets put an orbiter around the moon and stole the world's headlines. They were planning something big.

The leoport began to grow. Assemblers added rectennae to each hoop, checked it, primed the supercoolers, and jockeyed the new section of concentric coils into place, immediately starting with a fresh hoop. There was always immense excitement when a new load of 120 hoops was sent up and had to be docked. The crew enjoyed each other. There were a lot of jokes. They called themselves "congressmen" and their assembly factory the Capitol Dome and their creation "the national debt" because it grew longer every day. Sometimes Byron would laugh as he looked at the spiderwork dangling down below toward Mother Earth, linking them to the docks and the leoport.

Always there was work—checking out the lasers that kept the leoport linear, staying up all night to kill a bug in the controls, dismissing an assembler for smoking, hopping up to the powersat to comfort that vital project in its birthing pains. And there were the tests of the saucer prototypes. Boeing sent them up, and they eased them through the loops, monitoring and measuring. Systems would be tested and sometimes sent back to Earth for redesign.

Shantech expected the construction of the leoport to take years. The supply problem was enormous. The total tonnage needed was modest by Earth standards, but tonnage to orbit is expensive. Byron sometimes wished he could rent space on the huge Russian booster which lifted a freight load that even the shuttle derivatives couldn't match. But the Soviet's were busy expanding Mirograd and frantically carrying out their own SDI experiments—and perhaps (who knew?) planning moon ventures.

Once Byron had to shut down leoport construction for two months. The Soviets were testing a weapon to take out the MX and suddenly leoport cargos were being bounced by the military for rush American tests of an experimental ICBM killer. But Shantech never fell more than nine months behind schedule. The ground work got done on time, and the saucers and their feeder scramjets went into production only three months late.

They had one near catastrophe. Byron was a national hero for a week when a transfer vehicle took out eight hoops and smashed up some of their living quarters—but the accident proved out Armsiel's contingency plans for a leoport disaster. The damaged loops were just lifted out of the leoport and the line closed up. Construction returned to normal.

Then, in the middle of the hectic rush—when they were nudging the whole shebang into equatorial orbit for the first saucer flights from Namala—Byron was recalled to Earth for an emergency policy conference. The White House needed a lunar colony expert. The highest levels in Washington were brainstorming the continuous Soviet landings at Theophilus.

Byron gave talks to the politicians and their advisors. He brought his laser disks and showed off his lunar base proposal in detail to the technical people. He chatted with the generals over coffee about the strategic implications. He wished all of them had listened to him back in the eighties but he was a pragmatist and happy that they were listening now.

The United States was about six to eight years behind the Soviet lunar program, he told them, however, once the leoport transportation system was on line, the United States would be in a position to overwhelm the Soviet's very modest effort and make a profit doing it. To Byron the Soviets were simply atheists put there by God to be outwitted.

No one could better outwit the Soviet machine than Ray Armsiel. For the first time Byron began publically to discuss Armsiel's plan to import lunar oxygen into *leo* where its momentum could be used to keep the leoport in orbit under conditions of heavy thruput and then used again in orbital rocket maneuvers.

Byron was still young, but he had slight wrinkles around his eyes and the ease of an older man. By the end of the conference he knew that he would be the field commander of the second American lunar program. He already had the aura and national prestige that politicians admired; he was by birth a buddy of the military; NASA trusted and respected him; he spoke the language of business and got along with everyone in Shantech except old Charlie Bond who listened to his daughter too much.

It was a great ego booster. *This is how power feels before it corrupts you.*

But he was alone. Washington was an isolated city, cut off from everything that nourishes a man. With whom did one share the glory of triumph? He took a walk from his hotel and found himself in front of the White House where he had a fantasy of being an old man arriving here on weak legs to deliver a "Declaration of Lunar Independence". *Oh hell,* he thought, *I'll never find anyone in Washington who understands.*

The saloons didn't work out either. They were smokey Washington dives full of shop talk and rich con men from the boondocks looking for their daily handout and secretaries who reeked of cigaret. And so Byron ended the night in a glaring pizza place writing a letter to Amanda on the back of a place mat. He told her that he still winged over her Texas ranch once in a while to see if she had ever carried out her threat to bring home Petra's *Khasneh*.

After the conference he flew home. It irritated him that there was nothing to do in New Hampshire. He bought a dozen red roses from the Stonefield florist and laid them on the overgrown grave of the love letter Amanda had mailed to him more than a decade ago. He found himself in mourning. Of all of his mistresses, she was his favorite. He supposed she was still mad at him for being a Republican. He kept one rose for his wife.

That brat Charlie got on his nerves. The boy was always lying around in deck chairs instead of doing something! *He needs his father's disciplined hand.* Byron took off three days to march his son through one hundred miles of Vermont Green Mountain wilderness. It was good for the boy. And Byron certainly wasn't a bastard like his own father who force-marched children on rice and water; he made his son bring along decent food and made him cook it, too.

A McDougall frontiersman had to be tough if he was going to beat those Soviet Redskins out there on the lunar plains. It was Charlie's generation who would win or lose that battle.

CHAPTER 43

*"Yeah, but when you snip-neck the compact mode you gotta
F-wave the parameters or you get the squeaks."*
*"We should undercut the D-phase. Then you never kiss the
squeaks and you carve out range for all those sub-jollies—which
is what you wanna do. You're just hairy for high spice-flutter.
No one hears it."*

HEARD BY A GRANDMOTHER AS SHE RESCUED HER BEATLES
RECORDS FROM HER GRANDSONS.

Only gradually Charlie (Jr.) McDougall discovered the
superperfect shelter from his parents: digitanimal music, DM.
Electronic instruments frightened his mother. She had a PhD
in musicology from Mills but couldn't tell a fourier compact
series from a quartet concert series, a resistor had something to
do with the draft, and a chip was what an uncouth person
carried on his shoulder. Her music education was classical.
Though she claimed a range of knowledge up to the modern,
her training had never come closer to real-time than the compositions of Emerson, Lake, and Palmer.

As for Charlie's father, who polished off textbooks like most
slow readers polished off light novels, engineered music was in
the same category as purple smells or painted cooking. If it
didn't have its roots in rock, it wasn't music. So far as Charlie
was concerned his father could be as old as Mick Jagger.
Actually he wasn't *that* old or they wouldn't be planning to ship
him off to the moon. But he *was* too old to know how to dance
to trance music. Served him right. You sure couldn't rock on
the moon, but trancing in low-g would be a delight. He didn't
even know that there was a difference between trance and DM.

Waves, repetitions, pulsations, rumblings, the rise of a violin

taking off can all be described by a fourier series—an amalga-
mation of sine and cosine waves of different frequencies and
amplitudes. A frequency is a number. An amplitude is a number. Charlie constructed his DM by choosing those numbers
and deciding when they were to change. He used three of his
old junked computers to execute the commands. He could take
a compact disk from the 80s, rearrange it to his own instruments, and dijj it down to a hundred megabytes.

He got straight A's in high school but didn't want to go to
university. He was the tech man of a local group who practiced
in an old barn after Charlie rewired it for electricity. They had
big plans. Their leader, Snuffy, had contacts in Concord and
thought he could get a gig in a basement trancery.

Sitting on old bales of hay and eating ham sandwiches, Charlie
promised them that he could put together a demo disk. They
didn't even need a studio. He had all the DM tricks to take out
the noise and rebalance the sound—even to "improve" it. Carried away by the possibilities, he boasted that he would be able
to erase Artie's mistakes. Artie's weird musical slips were famous. He was the good-natured butt of the group's jokes. It
could be a sick horse, they said, but it was probably Artie.

Charlie really didn't know how to do all that he claimed, but
his friends trusted him and he wasn't about to disillusion them.
He *did* have all the books and it *seemed* simple. Charlie was
marvelously confident in himself as a quick study—he had
learned to obey his parents efficiently just to survive so he
could have some free time to lay around in the sun or collect
beetles or play with the pigs or make sod forts—the things that
were fun.

It was always chaos when his father dropped down out of
space. He gave demonstrations for his friends. "Attention!"

Therefore when his father and mother started to have little
arguments between themselves about where he should go to
college, slashing at each other with curved knives while they
ate their grapefruit, he decided for the first time in his life to
resist them openly. He started with passive resistance—continuing to do well in high school but neglecting to send away
for university application papers. They noticed. A few days
before Byron was off on some lunar training mission, they set
up an evening snack of cheese and crackers around a blazing
living room fire and invited him in for a pep talk.

He listened. Byron pointed out the opportunities facing such
an able student. Junie created images of applauding audiences.
Then Byron pulled out the application papers for the Massachu-

setts Institute of Technology, already filled out and awaiting his signature. Junie pulled out the papers for the Brilliano School of Fine Arts, already filled out and awaiting his signature. He protested that he wanted to pick out his own university, marveling all the while that he was *resisting*.

"It's too late for that, son."

Mama handed him a cracker, spread with Brie and cod livers. "There are deadlines. Are you aware of the *hordes* sieging Brilliano?"

He signed. He didn't see it as a compromise—after all he couldn't go to both places, and if he could refuse to go to one, he could refuse to go to the other. Hopefully, both might reject him. After he signed, Byron brought out the Irish Mist for his son, pouring a full glassful over the ice.

"You're turning into quite a man."

"He's still my little baby!" protested Junie.

Three days later Charlie woke up to the noise of his father cheerfully going through his closet and packing an overnight bag. Without being asked he was dragged off to Boston. They rented a car and had lunch with a gray-haired MIT professor. When the prof was off to the restroom and before the coffee came, Byron confided that his friend was on the admissions committee.

"Sometimes you embarrass me, Papa. I'm supposed to earn my way." How do you lecture your father on morality? Were all fathers corrupt?

"Bonds have never been adverse to a wee dab of nepotism."

"You're not a Bond! You're a McDougall and McDougalls have defended what is good and right for three generations!"

"I've been overpowered."

There were other surprises. Byron had already rented a four room apartment for his son in Cambridge, on a short back street a quarter of a mile from the Charles River. Yesterday it had been electrically rewired by permission of the landlord. A telephone crew had installed a fiber optics line that morning. Tomorrow the roof would get a dish.

"I'll be on the moon for most of your college life. I want us to keep in contact. If I recollect my own mind at your age, you'll be thinking you know it all. You don't. You'll need help. I'll be checking out your homework and we'll need a good fax line." He toured the rooms. "They did a damn good job of sanding the floors. What do you think? Are you going to be happy here?"

Charlie was stunned. His own apartment. Didn't college

students live in dorms and eat cafeteria food? He could bring girls up here! "What if Brilliano accepts me?"

"They won't. It's been arranged. And if you tell your mother that, you little bastard, I'll wring your neck."

"I'm not a bastard. I know you're my father because I have your blue eyes and black hair."

"Son, I'm sure I'm your father, too," he said sternly, "but how do I know Junie is your mother? She grew up during the sexual revolution. Those were hard days for macho men. You don't know how lucky you are with all the virgins around today."

I can never tell when he's pulling my leg, thought Charlie.

Byron took another tour of the apartment, inspecting the woodwork, turning the taps on and off, running a finger inside the stove, checking the upper windows for mobility. "Fantastic. You should see the barracks I had for a college! You are going to like this place. Don't bring any of those diseased Boston girls up here; you don't want to die before you're twenty-five. Has your mother given you your VD lecture?"

Charlie changed the subject quickly. "May I furnish it myself?" he asked hopefully, telling himself that it would be the last straw if his father hired an interior decorator.

"Of course; I always let you do what you want to do. I let you play the violin, don't I? And DM, you can do your DM at MIT. Do you think they know *anything* about electronics at Brilliano?"

Charlie was reluctant to tell Snuffy and the boys about MIT, and didn't even mention it until late August. Then they had a last jamming in the barn until the full moon was well above the horizon, before hiking into Stonefield to drown their sorrows in ice cream banana splits. Snuffy gave him a Motorola saxophone box with a 25 megahertz driver for a going away present.

CHAPTER 44

Karl Marx claimed that a developing capitalist country goes through stages which, by dint of their inhumanity, prepare the workers for revolution. It was his belief that a premature socialist revolution would abort. One does not shingle a house before framing it. That was how he explained the failure of the 1848 insurrections.

By 1917 Russia had not passed through the required pre-socialist stages. The necessary infrastructure was not yet in place. A correct application of Marxist theory in 1917 would have predicted the failure of the October revolution. Indeed, as if to chastise the Bolsheviks for trying to cheat historical determinism out of its hard preliminary sacrifices, the economy of Russia proceeded to develop relentlessly along the classical Marxist road toward the rise of a capitalist state.

Capitalization, according to Marx, begins by the extraction from the workers of what he called "surplus value." The selling of wheat taken at gunpoint from starving Ukrainian peasants in order to finance factory machines, the squeezing of slave labor from unwilling Gulag prisoners who worked long hours for no pay, little food, and no medical care, etc, are all classical Marxist examples of the methods by which capitalism takes root.

Marx spent many pages on capitalists who make their money hawking weapons to small countries and profiting from the misery of endless armed clashes. The foreign exchange earned by the Soviet Union in this way is the foul money of the cruelest of capitalists. The Soviet Union's penetration and use of Ethiopia is a textbook Marxist case of the acquisition of a colonial military base by a capitalist power.

In the final stages of capitalism, Marx saw an economy mov-

*ing toward monopoly. Monopolies give capitalists absolute con-
trol over their workers' "surplus value." Under monopoly the
capitalist class lives very well in luxurious country houses, with
special stores and special privileges, while the workers exist in
an artificially sparce economy, fleeced of the fruits of their
labor, with only drink and a state religion to ease their pain. It
is a remarkable irony that the Soviet Union is the only nation of
the twentieth century which ever developed a mature capitalist
economy of the kind defined for us by Karl Marx.*

*Persuasively, Marx predicted that these mature monopolies
would be the seeds of their own destruction. To exist a monopoly must centralize and coordinate its workers. Once centralized and coordinated they have the solidarity to remove the
capitalists. If Marxist theory is true, the Soviet Union/Empire is
now primed and ready for its first successful workers' revolution.*

LARRY SPACEKI, FROM THE PREFACE TO MARXSPEAK

The week that Charlie Bond died, the immensity that was
corporate Shantech held one of its many memorial services in
the Cathedral of Saint Sakharov. Sturdy beams gave off a solid
Russian Orthodox resignation. Tall slender windows—in myriad
shades of blue—blazed the defiant strength of science.

After the eulogy Kaissel wandered back through the maze to
his new office in the Cathedral of the Moon. Cathedrals were
springing up like mushrooms inside the citadel walls of the
SMB, this one honoring the Russian triumph at Theophilius.
Limon had a policy of lavish praise for things the Russians did
well—to balance the SMB's cruel awareness of Soviet weakness.

Peter was expecting to be alone with his thoughts for the rest
of the afternoon, but seated on his chair, relaxed, was Joseph
Synmann, long hair combed but unwashed for a week, Pushkin
outfit, once fresh and sporting, now going to seed, musty and in
need of a dry cleaning.

"It's been a year and a half!" exclaimed Kaissel.

"Two years," corrected the old hippy. "Been working hard.
The Reds are putting holes through our ABM defense so we're
busting ass to get the second generation of ABMs out of the
think tank. They're turning out four of their new missiles a
month. We haven't come up with any cost sensible counter-
measures. I've come up with an *insensible* countermeasure,"
he pronounced wryly. "Costwise it's perfect but the physics is
hairy."

"Need any help?"

"You could get your goddamned revolution cooking."

"The pieces are going into place."

"Not soon enough."

"*Violent* overthrows aren't change-time minimal," Kaissel said dogmatically in the terse language of simulations, repeating something Synmann already knew. "You've given up? You used to be very enthusiastic."

"It's like derailing a train with your bare hands. I used to think that when we got our ABM system in place, it would knock some sense into Soviet heads, and they'd just give up and put their own ABM system in place and forget it and start making shoes for their workers. Can't predict people. Instead they took the high ground and put the kibosh on our satellites. So we have hardened battlestations that can fight for a week and they have the moon and we have an ABM system that their new missiles can make Swiss cheese out of." The physicist threw up his hands. "It is going to cost them a couple of hundred billion to beat our ABMs. Can you believe it? How can they afford it?" Synmann laughed. "You guys are being lax on your job. Where are the Russian labor unions demanding a higher standard of living for Soviet workers when we need them?"

"We have a variant on a labor union structure that we're pushing—loosely similar to one of Lenin's wild ideas that he wrote down while living in a hut somewhere. We can trace it back to Marx with a little bit of Jesuit fasttalk."

"Lenin is going to save the world from the H-bomb by rising out of the grave and infecting Moscow with Solidarity? All by tomorrow? Good luck. Lenin was an asshole."

"Hey now. We treat Lenin with straight faces around here. Actually it's not *really* one of Lenin's ideas—we're using an idea of yours."

"That's better. I trust myself more. Which one?"

"It came out of the labor-unionoid simulations. But we have to give *Lenin* credit. Sorry about that. You know how it is when you deal with a dogmatically religious society. If it's good, God did it; if it's bad, Satan did it—people are only chess pieces. You make a good horse."

"Knight. Who wrote it up?"

"Joint effort of Limon and Spaceki. I did the mathematics. I think Limon and I postulated together the unionoid form that turned out to be optimal under Soviet constraints. We slogged through four hundred variations. It was like being a chemist for a medical drug company. Julian—he's new—did the similarity-sort through the works of Marx and Lenin to give it a proper transfer facade. Kraut did the targetting."

"Did you feed it through that program that turns all things into Leninist prose?"

"Of course."

Synmann laughed. "For the hell of it, I ran one of my physics papers through that program once. It sounded like bullshit straight out of the Novosti Press Agency Publishing House, but it was all there—Marxist-Leninist quantum field effect physics." He paused. "How can they buy the sudden arrival of a new idea by Lenin?"

"Easy. It was blocked by Stalin. In Moscow, Stalinist revanchism is an obscene subject too terrible to mention in polite society and absolutely taboo to mention in front of a non-Russian—but they *were* all victims of Stalin directly or indirectly and they know it. There are euphemisms by which one can discuss Stalin's crimes, and even a special vocabulary to talk about the horrible things he did to the true followers of Lenin. If you know the code words you can sell Stalin as a blocker of the advance of socialism who deflected key aspects of Marxist-Leninism into some incorrect eddy. But don't ever knock the Russian people while you do it! We've learned how to tippy-toe over that ground quite successfully."

"You have evidence that they are actually discussing ideas generated here at the SMB?"

"That's right."

"Of course, that doesn't mean a damn thing." Synmann had become a pessimist. "The Russian gestalt has always been able to isolate the intelligentsia from any kind of power."

"Yes—but it is not the intelligentsia who are in ferment. Stalin's millions of accomplices in crime ruled for a generation after his death and firmly discouraged any kind of serious study of Stalinism. Suddenly they all started to die. How many are left? A dozen? Not enough to hold down the manhole cover. The *inheritors* want to go back to Lenin and rediscover what Stalin destroyed. It seems the intelligentsia are cynical, but among the sons of the ruling class it is a mass movement. The SMB is just riding that wave like a surfboarder."

"Would John L. Lewis buy this 'unionoid'?"

"Who's he?"

"A coal miner with bushy eyebrows."

"An American union man?"

"Yeah."

"No, he wouldn't like it. It's a unionoid, for God's sake. He'd call it a company union. That's why we can sell it. How else could we sell a structure like that? Pass it off as the *Son of*

Solidarity and hope they smile? It's an easy sell. It ups production. Scads more surplus value for the State."

"More money to buy missiles to beat our ABM system? Just what I need."

"Yeah, but there are interesting delayed side effects. You know the kind—plantation cotton wealth today, marry your girl to some suave black executive a hundred years from now."

"There was a long time delay on that side effect. What's the delay on yours?"

"It's reasonable. Fifteen, maybe twenty years."

"Jesus, we'll all be dead by then. Blown up. The Lebanese will have atomic car bombs by then. I think I'll stick with the military. Good old generals. They're like women. You can't live with them and you can't live without them."

Kaissel showed Synmann the machine translation of several important Soviet articles. "Take a look at the kind of discussion we've been generating."

Synmann put on his glasses and read. "You're not doing very well. These are all *against*."

"Unionoids are generating flak in Moscow at the moment—which means they're getting support from somewhere. We suspect young men with clout whom the KGB can't touch—powerful parents. We even know some of their names." Kaissel pulled out a list.

"How did you smuggle in the idea?"

"We're not sure. We tried our first penetration of this item about three years ago. Not the whole thing, just the bait. We don't like these things to appear full blown out of the mind of God. They have word processors. We like them to add a bit, we comment, argue, expand; I think the full item went in only a year ago. We suspect that one of the computer clubs has been picking it up. They are quite effective in foiling government attempts to halt the illegal duplication of text files."

"So you *are* getting through sometimes?"

Kaissel smiled. "Hey, give us some credit. For years now we've had the kids playing *Socialist Victory*, the hottest computer game in the Soviet Union. We have versions for every one of their machines."

"I wish you had some games for the Soviet General Staff."

"Remember that jerk I was dumb enough to let into your leoport files?" Kaissel laughed. "I've kept him around. There are a thousand different channels to the Soviet General Staff."

"Disinformation?"

"Limon doesn't believe in disinformation. What did the So-

viet Union ever get out of their huge disinformation campaigns?
They got a reputation for fabricating lies, that's what they got.
Limon figures that someday, just like the KGB, we're going to
be caught red-handed and he wants to have the reputation of
having conned people with the truth. He's very demanding that
way."

Synmann snorted. "Limon lies with a straight face, and all
the time; you know that, don't you?"

"But he doesn't lie to the Russians. I'll let you look at the
report we dropped on them about strategic weaknesses in their
defense. They were having a fit for months. We couldn't have
lied about that and been believed. To cover those holes they must
reallocate about 50 billion dollars from their offensive budget."

"Oh, I like that," said Synmann.

"Have you seen General Savichev's report on our best version of *BalanceOfTerror*? He spent eight pages demolishing it
in the *Red Flight Review* and still you can see the cold sweat in
his conclusion. It was a worried man who wrote those eight
pages."

"You didn't tell me!"

"You weren't around. I'll have a Xerox made up for you. Can
you read Marxist military theology?"

"I'm quite familiar with Savichev, thank you."

Byron McDougall peeked in through the door. "Hey, Joe.
What are you doing here in this nest of commie lovers?"

Kaissel was offended but said nothing.

Synmann turned to Byron. "Attending a funeral, just like
you."

"I thought I heard war talk?"

"We were discussing General Pavel Savichev."

"Who's he?"

"One of their new hot-shot techies. Gives us lots of trouble,
that guy. Just finished rebuilding their big-bang button. He's
scared of us. He thinks we're going to nuke Russia one of these
days."

"Shivers in his boots, does he?"

"Don't you fear anything, Byron? I've never seen you afraid."

"Well, he can shiver in his boots, but *I'm* not afraid of
Americans. I trust Americans. I know them pretty well. I *know*
we're not going to use those bombs." At Synmann's silence,
Byron added glibly, "My mother told me."

"Obviously you didn't hear that rumor from a Jap," said the
physicist sarcastically. "Yeah, he's afraid of us but he's not
afraid of accidents."

"You're still flying that biplane about accidental war, eh?"

"Yeah. I sound like a broken record."

"Ever since they had records that broke, eh? Relax. Hey, that's right. Back in the days of Hiroshima they had wax records that cracked." Then, Byron, ever the gentleman, noticed that he had been ignoring Kaissel. "I think this Savichev doesn't believe in accidents because he's not expecting them. Why do *you* think General Savichev doesn't believe in accidents?"

Kaissel laughed. "That's a good question." He couldn't stay offended at Byron for very long. "I suppose the Russians believe in cause and effect—that was big in the nineteenth century. Marx certainly didn't believe in accidents; everything had its economic cause."

Byron pulled up a chair backwards and sat down. "They all plagiarized the same books, that generation. Freud didn't believe in accidents, either. If you broke a leg, it wasn't accidental—it was the will of your subconscious mind. I cut my toe the other day and my wife accused me of *punishing* myself. She reads Freud. I can't think of a single nineteenth century scientist who would even look at anything that he couldn't put into a causal structure. Accidents were taboo. Life had to be reduced to Newtonian determinism."

"Well, I've studied quantum mechanics and I believe in accidents," grumbled Synmann.

"General Savichev . . ."

But Kaissel wasn't listening to the conversation anymore. He had suddenly focused on the flaw in Savichev's reasoning. The general was assuming, without being able to stand away and look at his assumptions, that Marxist determinism implied a determined future that you could look up in a book. Since Marxist methods did not deduce such things as accidental nuclear wars, then no accidental nuclear war existed in the future. Therefore if the Americans were introducing the idea of "military accidents" into their defense planning it was because they were *planning* to have an "accident" with the Soviet people. No Soviet general wanted to be caught being deceived by such foul tricks . . . and so it went. Kaissel always found it difficult to follow the "logic" of non-mathematicians. Once he had spent months figuring out what was going on in Laurie's mind.

Let's see now . . . how did one fox such thinking? Always use a man's own logic against him. Peter thought about trying the direct approach; write Savichev a polite letter. But first he would have to look up the *Marxist analog* for "accident."

Hmmm . . . Marx never dealt with the subject, not being a

practical man. Stalin thought of accidents as "sabotage." That wouldn't do. The Russian Orthodox Church thought of accidents as "the will of God." No good. Kaissel was temporarily stymied. Then he laughed because he couldn't even find an equivalent *American* analog. American non-mathematicians had no concept for "accident" either; in the event of unpredicted and unpleasant happenings there was always some rich person/ corporation who was blameable enough to be sued.

Kaissel noticed that Byron was observing him quizzically and that no one was talking.

"Mathematicians go into unexpected trance states," Synmann explained. "It's a mild form of epilepsy."

"I was on the moon," said Kaissel.

"Maybe you can tell me how much Russian I'm going to need to speak when *I* get there," said Byron. "I'll be buying land from the locals in exchange for my beads—and sign language is difficult from inside a spacesuit."

"Our language labs are right downstairs."

"That's just where I came from. There must be an easier way. I was wandering up here looking for Phil Moser."

"Ah, Moser. Down the hall."

Kaissel took him to meet Phil and Moser showed Byron the SMB's prototype Pigeon, the size of a briefcase. Any document written in P-English was translated by the machine into an artificial language called Pigeon. If the operator selected for output in P-Russian, the machine, which was a sixty-four mode parallel processor, printed out a perfect translation instantly. P-English was a subset of English with a vocabulary of 8000 words and a fourth grade level grammar. It was not an elegant language but there was very little you couldn't say in it.

Byron typed in some James Joyce from memory and the Pigeon gave him error messages. *Word not in vocabulary.* *Unknown grammatical construction.* And with cryptic horror, *Idiom!* Byron laughed and typed in, "I am coming to visit you tomorrow across the sands of the moon. I am bringing my wife and a bottle of booze." The Pigeon rejected "booze." Byron substituted "alcohol" and the printer immediately spewed out two lines of Cyrillic print.

"I want it! I want it!" screeched Byron.

Kaissel, ignored, returned to his office to chat with Synmann. "Well, I know what brought *him* here. What are you here for?"

"I'm here because Byron's here. Been hunting him down all over the East Coast. Military project. I need mass and a vacuum. Earth has the mass but not the vacuum. Space has the vacuum but not the mass. That leaves the moon. Byron will have to tell me if it can be built."

"You should come and see us more often."

Synmann put his feet up on Kaissel's desk. "Can't. Too busy. It's your show." He looked very crestfallen, tired.

"We could use your input," said Kaissel gently.

"I've given up on you guys. It's too slow, too chancey. Who knows if we can make a science out of revolution? Or do it on time. In the meantime as long as the Russians are building missiles to penetrate our defense, I'm going to be building ABMs to stop them. I'm good at it. Who can do it better than I can?"

When Synmann left with Byron, chatting and morose no longer, Kaissel just stood there full of hollow. It was like being rejected by your own father. *Synmann* didn't believe. What a waste of a great man, to be hatching missiles like a hen! Kaissel tried to work. He shuffled papers. He let old games go by on the screen. Nothing happened to fill the hollow.

He picked up the phone and pressed an L and an I.

"Limon here."

"This is Peter. Laurie and I are having dinner in the back yard tonight. Thought you might like to join us."

"Hell yes. I feel like I'm growing wires into the Holy Mother. At six. I'm always prompt. Right on the nose."

Good old Limon. There was a man who never gave up. He'd hitch you to his wagon and beat you till he got where he was going. Now that was reliability!

CHAPTER 45

The little jet airplane buzzed south above the wilderness of Quebec, following the rocky stream bed of the Blanche at low altitude. It cut across the Ottawa River near Upper Duck Island and banked to the right over the city for a full U-turn, first along Highway 417 and then up the Rideau. A few strollers in Strathcona Park had time to see it fly straight into the southern wall of the Soviet Embassy which rose up out of the greenery by the river like an ancient blank embattlement. For the blink of an eye—a hole. Then the whole wall exploded outward, as if some satanic magic had converted the bricks into thunderclouds of flame. At the speed of sound the windows along Wilbrod and Stewart and Daly shattered. Above the wall the superstructure of penthouses stood for a surprised moment before gently collapsing into the inferno.

FROM *TERRORISM IN CANADA*, GREEN MAPLE PRESS.

It was marvelous to be on his own. All Charlie McDougall had to do was go to classes and follow directions. But the amount of study horrified him. It was like having *five* fathers loading on the extra work. He couldn't juggle the assignments in his head any more. Sometimes he couldn't even finish by six thirty. He liked to get his homework on the fax and delivered to his father before supper but at least once a week his plans went wrong and he had to slave on until nine or ten at night.

The day his father dropped down the lunar skyhook Charlie spent all afternoon in a Boston tavern watching the descent on TV. It was hard to sit around and drink beer with truck drivers to whom one's old man was a hero. They whooped it up like they had made a transcontinental run to the moon themselves. When Charlie arrived home at dusk, slightly drunk, he found his Dad's usual notes in his E-mail file: selected items from a lab report, a shortcut to take when solving dynamics problems, and a reminder about the diseased Boston girls who hung around Merrimac Street. There was no mention of the moon. Yet Byron had been writing his comments while the moon filled half his sky.

To save time Charlie took to eating meals with a group of four Afghan MIT students in the apartment below him. They were good cooks, even if it didn't taste like Junie's food, and he was glad to help them out with a little money which seemed to be in short supply down there. They were all from families which had been decimated by the socialist armies of the Soviet Union.

Not having to worry about food gave Charlie more evening time for the interesting work on his music. One night at home when he was on a high-f buzz—he'd been mixing drinks, half Pepsi and half Coke—he found he knew enough to be able to create his own language for simulating instruments. After that it was a simple matter for him to write a routine for oboe or violin or harmonica. He put ten violins on file, four of them matching in sound the finest violins ever crafted, the other six of a haunting timbre that could never come from a real violin, wood lacking the proper resonant qualities.

He had been programming ever since he had learned to read by typing to a screen. The courses that MIT gave in programming weren't even worth taking, except maybe their graduate courses, but he had a lot of trouble with the DM hardware. He just didn't know enough yet. His chief cook, Yahya Karargah, who was a graduate student in electronics, took pity and would sit for hours with him explaining the magic of silicon and wire over Afghan tea. Charlie, in return, did Yahya's programming.

Yahya was a quiet man who spoke little about his violent past. His right hand he couldn't lift above his shoulder because of an old wound. He wryly called it "Kalashnikov arthritis." It didn't stop him from repairing the tricycles and ray guns of the local children. Yahya had never seen a computer until he was eighteen and, though he could build them, he was never at ease programming even a simple von Neumann machine, to say nothing of a paralyzer. He would come upstairs and listen for long hours to Charlie's music, wondering at that weird use of a computer.

Charlie's DM strings moved with the freedom of an electron played by ghost equations. He couldn't stop exploring. He doodled up new instruments in pensive moments between studying for his courses and gave their sound-drivers frivolous names like the pooh and the eeyore and the kanga. His own kanga and pooh composition blasted into his ears while he studied the theory of light amplification in p-folded optical fibers.

One day a detailed questionaire arrived by fax from the moon. Who was Charlie seeing, when and why? Dutifully he replied. Back snapped a 5000 byte note, rolled out in six-character-per inch boldface, admonishing him to reorganize his social life. The social contacts he made at MIT were to last him his whole life. Charlie sighed. Something else to do. He joined an MIT aeronautical club—and found himself skimming over the river and sometimes flopping about on Dorchester Bay testing kite-driven boats.

Since Charlie didn't like getting wet he joined a subgroup of the club which had smuggled, from California, a laser disk CAD program that claimed to embody all that was known about aeronautical engineering in half a gigabyte. The rest of the disk contained a set of lavishly indexed aerospace reference books. Since Charlie had the only computer that could easily run the program, they met at his place.

They decided to try to design a cheap aircraft out of standard parts but they got bogged down on its function. Was it to be a weekend aircraft? a long-ranged flyer? a low-powered spy air-craft to overfly Harvard yachts? Someone even suggested that they build it—otherwise what was the point of restricting themselves to standard parts? Yahya Karargah, who was not a member of the group, suggested a homemade cruise missile. He wasn't serious, but there was a gleam in his eye. That struck them as an interesting challenge.

Charlie organized the group into four teams of two; Yahya fed them. It took one week of evenings to learn how to use the program—but only an intensive effort over the weekend to design the cruise missile itself, minus guidance. Range 900 kloms. Bomb load, half a ton. Monday morning they printed out the drawings on the big drafting plotter at MIT complete with a list of the parts and part suppliers.

Charlie's paralyzer was 250 times as fast as an old IBM PC, but it was still no Cray and it took a week of running non-stop to do the "wind tunnel" simulations. They learned that the vehicle performed very close to the design specifications. After that the group lost interest. But Charlie was a completist and spent the next year, off and on, putting the guidance package together with Yahya.

His research showed him that it had taken hundreds of engineers *years* to build the first cruise missile guidance system. But that was a long time ago. With Yahya, Charlie merely stripped down an autopilot toy that his mother had bought for the family Cessna and, after analysis, added a new board designed by the Afghan and programmed by Charlie. The original toy, which cost $2700, landed Junie's Cessna automatically at the Stonefield airport in any weather. It could land at any airport for which it had a memory. It used, but did not require, control tower assistance. Probably it was a direct descendant of the original cruise missile pilots.

Charlie stuck to the problem because it was a much faster way of learning electronics than taking a course from some professor who was restricted, by Einstein's University Law, to move slower than chalk. He needed the electronics for his DM and Yahya Karargah remained a tireless mentor. Once Yahya came back from a trip into the Massachusetts countryside with a whole goat and, over the camaraderie of goat stew, lowered his reserve and showed Charlie how to make a smart mine that plotted its attack in conference with other mines. Charlie listened patiently—he didn't really want to know how to blow up Soviet trucks—but if he was attentive then his Afghan friend was disposed to answer questions about, say, obscure aspects of high frequency sampling.

By using his knack with numbers as an open sesame into the trance underground, Charlie burrowed assiduously into this dark world his parents couldn't understand. He got to talk to wild women who seemed to be very plump for creatures dying of AIDS. For the three days that the notorious Tawn was in Boston, one of Tawn's wives (eVam) courted Charlie. He bought her a diamond mounted in gold for her pierced nipple and took her fishing on an authentically smelly trawler and fixed her mike's "shoe box" to handle the way her voice broke in the high ranges.

Theirs was a doomed romance and, on the last evening, eVam held Charlie's right foot against her naked breasts for hours while she tattooed a Japanese dragon upon its sole, all the while shedding tears from her long-lashed eyes for the lost youth of her twenties, deceased now for two years but not forgotten. The richness of her mournful croon made the needle bearable; partings are sad and must be celebrated with grief. When Tawn himself arrived to borrow a costume from his wife's wardrobe, Charlie frantically tried to slide under the covers.

"Look," eVam said, holding the foot away from her breasts for her husband to see. "Isn't my dragon beautifully ferocious?"

As Charlie traded his DM tricks with other practitioners in mysteriously lit trance halls, he slowly discovered that he was the one who had grasped the fundamentals better than anyone else in Boston. If he built a "shoe box" and listened to an output that displeased him, he could immediately identify whatever electronic alterations were necessary because he understood so well how electrons mimicked sound. He didn't have to doodle with forty variables. The power of it pleased him. He began to listen to trance rhythm constantly, even while he studied.

On Byron's first trip home from the moon, via Boston to pick up his son for a family reunion, Charlie was able to answer every single question his father asked with an oblique reference to trance. He slithered out of the Cessna in trance mode and rubbed noses with his mother. She held him off by the arms.

"They're not feeding my baby right; I can tell!"

His mother was excited when he told her that he was now dancing with the Boston Classic Group. But he took his time mentioning that the old director, Morrison—the one she knew—was dead and the new director was redoing all the old shows with on-line trance-action. Could he ever tell her what a tranced-up Swan Lake looked like, let alone what it sounded like? He felt again the brisance of the hunter flushing a panic of swans from the reeds. Now that was visual music!

Junie screamed when she found the dragon on the bottom of his foot staring at her the next morning as she brought him his scrambled eggs and orange juice in bed. It didn't matter. He could take it. He listened to his parents politely. But he talked a lot to the neighbor's pigs. He loved walking alone in the New Hampshire woods of pine and oak. Sometimes he would hang out at the Stonefield ice cream shop and practice stripping the local college girls with his eyes. He was getting good at it. You knew you were up there in the expert range when the girls turned their eyes away and couldn't look at you. The post office lady introduced him as "the moon man's son." What a bore.

By the time Charlie was a junior, he had MIT down to a science. For the really tough courses he organized five man study groups and ran them like a drill sergeant. He slept exactly six and a half hours per night. His Afghan friends were long gone so he mapped out the restaurants between him and the places he had to go, always ordering the same food to save time. The aeronautics club was out. He had the tranceries for his social life and the dancing for his exercise.

After dance rehearsals Charlie usually stopped for a few minutes in front of Berman's TV store to feed his intellectual life. Berman programmed the set in the window to endlessly replay the latest news. Charlie knew everything that was going on in the world that could be condensed into a twenty second slot and used his knowledge to keep most of his MIT friends posted on the outside world.

Tonight Berman's was featuring a bombing. He watched the replay of the roiling inferno of fire and the dazed, half-burned Canadian staggering out of the apartment next door. It was the Soviet Embassy in Canada that had gone up—killing all but four of the staff. Hey, somebody wasn't messing around!

Then the commentator mentioned . . . *kamikaze* . . . Afghan Jihad. The body of the suicide pilot had not yet been found, but neither had the body of the Soviet Ambassador to Canada.

Oh my God! thought Charlie who later found himself wandering along the Charles River in a daze. It was his cruise missile which had wiped out the staff of a Soviet Embassy. How could it be so easy? He tried to rationalize his way out of it. It was the laser disk's fault! And the guidance system had just been sitting there on the shelf!

That Russian child who had been playing on the lawn of the Embassy, blown against the iron fence, who died in the hospital three hours later—how could Yahya, who fixed children's tricycles, have done that? He remembered Yahya talking about an early memory—the Soviet helicopters circling, their flight somehow all the more frightening for being so slow and deliberate; the whine and the explosions reverberating off the sides of the valley; how he trusted his father as they climbed past refugee families huddled among the rocks while the Soviet ground troops hunted them from behind like animals, his four year old sister slowly dying from her wounds. They buried his sister somewhere on a mountain terrace in Afghanistan near a mulberry tree.

The Charles River was cold and damp, luminous wraiths flickering through the evening fog like lost children.

He remembered pragmatic old grandpa McDougall who enjoyed nothing better than to tell stories about war and soldiering to the children who would someday have to take on the duty of guarding America. "You can justify war on the grounds of *survival*, but I don't see war sitting on the side of *justice*.

War kills more of the innocent than the guilty. If you want justice, you can't get there with war. Damn fool idea!"

Charlie's routine was disrupted. He couldn't sleep. The more guilty he felt, the more he condemned Russia for starting the Afghan war so many many years ago. How long had it been going on now? The adrenaline in his blood made him rage at the casual high tech murder of feudal villagers. Only gross cowards arrayed helicopter gunships against bolt action rifles! What did those fools in the Kremlin expect as the fruit of their savagery after a generation of cultivating violence? Flowers? Praise?

Death in Ottawa was *their* fault.

To slaughter a people with the callousness of a Stalin, to make hundreds of thousands of enemies, to drive millions of those enemies into exile, to kill those enemies like flies fed on DDT, what else could such a policy breed but a superior cadre of dedicated Russian killers?

But intelligent land mines? Homemade cruise missiles?

He saw again the jumpy image of a six year old Russian boy being carried off in that Ottawa ambulance to die. *I did that.*

In the morning he had breakfast at a place where he usually ate dinner. He bought a newspaper. He never read newspapers— he didn't have time. And there it was in the headlines and splashed over the front page in pictures. Wreckage & Death. The Soviets were blaming the United States for the blast.

Morons! It could snow in Moscow and they'd blame the CIA. His hand trembled as it picked up the coffee cup. Did the CIA run the world? It was a nice theory. It simplified the mental effort of beanbrains. Maybe they'd blame their last crop failure on CIA inflitration of the Politburo! He read on. They were "protesting against the terrorist CIA covert sale of surplus 1980s Boeing cruise missiles to the Afghan bandits." He snorted into his coffee, draining the cup. Some people talked without knowing the difference between their mouths and their assholes!

Charlie ate his omelette in silence, the crumpled newspaper on the seat beside him. He *hated* stupid people. And then, slightly calmer, he told himself that they didn't have any KGB agents left in Ottawa to tell them differently. In any event he wasn't sure that a culture, which was having a hard time digesting cheap computers mated to printers, could ever understand the implications of cheap computers mated to weapons.

Aristocracies *never* believed in cheap weaponry when it came along. What could make an aristocrat reach for the smelling salts faster than the idea of a whole population armed to the teeth with an affordable means for killing them all? Especially a rich aristocracy which had been imposing its will through a monopoly on expensive weaponry.

Cheap iron swords and spears in the hands of yeomen swept away the bronze age aristocrat on his chariot—and in the end gave rise to the democracies of Greece and Rome. Muskets in the hands of farmers destroyed the noble aristocracy of the knight mounted on his ironclad horse—and in the end gave rise to the democracies of America and Europe. How many damn fools were killed in their chariots and shot off their horses before the survivors let themselves measure the truth?

There are times when military technology is expensive and there are times when it is cheap. Soldiers who are expensive to train and to equip tend to build around themselves aristocracies of imposed will. But when weapons are cheap and every ruler needs the consensus of his people just to stay alive, the times favor negotiation and democracy.

Charlie drank a second cup of coffee to that.

Million dollar tanks and two million dollar cruise missiles and ten million dollar helicopters and twenty million dollar fighter planes were the weapons of an aristocracy. Such tools outclassed rifles like armored horsemen had once outclassed the iron of the phalanx. But the tide flows in and out.

Certain outclassed yeomen had just voted with a homemade cruise missile. What if peasants could afford to buy a sackful of "brains" to be put into tank and aircraft killers designed on a village computer and then cobbled together by the village blacksmith with his robot machine tools? How long would the communist imperium last under that kind of technological stress? Was that what Marx meant by his "withering away of the state"?

Of course, thought a glum Charlie, a lack of negotiating skills mixed with cheap weapons leads to unpleasant learning experiences like the Thirty Years War of 1618–1648 and the Beirut of the seventies and eighties. Imagine Christians and Jews and Moslems all wearing hand-held cruise missiles in the Texan style! God forbid! But as grandpa McDougall used to say, "Warriors are what you need to tide you through the time when people are trying out mayhem as a substitute for the hard work it takes to make a set of just laws."

Jesus! Maybe I only have another day of freedom.

Charlie was thinking that by tomorrow the siftings from the rubble in Ottawa might reveal enough clues to bring the FBI knocking on his door.

He stayed away from classes. He couldn't get the deaths out

of his mind. For a while he paced to wear off the adrenaline alert. He tried to play the violin, for what could better sing the cry of fear in his lament? But his hands were shaking. And he needed his eeyore. What could be sadder than the tones of an eeyore in trance?

He plugged the special DM keybord into his paralyzer and began to compose the piece, "Requiem Recited by Violin & Three Eeyores Combined." He wrote and changed and played and revised the requiem until he had spoken his grief about a Russian boy in the Ottawa morgue and a four year old Afghan girl buried on a rocky hillside.

CHAPTER 46

Got a way with wimin
  When I'm struttin' down the street;
  They got to reach and touch me
  When I'm lookin' for sweet meat.

> *Got a way with wimin*
>   *When I'm swimmin' in the pool;*
>   *They got to rub and splash me*
>   *When I'm showin' off my tool.*

Got a way with wimin
  When I shoo her off to bed;
  She's got to moan and love me
  When I toss her on my spread.

> *Gotta run from all those wimin*
>   *Cause they're beating me instead;*
>   *Gotta run from all those wimin*
>   *Afor' I lose my big swelled head.*

TAKING THEM DOWN, THE TRANCELVANIANS

Charlie was twenty and deliriously celebrating the end of his junior year by smashing out in the popular Boston Trance Hall where the show was continuous and the waitresses sported silver pantsuits with cutout buttocks. All seven of his MIT classmates became dazzled by the nubility of the evening's singer. She was wearing a golden necklace from which her dress flowed, cupric green, so slashed in a thousand ribbons that one saw both all and none of her body as she sang. Betina

Marvelous was her stage name and she stamped with a trance herd called the Hot Buns.

". . . and I'll take you for a ride and you won't mind going blind . . ."

Charlie noted the ordinary voice—slightly brassy with a tendency to slurring—and rashly bet his friends she would date him. Gleefully they put $200 in the pot, impelling him to keep pace by taking her hand as she left the stage.

"You have a zorchy voice—a lot could be done with it."

She smiled coolly and let him hold her fingers—just long enough to appear unrude. It gave him time to press his card into that hand, a hand so cold his must have seemed tropical.

electronic madman
digitanimal music

Her eyes widened slightly when she read it—DM was a controversial thing on the pop music scene; one loved or hated its sounds and argued endlessly about the awesome scope of its territory. It wasn't just a style. You could do *anything* with it: classical, rock, trance. You could purify the sound. You could distort it, you could add emotional tones and alien themes. DM inspired mystery and resentment. Few musicians could handle its technical demands. But an ambitious woman with an ordinary voice would know what a DM magician could do for her.

She sat down and the cupric cloth rippled, sometimes revealing, sometimes hiding, always teasing. Seven adolescents who had been breathing heavily, stopped breathing. "What do you hear in my voice?" she asked—with a kind of appealing vanity.

"You'll have to come to my place and listen," he said, careful not to strip her with his eyes because he wanted to keep her looking straight at him. "It's beautiful," he said, covertly trying to get a peek at the skin of her breasts. *God, I'm in love with this woman.* He was already planning to take her to an Italian restaurant. "It's a stunningly beautiful voice."

"It's not! I don't think my mouth is the right shape."

"He'll fix it for you with a kiss," cracked a friend.

"I'll fix your kisser with my fist if you don't shut up," Charlie replied murderously.

She smiled and let a hint of a nipple peek through the slashes to silence the pimply intruder. "We were talking about my *voice*"—and she let her eyes slip back from the bigmouth with the MIT shirt to Charlie's face—"and how croaky it is."

"It's got an amoroso timbre to it," he sighed.

"Do you do Real Time or Augmented?"

"Both. I can feed your mike right into a shoebox."

She took his palm and read it silently. Then she looked into his face with crafty eyes. "What sign are you?"

"Aquarius."

"MIT rising," cracked his roommate.

Her face broke into a smile of relief, ignoring bigmouth, and bathing Charlie in sunshine. "Fantastic!" And she wouldn't let his hand go. Charlie's chums, conceding, shoved a money-filled envelope into the other hand.

Betina worked with him. He showed her many versions of her voice. He bathed her car. He rushed her clothes out for dry cleaning to give her extra sleep. One Sunday he called her while she was sleeping and was embarrassed by his rudeness but she only laughed and asked him over to make breakfast for her. She sat up in bed while she ate, letting the sheets fall to her waist.

"Get my kimono for me, will you, sweetheart. The red one." She pointed with a fork.

When she had a new gig, he set up for her. He worked late nights decoding the structure of her voice until he was able to customize a shoebox that transformed her into a siren at the wave of a mike. For that she hugged him and threw in a massage.

Solemnly Betina told him that they could never be lovers because he was twenty and she was, after all, twenty-four—but sometimes when she was stoned on several kinds of drug she let him give her a bath, let him soap her and rinse her and towel her, and when he *promised* to run the sound system so everyone else would be free, she sneaked him into wild parties where he learned to fry his brains on coke and nuke and bam to the strains of eastern music. Once he even got to share a large pillow with a naked girl while they were both paralyzed on bam.

"How you doin', honey," the naked girl said with adoring eyes fixated on the ceiling.

"It's the real thing," he answered lovingly, his mind fascinated by the pressure of the wall on his head.

Charlie's new life thrilled him. He spent all his time thinking about seducing Betina. Devious plans grew out of dreams and finally he convinced Betina to let him move into her place in what had once been the maid's room back in the century when cheap Irish labor was plentiful. It was only a fraction of what he had in his own apartment, but he had Betina.

He promised to cook and do the dishes and not molest her. His theory was that the way to a girl's heart was through her stomach and after a month of being taken care of by a man who loved her, she would melt. Maybe she would even consent to move in with *him*. In the meantime (when she wasn't home) he locked the maid's door and mooned over each cardboard mounted shot from her publicity portfolio, trying out different exotic positions on the tiny bed.

With great pleasure he shipped off a fax through the EM-hum via *geo* to the moon, telling his father that he was not returning to the dour halls of MIT. He was in love with a *musician* and this was it. Within a week his father arrived in Boston from orbit and set up house in Charlie's empty apartment.

Byron invited the couple out to dinner. He flirted with Betina outrageously. He turned up at the Boston Trance Hall and ground his teeth listening to music he hated. While shaving, Byron found a publicity picture of Betina (90% nude) that Charlie kept behind the bathroom mirror in his own apartment. Grinding his teeth, he gave Charlie a lecture about the sordidness of it all. "This is not the girl for you."

"I like wild women," Charlie said stubbornly.

"It's oil and water, Charlie. You're a hotshot up-and-coming engineer. She's a *singer* and God knows what else."

"I don't want to be an engineer," the boy said firmly.

Patiently Byron told him about the moon base. He talked at length to make an engineer's life sound exciting.

Charlie listened and was very careful to say nothing to encourage him. He waited until his father was finished. "I'm a musician and that's going to be my life. Betina and I have a whole life in common."

"It's a dead-end world!"

"What do you know about it? Music is different than when you were young. Then it was just ugly dull beat, beat, beat. It's all creative now. It's a magic renaissance."

"Bullshit!" said Byron. "*Chicago* played great music."

"What a bunch of scratchy shit!"

"You've only heard wornout 33s! I heard *Chicago* when they were *live*. We weren't spoiled like you kids with your antiseptic laser disks and electronic tricks. That was real music, and it had heart. And it's not a way to make your goddamned living!"

"I should be making missiles that kill little kids?" That was as close as Charlie could ever get to discussing Ottawa.

"I'm an engineer and I'm not making missiles."

"If you think Betina is so bad for me, why were *you* flirting with her! I didn't like that."

"I can handle that kind of woman; you can't."

"She and I do everything together!"

"What's this nonsense about giving up school to be with a flake? What kind of woman is that? She should be encouraging you in your studies."

"She thinks I have a great future in music. She's loyal."

Byron was cynical. "Is she a good lay? Never lay a woman unless you have your feet on the ground!"

"Why don't you go back to the moon where you came from!"

"Hey, son. You've got to be reasonable about these things."

"I'm not going to be reasonable!" Charlie raged.

So Byron took Betina out to dinner to have a serious talk with her. She made him laugh and tickled his sense of humor. He softened. They ended up chattering until three in the morning. Not once did she light a cigaret. That made it easier for him to kiss her, but he would have kissed her anyway. He charmed her off to Mexico City for a vacation.

Betina sent Charlie a letter from Xicotencatl with a picture of herself snuggled in Byron's arm, wishing in her large scrawl that he was there so she could have one McDougall lover at sunset and the other at dawn. The letter was forwarded to New Hampshire where his mother had abducted him by car, screaming at him all the time, insisting that if he wasn't going to continue his engineering he had to sign up for the Berlin Conservatory. In self-defense he reregistered at MIT, all the while plotting perfect murders.

It took him only two months to utterly crush his mother. He digitanimalized a secret recording of one of her screaming rages. Slowly he added harmonics. He mushed the words until they were lost against a pure emotion. Here he amplified the rage, there he added piteous undertones. Violins played at dramatic moments. Sobbing children filled the silences. He had the tape cut and sold the rights for the laser pressing to a company that pushed it up to thirty-second place on the hit parade.

Charlie figured it would take longer to crush his father. The bastard had shipped Betina to Paris and paid her off with a pension and gone back to the moon. His father was tough. He would have to bide his time and strike at an unexpected moment with overwhelming force.

CHAPTER 47

See through the mirror of the telescope
the longing moon that would with Earth elope
but circles far beyond the rim of hope.

Dry frost upon the lifeless mountain peak
and powdered ocean floods of lava speak
of hope that cannot touch a moon so bleak.

Yet if sweet life was never meant to be
on stormless oceans; still men, tempted, see
how they and love might seed maternity.

From thrusting loins of mighty commodores,
passion, across uncharted nighttime, soars
to kiss those stark and deadly barren shores.

Upon dark desert dunes such dreamers sow
their minds to make the solid oceans grow
the gift of leafy life, now row by row.

See through the glass of telescopic piece
the moon that with the Earth has found release;
along the crescent edge, a green increase.

ANONYMOUS ASTRONOMER, 1903

Billions of years ago splashings thrown out from the crater
Rhaeticus had cast, along the shoreline of the Sinus Medii, a
bay of molten magma. The initial American lunar base was
built there on the equator so that it could be served by a

skyhook. Every three hours and forty minutes the skyhook drifted overhead and dropped a midget supply rocket down onto the sterile desert.

The upper level buildings of the colony cowered from the naked sun under gray mounds of moon. Byron referred to the locality as Massachusetts Bay and the base camp as New Boston, in honor of the lack of any cultural life, but everybody else called the place Medea Bay and their spartan diggings, Medea.

Spindly carts regularly emerged from the anthills of Medea to unload each awkward skyhook vessel and fill its tanks with liquid oxygen. The men who controlled the carts remained below. Then, three hours and forty minutes later, the ship would rise again on its rocket motors as a new supply ship flamed down to a dusty landing. The lunar base received approximately fourteen tons of payload every twenty-four hours. It took two seconds to order supplies and a fortnight to bring them in.

Medea's considerable daytime power needs were served by an orchard of solar mirrors focused on an array of micro-rectenna panels. As fast as the colony could manufacture them, more panels and mirrors were added—the assembly factory being a robot-equipped tunnel without atmosphere, run by three men who were fanatical about substituting lunar materials for everything that was supposed to come from Earth.

When darkness fell the whole base had to shut down all energy-intensive processing and rely on a small 200 kilowatt nuclear reactor for basic requirements. No one was satisfied. Beyond the bay, the Sinus Medii had lately grown a rectenna web of wires to receive microwaves from a small eighteen megawatt solar powersat that had been built in low Earth orbit and towed up to the Lagrange One position 58,000 kloms above the moon. Even that was thought of as just another backup. The colony's primary nighttime energy effort was going into the construction of Byron's huge underground storage torus.

Each new addition was part of a carefully planned expansion to increase exports. The colony's chief export demand was for an unconventional product—momentum—which the moon was eventually going to be able to supply to the *leo* factories at far cheaper prices than any Earth-bought momentum. Momentum is mass times velocity—lunar mass, with the velocity being added during the Earthward fall.

It didn't matter what kind of mass. If the mass had some byproduct use, all to the better. The export of choice was oxygen, which the moon had in abundance, and which was needed down at *leo* as a rocket propellant. The present stopgap method of delivering the oxygen was to ship it to the skyhook via suborbital rocket, then to pump it as a gas up the skyhook's pipeline, where, at the tip, moving at lunar escape velocity for that altitude, it was reliquified and dropped toward Earth. The procedure was a cumbersome bottleneck waiting to be broken by the completion of the lunar electromagnetic track.

When Byron McDougall took the assignment to construct the initial lunar base he was given one-third of the money originally allocated for that task. He grumbled, even raged. But he had the thinking reflexes of a soldier who was still willing to fight even when his supply lines had been cut. McDougall's base had shafts without elevators. He used cast or spun basalt instead of aluminum whenever he could. He imported only the critical components of the machines he needed, manufacturing eighty to ninety-five percent of the weight of the remaining parts out of lunar metals and ceramics and glasses on easily reprogrammable machine tools. Food was raised locally. The lunar day was devoted to energy intensive tasks such as metals and oxygen production. The lunar night was given over to effort intensive tasks such as design work and machining.

Byron didn't like to admit it but the anti-proton facility he was setting up for DOD was the financial difference between swimming and insolvency. He had qualms about it—it was so secret that the men building it were told only that it was part of the energy storage torus—but his qualms didn't bother him too much; the damn thing was paying their bills.

From his tiny office Byron called Louise who was his chief executive honcho. "Sweetheart, you have a bottle of champagne tucked away for the celebration?" He knew she didn't.

"Champagne? How about a liter of Ralph's turnip rotgut?"

"Any last minute hassles with the powersat?"

"No. We should have power exactly on time."

"Good."

"Your son has been trying to reach you. We'll have the connection set up in fifteen minutes."

"I'll hop right up to the control room."

Byron switched off, smiling slyly. He took out a half bottle of champagne he had hidden, all he could afford to smuggle via rocket and that turtle-paced skyhook, but enough to give them a taste of victory. It wasn't really victory: getting the powersat up so that they weren't ransomed to their nuke was just another milestone, but one certainly worth celebrating. They'd be up

Shit's Creek if they ever had to shut down the nuke for repairs
and couldn't get it up again by nightfall.

Maybe there never would be a final triumph. Byron sometimes despaired. Maybe in a few years this effort might be
just another ghost town of tunnelings to be sifted through by
some future Amanda in spite of all the billions that had been
invested in it. Risk funding was so damned erratic.

Support waxed and waned in Congress. Sometimes DOD
was told to go ahead with the second generation ABM system,
and sometimes after an election the rules changed. Politicians
saw the specs of the new Soviet ICBM and fainted and voted
money—but within the year, and new advisors later, were
grumbling that it wasn't worth it, that the old battlestations
were good enough to contain the Soviets who had been getting
less and less aggressive and had promised, cross their hearts,
never to get mad.

Defense wasn't the only lunar commitment from Washington
but the wavering was even worse on allocations for straight
benefits. Politicians don't like long term risks, not being far-
sighted enough to know how to evaluate crop futures. Some
projects need seed money that will eventually provide a vast
harvest in future taxes from an enriched citizenry. Others are
boondoggle which deflect the same seed money directly into
the millstones of hungry men who are too impatient to plant.
Few politicians can tell the difference. Of course, Medea's
money wasn't all government money . . .

But God help the colony's *business* funding in the event of a
deep recession. Business support had been waning now for
years—almost since the beginning—even though the medium-
term payoff was a certainty. A sixty year old corporation executive wanted his dividend before he was 65. Maybe, thought
Byron, he could sell "New Boston" to the Finns if worst came
to worst—nobody in Europe was doing better than that little
country. Or maybe King Charles would buy the place. "British
Interplanetary Empire" had a nice ring to it.

He slipped out of his office, soared up the shaft, caught
himself, and made his slow leap into the control room with the
bottle high in his hand. "Who's got strong thumbs?"

"How did you get that!" Louise's nature lent itself to excla-
mations. "Did you bribe customs?"

"False bottomed suitcase."

One of the men turned to Byron from the console display
with a smile. "The powersat is up and checking through beautifully. We should get the first beam down soon."

"Is your son as handsome as you?" asked Louise dreamily.

"Why should you care?"

"Braithwaite was telling me he's coming up here to work on the track as soon as he graduates from MIT."

"As a matter of fact, I'm much better looking than my son. You should try older men once in a while."

"Not a chance. You'd see through all of my tricks. I *might* get away with batting my eyes at your son. He's six years younger than I am."

"Actually you might have a chance. When he gets here I'll set you up. He chases older women. I took a girlfriend of his off to Mexico City on my last trip back to the old country. She was a great lay—I've got to give him credit for his taste in bodies—but I was bored to death with her chatter. But what the hell, a lay is a lay."

"Byron! You stole your son's girlfriend? How could you be so cruel? And I always thought you were such a *nice* man!"

"Ask my wife. She'll set you straight."

"But Byron, you know young boys have such a hard time when they're in love—you should leave him what he has."

"I did him a favor. She was using him," he said bitterly.

"He probably needed her!"

That stung Byron's anger. "Like hell he needed her. She didn't have enough sense to send him back to school when he quit to take care of her. For that I could have killed the bitch. I shipped her off to Paris with enough gold to keep her amused."

Louise was grinning. "How did your wife take it?"

"She's divorcing me."

"Byron!"

He laughed. "Something else to celebrate."

The phone rang. Louise took it and chatted with the operator. "Byron. It's your son."

"Hi Papa."

"Charlie!"

Two second pause.

"I'm calling you up to congratulate you. I hear you're not going to need candles at night anymore. Hey, pretty soon you'll have hot running water in the trenches."

"Yeah, I'm pleased. Good backup for the nuke."

Two second pause.

"I just got your comments on my last batch of homework. You're two days faster than my profs. I'm glad I'm getting clever enough with my mistakes so even you can't see them."

Byron was smiling. "While you're on the line I want you to

talk to Braithwaite. You'll be working with him on the lunar track. He's anxious to get you after all he's heard about you."

Byron motioned frantically for Braithwaite to come over while his voice travelled to Earth and his son's came back.

"You still want me to get involved in that thing, eh?"

"You bet. When we get it built this place is going to start to pay. She'll mushroom. We've been tooling up for the track and now that we have the power to do more work at night, we're ready to roll. Boeing is already doing tests on the track ships. We're going to need men. We want you here."

"Say Papa, I'm calling to tell you not to bother to come back to Earth for my graduation."

"But of course I'm coming. I need the vacation."

Two second pause.

"*Another* vacation!"

"Business trip. I'm away too much. Got to see the family."

Two second pause.

"What family? You're divorced."

"*You're* my family. Got to celebrate with the kid."

Two second pause.

"Yeah, but I just quit school."

"You're at the top of your class! It's your fourth year! It's exam time!"

Two second pause.

"Yeah, that's why I quit. It would be silly to quit after putting so much sweat into the exams. I decided I don't want your job and I don't want to be an engineer. I just want to play around and listen to the birds sing. Why put myself in the position where I need a Mexican vacation when I can have one all the time? Where are you going to take your vacation this time down? Paris?"

Byron thought frantically. Was it another woman? "It's the chance of your lifetime! It will make your career! From this job you can go anywhere!"

The pause lasted an eternity. There was no real way to argue over this distance. He had caught a barracuda—and the line was too light.

"I never liked engineering. Good luck in your log cabin. I'm hanging up now."

"Charlie!" The line went dead. *They never appreciate what you do for them!* Byron waited for two seconds, stunned, then he smashed his bottle against the bulkhead wall. Gracefully the champagne foamed as it arched in a slow motion spatter.

"She's ready," said the operations man, as calmly as if he had witnessed a christening. "That's it! The grid is powered."

Louise was rushing over to Byron. "It's all right."

Byron was frozen, his hand outstretched where it had grasped sudden defeat from victory. "No," he said in pain.

"Are you going back to Earth to talk to him?"

"No." Byron paused for two thoughtful seconds, his hand slowly sinking. "I had to push him and push him, the little bastard. He did so well, I couldn't resist. If I didn't push him, he didn't move. So I pushed him. God, how I wanted him here under my thumb where I could make a man out of him." He shrugged bitterly. "It's no use. If you have to push a man, he's not going to move anywhere."

"He'll settle out," said Louise with affectionate sympathy.

"Yeah, he'll settle out. He'll settle out as a third rate musician."

CHAPTER 48

You will remember me for a thousand years.

ADOLPH HITLER

The stalwart defender who faces the past, remembering Hitler, who is ready at a moment's notice with a vast military machine to crush Hitler's next assault, will not live a thousand years. He will be shot in the back by some apparition from the future.

DMK

Fellow mujahideen called Yahya Karargah a mule who shape-changed into a tiger at night. He was alive because he planned his moves completely, cautiously. He did not believe in hand-to-hand combat against an enemy with greater fire-power. Kill them in the never-present. He cast his traps across the fabric of time at places where he wasn't and when his Boolean fingers snatched their victims into the long dark, only Yahya's robot sensors were watching.

By the nineties, endless war against their villages had scattered a million Afghans to the winds, like the Armenians before them, and so Yahya could move over the face of the Earth invisibly, always among friends. Briefly he headed a Paris-based assassination team, worked in armaments, ran a training camp. He was sent to MIT to sharpen his weapon-making skills.

In those long gone days Yahya's boundless ambition had been caged by small arms goals. He did not think like a man with vast resources at his disposal. He was interested in mines and radios, silencers and electronic sentries—the things a one man army might like to carry in his packsack. He conceived military

316

actions in limited terms—of killing one Russian at a time and arranging his life so that he would remain alive to kill another.

Then, with Allah's guidance, he met the son of Moon Conquerer.

A man of a different culture will often think of his new associates as mad. He will watch a friend's antics with amused fascination as Yahya had watched Charlie. Charlie was indeed half a lunatic. He thought like a wholly self-contained Military Industrial Complex. Utter madness! When Charlie wanted a cruise missile he . . . in Yahya's world there was no concept for what he did . . . he became his own Pentagon!

To Yahya who had dreamed only of killing Russians since the age of eight, expert systems were a revelation. He could buy an iridescent disk that, like some Aladdin's lamp, would conjure up at his command an endless army of helpers! There between the cup of his fingers was all that the Americans had learned in a hundred years about building lethal aircraft. It was like being thrown drugged into a heaven full of houris and being unable to choose which one to embrace. He never looked back.

Yahya was careful about whom he involved in any operation. When he decided to build the *Revenge*, he asked his commander to give him only veteran survivors. He was in no hurry. A smart general does not test a new weapon in a critical battle, does not try to invent a whole new form of warfare overnight. He builds a disciplined team.

Yahya selected the Soviet Union's Ottawa Embassy as his first test target precisely because it was an undefended sitting duck. For a man who had played tag with secret police killer Najibullah, evading the RCMP was child's play. His teammates learned, refined their weapon, built more. In Africa they tested a staged carrier that turned the *Revenge* into a deep penetration threat, and he designed an all new, deadly sprinter.

The technologically advanced, but unimaginative, Western press had whined for years that they were unable to cover the Afghan Serial Horror Show because the Russians wouldn't give them Press Passes and lodging at the Kabul Hilton. Yahya, peasant, solved the problem in months. He needed communications with his ground troops; press coverage was only a side effect. He used a variable frequency fax transmission system that broadcast the digitalized images from seventeen dollar Japanese cameras into space for relay. How could the Russians stop or even find a beam that went straight up?

On the morning when grisly pictures appeared in the New York Times showing Soviet Elite Troops commanding the Jerali massacre, Yahya Karargah lost some of the caution which had been the mark of his survival over decades of fighting. He slightly modified his formative plans for a massive attack on the Soviet Air Force in Afghanistan to include the Kremlin as a target.

That the Kremlin was the most heavily defended point on Earth only challenged his rage. The brutality at Jerali had recalled to his mind two events from half a lifetime ago: the *sound* of Russian troops Kalashnikoving the men in Yahya's village and the *sound*—forever unchanging—of that Soviet *Stuka* poised in the air above his childhood home, suspended in time at that last moment before the bombs were released, the final moment when the Soviet pilot could have decided on mercy over murder.

If the Kremlin was heavily defended, so much the better. No one expects attack at a strong point. Surprise is the handmaiden of Victory. And disgust for a strong enemy who terrorizes the weak is the source of meticulous planning. Piss on the Kremlin!

But even the finest of surprises are themselves the subject of surprise. Yahya found himself forced into a premature move. He was covertly using a Saudi Arabian comsat as the hub of his comnet. The suddenness of the revolt there against the House of Saud was catching him at an awkward moment. His plan had already acquired too much inertia to stop, and because multiple attacks require coordination, he could not afford to lose his comsat link. He needed it throughout the week of the strike.

Karargah did not trust his Moslem brothers. The Syrian dogs had long turned their backs on Afghanistan to curry Soviet favor. And Yahya had been sent to MIT on Saudi money. He was not betting his schemes on the goodwill of an unknown Marxist regime in Saudi Arabia. Bijad ibn Jamal was a Marxist and that meant he was an atheist, as untrustworthy as any Russian dog.

Yahya delayed the strike as long as he could, at the same time accelerating the preparations. The Saudi Royalists had a rally and then suffered grievous losses. Americans were being slaughtered. That decided him. His hand was forced. Even then he waited another day because he read the weather reports. A storm, a beautiful missile-shielding storm, was converging upon the worst part of his flight path all along the route to Moscow.

No one questioned the sudden change of plans. The precision with which Yahya could react to an emergency was a survivor's legacy. His comrades trusted his gift. He was a legend within the inner councils.

At the rebel command post, a five hundred year old ruin in a northern mountain valley, Karargah's men launched three missiles in loose formation, each cradled in the arms of a larger winged tanker. The pairs were programmed to separate over the Ust'-Urt Plateau, the tankers to crash into the Caspian Sea.

Each of Karargah's vehicles was more maneuverable than any of the Soviet Air Force's obsolete twentieth century fighter planes. They would not run into any modern fighters until they reached Moscow, and the best of the Soviet fighters were still manned and used a down-looking radar that hadn't been updated since 2001. His warplanes could outfly any human pilot and bollix the brains of any known Soviet computer.

The *Revenge* carried a commerical autopilot, a civilian version of the US Air Force's AI unmanned fighter brain, remodified to fighter pilot behavior with added Karargah touches. That was for emergencies and for the final run over Moscow. The main brain was an inertial and pattern seeking navigator once used in geological surveys. The third sub-brain was the missile's electronics warfare expert. Altogether it was a nice package he had assembled in his Casablanca workshop.

As a crowning insult, Yahya simply filed a counterfeit flight plan to Moscow. Long ago the Afghans had learned to smile at the Russians and tell them what they wanted to hear. The Russians saw only good socialists among the Afghans they dealt with. But there was nothing a Russian did that was not relayed back to the mountains and from the mountains to space and from space to the command center which kept all its records in unbreakable code on portable computers that were always being moved. Soviet air control procedures were known. No enemy, however powerful, is immune from treachery.

It didn't really matter to Yahya if the three missiles got through. He smiled and used an expression he had picked up in Boston. "That's just the icing on the cake."

The main mission was the Soviet Air Force in Afghanistan. He had seventy-four homemade sprinters ready for launch. They were programmed at three priority levels: (1) to attack any aircraft that threatened them, (2) to attack any moving aircraft they detected, and (3) if they reached their target airfield, to attack parked aircraft, control towers, fuel dumps, barracks, in that order. Their cost, minus labor, was about the price of one Mercedes car bomb.

To distract the infidel dogs he had 950 low-IQ missiles with a range of only 30 kilometers. They had propellers, a French pillbox charge that blasted the remaining fuel through a hole that it was quite efficient at making, and a simple brain that could only home on a single preset target. It flew at 160 kloms per hour at housetop level and was designed to penetrate Soviet compounds, government buildings, the Soviet Embassy in Kabul, KGB rest homes, Soviet barracks and the like. Parts of substantial numbers of these had been captured, but none in an assembled state. The brain was mistaken for an electronic camera. The body, with Brazilian manufacturing marks, was dismissed as a poor attempt at a reconnaissance drone. The unassembled bomb blew up when it was handled by personnel unaware of the passcode and was considered to be dangerous by Soviet occupation troops.

Yahya, from long association with the enemy, anticipated nazi-like reprisals after his massive attack. With this in mind he had distributed a thousand digiphones and photophones so that the Soviet reaction might be fully documented in the Western press. How do you disconnect a thousand phones that aren't routed through a central exchange controlled by the Soviets?

On the critical afternoon, the Politburo was in emergency session to discuss the American response to the Saudi revolution. The best intelligence indicated a rapid mobilization of American Fast Strike forces. Already a twenty-four hour airlift was resupplying loyal troops of the Royal Army. It was a crisis.

In the middle of the meeting a series of stunning reports began to arrive . . . 65 warplanes destroyed at Bagram . . . 16 destroyed at Kandahar airfield . . . 47 at Kabul . . . a vicious attack by an unknown high-tech weapon . . . fifty Air Force officers in one barrcks burned alive . . . dumps on fire. Did the Americans want those airfields as an advance striking base? The information officers decided that they had better interrupt the Politburo.

Still the conflict was a distant battle. No one in the Soviet aristocracy even questioned their safety behind the bristling defenses of Moscow. At precisely 15:36 the Moscow Defense Command noticed that a flight of military aircraft from Afghanistan was deviating from its flight plan. They reacted instantly. The errant aircraft replied to their demands, in Russian, casually asking why permission to land had been denied. (Talking cruise missiles?) For a second that caused confusion, but for only a second. Too late, they reacted. One of the intruders went down but two missiles flew right through the walls of the main Kremlin offices, there killing the General Secretary, eight members of the Politburo, and seventy others.

Uproar! A nest of hornets had been bashed. Frantic Moscow

bureacrats could not comprehend what had happened. They did not believe in the power of the workers. They held all peasants in contempt. Their ears had long ago been deafened to Marxist compassion by a boiler room of Marxist rhetoric. Thus they could not even begin to perceive the vile attack on the Kremlin and the morning's events in Afghanistan as a classical rising of the people. Not one of them would have understood Lenin's cry, "Arm the workers to pull down the imperialist exploiters!"

What these men *did* see was high-tech weapons. The attack was, therefore, an American plot.

The alarming reports continued to come in. The KGB offices in Kabul were burning. Dozens of Soviet Army barracks had been attacked. The offices of the USSR-Afghanistan Friendship League were burning. Twenty gasoline tanker trucks were burning. While the relevant *aparatchiki* in Moscow were trying to deal with the emergency, ambulances screamed to the Kremlin. Soldiers raced about in trucks.

Within minutes rumors were awash in Moscow. For one whole lifetime the Soviet nation had prepared to defend itself against another Hitler. Their children had been cautioned. They had even programmed their computers to defend them against Hitler. *Eternal Vigilance!* But *again* they had been fooled. *Again* they had let their guard down. The Americans had betrayed them. The CIA had done it to behead them on the eve of a sneak attack. The Americans smiled but they were just Germans all over again. And the bodies lay across the floors of the Kremlin. Some of them crawled. Heroes came to their aid. The sirens screamed.

What happens when a whole nation looks north, as one, and sees another Hitler, even if only for a moment of panic?

CHAPTER 49

*One day farmer Arcuat went to his local church and heard a
fire-breathing sermon extolling the great Christian benefits that
accrued from self denial. Six months later at the local tavern he
was heard bewailing his luck.*

*"I got no luck at all, nohow. Jist as I was gettin' my mule
trained to work without eatin', she has to up and die on me!"*

Joke circulating across the screens of Medea Base after
Congressman Arcuat (Dem, S.C.) spearheaded passage
of a bill slashing lunar appropriations by 30%.

Byron's staff poked at the budget cuts that had just come
through, and went over their own expenses from five different
angles. They varied numbers and watched the computer dis-
plays recalculate. No sane way of handling the arbitrary cut
emerged.

During the next shift out on the lunar plain Byron chewed
over his anger. He bounced the surface truck along the rutted
regolith. The raised track beside the road swept across the
surface of the Sinus Medii, seeming to pierce to the very edge
of the universe where God's knife separated the light of the
plain's glare from the starry darkness.

There was no doubt that they'd have to shut down track
construction. It was heart-breaking. His mind kept wandering
off to Earth, that goddess of inconsistency. How damned annoying to be working to commitments that the other party kept
violating. *If* they were allowed to finish, within four months the
first graceful test ship would be skimming in tangentially at
orbital velocity, and the electromagnetic link with the leoport
would be closed: with volume, travel to the moon would become
as cheap as a ride on American Airlines from L.A. to New York.

322

One year you had Congress convinced that what you were doing was in the economic self-interest of the United States. You'd ask them if they were *sure* before you went ahead. Yes, Congress was sure. And they backed you to the hilt. They made laws. But the next year they were riding some new fad.

Right now Byron's staff was installing auxiliary systems in little huts along the right-of-way, a series of flywheel energy buffers between the track circuitry and the storage torus. They were there to soak up the energy of a landing—or feed out energy in the case of a take-off. A fifteen-ton ship coming in at 1,680 meters/sec and decelerating at four Earth gravities generates a gigawatt of electricity, enough to power a large city.

The work would have to wait.

Back at the base Byron wandered through every tunnel and shaft, looking for cash cuts. He found a crew repairing the air conditioning. Well, they couldn't shut down Life Support. Maybe they could open a consulting firm to all those awful Earthside towers built in the seventies and eighties that gassed their occupants with recycled tobacco carcinogens—his engineers knew more than anybody on Earth about cleaning old air. It was a thought, but there was no money in it.

He found himself behind the security bulkheads of the "sewer line"—code name for the anti-proton facility which barreled on for kilometers in its tunnel through the lunar crust. This was Joseph Synmann's baby. He was a funny guy. The major part of his lifetime's work was in space—the coils of the leoport, the battlestations, and now a 200 billion electron volt linear accelerator on the moon—but you couldn't drag Synmann off his planet. He was afraid of rockets.

Jaimison was alone on duty. "How goes it?" asked Byron, stooping under a pipe.

"Fine tuning. I'm up to recovering 42% of the anti-protons that pop out of the target. Not bad for the first six months of operation."

The man was modest. That was three orders of magnitude better than the capture rates of the eighties. Byron wondered what it was all for. They shipped off tiny bottles of anti-hydrogen and never saw them again. In the long run he knew what it was for—anti-hydrogen was the nuclear rocket fuel of the future and was going to open up the solar system—but right now its use was still a secret.

Couldn't shut this place down, either. The Department of Defense was already waiting impatiently for the torus to go on line so that they could double their production by running the energy hungry proton beams during the lunar night. Anti-hydrogen was half of Medea Base's reason for being but it wasn't something they could advertise—most congressmen didn't even know they were making the ultimate nuclear fuel, and God forbid that they should ever find out. Some of them were Democrats.

Byron was resigned to a trip back to Earth. More politics. DOD would be a great help in keeping the shop open, but the Defense Department wasn't the power it used to be. Defense spending was declining in both the Soviet Union and the United States—for some strange economic reason—and DOD could hardly afford to pay its own salaries these days.

Byron took dinner in his room. He cut off the intercom and tended his climbing vines, still churning his mind for a solution to the latest change in the financial rules. Adam Smith was wrong; men were not motivated by self-interest—they were too myopic to perceive self-interest farther than a centimeter away. A man would grab for that cigaret because the pleasure was immediate; the surgeon's knife cutting out his cancerous lung lay an unreal fifteen years in the future. He lay down.

Byron's eyes blurred and for a moment, in his hammock, he beheld a religious vision. A luminous hand was reaching out for the stars and that hand was a mosaic of little men held together by little hands in the pockets of the men above. Each little man was complaining about someone else's greed. The conquest of space was not, at the moment, a gloriously cooperative venture. It was a war of pickpockets. But war gave him an edge. He smiled. Once a fighter pilot, always a fighter pilot.

His fingers keyed off the lights so that he was in darkness, the netting easy under his body. What did a soldier do when he was cornered? Byron remembered one of the favorite maxims of his father. "To a *real* soldier there is no such thing as losing," said that very stern man—an absurd maxim, parochially American, but one his father could imbue with a peculiar vitality.

As a ten year old Byron had been no fool. "That's what Hitler said at Stalingrad," he had argued hotly.

"Ah, but Hitler confused winning with being on the offensive. You and I would have retreated and won."

"We retreated all over the place in Vietnam and lost!"

"*Real* soldiers aren't trying to defend something by destroying it."

"What's a real soldier?"

"A common soldier fights well when he is grandly equipped.

A *real* soldier can still fight after his supply lines have been cut. A real soldier doesn't even need any help from Congress!"

Once, on a 300-klom hike with his father, he had crumpled, refusing to go farther, the pain overwhelming.

"A man inured to hell cannot lose!"

"He can die," Byron remembered himself whining.

His son-of-a-bitch father had then bodily lifted him to his feet. "No. You forget. Death comes first—*then* hell. Get moving. McDougalls are tough enough to walk out of hell. Where in hell do you think we came from! You're that tough. We make camp in two hours."

Was life one hell after another? When Byron had walked out of his father's hell into an Air Force recruiting office, the Air Force had groomed him, disciplined him, toughened him, and then sent him to Saudi Arabia to train Bedouins to fly the F-15. It was hell. He coped with that empty time in the desert like a good commander might use a lull in the fighting—to build up striking power. He sweated out an engineering education by correspondence course.

And here he was, out of the Air Force, the inhabitant of another surreal hell, more unforgiving than any Saudi Arabia.

It's always war, he thought, *and war is hell.* This one was a battle to take the high ground from the Soviets. The battle up the slope always cost more than you wanted to pay. Sometimes the home front got tired of the war. Still you kept on fighting your way higher in the hope that once you reached the peak you could dig in and hold it cheaply.

How happy the troops had been to get the shuttle—and then the Soviets began to fly their Snowfoxes to *geo*! Maddened, the USA had built the leoport. But that wasn't the end of the battle; the leoport was only a ridge, a defense line, a trench. Low Earth orbit wasn't high enough. The battlestations to protect the *geo* satellites weren't high enough. Strategists had begun to covet the really high ground, the moon.

It wasn't only the invulnerability of the moon in a world where no fortress on Earth was more than a few minutes away from a surprise death. If lunar mass could be delivered to Earth through the leoport, momentum balancing of the leoport would cease to depend upon auxiliary power: the inner solar system would belong to the men who controlled the moon *and* the leoport.

The dust at the bottom of a minor lunar crater holds more energy reserves than in the whole of the Arabian peninsula. The potential energy of the moon is enough to power the wildest space program for millions of years. Damn the cost! Capture the high ground! Economics demanded it!

And so the war went on. But congressional support was disintegrating because the Russian tortoise had fallen behind again. Wars are not fought on the battlefield alone. They are backed up by a whole support structure, and a loot-hungry-populace is impatient with long sieges.

Byron's father had something to say about long wars. "When the enemy's line is solid, endure, survive, and observe. Do not expect a break to appear at an enemy strong point. The break appears where *no one* expects trouble. Once the break develops, victory goes to the swift. A place which has no strategic import may achieve importance simply because it is not being defended."

The next morning Byron was in the materials factory talking with the man who made the colony's fused quartz fibers. What equipment could he do without in the coming months?

Braithwaite popped down through the hatch. "McDougall. Louise hasn't been able to find you. You aren't wearing your beeper. She has an urgent call from Earth."

"Goddamn that phone! I go all the way to the moon to get away from it—and they still call. What is it this time? Are they going to cancel our transportation passes and leave us up here stranded?"

"I think it was Sam Brontz about the crisis," said Braithwaite.

"Which of ten on-going crises!" snarled McDougall.

"The revolution."

"What revolution?"

"In Saudi Arabia."

"Yeah, yeah. Saudi Arabia is going to revolt when hell freezes over. I know those sand eaters. I know Abdul Zamani, the defense minister. I taught him how to fly the F-15."

"Abdul Zamani is dead. Where have you been? The last I heard the refinery complex at Dhahran was in flames."

"Abdul Zamani is *dead?*"

"Old Poker Face raced in from Camp David and seems to be trying to gather support to send in the marines—but hell, it seems pretty late. The Royalists who were yelling for help are already dead."

"You're kidding me," said McDougall, stunned, but he was no longer sure it couldn't happen.

"You didn't scan the news this morning? We saw rows of royal bodies hanging headless by their feet from the lampposts in Riyadh. Along with a CBS cameraman. The king was murdered three hours ago along with a couple of his brothers.

"My God! And you didn't tell me!"

"I automatically assume you know everything."

"Sweet Jesus son of Allah!"

Back up top Byron replayed the late news on his console screen. The CIA had heard of the superbly coordinated revolt via a shaken CBS camera team. Evidently modern Arab coups weren't the clumsy affairs of yesterday.

Swat! Just like that.

He felt disoriented, remembering the tough men he had trained. Those Saudi fighter pilots had been Royalist to the core. He couldn't imagine a coup succeeding without them and he couldn't imagine them siding with the Palestinians and the Pakistanis and the other immigrants who chafed under Royal rule. Iranian subversion? Impossible! They had never recovered from the war. McDougall didn't let his disorientation stop him from sensing that here was an extraordinary battlefield situation to be exploited *immediately*.

He called up Sam Brontz and they discussed the effect of the revolution on future oil markets. Saudi Arabia still owned half the world's oil reserves, and all of its cheap reserves. Sam had in mind saving the lunar program by reviving the old idea of huge powersats beaming down electricity to Earth. After this affair Americans would want a secure power source. They had neither oil nor nuclear power plants.

Zimmerman came into his office with a worried look. "Such bad news. You heard the news?"

"Yeah. I still don't believe it."

"Look, no American should try already to understand an Arab intrigue."

Byron glanced at his watch. "Hungry?"

"It's cucumber salad day," said Zimmerman disconsolately.

"I'm going to have to crack that whip to get that landing track finished so we can ship in some beef."

"With whose money?"

"You think money will be a problem after today?"

"I see a depression," Zimmerman said gloomily. "No money for the moon. No oil."

Byron was grinning as they drifted off toward the cafeteria. "I see gas rationing in the States, and I'm dying laughing. I'm seeing the pipes bursting in the middle of winter and I'm rolling in the aisles. I'm seeing the Soviets trading weapons for Saudi oil and I'm grinning from ear to ear."

"That bad you see it?"

"I used to like Americans," said Byron with amused savagery. "I'm an American. It used to feel great to go to them and say, 'Here's a solution to a problem that hasn't happened yet.' So how do they react? They sniff daisies and snort coke. And think they are smart asses; even my son. Zimmerman, if an American jumps out of an airplane, you can't sell him a parachute until *after* he hits the ground. I don't even flap about it anymore. Americans are manic freaks who slack off suicidally between crises and then work their elbows to a bone to meet a crisis *after* it has bashed them in the face—all the time bitching bitterly that no one ever told them the fist was on the way. Well, *I* told them. *I* was on my knees begging them, for Christ's sake. It's a mania that will kill us all dead one day, and our Constitution besides, that one last crisis too many, but in the meantime it is no use yammering to deaf ears about how to prevent a coming crisis, you just have to be cool and work quietly until you know exactly what to tell them to do *after* the crisis has them screaming in pain—and hope to God they can get their silly asses in gear as fast as they always have before. Don't have the parachutes ready! Know all about splints!"

"Well done!" exclaimed Zimmerman. "I haven't heard you rant that well for three days."

Braithwaite appeared from behind the potted plants and joined them at their table. "Have you phoned Boston yet?"

"Yeah. Sam's going to send me back to DC to try to sell Congress on putting up the risk capital to set up a production line that will crank out one ten-gigawatt solar power satellite per month. I'll go; I'll make salvation noises, and Congress will stand there with their knees shaking, those Georges who have cut us colonials down to the bone, and they'll kiss my ass and they'll buy it."

"You're so happy it depresses me," moped Zimmerman. The State Department is having a morbid nightmare, and you're happy."

"Give us a smile, Zim."

"How can I give you a smile? My son is in Israel."

"Arabs are killing each other and he's worried. Give us a smile. This is the break we've been praying for. Now the bureaucrats need us in a bad way."

"You really think DC is going to buy anything? With our luck they'll revoke our return tickets and turn off the air. We'll starve. Here, maybe have some cucumber salad before it's gone already."

The next days were hectic. Byron put aside his plans to mothball the colony and started to look at what a real oil shortage would do to lunar prospects. Nobody knew how close they were to paying their own way through slashed transportation costs. The numbers kept coming out right! Boom times right around the corner!

. . . beep . . . beep . . . beep . . . *Goddamned phone*. "Yeah? McDougall here."

"This is Colonel Samson, sir. Please, I must see you up here right away, sir."

"Hey, Joey . . ."

"That's an order, sir."

The lunar colony was stuck with one battlestation and Colonel Samson. Their gun could spew out pellets at greater than lunar escape velocity or muzzle down to circular velocity to shred anything coming in horizontally even though this far from *leo* there wasn't anything to shoot at.

McDougall entered through the hatch without protocol. "Joey, I'm a busy man."

Colonel Samson saluted. He was white-faced. "The Third World War has just started, sir. I thought you should be the first to know. We are in no immediate danger."

Nervous Colonel Samson was not a man anyone took seriously. "And when did all this happen?"

"One minute before I called you, sir."

Byron eased into his fighter pilot role and took over the console, believing nothing. He read the signals professionally. He remembered the men who did not believe the radar operators at Pearl Harbor when they reported a fleet of approaching aircraft. The news from *leo* was two seconds old but it looked like more than a hundred Soviet ICBM missiles had been launched.

He nodded. "Thanks, Joe." And pulled out a microphone and collected his thoughts. So . . . for the third time this week he had to make a major revision of his plans. His first thought was: *If the Reds get the leoport we're up Shit's Creek*. Still it could take a lot of punishment. Even if whole kilometers of hoops were blown out, the undamaged sections could be reformed.

What assets would Medea have if cut off from Earth? A lot. But they didn't have hydrogen or carbon or nitrogen. His mind raced. The Soviets had proved out some nearby carbonaceous asteroids. The Soviet Mars fleet was sitting there with hydrogen in its tanks. Lots of problems. Probably solvable. He'd have to wait for a planetary damage report. He switched the mike on.

"Attention. Major alert. All hands attention. This is Byron McDougall up at the guns. No danger in sight here but the US defensive shield down below is signalling a major Soviet ICBM attack. I suspect that in the next half-hour our financing from Earth will be wiped out. Repeat: ICBM attack. That's bad news. A lot of those will be 78s and the 78 can make Swiss cheese out of the shield which hasn't been kept up to date. Same budget problems as we've had." He paused. His voice was cracking and he had tears in his eyes.

He was thinking of his son. *Damn fool kid, he could be up here now where it's safe.* In hell.

CHAPTER 50

Now the seven angels who had the seven trumpets made ready to blow them.

REVELATIONS 8-6

Charlie McDougall's mother was in Florida living with some rich man, and his father was running around on the Sinus Medii building his crazy landing track. They had the sun and he had the winter snow blasting and rippling in the wind all this day. It was peaceful to be alone without the nagging.

He pulled the truck into a snowbound EXXON station and pumped a single liter of gas which was six percent alcohol and six percent synfuel. The wind was freezing his ears as he tried to keep the snow from blowing into the tank. Damn these self-serve stations. He waded up to the insulated booth and presented his dollar bill.

"Ain't goin' far," stated the laconic attendant emphatically.

"My last dollar," said Charlie.

"Only car I seed all morning."

"4-wheel drive."

Three times when he was off the highway he had to back up and ram drifts. He could hardly see. Pelting dry snow did not leave shadows. But he made it around the bend and up into the trees beside the McDougall house. Stone fences were buried. The flagstone stairs were buried. In all that silence the furcate forms of the winter trees and the lines of the house stood like speechifying revivalists at a convocation of mute white nuns.

Charlie gripped the collar of his coat, took a deep breath, jumped out with his groceries and staggered to the house through the knee high drifts. On days like this he could believe his father's yammerings about energy. New England was going

331

to freeze them all to death yet. But better New England than the moon. God, here in the summer you had the smell of mowed hay and the little swampy brook and the daisies to pluck.

Sophia met him at the door. She was his girlfriend and came from the farm next door. He was pretty desperate for girls because she was flat-chested and eleven years old. There were no trancers in this neck of the woods. "You're late," she sulked.

"Jesus. It's snowing. Can't you see it's snowing out? It took me an hour just to get to the store."

"I've been waiting and waiting!"

"You should be in school!"

"School's cancelled today. Can't you see it's snowing out?"

"How did you get in?"

"You left the door open."

"I'll have to remember not to do that anymore, Softy."

"Sophia! Don't call me *Softy* or I won't eat with you!"

"Did I invite you for breakfast?"

She hesitated. "My mummy said I could eat with you—if it was all right with you."

"You're a pest. Why don't you go home?" he said fondly.

"You'd have to carry me piggyback." She giggled. "The snow is too deep for me in the shortcut and the road is too long."

"We're having macaroni."

"Macaroni! For breakfast?"

"I told you my father is starving me out."

"How can he starve you out? You're the son he loves."

"He loves to boot my ass. He's bigger than I am. He's always been bigger than I am, ever since I can remember."

"Even if he doesn't love you, he's rich. He can afford a shmuck for a son." She grinned shyly and punched him in the stomach. "You shmuck!"

"Softy! I've warned you not to do that. I'm bigger than you are. I'll kiss you."

She punched him in the stomach again. "That's for calling me *Softy*." He tried to grab her to kiss her, but she scooted away and ducked under the table out of reach. "Kissing! Me kiss an onion eater?" She made mock vomiting noises.

"Ha, sauce for the macaroni," he countered gleefully, bringing out a pot to put under her face.

"Doesn't he leave you *any* money?"

"Enough for bread and water."

"You *could* get a job. I've seen your engineer books."

He sighed. "You know what I was doing when *I* was eleven?

I was up to my ears in mathematics, learning how to be some kind of a nut civil engineer who builds things in space because that's what my old man wanted me to do. I could build you a lovely hotel on the moon. But it would fall down on Earth. They forgot to tell me about gravity."

"You could learn."

"I could get a job on the moon, that's what I could do."

"That would be fun," she teased.

"Fun? It would be like New Hampshire in January with the air missing."

"Don't you have *something* to put in the macaroni? Just butter sauce? You're not a good cook!"

"While I'm cooking, you can do the shoveling," he said.

She turned her back on him angrily. "No!"

"Twerp, you want to eat my macaroni, get out there with the shovel!" he said sternly.

"It's still snowing!" she cried.

"Naw. It's just the wind stirring up the drifts."

Stubbornly she marched over to the kitchen radio and switched it on. "That's not what the weather report said! They said it would keep snowing till tomorrow!"

". . . oilfields in flames. A secondary attack seems to be centered in and around Jiddah. It is reported that the anti-monarchists control the airfield. . . ."

"That's New York, real-time," he said. "If you want the weather report you better punch CONCORD WTHR." The radio listened continuously to eight stations and stored and sorted the programs so that anything one wanted was immediately on call with the right code word.

"Is that *another* war!"

"Yeah, they've been killing each other for days now. If they aren't killing Jews or getting themselves bashed by Jews, they spend their time killing each other. Old cradle-of-civilization pastime. It never ends. For God's sake, my father even used to *train* them how to kill each other with modern weapons—as if they needed to know."

"It sounds like Europe."

"Been reading your history again, eh?" Charlie punched out CONCORD WTHR. Sophia was right; the snow was supposed to continue all day until after midnight. "Okay, just dig through the worst of the snow. You don't have to finish. When you're done, how would you like a sniff of my father's best brandy?"

"Yes!"

"You're not to tell your mummy."

"You're bribing me," she accused. Then she sulked and put on her coat and took the shovel and banged the door.

Charlie did a mental calculation, deciding that he could splurge a whole quarter of a kilo of hamburger for the macaroni casserole. He whistled while he crushed a garlic bud, listening for the sounds of shoveling. When he didn't hear any he became suspicious and hunted through the house for Sophie. He found her in the upstairs bedroom, still in her coat and mittens, attached to the upstairs radio by earphones so he wouldn't catch her.

"Don't you have a TV?" she complained.

"I had to hock it. You're supposed to be shoveling."

"Lemme wait for more snow. It's easier that way. Besides there's a new war and I'm interested."

"What war is it this time? The War against Poverty? The War of the Sexes?"

"Nope. It's Russia against the USA."

"Can't be. It's not world series time."

"Is so!" She punched the radio's replay button and activated the sound.

The commentator was freaked out of his mind, but he was telling everybody to be calm. He told people not to stand in front of their windows.

"Hey, you're right for once." Charlie's heart skipped a beat. Zowie. There goes Boston. "I'm glad I'm not in Boston right now." It was an inane comment but his mind was paralyzed.

"They're not playing in *Boston*. You don't have wars in Boston, stupid!"

"This is a rough game, Softy. They're going to *nuke* Boston." He still couldn't move.

"They'd better not! We'll nuke Moscow!"

"Yeah, you got the right game."

"Can we phone them up and tell them to stop? If *everybody* phones up?"

"It's not a game you can stop. You sell your soul to the devil for a few years of peace—and then he takes you anyway."

"They're going to *nuke* Boston?" She was horrified. "When?"

Charlie looked at his watch. "Twenty . . . thirty minutes."

Sophie dived under the bed.

Somehow that released Charlie and he could move. He sat on the bed and peered down at Sophie between his legs. "You don't think the Russians will find you there?" It was funny and he started to laugh.

"You better come down here, too."

"No, Softy. I'm an engineer. I know just the place in the basement to sit where the house won't fall on us.

He took the time to bring the macaroni and two plates with them. It was cooked.

Sophie brought the bottle of brandy. "I get to make the goodbye toast to Boston! I *like* that town."

CHAPTER 51

Men make their own history, but they do not make it just as they please; they do not make it under circumstances chosen by themselves, but under circumstances directly encountered, given and transmitted from the past. The tradition of all the dead generations weighs like a nightmare on the minds of the living.

KARL MARX, *THE 18TH BRUMAIRE OF L. BONAPARTE*

The rampart's flagstones, blown free of snow by the wind, accepted Limon Barnes's pace as it fell with measured leisure. Looking back from the parapet, this winter's view of his shadow Kremlin was somberly Russian. The old Cathedral of Saint Marx the Benefactor was dominated by the elaborate walls and golden cupolas of the Cathedral of Saint Sakharov, asymmetrically blending with the white marble domes of the almost mosque-like Cathedral of the Moon which Limon had commissioned in honor of the founding of the Russian colony at Theophilus. Snow blurred the scene while little tempests of wind-borne flakes pirouetted as they built snowbanks.

Carving out his principality had taken him far longer than it should have. Years longer. Decades longer. The heroic youth who rode horses and carried a sword and had witty conversations with dragons had set out on a trail to victory worried only about the trolls under bridges. Ah youth! But the gaming conflicts between two competing imperialisms were deeper and more intractable than any a mere youth might have imagined.

Yet Limon Barnes was not unhappy with what he had been able to do. The research base his friends had constructed still amazed him. How white-haired Sam Brontz bent all the rules to use that base amazed him even more.

Looking out over his estates, over the white ghost of a New England forest through which he had once sent a Mongol escort to bring Prince Samislav to court, Limon remembered a boy who had been convinced that all Sam Brontz wanted was to market a mildly educational board-game, a boy unable even to conceive that Sam's dreams included a high-powered military-strategy think-tank *simultaneously* capable of modifying both American and Soviet military thought into saner channels.

Sam's task had consumed Limon. He could hardly recall the beardless knight who would spend hours forging chain-mail. He had become half-man, half-library and was now addicted to the company of the Holy Mother. Long ago Limon had settled into the triumvirate role of tyrant and scholar and administrator—but it was the scholar who found time, every day, to talk to his silver-tongued silicon mistress.

Sometimes he translated a poem, struggling with it until he couldn't tell whether he was thinking in Russian or English. Or he might be travelling in time or he might be calling up a Soviet dialectic tomb of the late thirties to flay his mind into the mystical state that came with self-inflicted torture, paring the dry logic down to its essence, following the *correct* Marxist lines to their *correct* conclusion, like some infallible St. Thomas guiding the steps of a blind Pope. Sometimes Limon talked to the Holy Mother aloud though her aural receptors were hardly better than those of a deaf old woman.

He walked along the wind-swept stones.

Karl Marx had his British Museum. Limon had the Cathedral library. He did not doubt that because of his library he was the most powerful political thinker of his generation, and more, that he was a master of global manipulation.

Yet he was wholly aware that he was totally limited. There is a central paradox to power that every man who aspires to godhood must handle in one way or another.

Any god who is a major thinker and a master manipulator can build magnificently to his own design, but, alas, his palace will always crumble for he will have to build it of unfired bricks. There is only one fire in the universe strong enough to bake enduring bricks: the flame of thought. And yet, whoever builds his edifice out of thinking men, *cannot* build to his own design for his bricks will be having a say about where they are put. Alas to be a god!

Limon had never wished to emulate Lenin's failure. Lenin was a master manipulator and he build magnificently to his own design out of men who could parrot Lenin and Marx—but not a single thinker among them. Lenin was vain and thought the fire from his own mind was strong enough to harden the bricks of other men—*his* men, the Bolsheviks. Yet, when Stalin rained on them, these men signed their own death warrants, mindlessly, and hence were liquidated in the thunderstorm, like adobe back to clay, and were no more.

Better to die in an unmarked grave than to be celebrated by 200 million men in the wreckage of your dream, as they chant out the glory of your words, mindlessly.

Limon had long been aware that he could outthink the ponderous Politburo. When the leverage was right, he could even step them through his script. He could monitor the Soviet General Staff and generously offer to give them back a move when they took a fatal step. He could see the nudge that would push the Pentagon away from hasty error. He could lock himself in his office and turn the lights down to dim gloom and call up the giant screen to converse for hours across the paths of machine consciousness with the Holy Mother. It was the graceful decline of the arms race that was the jewel in his crown. No one in the world, except perhaps Sam, suspected that it was he who had pulled off that "impossible" pool shot.

However, nothing that one did by manipulating unthinking men was stable. Perhaps, thought Limon, he could have built palaces—at one flash point there had been a way to turn the Polish people against the Soviet Army. Lenin would have done exactly that. Yet it was more interesting to be a brickmaker, and probe the internal fires that made men strong. Let the bricks find their own place in destiny's higgledy-piggledy palace— which somehow had left a corner for his own beloved Massachusetts Kremlin.

The wind was beginning to howl. He ducked down into the arched interior of the medieval wall. Enough of this useless nostalgia and egomania. Had to get back to work. Work, work, work. And he bumped into Monk Krupskaya, at least that's what she called herself. She was twenty years old and hailed from some hick village around San Francisco. Out of politeness he doffed his fedora. Only America had female monks. It was a peculiar place. He was wearing his Nikita Khrushchev disguise these days, a baggy Italian business suit with large lapels.

"Hi," she said, awkwardly sidestepping, as if she had suddenly decided to follow him and then, in the middle of the decision, decided that she shouldn't. Her wise eyes never blinked. "Kaissel was looking for you."

"I was up on the wall admiring my handiwork." He took pity

on her indecision and gestured with a slightly spastic wave of his hand for her to follow him. He watched the sudden rush of pleasure in her cowled face.

I'm getting old, he thought, *when twenty seems too young.*

Sometimes he regretted that he had been too busy ever to marry. Perhaps he hadn't because the Cathedrals, in their own peculiar social way, provided him with a mistress often enough to remind him how much trouble women really were. He had a love daughter, all of twelve years old, who lived in Arizona and who flew out on her own to visit him once in a while expressly to disorganize his life.

He remembered when his daughter, in a very loud voice, had ordered the Holy Mother to take better care of her Limon, and, not quite sure what the daughter had requested but too proud to call for a clarification, the library computer had muttered on about maternal care in twelfth century byelorussia.

"I brought Kaissel the new batch of samizdat-disks," said Krupskaya. "He seemed distracted."

"Peter is always distracted. This time it's probably the war in Saudi Arabia."

So, he thought, they had smuggled out some more of the samizdats. Russian computer kids were wary of "bulletin boards" because they were too easily monitored by the police, but a samizdat-on-a-disk was a different thing. Its essential form had been invented by Limon but long ago modified into a rich phylum by an enthusiastic class of Russians who called themselves *Bogatyri*—a name referring both to mythical Russian supermen and the most common of the Soviet personal computers. It was not a literary form encouraged by the police.

Limon plugged his vox-card into a slot. "Peter Kaissel."

"Kaissel here," replied the speaker after a short pause.

"Where are you?"

"The Old Lubyanka. Been up all night."

"Haven't they let you out of prison *yet*? I'm sure I ordered your release back in nineteen ninety-something . . ."

Peter laughed.

"What was that?" asked Krupskaya.

"A rumble before your time. Just one of my stunts."

"You like stunts, don't you?" she said admiringly.

"I'm more formal these days. Stunts are a bit scattershot. They miss, sometimes." Limon continued to reminisce. "I lost a good man once. He still won't speak to me—has a good job as a professor at UCLA. I used to like to play Stalin. Heavy role. When you get older you prefer shoe-banging."

"What is a Limon-Stalin like?"

He smiled. "Fierce." He couldn't explain.

When Limon and Krupskaya came out of the wall, while they hurried through the snow, he asked her if she knew that Peter Kaissel was the SMB's greatest expert on Russian Law.

She was still with him when they reached the Old Lubyanka.

Peter's accomplices sat at the new terminal, checking through the latest iteration of Scenario 14. It was an overserious document, almost a satire of an American response to a Soviet "provocation," and not something a typical above-average American general would have conceived—the scenario was afflicted by the short-sighted thinking of a 1930s German Field Marshall who couldn't plan much farther than a six week campaign. It lacked—deliberately—both the imperial patience and the long range pragmatism which appealed to the American military.

The basic assumptions of all such SMB scenarios, in fact, had been derived from a careful analysis of the attitudes of the majority of the real Soviet General Staff about the way they *thought* an American general thought—the mirror image of a mirror image. If you want to tease a paranoid, as Limon Barnes well knew, you brought alive a role right out of his most dreaded fantasy—and added special details. As they had in the past, the real Soviet General Staff would find the scenario a plausible artifact of the American military mind and respond to it.

The strength of this scenario was that it identified three vulnerabilities in the USSR defenses that would cost about one percent of the Soviet economic resources to plug—without, at the same time, adding to Soviet offensive capability.

"Looks good," said Limon.

Kaissel interrupted. "Let's take a break. I'd rather talk about the actual reason I got you down here. I want to put this scenario on hold. I want to run it through the analyzer again. Too many big changes this week."

"The revolution in Saudi Arabia? I'm not so sure that's a change. That whole area has been one big firecracker string ever since the Turkish Empire broke up."

"Heard the latest news this morning? At least a *thousand* Americans have been killed. That's not going down well. State is screaming."

"Blaming the Russians?"

"They may not be screaming out of reflex. I've been on the Holy Mother all night running a search on this guy Bijad ibn Jamal who surfaced yesterday."

"You didn't expect to find anything!"

"Jesus Limon, do you understand that library we've created? We added two new computers to the network last month. Nobody understands her operating system anymore."

"She's biased to correlate data about Soviet affairs."

"Yeah, and that's why she put ibn Jamal's profile together so quickly. She came up with 27 items, none of them meaningful by themselves. He may not be a KGB man but he's up to his ears in KGB money and connections. They even rebuilt his face."

"Shit," said Limon.

Kaissel was talking to the Holy Mother and she was putting maps of world oil reserves onto the screen in various different overlays—all from the Soviet viewpoint but that didn't matter. Saudi Arabia still had the world's lowest wellhead costs and the largest reserves and had patiently waited for the depletion of the West's higher cost reserves. She was in a stronger position than at any time since 1972.

Everybody but the United States had gone over to nuclear power. The best estimate for a minimal-sized fusion power station was 120 gigawatts, far too huge and expensive to build. The United States could get along without Saudi Arabia—but they would be *very* unhappy about it—and, if a Soviet finger was found in that mess, the whole USA would be a nest of fury.

"So much for the Soviet trend away from 19th century imperialist intrigues," muttered Kaissel wistfully.

Limon sighed. "The tempting thing about Marxist historical determinism is that you don't have to be responsible for your foreign policy. Whatever happens is *the result of historical necessity*. Meddlers love not being responsible for their sins." He knew Kovalyov was no adventurist—and never would be one. But it was an old Russian story. The right hand didn't know what the left hand was doing. Centralism generally meant that no leader knew what was going on because there were too many communication bottlenecks. Whole fiefdoms operated on their own. "Maybe yesterday was the first time Kovalyov was ever briefed about ibn Jamal. You're right. We'll run your stuff through again before we put it into covert channels."

Limon couldn't help but peek at one of the samizdats. They were on Belgian disks because they had been smuggled out the usual way, over the telephone, coded on the voice track in the noise. Let a Russian loose and he turned out really good stuff that was exciting to read.

Samizdat-disks were the hottest creative artform circulating in Moscow, precisely because there was no way that the state could control them short of confiscating the computers or limiting their use which they couldn't do without crippling the Soviet economy. The Soviet Writer's Union had been very threatened by the process and had tried to flood the market with sanitized disks—which were immediately gobbled up, erased, and reused. (Blank disks were controlled.)

The permutations were endless. A *Bogatyr* would copy things out of print for distribution to his friends. He would take someone else's collection and "improve" upon it by deleting what he didn't like and adding what he did. Arguments and philosophical discussions were carried on that way—sometimes with great passion because the authors were untraceable. The disks often included hot little utility programs as a come-on. Tips about government falsehoods and scandals circulated.

Limon used them as a constant source of information and as a vehicle to distribute his heretical versions of socialism tailored to the young *apparatchik* with a computer. He kept track of which of his essays were copied and which were erased. His staff used many styles and many themes. Limon was probably the best read author in Moscow among the computer literati and loved the feedback.

Leaning over his shoulder, Krupskaya sighed. He smiled. "When your Russian is more polished, I'll have you published in Moscow. Best audience in the world. They're *hungry*."

"Have dinner with me," she blurted.

Limon did not have time to reply. Suddenly the loudspeakers kicked in, carrying a shaken Boston newscaster repeating himself.

"Shit!" said Limon.

He recognized the dreaded Synmann Accident immediately. He got up and went over to the master console. The disk drives whined.

"What are you doing?" asked a white-faced Kaissel.

"Backing up all our files to the lower vault. Isn't that what the engineers say? When you expect a hardware failure, back up your files. We haven't backed up to the Doomsday vault for a week. Don't want to lose all that data."

"What are we going to do?" asked Kaissel.

"There's *nothing* we can do," snarled Limon, and his head jerked before he could bring it under control. "We've *failed*! We *die*!"

CHAPTER 52

You millions from the West,
Eager to march unrested,
Served by cannon's roar,
Across our plains in test of strength and will
Shall only meet
with hordes
and hordes
Of slant and avaricious eyes!

Whole ages passed for you;
For us one single winter's day
Freezing in the wind
To hold the shield between two hostile men:
White, and Mongol
riding,
riding
Out of an endless grassy steppe.

While you are still in life
And filled with strifing sweetness,
Warm about your hearth,
Go listen to the teachings of your many wars
Beseeching you
to pause,
to pause
before you pass the ancient Sphinx!

Our Russia is a Sphinx!
   Exultant and afflicted,
Drenched in blackest blood,
There in shadow she is gazing at your soul.
Scythian eyes
     gazing,
       gazing,
         With hatred and with steadfast love!

Old World, come to us!
   There's joy in a peaceful hug.
Washed of war and clean,
Slip your sword into its gilded leather sheath.
My cry to you:
     comrades,
       comrades,
         We must seize the day as brothers!

If not—then I curse you!
   We will close ranks like the Hun,
Rob food from corpses;
Herd frightened hordes of humankind to church;
Torch screaming towns—
     burn them,
       burn them,
         Roasting our brother's flesh!

No more will I call you!
   For the last time I speak out!
The table is laden,
A radiant feasting of peace and labor.
I call you all.
     Trumpets!
       Trumpets!
     My barbaric trumpet calls you!

> ALEXANDER BLOK 1880–1921, RUSSIAN
> POET IN CONVERSATION WITH THE WEST.

The Soviet General Staff had planned and prepared for every conceivable kind of American attack—but not this one. As is usually the case when a complacent military command has been totally surprised, the sudden chaos in the caves under the Urals was not quickly being disciplined—communications were blocked and jamming, complicated by the worst storm to hit Central Russia in a century. Contradictions were arriving over non-standard emergency channels.

General Pavel Tikonovich Savichev was pissing into one of a smelly row of urinals in a tiled room with a defective public address speaker when the war began and only found out about it when he stepped out of the urinal and an officer rushed past him, turning to mutter about something terrible at the Kremlin. War was so inconceivable that Savichev's first thoughts supposed a Palace Coup gone amuck. He felt himself insulated from Party politics—but, still, a coup was a surprise. Anyone who set off a bomb in the Kremlin should be shot. He wasn't sympathetic.

But when he reached his duty station he was chilled into action. This was no coup. The Soviet Union was at war!

Wildly different reports suggested that all senior members of the Politburo had been killed in the treacherous attack, probably along with key members of the Moscow military staff. Savichev had not been missed in the preliminary confusion. He was not part of the chain of command which had been set up to initiate retaliation against American adventurist aggression. Savichev was the man who carried the responsibility for a calculated secondary Soviet response. It was his duty to assess the damage done to Soviet defenses after an American first strike, and to assess the degree to which the Russian response had failed, and to prepare, and execute, a second strike.

The precipitate disorder of the Soviet response had appalled Savichev. Once begun, however, the operation had been smoothly correct and the enormous planning had paid off. The computers were working flawlessly. When the maximally permitted response time is six minutes, every detail has to be anticipated in advance and programmed and executed by computers which are not crippled by emotion or hesitation or befuddled thinking. Even the fastest mind of the best general is too slow.

Savichev's mind was in turmoil, and yet he did his job. Part of him was thinking of his wife and beloved children in Moscow—they would not escape—no one would escape—the Americans were insane—and the other part of his mind was the perfect professional soldier, gathering the information he was going to need to finish the destruction of a wounded United States before he, too, died.

Savichev was horrified at the speed with which the Americans were taking out his satellite eyes. At that rate he would be blind in an hour and would have to make his strike in the dark. It wouldn't stop him. He had ample reserves of mobile miniature ICBMs. Another satellite went dead. His mind raced. They were taking them out at ten times the expected rate. Maybe those madmen had secret capabilities that they had managed to hide from Soviet intelligence.

An awful thought crossed his mind. War is the art of deception; was he being deceived? The obvious weakness of the Americans was that they squabbled in public. They warred with each other. They babbled out everything and could keep no secrets. Congress had been publically crippling the American space defense system—refusing money to upgrade the system to counter the new Soviet ICBMs. But what if that charade had been orchestrated to lull the Soviets? What if they *did* have weapons that made them invulnerable? *There* might be the central assurance behind an otherwise senseless strike.

The American attack on the Afghan airfields *seemed* like an incredible blunder. Two of Savichev's aides were speculating out loud that the Americans had beheaded the Kremlin and were now planning a fast airborne advance into the depths of Russia via Afghanistan before the Soviets could recover from confusion—but on any kind of time scale that hypothesis was absurd. The war would be over long before the troops arrived, unless . . . Again, what if the Americans had *reason* to consider themselves invulnerable?

This whole cacophony of thought was passing through his head in mere minutes while the professional soldier assimilated with his eyes a whole world of Soviet sensors and a stream of information that would have meant nothing to an untrained man. It was unbelievably noisy under battle conditions. Sectors went out and faded in. Nevertheless the flux of data on his screens was disturbing. There was no real pattern. It was a masterful surprise attack. Unpredictable. The enemy was destroying vintage Soviet missiles almost before they got out of the atmosphere but the SS-76s and 78s which had been designed to penetrate the shield were, in fact, having no launch problems.

What was beginning to bother Savichev was that there were no enemy ICBMs. Had the Americans been able to apply stealth technology to their missiles? That seemed incredible. What if they had a second generation of ICBMs which were invisible to the Soviet shield? No, not incredible—impossible. Then what *was* the pattern of the imperialist attack?

"No American warheads are coming in," he said to his aide.

It didn't even surprise him to say this because he had not yet noticed his own thought. Once a man is committed, totally, to doing what he has been trained to do all his life, his mind reacts before it thinks, seeing what it has been trained to see. He continued to believe that the Americans were mad to attack while another frantic part of his mind searched desperately for the method in the madness so that it might be foiled. Only in a third mental corner, unnoticed even by himself, was he examining the input of his senses without filtering it through dogma.

A pale reflection of the flaring battle in space flickered across his screens. He was asking questions now. He talked briefly to the military men on Mirograd. He made a frantic call to the Dzhevenki radar station. Nothing could be rationalized. The Americans were responding *defensively*.

For no apparent reason an article he had read long ago flashed across his mind. Accidental war. (The paper had disturbed him then and he had ranted about it to his colleagues. His rebuttal appeared in *Red Flight*. But in spite of the official position, and his own *public* position, he had never been able to convince himself that accidental war was impossible.)

By now the signs of an accidental war were unmistakable.

He did not have time to test this hypothesis.

He did not have the weeks he would need to convince his colleagues. The war was already minutes old.

Two factors commanded Savichev's decisive action: (1) the United States was holding its fire and (2) he understood every facet of the communications system he was dealing with, having rebuilt it from the ground up. Knowing what he controlled and what he could do, he ordered all ICBM launches halted.

Back in the primary command theater, General Volkovoy first tried to countermand Savichev's orders and found that he couldn't because the computer programs, designed with safety in mind, now required Savichev's consent.

Within fifteen seconds Volkovoy stormed through the tunnels to Savichev's command station, shouting to Savichev's aides that their general was a CIA infiltrator and was aborting the defensive strike *so that the Americans could finish them off*. He was wild with fury. He had his revolver out.

Savichev turned, took in Volkovoy's face, and fully expected to die. He did not have time to reach his own revolver.

Captain Sergei Dal executed Volkovoy with a single bullet to the head, then stood stunned at the magnitude of his deed.

Savichev never gave the Captain time to regret this instinctive move of loyalty. He rose. "Well done!" While his other aides were just beginning to react, Savichev was checking the dead general, disarming the corpse and dragging it aside.

Back at the console he paused. He had only seconds to convince his fellow officers of the magnitude of the Soviet error—and no amount of reasoning would do. His simple message, heard at every station inside the Ural fortress, was loaded with emotion. "General Volkovoy has just admitted a fatal act of judgment and has committed suicide. This is General Savichev. I am taking command." He spoke with the voice of the Angel of Death acting on God's command. "There will be no more military action until the situation has clarified. Our reserves are ample to destroy the United States several times over. At the moment we have no evidence of an American ICBM attack. Stand by for new instructions! Stations acknowledge!"

Within seconds he knew he had control. The years of forging a loyal following had paid off, but he suspected that no one else wanted responsibility for the truly awful situation they were in.

The American command had been trying to reach them by phone. Savichev took the call and answered in his flawless English—though he knew the men at the other end spoke Russian. "This is General Pavel Savichev in command of all Soviet nuclear forces as of a few moments ago. Our attack was an error. All Soviet ICBM launchings have ceased. I am aware that the United States has not yet responded. I am *not* aware of the decisions which led to our launchings. The Kremlin seems to have been bombed. We are losing eyes at an alarming rate. I will be able to restrain my own forces with a firm hand *only* if I can continue to monitor your response."

"Are you asking us to stop killing your eyes?"

"That would be appreciated."

"Just a moment." There was a long pause in which another American took over the conversation in Russian. "What's going on over there? We're puzzled."

"How should I know?" Savichev spoke with irritation. "I was taking a piss when it happened. It's running on computer time—too fast for me."

The first American voice came back. "Yes, we will be able to stop terminating your eyes—temporarily. It should take about 30 seconds for the order to go into effect. Please be patient."

Savichev continued. "I've already requested our defensive battlestations to take out as many Soviet missiles as they can. I'm not optimistic about battlestation effectiveness—never was.

I'm afraid your country will take hits. I have to warn you that I will be obliged by circumstance to retaliate if you respond."

"Acknowledged."

There was a pause while the American took that in. To Savichev his own words had sounded like the most arrogant line of his life. "How are your Reagan contraptions doing?" he asked without much hope.

"Your 76s and 78s are penetrating our defenses admirably. Excellent missiles."

"Thank you! But are you going to *kill* any of them!"

"That information is classified. I don't believe you have the proper security clearance."

While they talked, the Star Wars raged.

CHAPTER 53

"If you want to know the difference between a defense and an offense," Joe Synmann had a habit of saying, *"assume that your enemy is* willing to commit suicide *when he attacks. If you can stop him while saving yourself under those conditions, then what you have qualifies as a defense."*

USAF LT. GENERAL WILLIE HARMONY
FROM *LARGE SCALE SIMULATIONS*

In a Synmann Game—using the strict Synmann definition of defense—the probability of war is decreased dramatically by moves which force offensive strength to be given up for defensive strength, and defensive strength to be given up for cooperative effort. The Synmann Game rules do not allow the use of double-talk. For instance, nuclear deterrence cannot be classified as a defensive strategy, for though nuclear weapons may be used to prevent the victory of an enemy, they cannot be used to provide a safe haven for one's own tribe.

DR. PETER KAISSEL FROM *THE MATHEMATICS OF WAR GAMES*

Horrible-Bill Maltby liked to talk to his machines. They were all women to him and he patted them on the rump. He never kicked malfunctioning TV sets. He sweet-talked them into giving him a picture. When a candy machine politely delivered him a chocolate bar after he deposited his money, he thanked it. He especially liked coffee machines because they were nice to him in the morning. "Treat her right, and she'll serve you well," he was known to say to his young nephews back in Texas. His nephews were wary of him because he had once paddled them for cursing a lawn mower that wouldn't start.

Though he loved machines, he didn't approve of *intelligent* machines. Giving them *some* intelligence at the factory was all right but with too much smarts they got hard to live with, and, worse, when they were over-educated they took off and flew combat missions by themselves, acting like a *man*, and taking a *man's* job. He grumbled. Horrible-Bill, a fighter pilot, had been relegated to driving sexy blond trucks in L.A.

So when the Air Force called him up and offered him a gig with the most beautiful machine a recruiting officer had ever described, he was both excited and wary. They showed him pics. He was wary because she looked like one of those smart jobs. But God, she had sleek lines and she had power to knock your balls off. In the end, he couldn't resist. He had to touch her.

"But what will she need me for?" he asked, remembering those factory installed brains. Maybe she could even read.

"Maltby, she'll love you. You've got the touch."

She lived in space. When he first slipped into her plush cockpit he patted her gently on the range-finder and said, "Now you no-good good-looker, don't look to give me no trouble, and I'll treat you right." She fed him and massaged him, and he thanked her. She played chess with him and was decent enough to lose from time to time. "I beat you fair and square that time, didn't I? You didn't cheat and let me win just to make me feel good, now did you?" Tactfully, she said nothing and put on the music he liked. He named her Horrible-Bill's Whore and wondered what he'd do without her when his tour of duty was over.

It wasn't all play, and the defense command put them through their paces testing her systems. "Little Whore," he'd always say after one of her impressive workouts, "you got a strong arm. Now don't you go getting mad at me!"

Horrible-Bill was just as surprised as anyone else one day when his Whore called him to full alert. "Pirates? Jimminy-Goddamn! There be pirates out in this wild black yonder!" Maltby and his battlestation were cruising high, upside down, overtaking a dark California far below, or far above, depending upon the orientation of your semi-circular canals.

There wasn't even time to get dressed. He fought in his pajamas, that's how surprised he was, with his command helmet locked over his head. The Whore was murmuring already, her battle systems up, receiving and sending to her cousins. He

had a twenty-eight minute window within which to be effective—
and an untried weapon. That made him sweat.

The hydra weapon had been tested in the field exactly once,
on the other side of the moon when the Russkies weren't
looking. But what the hell. The Almogordo bomb hadn't been
a production weapon either, and the Nagasaki and Hiroshima
designs were first tried out in battle. A weapon that accelerates
at 100 gs and tops off at ten Earth escape velocities can't be put
through its paces without having the Red team notice.

Horrible-Bill listened to the battle in awe. The golden-oldies
could hardly lift off Soviet soil before blossoming into the colors
of flame. But the 76s and 78s were doing well, sifting through
the screen. Soon they would be coming in "over the ball" and
at an altitude two thousand kilometers below the Whore. He'd
have to fine-tune his hits. His rack had place for twenty of the
hydras—but at the moment Horrible-Bill and his Whore carried only three. They'd run out of hydras before the Red team
ran out of pirates. Anti-hydrogen was still scarce.

The Whore rolled to aim herself at the horizon, her first
hydra already armed and pointing at a million decoys running
interference for the warheads. Earth loomed underneath them,
huge, a half-lit North American continent lazy with clouds.
High frequency pulse lasers were probing the pirate swarm
using Newton's laws to separate out the wheat from the chaff—
the light chaff recoiling more than the warheads.

Holographic computers in the battlestations were chittering
and chattering among themselves, picking, choosing, singing
among more lines of computer programming than had been
written for all other systems combined since God had created
Mark I and Univac. Most of their programs had been written
by the computers themselves.

Captain Maltby waited tensely, in his pajamas, for the assignment of targets. He and his Whore wouldn't be on their own
unless the main command system failed. In those slow moments he patted his woman encouragingly. "We'll get 'em,
baby." This girl he trusted. After 143 tests of her laser targetting
locks, he was impressed. It amused him that the Soviets thought
this deadly broad was just another laser battlestation. And she
learned! Everytime she made a mistake, she learned! He had
honed her into the fastest draw outside of Texas. God, these
holos were smart!

His speakers crackled. "Horrible—you're on. Targets transmitted. Your pirates targetted on US cities. Every one you hit

saves a city. Make it good." Somebody was figuring that the point-defended hard silos could take care of themselves.

Thirteen laser beams shot out toward the horizon, seeking, locking one after the other. "Good draw! Hey, baby!"

Her electromagnetic gun spat out the first hydra. He felt the recoil, surprised, but his woman wasn't surprised. She held her thirteen laser locks.

The first whack of the launch woke the sleeping weapon, releasing the anti-hydrogen genie from its bottle. Outnumbered anti-matter fought viciously with matter. Pions flew. Porous tungsten soaked up the gamma ray disintegration of the neutral pions. Synmann's ingenious magnetic chamber grabbed the charged pions before they died and whirled them into a reaction that combined them with the hydrogen cooling the tungsten and sent a thin stream of ionized gas out of the rocket at twenty times the velocity of the best hydrogen-oxygen reaction.

The rocket leaped down its beam, weaving among the lasers that stabbed out the target cone.

After 52 seconds the hydra was already moving at seven times the velocity of the pirate ICBMs. Then it shed the first of its warheads, a chemically-powered mini-rocket that followed beam-one to a preordained destiny. Still accelerating, the hydra weaved into the path of laser-beam-two, to shed its second head. At four second intervals it lost new heads until there were none left. And then the headless hydra followed the thirteenth beam down to a target of its own.

At one hundred thousand meters per second a tiny warhead needs no explosive punch. One gram at that velocity carries the energy of one pound of TNT. Anything it hits is shattered down a cone of spreading debris. At that velocity a 22 caliber bullet would knife a hole through a T92 tank like so much cream cheese.

The last released head hit first and the first head hit last. There were nine impacts out of thirteen shots. With their probes, command center confirmed the kills. "Hey, sweet baby," crooned Maltby. "You're a knockout!"

Horrible-Bill's Whore wasn't paying any attention. The seconds were precious, and in that time between targettings she was reprogramming her reflexes so that she would not repeat the four misses. During the next attack, over a wider angle and a more difficult shot, she got thirteen out of thirteen, and, on the next shot, twelve out of thirteen.

"What do you want for a present, sweetheart! I love you.

You're a damn smart broad! You've got the brains; I've got the brawn!" He caressed her range-finder with real affection.

Captain Maltby and his Whore with a golden heart had no more sting—but Wilson's Lady was drifting into Pirate range. The two machines were exchanging recipes, revising the algebra of their algorithms, humming, and gossiping over the com lines with the other holos.

Ten of the Soviet 76s made it to re-entry. None of them reached the ground through the hypervelocity hail thrown up by Earth bound chewers.

Eighteen 78s made it through. Fifteen of them died in the atmosphere. Two hit Montana and one of them bloomed over North Dakota, destroying Ruthville.

CHAPTER 54

The men stuck their heads above the lunar crater. Sergeant
Baen pushed aside the frond that blocked his view. Dew dropped
from the moon fern. In the glaring light of the Imbrian plain
the sergeant gasped. There squatted the slimy moon crawler
drying its multiple feet in the sun.
"Back, back," Baen said frantically.

FROM *THE MOON CRAWLERS* BY DIANA GROVE

It was named many things but within three days everyone
was calling *it* the Great Accidental War. In the United States
Joseph Synmann was a national hero to people who were stunned
to find themselves still alive. Newspapers were reprinting old
Ronald Reagan speeches with a kind of sobered reverence. A
rash of bumper stickers screamed: *Remember Ruthville!* or
Nuke the Reds! or *God Saves!*

The United States Expeditionary Forces were having a rough
time in Saudi Arabia, barely managing to evacuate and protect
the Americans there who hadn't already been killed. They were
losing about five trucks a day. In the Soviet Union an intense
power struggle, following the virtual elimination of the Politburo, was making urgent negotiations with Washington almost
impossible. General Savichev had seized control of the Soviet
Armed Forces, reassuring an indignant French Premier that
the Soviet peoples stood by their vow never to be the first to
use nuclear weapons. Poland was erupting after the assassination of the Zomo's Marshal Pryzewiocki. Afghanistan was under
strict censorship. The Italian government had fallen. Forty-
thousand Germans came to hear an American Baptist preacher.

But to Diana, a resilient youth, it was "just a war scare." She

355

celebrated the death and resurrection of the world by reading a romance novel in free fall and writing a 500 word short story for *Planet Stories* so her byline could appear on the restaurant's front cover.

Diana was late for work for the first time. It wasn't her fault. There had been a minor malfunction on the transport line between eyries. Even though she was late she had to stop and admire the *Planet Stories* cover. The ten loving eyes of the monster were still gazing at the blonde woman he was fondling with his tentacles, and the Swede, in his cylindrical spaceman's helmet, was still racing to the rescue, jet packs ablaze. But now *she* was on the cover, too! Diana smiled broadly. And in Chinese red and sparkling green type!

the MOON CRAWLERS
a chilling adventure
by Diana Grove

the DIMENTIONAL FORTUNES OF DR. SAM
by Susan Foibbs

ALONG THE DREADED WARLANES OF BALMUKARI
the man from the atom meets the immortal siren warriors of Io!
George Allan Gardener's latest Odyssey thru interplanetary space.

Ducking under the hatch she apologized to the Rocketship Captain of the Tri-Planetary Space Fleet, quickly so he wouldn't have time to chew her out, then disappeared into the lady's room. Because she was in a hurry she had a difficult time squeezing into her brass scanties. She primped in front of the mirror, fixing her hair just right under the helmet phones.

"Mr. Ling!" she said admiringly to her own image, "you are a dirty old man!"

She eased herself into the bar above the dining room with nonchalance, flowing in as part of the furnishings, as if she had always been there. She hated to be noticed when she was late and she pretended to ignore the customers. If she had arrived on time they would long ago have been served and be ignoring her.

"Diana!"

She turned. A man with pepper hair and blue eyes was smiling lazily at her. He wore lunar togs. He had a strong aura about him and she thought she saw in his face a gentle fondness

for women. That strange heady feeling of love at first sight
struck. She let the emotion tingle through her mainly because
he was an older man and that made him safe. Three other men
hovered with him at a service booth. She glided over, her
willingness to serve at a level above and beyond the call of
duty.

"How do you know I'm Diana?"

"I've kissed all the other bylines."

"And they rejected your clever pass, so you're trying me as a
last resort?" *What a handsome man,* she thought.

"Watch out," said one of the others, "she's armed."

"And beautiful arms they are," said the distinguished blue-
eyed man, undiscouraged.

"I've become a famous writer," she said proudly.

"And tell me, love of my life, what's a Moon Crawler?"

"A Moon Crawler," replied Diana, "is a slimy worm from
outer space who telepathically poses as an irresistible woman.
All that's left of the man in the morning is his toenails."

"Ouch. Let's hug and make up."

"You wouldn't survive. Now what do you want to order?"

He was amused. "I'm rich and charming and experienced, a
classic winner. What did I do to deserve you?"

At the first opportunity Diana asked her captain in his Tri-
planet Rocketforce uniform, "Who is that distinguished one with
those accountant types? He's a regular here, isn't he?"

"McDougall."

"McDougall? *Byron* McDougall?"

"Yeah. The one and only. He has a few interesting stories up
his sleeve. He's an old fighter pilot."

But Diana wasn't listening. She was staring. He certainly
looked like Byron McDougall—only much more alive. So *that's*
why she had fallen in love with him the minute their eyes met!

"He just came in from the moon?" Her eyes darted back to
the corner.

"He *commutes* to the moon."

She leaned conspiratorially over the 1940's space battle cruiser
weapons control array. "Why do I like married men?"

"He's divorced."

"He is?" She shivered at that news. "He likes me, did you
notice?"

"Diana sweetheart, listen to me. You have a superlative bod.
He's a make-em and leave-em man. He's out of your class."

"What do you know about trapping men!" she flared and left
with the dinners.

One thing she liked about her job, the girls were supposed to entertain intellectually as well as serve and be sexy. Ling never sent a woman to *Planet Stories* who wasn't a good talker. It was easy to wedge into this group and dominate the chat. She made her points by touching the men lightly with excited hands—except McDougall. But while his companions caressed her brass armor, she flirted with those flecked blue eyes.

Duties called her away, yet she made special trips back to *his* corner. Only as they finished their after-dinner drinks did she tousle Byron's hair and whisper in his ear, "I'm off at two this evening. Why don't you pick me up then?" She was trembling with embarrassment.

He smiled. "Too bad I'm not on vacation. This war mess downstairs has a stake up all our asses." He scribbled something and handed her a note. "God you're beautiful. For you I could give up working."

Diana didn't dare look at his note until he left, and then she couldn't open it quick enough. It was only his Hilton Hotel room number, the executive suite. She had a flash of anger. *I won't go.* He wanted *her* to chase *him.* It was humiliating. *I'll go home and chain myself to my hammock!*

On the wall hung an original *Planet Stories* illustration of the Princess of Ganymede, wearing a World War II hairdo and burlesque costume, racing between the moons of Jupiter on her rocket sled and being pursued. *Some women have all the luck!*

It was a long ride to the Hilton in the maglev car. She stared at the golden rings of the leoport stretching out to a point at infinity above the Earth's horizon. Close by one could look between the coils and sometimes see a saucer coming through or being shot out: the coils jerked and a glimmer of ripples travelled up and down the golden snake.

The eyries were mostly at the ends of the leoport. *Planet Stories* was in the trailing edge. The fragile connectors which held the city of eyries together seemed like a fairy world that the wind could blow away—only there was no wind. The moon was so bright she could hardly look at it and the sun was blocked off by her car's screens, obscuring her destination.

Tremulously, at two-thirty, she was at McDougall's door, knocking. He opened. Behind him papers were maglocked to the walls. The console that went with the executive suite was alive with readout. He seemed confused to see her.

"Didn't you invite me?" She clutched his note, unsure of herself on his territory.

He shook himself. "I wasn't expecting you."

"I thought you invited me."

He eased her inside. "And I thought you were pulling my leg. Pretty wench, you pulled my leg all evening! So I pulled yours. If I'd known you were serious I would have been after you with roses. I hate being stood up."

Slightly mollified she said, "Where would you get roses?"

"There are ways, my little Moon Crawler."

She watched the tension lift from his face. A lined face could not hide tension as easily as a young face. *He's happy to have me.* He took her in his arms and held her warmly. She let him. *What am I doing here? He's going to try to lay me. I've got to get out of here.* "Did I interrupt something?"

"You most certainly did."

"I'm sorry. I won't bother you. I'll just watch. I love to watch men work. They're so involved."

"Give me another hour. I'm making up a presentation for a congressional committee. Looking at energy alternatives with Saudi oil probably knocked out. It's easier to bring in energy from the moon than dig it up from under the North Pole."

"I thought we weren't importing as much oil from Saudi Arabia as we used to." *Always get a man to talk about his work.*

"We're not. But try turning off fifteen percent of your oil supply when you are all geared up for it, and when it represents sixty percent of your reserves for the next thirty years. That new crew of camel-smelling sister-beaters are throwing out their American oil men. They killed more than three thousand of their own American-trained men in the battle. There isn't going to be *any* production for a while."

Her eyes were glowing. "Will we have to build solar power satellites now? We'll need the moon for that," she said loyally.

"There's a good chance."

"They'll probably just dig more coal," she said with scorn. "I used to live in Ohio. *Everything* was done with coal."

He snorted. "Coal has been having problems for a long time. I could buy a lunar colony for the billions of dollars the government spends on coal related disabilities and acid rain." He called up another display on the screen—hydrogen fusion was still impossibly expensive. "That leaves oil shale, breeder reactors, and solar power satellites. I'm trying to figure out the trade-offs."

"Is there anything I can do? Sort papers or something?"

"Diana," he said warmly, "you've had a hard day. You've had a whole shift for God's sake. Get to bed. I'll join you later."

"I'd rather watch." With a cringing fascination she noticed the terror that was beginning to rise in her.

"And *I'd* rather see some rosy cheeks in the morning." He took her behind the room screen and pulled out the bed netting and casually began to undress her.

She froze.

He backed off. "We've made different postulates?"

She was panicky. She didn't know how to explain. "I have to be between you and the door. I'm crazy."

He changed positions with her, careful not to touch her, instantly willing to put her at ease. "Is that better?" He was puzzled and half-amused.

She nodded.

"Have you ever made love in space?" he asked.

"No." She had never done *that* anywhere.

"You'll enjoy it."

"I'm getting out of here."

"Stay." It was a command. He did not raise his hands.

She stared at those blue eyes which held her own eyes, knowing that he would let her go if she had the strength to leave. "I can undress myself!" She did so, swiftly, awkwardly, and slipped into the net. "Kiss me goodnight."

Quietly, at six in the morning, he woke her. His body was comfortably warm. That part was like Mr. Ling and she enjoyed it. But Byron's body was also hungry. That part confused her. She tried to be like the girls in the videos. It didn't work. It was like trying to take control of a runaway horse.

He stopped. "How old did you say you were?"

"Twenty-one."

"But you're a virgin?"

"Is that bad?"

"Holy Jesus Allah."

"I'm sorry. It's not my fault I was born that way!"

"I'm rattled. You aren't in the space I thought you were in, and I'm astonished that I missed it."

"You don't want me?" She was horny and ready to cry.

He didn't stop making love to her, but he was slower and carefully gentle, less intense, more propitiative, and he took contraceptive precautions because he didn't trust her innocence. The pleasure of it astonished her and she clung to him and wouldn't let go.

"My father used to beat me," she said with her arms holding Byron tightly and her cheek on his chest. "I've had a hard time liking men. You're a good lover."

"How would you know? I'm a lousy lover."

She nibbled him. "You're so delicious. All that's going to be left of you this morning is toenails."

"Maybe it's just space. The first time you try it on Earth, you'll be shocked—especially if you are stuck with a 200-pound man like me."

"I'm never going back to Earth!"

"I am. In three days."

She began to cry in earnest. "Are you going to marry me?"

"Sweet Jesus. I could be your father."

"It doesn't matter. I love you. I've always loved you. When I was a little girl I kissed your picture till the print blurred. I remember everything about you. And just yesterday in *Planet Stories* you said you'd never met a woman who could love both you and space. Well, I love you and I love space and I want to settle down on the moon just like you do."

"Wench, we will discuss this later when you are sober."

Diana called up one of the other girls and arranged an exchange of days off. She did her best not to let Byron out of her sight. He didn't seem to mind. She let Byron work. She helped him when she could. But the minute he showed signs of relaxing, she seduced him with every wile she knew. Sex, for two whole days, was her entire universe.

Only on the third day when he pleaded business was she left alone to think. She took a bath in the massager. She pasted together a paper elephant like she had done long ago in school and hung it over his hammock, with two strings, not one, because there was no gravity. *He's nice*, she thought while drifting in the lotus position, nude, idly fingering the small scars on her belly where her father had once stabbed her. How could a man be so nice? If men were that nice, then she could *have* one and not just dream about them. *I knew it!* she told herself. *I knew there were nice men in the world!*

The hatch of the Hilton room slid open, slowly. Byron's eyes were blazing with blue fire. "Get dressed!" Suddenly terrified, she slipped into her blouse, but his anger couldn't wait and he gathered the collar of the blouse in his fist and shoved her against the wall. "You lied to me!"

She loved him too much to hit him or struggle.

"There is no Diana Grove." He shook her like a dog shakes a rat. "Your name is Osborne and you are sixteen years old. You are jailbait!" He let her go. "Do you realize how much trouble you could get me into?"

"Don't hit me! Don't hit me!" She was cringing.

"You slipped up on some of your stories. I got to thinking.

And the company has ways of checking up on people. We can't tolerate fools in space. Sixteen. My God. Sixteen! You should be home with your parents!"

"My father beats me," she said piteously. "That's why I ran away when I was twelve."

Byron remained angry. Kids always blamed their fathers. A favorite sport. "Fathers happen to be nice guys. Maybe you just never understood what your father was saying. Maybe you are headstrong and willful and don't see the dangers a father sees. You're young. Fathers know, kid. They *know*."

Her face twisted into agony. "You don't love me anymore."

A single tear rolled out of his eye. "Jesus, what a damn fool I am. Yes, I love you. And I'm responsible for you. I'm leaving tomorrow and you're coming with me."

Sometimes the sun breaks through the clouds. "You're going to marry me?"

"I'm going to take you home to your family."

The sun can disappear again behind a thundercloud. "I *hate* my father!"

He took Diana in his arms and soothed her. "Can you remember something nice about him?"

"Why should I?"

"For me?"

She paused, wanting to please Byron. "He bought me a rug."

"Did you like the rug?"

"Yeah."

"Remember something else nice."

She thought a long time, her eyes staring off in the direction of Arcturus. "He always made lemon and honey for my mother when she was sick."

"See? He's a nice man. It's been a long time. Our minds don't remember things well because we are committed to proving that our decisions were right. You'll like him. You'll see."

"Mr. Ling will never forgive me," she said petulantly.

"I'm buying your contract."

"You can't make me go!"

"Oh, yes I can," he said grimly.

CHAPTER 55

Nuclear weapons are the horrible god-face painted on our Soviet Socialist shield, promising the wrath of heaven to any Imperialist Aggressor—but fooling no one. It is the hide of the shield, not the painted face, that must ward off the Imperialist blows.

Even children know that we cannot use nuclear weapons to defend Our Socialism. Call on the aid of the nuclear god—and, with total lack of loyalty, his grim pall bearers will carry to the grave, in deathly repose upon that same painted shield, the very socialist workers on whose heroism Our Socialism stands.

Of what use is a god one cannot invoke without dying? If we are afraid of our own god, can we expect cynical Imperialist Aggressors to restrain from striking us? Will burnt-umber and dragon-red and flame-blue pigments mixed in oil save us? Will ferocious ornamentation save us? No! It is the quality of the leather out of which our shield is made that will save us!

The leather must be stretched on a frame of law, it must be tanned by integrity, and it must be cared for every day, waxed and soaped and rubbed with constant vigilance and duty. The barest crack in the leather must be tended immediately, no matter what the cost, lest we again find our shield penetrated and ourselves bearing false testimony against our neighbors and, in the chaos that follows, again working as katorzhane, slave laborers, in the Gulags of some Cult of Personality.

The Soviet Union will earn respect through the fairness of its laws. And if, by patience and responsibility, we build the greatest legal work that man has ever known, then we shall be respected above all by all nations. When we can say with true humility that even Karl Marx would respect the smallest of our

*laws, then we will have built our mighty fortress impenetrable
to the vilest of Imperial Conquerors!*

LIMON BARNES WRITING AS ALEKSANDR ZDOROVOI
IN THE SAMIZDAT-DISK *BYLINA*

A strange thing had been happening to the mind of Pavel
Tikonovich Savichev. He had been cast by his decisiveness
into the mythos of Russian heroism. Acting out the myth had
given him power. And power had given him choices!

If we look at the history of the Russian people, rather than at
the history of the Russian overlords, we see a Great Thousand
Year Patriotic War against an invader who *did* conquer them:
rebellions, incredible acts of defiance, minor victories, stoic
bravery, sabotage, terrible battles and terrible losses, noble
deeds, fleeings, retreats, treachery and betrayal, sometimes
cowardice in the face of overwhelming odds, sly collaborations,
sullen captivity, recklessness, resignation—a crucible of woes
from which has poured a steady flow of molten heroes.

In Russian folk tales it is the peasant hero who always saves
the foolish prince from himself.

Over the millennium hundreds of thousands of tales of bravery
merged into one archetypical hero. All Russians see him in
their souls. He is a man acting alone from moral principles
against terrible odds. He is Eupaty the Fearless who went into
single combat against an entire Mongol army. He is Andrei
Dmitriyevich Sakharov who went into single combat against the
whole of the Soviet State in defense of the socialist rights of the
weak.

Why does a Russian see his hero acting alone? Why are
Russian workers unable to grasp the Marxist concept of collective action? Some of them even view a man who believes in
collective action as slightly insane. When the state sends such
men, not to prison, but to the insane asylum—it does so with
the concurrence of the populace. The propensity of Americans
to form unions and committees and rights groups and defense
funds at the first hint of wrong is a total wonder to a Russian.

Slavic culture remains one of intransigent individualism—and
perhaps that is why it does so poorly against repression. When
the KGB takes a man, it is seen as a problem which the man
has to deal with as an *individual*. Another may decide to help,
but in doing so sees himself as *another* individual taking on the
KGB in single combat. He does not see himself as a cog in a
mutually self-protecting army.

In such a culture the mythology of the hero is central. His deeds are sung with amazement and awe, and the songs cannot be silenced. The hero is tsar. Not the union. Not the collective. Not the *apparatchik*. Even the cowards and the thieves and the torturers of Russia retell the stories of the national heroes with reverence. Especially the cowards. The Russian mind is medieval in its worship of the hero who stands alone in battle.

Savichev had seen disaster and took his stand and, in the Soviet eye, saved the world in single combat. The story as told by a simple Russian tongue might sound odd to an American ear but not to the Russian heart. Listen to them tell the story . . . General Savichev strangled Volkovoy with bare hands . . . General Savichev physically pulled General Volkovoy away from the lever that was launching the doomsday missiles . . . General Savichev rushed to the podium and gave a fiery speech that brought all men to his side with tears in their eyes, and *they* turned to Volkovoy the Adamant and shot him . . . *our* Pavel called up the Americans with a voice that brought such fear to their minds that they did not *dare* retaliate. A thousand versions of the story circulated, fitted and spun around the archetype.

Yes, he had saved all of Russia, and the lives of the foolish Americans, too! (Russian heroes always save the foolish prince!) He was decisive, that Pavel! He could lead men!

At first Pavel was puzzled by his fame. Then he used it to save himself from conspiracy. And then . . .

Pavel Savichev worked through the evening in his softly lit Moscow study. His son, who was his constant companion, brought him a plate of food. "So," the father said, "Doroshevich seems to think he is taking charge." The two men were discussing the negotiations with the American delegation.

"He is abrasive," replied Pyotr.

"I will be reassigning Doroshevich tomorrow. Think of a tedious position paper I can have him write for my wastebasket. He is showing the coins of his house. I believe he is working for Kasatkin." One had to keep track of the intrigues.

"What kind of paper?"

"A morass!" Savichev returned to the main subject. "And your opinion of Jackson?" He had deliberately met none of the American delegates as yet.

"A man who treads carefully—a smooth diplomat waiting patiently for the talk to die down and the points to stick him."

"Have you observed Jackson and Limon Barnes together?"

"Their relationship seems friendly but formal."

Barnes was here in Moscow only because Savichev had quietly stalled the talks until Barnes had been included. It was not possible for the general to deal with this provocateur openly, certainly not while he was in the United States . . . but there were many ways to buy a cow.

"Tomorrow morning I will be rousing Barnes for an early breakfast." Savichev smiled dourly. Let others deal with Jackson while Barnes was humored and fattened with good food and wine. "Do you suppose this Barnes is as dogmatic as he sounds?" The Acting Secretary of the Soviet Union then replaced his spectacles and went back to reading.

American newspapers, he saw, were forming an odd sort of picture of their "mystery general," a sober soldier keeping the country together while a "power struggle" raged to reconstitute the Politburo. He harumphed. In fact, he was feeling as much enthusiasm for Lenin's invention as Lenin had once felt for the Constituent Assembly. When a man achieves Lenin's power, why should he be bound by Lenin's mistakes? Let the Yankees think him bound! Let his own people think the same! He was not bound!

General Savichev arranged for the breakfast to be an informal family affair. There were limits to what he was willing to provide Barnes—corn flakes, for instance. But he had orange juice and coffee and toast with marmalade and a variety of special jams. He had a cook ready to produce everything from simple soft-boiled eggs to exotic omelets. And he had dishes like smoked salmon that one wouldn't expect to find on an American breakfast table.

Savichev knew exactly what he wanted.

His first impression of Limon Barnes was negative. He felt disappointment. This archenemy of the Soviet peoples was not imposing. He had a slight spastic movement to his walk. His suit was impeccable but he wore a blue velvet shirt in terrible taste. Even his American friendliness was cold. Formally the general introduced his wife and his teenage daughter, Lida, and his son, Pyotr. Savichev raged inwardly as the formalisms seemed to go on forever—he trying to break the ice, and Barnes replying with an absolutely correct and accentless ritual.

He's a dogmatist, thought Savichev, already beginning to revise his plans, preparing himself for an unpleasant morning.

It made matters worse that Lida, who was usually so composed, was scared to death to meet her first American.

She dropped a knife.

Limon picked it up, put it back on the table, and covered her mistake with flawless Russian etiquette.

"How is it that you do not have the accent?" Lida replied shyly in heavily accented American.

He told her about the error-correcting feedback machines he had in his language lab. He made sure she understood and he listened to her questions and answers.

Ah, the man listens, thought Savichev. *And he is kind.*

Limon turned to Pavel's wife and chatted with her formally about Moscow, a little bit heavy on the historical references, but not bad for a man who never travelled.

Pyotr did not wait long with a question of his own. He asked about *Dungeons and Dragons* and Savichev was surprised to see a real smile cross the American's face. Serious talk about the three-headed dragons who were the sons of Baba Yaga and all that rot was not the sort of topic he expected from a Marxist theoretician who was, possibly, a front for the CIA.

Still, Savichev decided to pursue his plan. Obliquely, of course. He waited until Limon's mouth was full of smoked salmon. "I believe you know Joseph Synmann personally."

"He was one of my main theoreticians before he got caught up in defense work. You once wrote a rebuttal of a paper he wrote for me."

Savichev laughed like a bear. "You read that?"

"Of course."

There was a dramatic pause. Savichev rose as if he were to present a toast but there was no vodka. "I have invited you here today so that I can thank you for publishing that paper of Synmann's. I cannot say that, without it, I would not have come to the same conclusion during the emergency. But I would have been slower in focusing my wits, *certainly* ten minutes slower. I'm not privy to your country's defense secrets but by *my* best estimates, if I had waited another ten minutes before acting, the United States would have suffered at least 30 million casualties. That would have been the first round. Both you and I, and our nations, would be dead by now."

He reached over the table and shook Limon's hand warmly. Pyotr waited until the exchange had been complete and then shook Limon's hand himself. Lida gave him a shy peck on the cheek.

"So, you see," said a smiling Savichev, "you aren't all bad. However, sometimes you are very, very bad! I'm inviting you into my study for a discussion. I should like to show you the KGB files we keep on you."

But Savichev, with Pyotr by his side, would not show Limon the files. Instead he played riddles. The general deliberately posed a problem to Barnes concerning the Soviet economy, boxing it within a strict Marxist-Leninist framework.

Limon analyzed the puzzle with Marxist-Leninist tools and put it back together again in a tentative solution. All the while Savichev listened to where this chain of cant was taking them, astonished to find his guest *thinking* in cant. He was ready to pounce on the first unorthodox twist. But the argument was straight; only the destination was unorthodox.

"You are a master deviationist!" he exclaimed.

"If the pendulum of a clock never deviates, the clock is stopped," Limon replied in Russian.

"Ah, and a peasant philosopher, too!"

"My mathematicians tell me that Marxist-Leninist thought is not consistent, and therefore can be used to prove anything."

"So you admit it! You are not a *sincere* Marxist-Leninist!" That was what he had wanted to establish.

Limon was beginning to enjoy himself. "I'm as sincere as the best of the Soviet Marxist-Leninist theoreticians."

"And a comedian!" He poured three small glasses of brandy. He smiled broadly. "I've been interested in you ever since I found my son playing one of your games on his Bogatyr. You've been meddling in our internal affairs."

"A normal Marxist activity."

"An imperialist activity!"

"Yes," said Limon.

"The KGB's theory about you, Mr. Barnes, is that you are a paid operative of the CIA plotting the overthrow of the Soviet government by inflaming counterrevolutionary thought."

"A near-miss," said Limon.

Savichev handed Limon his brandy. "My own opinion differs. I'm a student of Americans. I admit, you are the first American I've ever met personally, but I read. We Soviets make the error of seeing central authority in everything an American does. If we can't find it, we think it hidden. I see a different pattern. Americans are meddlers. No one has to tell you to meddle. It's instinctive. It's like gambling and Las Vegas girls. Americans can't resist meddling. There are *hordes* of you meddlers, all acting independently. Astonishing! Independently! Kill one and seven other American meddlers crawl out of the woodwork! Am I right?"

"I prefer the word revolutionary. It has more dignity."

"What do you hope to gain? Do you wish to make capitalists of us? Do you plot to have a voting booth on every corner in Moscow? Would it make you happy to see a Marxist-Leninist

Party and a Leninist-Marxist Party and the Cadets and the
Socialist Universalists and the Left Socialist Revolutionaries and
the Feminine League for the Salvation of the Country and the
Orthodox Parishes and the Liberal Stalinists all fighting to
represent the masses? Or are those parties not *Russian* enough
for you? Would you impose on us the Democrats and the
Republicans?"

Savichev stopped, curiously waiting for Limon's response,
hoping that he had goaded the man sufficiently.

Limon merely swished his brandy glass. "You are accusing
my countrymen of a lack of imagination. You may be right."

Savichev, in frustration, changed his tack. He talked about
his years of rebuilding the military communications system—
the immense problems. He had found it necessary to assemble
a huge personal apparatus to work around the bureaucratic
bottlenecks. "Recently I have been reading everything I can
find by Synmann. I have also been reading the papers you people
distribute. I was startled to find that one of the SMB papers
was a detailed analysis of how to work around the Soviet bureaucracy by building up a personal apparatus." His voice held a
hint of sarcasm. "I first read it years ago on a Samizdat-disk
under some pseudonym."

"You may not have been unduly influenced by it," Limon
chuckled. "We simply formalized a procedure long used by
some of your better people. It's not a skill you can teach in a
paper."

"But there was a structural analysis behind the report, that's
what I want to know about."

"Hmm. The theory would have come out of one of the
Synmann games. Good stuff, that." He didn't elaborate.

It was *extremely* frustrating, talking to Limon Barnes.

But they got along. On the third day Savichev brought up
Leninist concepts for furthering socialist revolutions by military
means. Limon went down to his room and brought back a
console by which he could network with Massachusetts. They
played games all afternoon. Limon made a very convincing case
that intervention in Afghanistan in 1979 had not only *not* saved
the socialist revolution there but had retarded the conditions
for a successful socialist regime by a hundred years.

It was the first time Savichev had seen with his own eyes the
thing he was trying to get his hands on—a weapon more powerful than any nuclear arsenal, a tool to predict when and where
and how to apply the forces of social change. You could build
empires with this thing! Did Barnes know what he had?

General Savichev normally spent his days talking with one official and then another. He was a one man Politburo. Still, he managed to find time for Limon. The man chilled him. Limon would casually discuss socialist revolutions and then map them out in some model that he would play with until it bored him. He just smiled and said that all politicians had models in their heads—he just had a better one. He would plot capitalist revolutions or Zulu revolutions—he seemed to have no commitment to any ideology. The closest that Savichev heard him come to a moral statement was that assassination was counterproductive!

On the seventh day Savichev decided to brazen it out and offered to *buy* Limon's technology of revolution or gaming models or whatever it was that he was doing. With all these damn pseudo-Leninists plotting against him, Savichev needed an edge.

Limon didn't blink an eye. "Good idea. Change moves faster from the top down than from the bottom up. Why don't you let me take Pyotr to Boston for three months? I'll have him set up a branch office in Moscow. Once you have enough people trained up, you can set them to writing a new Soviet constitution that will give you real power. Right now you've got a dead turkey."

Savichev groaned. A reply like that served him right for being brazen. Limon was the ultimate in sarcasm.

"I'm quite serious—if you are," smiled Limon.

Now Savichev was suspicious. He took an extreme position. "You're a creature of the CIA. Why would you give me tools to make effective revolution anywhere on Earth?"

Limon was still smiling. "Because there's a catch."

"A *catch*?"

Limon explained what the American idiom meant. You could conjure up a genie out of a bottle who would grant you any three wishes you wanted, but there was always a catch.

"A trap?"

"No, a *catch*. This one falls out as a theorem of the Synmann game mathematics. We have a name for it. The god's dilemma. If you want to make a world in your own image you have to make it with men who can't do any original thinking. Lenin's revolution died in 1937 because when circumstances came up which Lenin had not anticipated, there were no Bolsheviks around who could think a non-Leninist thought.

"On the other hand, if you want to make a world that lasts, you have to make it with thinking men. But once you align yourself with thinking men, you lose control of your creation. You get something like science rather than religion."

"You've been trying to lay the foundation for a revolution in the Soviet Union," accused Savichev.

"Of course. I'm a meddler."

"And you've been brainwashing my son."

"I like your son. He can outthink Lenin."

Savichev did not reply. He refilled the brandy glasses.

"Suppose," continued Limon, "that I was making my revolution in collaboration with thinking Russians. Suppose the effort was overwhelmingly successful. Suppose all was accomplished without violence or bloodshed. In the end whose revolution would it be?"

The hero of the Great Accidental War scowled. "Yes, yes," he muttered. He clinked glasses. "To the American Revolution!"

"To the Russian Revolution!"

CHAPTER 56

When the lamp is shattered
The light in the dust lies dead—
When the cloud is scattered,
The rainbow's glory is shed.

PERCY BYSSHE SHELLEY

Last week's snow was dirty with Ohio coal dust. Coal smells were on the air because the wind blew from that direction. Diana was surprised to see her father smiling, surprised to see him contrite, surprised at the warmth of the welcome he gave the distinguished Mr. McDougall whose power awed him.

She arrived back in her familiar rat warren of factories and dry cleaning stores and chunky houses on tiny lots with potholes in the streets, a prisoner of the man she loved, determined to be emotionless—instead she cried with her mother.

Both her parents lavished her with affection. They bought her clothes and a new golden bedspread. They surprised her by bringing home a Kobatsu symphony orchestra with a full set of violas and violins, clarinets and flutes and oboes and bassoons, trombones and tubas and french horns, drums, cymbals, and harps. It was on sale. Her father showed her how to plug in the conductors (there were five of them) and her mother unwrapped the 10,000 best orchestra pieces of the 19th century coded on a compact disk; (the 18th century was on back-order.) They took her to the movies and helped her with school.

It was weird to go back to school with kids who hadn't changed since they were twelve because they hadn't done anything since they were twelve. They thought going to Kansas City was a trip. The boys giggled when they said "boobs" and the girls were virgins who thought SPS was a new thing to put in face cream to keep your pores clean. They wouldn't have known a Solar Power Satellite from a star.

One freckled gawky girl took a liking to Diana and Diana spent hours with this creature spinning stories for her of the spaceways, mixing up tales of the leoport with the Warlanes of Balmukari and the Immortal Siren Warriors of Io. Diana liked to lie. She became a princess of the stars watching from her eyrie's blister the great space battle between the Americans and the Soviets, never mentioning the nameless fear of being crouched inside the "snowball's chance." She told stories about the wickedly erotic underground cities of the moon and those were the hardest to tell because they wracked her soul with sorrow.

But in the end her friend abandoned her for a scarecrow boy with real straw growing out of his ears.

Diana introverted into thoughts of Byron, suppressing all the evidence that might tell her that she had been abandoned. He had hairs on his chest like Samson and she had some of them in an old perfume bottle. He was a hero angel who built stairways to the stars for men who were as yet too savage to understand. His fingers were pleasure, his eyes an ultimate beauty.

In her loneliness she began a letter to him. She wasn't sure she was going to mail it but the poetry of her love ached on her tongue. "Dearest Byron, I had a dream that there was nothing left of you but toenails and woke up in my bed nude (and beautiful as you well know) and imagined sweet touches . . ." She redrafted the letter again and again, hiding it under the lacquered beauty of the symphony orchestra on her desk.

One day—it seemed so long ago that she had been in space— when she came home from an errand to buy milk, her father chased her up the stairs, raging against the depraved McDougall and against his daughter's pornographic mind. He cornered her in her room, crumpling the letter in his fist, spitting on it. Where had he found it? She hadn't seen him this violent for a year but here was the man she remembered.

Karate habits told her to assume a defensive posture. She found herself cringing instead but when he advanced on her, eyes cold, his fist cocked to hit, her reflexes took over. A precisely placed foot smashed into his elbow, breaking it. She never looked back. She grabbed her Diana Grove papers from hiding and leaped through the window onto the porch roof and down into the snow on the ground, rebounding in a run, unprotected against the winter cold.

A man and his wife found her on the highway, half frozen to death, thumbing a ride. They wrapped her in a car blanket and turned up the heat. She told them that she had run away from her mother to visit her father and that he had beaten her and now she understood why her mother had divorced him and she wanted to go back home to New Hampshire. She cried. Only after she said New Hampshire did she remember that Byron's home was there. She knew nothing about New England and had never been there.

The couple were active Christians and though they gave her endless advice about God and finding Jesus they were also practical. They insisted on taking her home, feeding her and finding winter clothes for her from their friends. They insisted on paying her bus fare and, when she protested, they merely smiled and told her that she could pay them back by helping someone else someday.

On the bus she prepared the scathing lecture with which she intended to axe-murder Byron. She wrote in a tight, neat script.

(1) You are a monster!

(2) You seduced me and, not content with just rejecting me, you ruthlessly destroyed the whole wonderful life that I was building for myself.

(3) And once you smashed my life, you weren't satisfied; you had to deliver me to a sadist for safekeeping, just so you could walk away without any burden.

(4) How am I ever going to get a job like that leoport job again?

(5) It's not my fault that I had to pretend to be five years older than I really am. The government is stupid. They won't let me work and they won't take care of me.

I'll strangle him. He better give me some money. He better give me a job on the moon.

Halfway to New Hampshire she realized she didn't have a mark on her body and she wouldn't have a story to tell Byron that he would believe. At one of the lunch stops she went out to a brick wall and bashed her head against it until the side of her face was bloody and swollen. When some friendly passengers tried to ask her what had happened she queered them by talking up the joys of head-pounding.

Looking like an accident victim and in a state of confusion, she stepped off the bus, penniless, at a roadside terminal in a little New Hampshire town. It was madness to think that Byron would be home. He would be in DC or Seattle or anywhere but New Hampshire. She was going to a shuttered home buried in snow. His ex-wife, she knew, was in Florida.

She had to cry in the ladies' room before she went over to the post office to ask about Mr. McDougall. The woman told her he wasn't home, but that his son was, and a no good shifter he had for a son, a good boy gone wrong. Diana panhandled two quarters for a phone call and when she heard the son's voice, hung up without saying a word. She walked in the snow, ten kloms, feet frozen, until she reached the McDougall place.

A dark-haired young man with Byron's blue eyes answered the door. "You've been walking. Your car is stuck? Hey, I have a truck!"

"No." Frigidly. "I'm your father's mistress."

He tried to say seven things in reply and only a squeak came out. She walked past him, hugging herself. He rushed after her. "Hey, you're cold."

"Well, take me to your radiator."

"You've had an accident."

She touched her face. The swelling was down. "The black eye is pretty awful, isn't it? My old man beat me up for sleeping with your old man."

"My father abandoned you?"

"Yeah."

"Didn't he give you a free year in Paris?"

"He gave me a free year in an Ohio coal town."

"You could have asked for more! You have to bargain with him."

"You don't ask for things when you're in love."

"You're too young for him."

"I *don't* think *that* is *any* of your *business!*"

"Are you pregnant?"

"*No* I'm *not* pregnant," she said through gritted teeth.

"I'll have some hot tea ready in a minute."

She sat down in the kitchen by the radiator and took her boots off. Her feet were white and numb. "Where is he?"

"I just got a check from Houston, but that was a week ago."

"A lot of good that does me." She started to cry.

"Aw, hey now. It can't be that bad."

"If you come over here with your big blue eyes and try to comfort me, I'll slug you!"

CHAPTER 57

And if I ever meet her
I might never say goodbye;
and if I ever see her soul
then mine will light the sky.

She roams within my haunting place,
a melody of moving grace,
behind my conscious stare—and oh,
I yearn to turn my face and find her there.

A TRACER'S LAMENT

Diana sulked in the master bedroom except for meals. Across the veranda she had a view of snowed-in farmlands, the kind of rolling landscape rich people purchase when they are bored by the city. The room had a handcrafted look with walnut trim and carved walnut doors. It was wholly a woman's room. Perfume bottles were on display, but things like brass hairbrushes were neatly placed in drawers. Two portraits hung over the bed: a woman lit by sun reflected from spring leaves and a man glooming beneath some autumnal overcast in a fighter pilot uniform. The portrait of Mrs. McDougall, Diana hid under the bed. *His* portrait she launched upon the bed, a raft for a lonely girl to cling to in a king-sized ocean of softness. But Byron's face was as cold as glass to her cheeks.

Sulking made Diana restless. She had never tried it before and didn't like it. After three days she took a couple of hours off to bake a chicken casserole and that was such a relief that she began trying on Mrs. McDougall's clothes, modifying the ones she liked on the sewing machine.

The only excitement came during her fourth day of sewing when a rock crashed through the window and Charlie ran outdoors to yell at someone. Afterwards he came to the master bedroom with glass and cutting tools and putty.

"What was that?"

Charlie laughed. "Just the girl next door. She has a crush on me and is jealous of you."

"You can tell her that I'm your father's private slut."

"I would never say that about you. You're one of my father's *victims*."

Her eyes narrowed. "Your father has *victims*, eh? And you think I'm one of them? Is that how *you* got to be a basket case?"

The next day a timid knock interrupted her concentration. "Like to come to the village? I'm going for groceries."

"Thank God! Did Byron finally send you more money?"

"Naw. I did some electrical work at the Hodge farm."

"You worked?" she exclaimed incredulously.

"Yeah, you're eating me out of house and home."

"And here I thought I was starving!"

"So today we'll have steak. I figured that if my father can keep *my* girlfriend in Paris, I can at least buy *his* girlfriend a steak."

In the village she noticed that the highway restaurant needed a waitress and she went in and took the job. It was a drag to live with a wastrel like Charlie who ate macaroni every night, sweet as he was. She was used to money.

Sometimes she hitchhiked home after work. Sometimes Charlie was waiting for her if she paid for the gas. Once he arrived to pick her up and found her being hassled by three toughs. The leader blew smoke in Charlie's face.

"You being bothered by these lung disease cases?" he asked.

"Stay out of this, Charlie. I know karate."

"It's not a job for a lady." He assumed the stance of a battle-tried colonel. "Leave!"

They left.

"How did you do that?" She was amazed.

He laughed. "Ordering men around and saving women and children runs in the family. Old military tradition. I'm considered the sissy of the McDougalls."

Diana decided to become independent of Charlie and bought a three-hundred dollar car and a pay-by-the-week insurance policy after she had wangled some gas ration tickets. The car got her halfway home.

"Charlie," said a plaintive voice over the phone. "I'm stuck on the Stonefield Road at the hairpin. Would it be too much trouble for you to come and get me? Bring a chain."

"A chain?"

"To pull my car."

"Your car!"

"I bought a car."

"How much did you pay?"

She muttered an answer.

"Good God! You can't buy an unrusted hubcap for that!"

"It made noises and quit. Can you fix it?"

He sighed. "Maybe it's the spark plugs."

The engine had seized. "How much does a new engine cost?" she whined.

"Oh, maybe a thousand dollars for a second-hand clunker."

"But it's such a small car!"

She cried all the way home. He tried to console her by telling her he could get something for the tires, and maybe sell the map display and a few other parts, but she was unconsolable. He began to feel so sorry for her that the next day he towed the car off to a friend's garage and spent all weekend doing an engine job. Monday evening he picked her up.

"Where's the truck?"

"I came in your car. It's parked out back."

"I didn't know you could fix cars!"

"I can't but I used to repair obsolete jet engines at MIT."

"Where did you get the money for parts?"

Charlie grinned like a man who has just won somebody else's gambling money. "My father is a millionaire. I have a kind of credit around here. He grumbles like hell but he pays up."

"I don't understand you. Why do you loaf around when you could get a job as a mechanic?"

"Diana! That's work! I only did it for you."

"You're a sweetie pie. How can I sacrifice myself for you?"

"Entertain me in bed."

"I belong to your father!" she said indignantly.

"What kind of garbage is that," he lamented.

"A woman belongs to the man who took her virginity."

He guffawed. "You believe that drivel?"

"I certainly do!"

"You sound like my grandfather."

"I'm *not* your grandfather."

"Well, all right. I won't go that far. But you sound like someone right out of the flaky-eighties."

"Are you in love with me?" asked warily.

"An inch, going on an inch and a quarter."

"How many centimeters is that?"

"Almost three."

"Even your father can do better than that," she replied stiffly. But as they were thrown around the hairpin turn on Stonefield Road she kissed him. "If I hadn't met your father first, I'd love you an inch and a quarter, too."

"Watch that stuff. You'll get dirty. I couldn't wash all the grease off."

"I don't care. I want to be nice to you. What was the nicest thing that ever happened to you—besides sexing with the neighbor's sow."

A faraway smile crossed his face. He danced the car in a little back-and-forth skid. "Betina let me give her a bath."

Diana screeched. "I'll give you a bath!"

She sudsed him carefully, in no hurry to finish caressing away the intractable black grease. It made her lonely to touch him, and happy at the same time. He tried to convince her to join him in the tub but she refused. When she was toweling him afterwards, he tried to kiss her and was almost rough in the way he held her wrist and wouldn't let her go. She hit him and they had a fight. She ran to the master bedroom and locked the door—but hugging Byron's angular portrait proved to be no way to go to sleep. She kept thinking about crazy Charlie with the dragon on the bottom of his foot.

At four in the morning she wrapped a sheet around her body and shuffled to the kitchen for a glass of milk. She returned by way of Charlie's study, curiosity driving her to rifle through his papers—schoolwork, equations, printouts, drawings, projects.

Charlie appeared at the door in his pajamas. "You're not asleep." He paused. "I'm sorry about the fight."

"I'm not mad at you. What are all those things?"

"I used to go to MIT."

"What are you?"

"I make buzz-bombs that kill babies. Naw. I'm a lunar engineer." He thought about his answer. "Actually, I don't know what I am; I didn't specialize in lunar construction problems until my last year."

"Is that what these diagrams are?"

"Yeah?"

"You never told me."

"It's not important to me."

It was to her. Like a dash of hot Tabasco, the familiar excitement was in her body. "Did you flunk?"

"I was at the top of my class."

"Then why aren't you building houses on the moon?"

"Why work on the moon when the worst that can happen to you on Earth is to be staked to an anthill in Nevada? At least you can breathe in Nevada."

"But you could go if you wanted?"

"My father would love it. Staking me to an anthill isn't good enough for him."

A small adjustment of her shoulders let one curious nipple peek over the sheet at his blue eyes. She pretended to pull the sheet tighter, but a shoulder popped out. "And what's all that electronic junk?"

"My music."

"Is that the weird stuff I hear once in a while?"

"No. The weird stuff is when I'm composing. That's just experiments and subthemes. Sometimes its a foundation-sound on which I'm going to build." Then he added shyly, "I've been composing a piece for you."

"Oh, you *are* in love with me!" she teased. "May I hear it?"

"You sing this wild stuff in the shower. I built it on that. You'll have to forgive me for bugging your shower."

"You *record* me while I'm naked? I think that's disgusting!"

"Such sweet sounds."

"But I have a slug's voice."

"I hear only the most beautiful throaty wonders."

"You're Byron's son, all right!"

"You know what I call it?" He was shy now. "It's called *Diana in the Rain*. You inspire me."

Men were queer when they were in love. "I'm not really a muse. It's all an illusion in your head." She threw her hair back. "All right. Play it. I'm ready to suffer. But if I sound like a slug gargling, I won't let you play it for anyone else!"

Nothing larval was left in the voice he had transformed with his silken touch. Mostly it wasn't even human. Diana in the rain. Perhaps a nymph bathing in a mountain waterfall would sing that way. The sound folded and unfolded wings of joy so festive that even she failed to recognize herself as the music gripped her with her own emotion. Background instruments capered in the tonal patterns of no wooden instrument. Captured by his net, she recalled mythical worlds never seen.

He stood breathless, anxious, watching her reaction. Slowly becoming aware of what his metamorphic magic had done to her, she worked out of her percale cocoon with little jerking cries of pleased embarrassment. The sheet became her wings.

"Golly."

He was drugged with happiness just watching her.

"Don't stare at me like that or I'll turn you into a stag and your own hounds will hunt you down!"

Gently he carried her off to his parent's room. Responding to his memory of her earlier anger at his forwardness, he laid her gently on the bed, pecked her cheek, and withdrew. She would not let him go. What is true one hour is false the next.

"Stay with me and cuddle. As long as I get the door side of the bed. Your father was very kind to me and always let me sleep next to the door. You can make love to me in the morning. I have to have time to get used to you. Is that all right?" She kissed his fingers. "I won't eat your toenails."

When she woke she found him staring at her with his blue eyes. Blue eyes were the most romantic eyes in the whole galaxy. Sleepily, she rubbed noses with him. "Hi," he said, wide awake. "Is it morning yet?"

Their sexing was an awkward disaster. The gravity threw her off and the only woman he had ever known was the very experienced eVam. Alternately they swore at each other and laughed. Finally they decided that at least they knew how to hug.

"It reminds me of a story that my grandfather loves to tell," he sighed. "Once upon a time there was a new recruit for the 43rd Cavalry Regiment and the commanding officer asked him, 'Have you ever ridden before, my boy?' 'No, sir,' said the boy. 'Hmmm,' replied the colonel, 'I have just the horse for you; she's never been ridden, either.' "

"Let's have breakfast and try it again," she said.

For three days Diana ran around in a daze, baking, washing his clothes, laughing at his jokes, buying him presents with her tip money and hugging him every time she met him. But the second time she found herself scrubbing the kitchen floor in one week, she frowned. Did sex always make a woman feel this way? Byron had given her the goosebumps, too. Were men similarly affected? She peeked out the kitchen window and saw Charlie freezing his fingers off changing a bearing on her car's right front wheel.

By Friday she was enough in control of her emotions to begin the Great Plan. (1) Get Charlie a job. (2) Get him to finish school. (3) Get him a job on the moon. (4) Marry him. (5) Have children. She wasn't going to do it by nagging. She hated nagging a man. She'd rather leave a man than nag him. She was going to do it by worshipping him.

A trucker's mother died and the man took his truck off to New Jersey for the funeral so Charlie picked up a contract to haul potatoes for three days; Diana let him make love to her for three evenings and three mornings. A neighbor's pipes froze and he joined the plumbing crew; she cooked him a full course meal. Slyly she began to encourage him to be more ambitious. He took a weekend gig in Concord with his music. But spring came and he was still only doing odd jobs. Happiness gave her patience. They went walking in the woods when the buds sprouted. They splashed nude in a brook that was rampant with the freezing spring runoff.

She began to read to him from the papers about the big new push into space. Money was flooding into the effort. A consortium was even building a test solar power station. The Soviets were off to Mars. Old high risk investments in the leoport factories were making money and that was seducing the timid money out of the woodwork. The lunar landing track was operational. Overnight, it seemed, the high frontier had become a business almost half as big as the American cigaret, dope, and cosmetics trade.

Charlie was never interested. She hid her hurt.

The Saudi Arabian situation improved. Escaped Royalists had money in America and Europe with which to influence politics at home. Intrigues prospered. Assassinations were frequent. The new leaders found it easier to conquer than to rule, and found some appeasement of the western capitalists necessary. Still the oil situation was grim and, as reserves were depleted, the United States imposed draconian gasoline rationing. Synthigas plants were being pushed to full capacity in spite of a coal strike which had been suppressed by the Army and acid rain riots. Sabotage and slow-downs continued to decimate coal tonnage.

Red tape was cut so that breeder reactors could be put on line in four years but protests continued to mount. A new tarsands plant was financed for Alberta. The physicists were promising that hydrogen fusion power would be on line in twenty years. A new gas field was discovered at great depth in the Gulf of Mexico. Mainly the economy was gearing up for solar power satellite production.

She read to Charlie the fabulous job offers in the *Boston Globe* and the *Manchester Times Leader* and the *Los Angeles Times*. He wasn't interested. She sulked.

One day like a bolt from Jupiter Charlie's father called and Diana listened on the upstairs phone, tears rolling out of her eyes. *There* was a man. He could build. He could fight. His very voice called forth loyalty. He was on the cover of *Time* magazine again! He could even be tender to virgins. His kind forged the glory of man. She ached to hold him. Could a woman ever forget her first man?

That noon Diana cooked pies and a mouth watering lasagna. She made a fresh spring salad of new asparagus tips. She adjusted Charlie's collar. She teased him and in all ways was free and easy with her love. When she went to work she left a note in the truck's windshield wiper. "I have a job on the moon." Which wasn't true. "I'll *always* love you." Which was true for the moment. "Keep in touch."

She stopped at the restaurant only long enough to collect her pay and buy a packet of black market gas stamps and a trans-continental laser disk for the map reader. She got as far as Montana before she had a breakdown. In Butte she abandoned the car and took a bus to Seattle, curled over two seats with her head pressed against her wadded jacket, dreaming that she was asleep next to Byron's facial stubble.

CHAPTER 58

When the stars threw down their spears,
And watered heaven with their tears,
Did He smile His work to see?
Did He who made the Lamb, make thee?

DIANA GROVE IN A MASH NOTE TO BYRON,
QUOTING WILLIAM BLAKE.

For three hours a nervous girl waited in the hotel lobby where that flighty secretary said he was staying for the astronautics conference. It stunned her when he sailed by, his weathered eyes scanning over her like a reef to be avoided, his wake washing away the hello in her throat. She buttoned the decolleté she had arranged to remind him of her womanhood and followed him into the waiting elevator, ignoring him while they touched shoulders. She was, she observed, pretending he didn't exist about as well as a Soviet fishing boat, packed with electronics, pretended to be fishing in the vicinity of an American battleship.

Byron left the elevator. She followed silently. He stopped and took out his key-card. She waited.

"Diana! For the love of God!"

"So you finally noticed," she said petulantly.

"I had you pegged as one of the convention girls," he apologized, somewhat untactfully, switching on the light and walking over to the telephone. "What'll I order for you?"

"Poison darts!"

He spoke into the phone. "A double whiskey for room 412. Also glasses, a bucket of ice and three bottles of ginger ale." Carefully he cradled the receiver. "So you ran away again?"

384

"He started to beat me up the minute you left!" Which wasn't true but she wanted Byron to feel guilty. "I mistook myself for a gong. I escaped the last time by jumping two stories into the snow. A couple of good samaritans found me frozen to death at the end of a trail of blood. It was a very good lesson you taught me. I learned about fathers what I already know."

He was gazing at her with quizzical amusement. "Any scars?"

"No sir!" She snapped to her heels. "Regrouped, resupplied, rested, and ready for active duty, you son-of-a-bitch, sir!" A clipped salute finished her report.

"*Now* I remember you," he said amiably. "You're the tough one with the smile. And how have you been spending your AWOL?"

Diana had already assumed a fighting stance. Expertly she seized this opening and jabbed. "I've been living with your son." She withdrew and waited for the effect.

His face crumpled like a piece of paper being prepared for a bureaucrat's wastebasket. "You've seen Charlie?"

He was suddenly groggy and she moved in again. "We're lovers." She danced away.

McDougall began to steel himself for the blows. "Did he send you here for money?"

She relented. "Oh Byron! I heard your voice last week on the phone. I became nostalgic. I came here to marry *you*. We're going to have three children and live on the moon."

"A minute ago you were ready to kill me with poison darts."

"That was a minute ago. Before I decided to marry you." She touched him. "I'd be a good wife."

He was still shaken by the news about Charlie, still trying to focus on this girl who had seduced him on the leoport—and then, safely out of sight, had transmogrified into his son's lover. Was that possible? his son wrapped in this imp's embrace? "Changeable little wench, aren't you?"

"No. I've always loved you. Since I was six."

"Hmmm," he muttered.

"Look, you haven't even unpacked your suitcase yet and your dirty socks are under the bed. Hotels don't take care of men very well. You need a wife."

"I'm tempted," he said.

"Yeah?" She unbuttoned her decollete.

"But my good sense remains. I'll give you a choice. I'll argue with you or send you to an orphan asylum."

"Argue with me."

"You laid Charlie, eh?"

"What's it to you! The last I heard from you, just before you abandoned me to that prick father of mine, you wanted me to live in the coal dust and be virtuous."

Byron was trying to visualize being married to her. "I was thinking that you are young, even for Charlie."

"Yaah! Charlie's young, even for me."

"It wouldn't work between you and me," he said decisively.

"Why not!"

"I'm more than thirty years older than you are. I'm dying. You are beginning to flower."

She undid another button and rummaged around under the bed for his dirty socks which she angrily threw into a plastic bag. "Corpses make good fertilizer for flowers. Your power and my youth; it's a fair exchange. Jesus, Byron," she turned to him with regret, "I swooned when I saw you on *Time*. I was horny for a day."

"You'd tire of an old man."

"But it's *men* who are fickle. Women aren't like that. They're faithful. When they love a man, they *love* him. I'd be faithful to you. I'd forgive you anything."

He was settling into his decision. "That's what they all say when they are seventeen. When they are twenty-seven it's a different story."

"Already you're complaining about ten glorious years?" she stormed. "I'll bet you think you deserve fifty!"

There was a polite knock on the door.

"Young girls tend to bore experienced men," he reminded her.

She flung open the door and took the double whiskey from the bellhop's cart before he had fully entered the room. She set the glasses on the dresser, imperiously tipped the man, and poured Byron a ginger ale. "For your liver, old man." She took the whiskey. "So I bore you, do I?"

"You started me thinking about those fifty years."

She half finished her drink in one slurp.

"Can't I even have a sip of my whiskey?" he complained.

"I've decided to blackmail you instead of marry you," she answered calmly.

"Blackmail me!" She had his attention. "We're not even married yet and you're being a bitch. I hope your lawyers are cheaper than my lawyers! You've stolen my whiskey. What else do you want?"

"A job on the moon."

His humor left him. "No. That's final. What's your counter-move?"

"You damn fool!" she flared. "Your son is in love with me! He'll follow me to the moon! That's where you want him!"

"And do you love Charlie?"

"No! I can't *stand* drifters. Yes. He's very kind."

Byron gripped her arms in the iron curl of his fingers . . . "Diana. He *won't* follow you to the moon."

"Yes." . . . while the fingers squeezed . . .

"*No.* I know my son." . . . the blood from her arms.

"You've seen him lately with my legs around him?" she lilted sarcastically, not even trying to escape his crushing hold. "He goes crazy just looking at me—even when I have clothes on. I've watched him butter my toast. I've watched him scatter men who were trying to molest me. I've seen his eyes in the morning. You know *nothing* about your son. You're a dried up old man, remember, who has forgotten what it's like to be driven by his juices. Charlie would follow me to hell. I planned it that way." She started to cry. "At least he'll follow me if we move fast enough before he has time to sober up and get another girl."

Byron went limp. "He could follow you and refuse to work."

"Then I'd let him *die*. No man of mine is a suck." She smiled through her tears. "But for me he'd work."

Byron began to march around the room, shaking ice from the ginger ale glass he had exchanged for her arm. "And you think I give a *damn* whether he goes to space? I don't give a *damn* anymore. I used to care. Now I'd be happy if he did anything. *Anything*. Wash cars even. How is his *damned* music going?"

"Like his engineering. He piddles at it."

"Is he healthy?"

"He's fine. I took good care of him. He's probably very unhappy right now."

"Suffering, eh?" Byron was smiling again. "A couple of months in the trenches will do him good. Finish your whiskey and let's go. You've earned a dinner at Seattle's finest."

At dinner he refused to gossip about his son. He ordered the best meal on the menu, the third most expensive. He tucked a bib under his collar. "It's good to eat like this again. It used to be better when they had a real Frenchman for a waiter who would just as soon spit in your eye as serve you." He looked about at the paneled decor and the wine bottles on the rack. "It makes me feel human again. For a while I didn't even have an expense account. I was beginning to feel like a schlimazl."

She was breaking hard bread, waiting for the waiter to bring their drinks and take their order. The butter was shaped like chickens and eggs and leaves. "What's a schlimazl?"

"According to my friend Zimmerman, who is our freak carbothermal chemist on the moon, a schlimazl is a poor jerk who is good at everything—he grows a perfect potato crop . . . the year of the great potato blight. The next year, when he tries to make up his losses by opening a funeral parlor, someone discovers immortality. Zim differentiates between a schlimazl and a schlemihl. A schlimazl is the one who is good at having the soup spilled on him by a schlemihl. Those schlemihls in Washington were good at spilling soup. I was the schlimazl."

"I'll have the vichyssoise. I love cold soup. It doesn't burn as bad when it's spilled."

"Go right ahead. Those schlemihls in Washington are paying for it. I got out their anti-hydrogen when they needed it and they love me."

"I'm on your expense account?"

"You're goddamned right. This year we're doubling the size of the lunar colony. I wouldn't have believed that last year. And you should see the assembly line we have in mind for the solar power satellites; subcontracts all over the nation."

Her eyes were grinning. "I heard rumors that next year hydrogen fusion prices will drop to one cent a kilowatt-hour."

Byron almost didn't laugh. "How could I let my boy marry a girl with such a macabre sense of humor!"

He took her walking along the night beach, barefoot, sometimes on the sand, sometimes over the great driftwood trees, his shoes tied by the shoelaces over his shoulder and hers stuffed in his jacket pockets. The Pacific wind was cold and she sheltered herself behind his body, wondering at his silence that lasted for miles, not daring to invade his thoughts. The waves came and broke and went. Their feet were alternately drowned by foam and then free to make wet tracks in the moonlit sand.

"I'm not sure a romantic girl like you would like it up there. There's no lover's moon in the lunar sky."

"I can make poems about the Earth."

"You still have your Diana Grove papers?"

"Sure."

"They need to be made more solid. I'll spend some money."

She hugged his arm, thanking him silently, the glory and the triumph rising in her bosom to shout down the Pacific wind.

"I'm shipping out in two weeks. I'll take you with me. Not because of Charlie. Charlie can go to hell. For you. Of course, if by some miracle Charlie follows, well, there'll be a job for him. We're extending the length of the electromagnetic track so we can handle softer accelerations and decelerations."

Blackmail works! She was amazed. "What will I be doing?"

"Who knows."

"May I sleep with you tonight? I'm a much better lover than I used to be."

"No!"

"My hotel by the bus station has cockroaches!"

They were halfway back along the beach before he answered. "Zimmerman tells this story about some New York cockroaches that followed him to the moon. He claims to have spaced them out the hatch but that they didn't die and are running around the crater Aristarchus to this day."

CHAPTER 59

So we stole away together,
On the road that has no end,
With a new coined day to fling away
And all the stars to spend.

Dana Burnet

Diana teased Byron about whisking off his son's paramour and setting her up in Paris. He pretended not to hear but suddenly confided that he thought a vacation in the South Pacific would be good for him and would she like to tag along? So he arranged a side trip through Samoa before their Namala launch. They stayed for a week on Tutuila at the Rainmaker Hotel overlooking Pago Pago Bay, catching taxis in the morning to go scuba diving at the Taema Banks. Byron got them aboard a tuna boat.

But the excursion she was to remember the most started with a pillow fight at dawn, then a flight to Western Samoa's Upolu in a light plane that Byron rented. After he showed her the emerald mountains he put down at the Faleolo airfield and they walked all over Upolo, catching the occasional wooden-seated bus when they got tired. She saw storming waterfalls and once came up behind Byron as they emerged from a forested trail to catch a mountain view of the ocean that staggered her.

"Byron!" she gasped, holding his elbow.

"Yeah, the moon was never like this," he agreed.

When finally they caught a commercial flight to Namala it was she who took Byron around the island and showed *him* everything. That night they visited Ling's Kaleidoscope. Madam Lilly was doing a revival of a late sixties hippy farm. She combed out Diana's hair and lent her jeans and an embroidered jean jacket. The food was chicken roasted on an old bedspring over ruddy coals. One of the young waitresses loved her Ewan MacColl and, between serving customers, would sing his songs in an old fashioned voice while playing her guitar.

"The first time ever I saw your face . . . I thought the sun . . . rose in your eyes . . . and the moon and the stars were the gifts you gave . . . to the dark and the endless skies . . ."†

Byron liked the part where the girls went skinny-dipping in the pool. Diana, who was in a very good mood, joined them. So did one of the oldsters who had been sitting around with his wife and several other graying couples.

"Harry! You're too old for that!" said his wife, chewing on the beads lent her by Madam Lilly.

A prim companion of the wife took a last puff and passed over the table's common joint to calm her friend's nerves. Out of a distant speaker, the Beatles began to croon one of their nostalgically quaint songs while the prim companion rolled another. "When I get older, losing my hair . . . many years from now . . . Will you still need me, will you still feed me . . . when I'm sixty-four?"* With a pin in the roach, smoke lazily climbing her fingers, the wife watched her husband as he sported with all those nubile bodies in the psychedelic lights around the poolside. Finally returning, naked as a jaybird, he kissed her on the forehead and took the last toke, carefully sucking and holding his breath.

Madam Lilly provided him with a bathtowel to preserve the modesty of her place.

Next morning Byron and Diana checked into the spaceport's staging area two hours before launch. Diana felt like a veteran. On her first trip up and out, from the Kennedy Spaceport in Florida, she had been thrown into orbit by a rattletrap Rockwell Mark VI transport, a much modified version of the original Rockwell shuttle but still launched essentially by the means pioneered during the 1980s. Now she was "going up" from Namala aboard the latest in eight-passenger saucers, its very design younger than her "Grove" identity. Their saucer was fresh from the factory in Seattle. Even the upholstery smelled clean.

"I feel like a sardine packed for the giant at the top of the beanstalk," grumbled Byron, after he had been wedged in beside her. Not a patch of their bodies was unsupported.

---

†Copyright 1962 Stormking Music Inc.
*Copyright 1967 Northern Songs Limited.

Diana marveled. "I'm going to heaven!"

"Me, I get nervous out of the cockpit."

There was no stewardess, no human crew. A robopilot spoke words of comfort, explaining procedures while their saucer was picked up like any freighter and loaded into its assigned scramjet with the other saucers, mostly freighters. Diana happily recapitulated an Edgar Allen Poe story she had once read about a man who had been buried alive in a silk-lined coffin.

"Shut up," said Byron.

Invisible sensors monitored each passenger, checking that all regulations were being complied with during the countdown. To a gentle hiss, fast-setting foam filled out the seat contours to fit their bodies. ". . . three . . . two . . . one . . ."

The blast-off was easy but the force built up for a long minute before subsiding into a caressing pressure as the scramjet took over. The passengers were sightless and immobile.

"I need a piss," said Byron.

Diana told him stories to keep his courage up. They felt the slight lurch as the scramjet released their saucer. "Bombs away!" said Diana happily. The silicon pilot kept them informed. It told them when the saucer's rockets ignited. It told them their distance from the leoport. "Can't anybody shut off that damn mother?" complained Byron. The rings were closing in on them rapidly. "Twenty-five kloms . . . twenty kloms . . ."

Then, as the saucer found the apogee of its orbit among the blaze of stars, the leoport met them, an express to hell hitting them so hard that they sank into their couches with the grace of elephants while they raced through the monster's electromagnetic intestine, their backs against the action, eyes blind, bodies too heavy even to allow thought.

After 80 seconds the weight was gone. "Orbital injection complete," said the robopilot redundantly. "Please remain seated. Thank you for flying Shantech."

"Poor little Byron, you can relax now. We're here."

"Whew! The old shuttle was a piece of cake compared with this sobering ride. I feel like I've just been cut down by a firing squad after sassing a machine-gun with my bare ass!"

"You're such a stick-in-the-mud. You're too *old* for me."

They ate at *Planet Stories* with leisurely gusto. Diana drank too much. She told Shaggy Dog jokes and, when she had the attention of five booths, tried to dance on the tabletop in null gravity and ended up manning the ceiling. When she passed out, Byron took her back to the Hilton.

The next day they caught a ferry to geosync orbit at the

construction site of the first test solar power satellite. For eleven hours the five passengers played poker while the ferry captain distributed sandwiches and made coffee.

The ship continued to maneuver. When they established parking orbit, the captain called Diana into the cockpit. "Take a gander." The matchstick framework of the SPS angled away into the star-laden blackness. "It's hard to comprehend how immense it's going to be. Look, see that crane over there? It's a whopping big crane. The little dot is a cabin for two men."

"Wow."

"That thing is going to be half as big as Manhattan Island. What you see is only the first of eight modules. We've only got Greenwich Village built."

McDougall was laughing behind them. "Tell her how to go from the A-train to the Seventh Avenue line."

Within the hour they docked with a lunar transfer vehicle that was exchanging oxygen for terran hydrogen. The boss of the LTV stuck his head through the hatch, mainly to get a chance to razz McDougall. He was wearing a ten gallon hat. Byron didn't introduce him to Diana until the visit was almost over.

"Captain Horrible Maltby. Lady Diana Grove."

"Pleased," said Maltby, tipping his hat.

"Horrible and I used to fly in Saudi Arabia under the same command. And he used to be a battlestation man not so long ago on the Reagan shield. I'm going to have to stay here at the SPS construction site for a while and ride herd. It's my company that builds the solar panels. Captain Horrible will be taking care of you from here in. He'll get you down to moondust okay. But watch him. He's a rascal. Take care of yourself. Write Charlie. And don't let any of Horrible's friends send your bags on to Mexico City. Ciao."

Maltby took her back through the airseal tunnel.

"You sit copilot with me," he said.

"Where's your real copilot?"

"He's too fat. I left him home. Where would I put you if he was here? This ain't no taxicab. This here boat is a freighter. You want to fly the beast?"

"You're scaring me."

"Seems complicated to you? Shucks, you just say 'giddiap' and the beast goes. She has a brain of her own. Smart woman. She knows where home is. The smell of oats."

"Giddiap," said Diana. Nothing happened.

Maltby did a few quick things with his fingers and the ship

swung around. Then he yelled "Giddiap!" with an ear piercing Texas drawl and the ship roared to life.

This trip, instead of poker, Diana learned how to play chess. He gave her a two-pawn-and-a-rook handicap and she won one out of five games in the next two days until they docked at the small Penthouse station on top of the lunar skyhook. The maneuver cost them very little energy because the station was moving at lunar escape velocity for its altitude, anchored from flying away by the main Jed Cline station in orbit below, named after the first man who had proposed a lunar skyhook.

The skyhook had to be redesigned after the Mediian electromagnetic landing track went into operation on the surface. Cables were shortened and strengthened by busy spiders weaving with fused and spun lunar quartz. Elevators were rebuilt to move heavier loads at respectable speeds. The center of mass of the skyhook was lowered to increase its orbital speed.

"We've got to crawl down that?" Diana was skeptical. It looked like it dropped all the way to the lunar surface even though she knew it didn't get close. She couldn't even *see* the bulge of the Jed Cline hub, it was so far away.

They left their LTV at the Penthouse for another pilot who might want to go to geosync and Maltby loaded Diana and a pile of high tech plastic parts into one of the elevators with life support. Down to Jed Cline they dropped. They had time for chess. It was like going Greyhound Bus instead of American Airlines. It took *forever*. When they finally arrived, the hub turned out to be a lot larger than the Penthouse, but still they were assigned to sleep in tiny coffin bunks and ate in shifts with the station crew.

Diana stared at the pock-marked moon turning below them. She had never been so close! "Hey, some wall poster!" she told Maltby. Then she sat in the roundhouse watching the Ground to Station Vehicles glide in and dock. Later, Maltby came for her. Below deck in the honeycomb of hangars he picked up his own GSV.

The ship was lowered down the hook, a few hundred meters, and then released somewhere over the backside of the moon. Maltby made rocket adjustments to his orbit, but not many. Fuel was scarce this far from Earth and a good pilot used it sparingly, preferring to bleed gravity whenever he could.

The ship's small jets fired intermittently, making tiny vernier adjustments to their velocity as they came in for the horizontal landing, ass-end-to. Lazily the barren moon flowed by, slowly rising to meet them, but only when they were skimming the plain at crater-rim height did their enormous speed become evident to Diana. A mile every second. Nearby features to the side ran together in a watercolor blur. It unsettled her to be facing the wrong way, to see only the lunarscape they had already passed over. She had a moment of panic when she thought they were dropping too fast and would hit the ground.

Suddenly a line of track appeared, another blur as if from a train's caboose. She knew that behind their backs, the catcher-cradle was racing along the track ahead of them, accelerating to match the GSV's velocity. (She remembered her bicycle and the spaniel who used to trot leisurely from the neighbor's house, heading her off upstreet, but already madly galloping beside her as she reached him, nipping at her heels.) The cradle, moving with them now, positioned itself underneath them—she could see its rear extensions—grabbing with gentle jaws until the ship and the maglev vehicle became one with the slightest of jolts.

Maltby was yelling "Whoa!" at the blood-curdling top of his Texas voice. Electromagnetic fields cut in to convert fifteen tons of mass-flow into an electron flood. Force hit then, two gravities that slowly built to five. The blur beyond the windows resolved into the majesty of the lunar desert, and finally they were moving sedately along a shunt line towards a shed. Maltby was fondly patting the control panel, smiling. "Atta girl."

I'm here, Diana thought and wonder was all within her.

She was assigned to the hydroponic gardens under a scowling beak-nosed boss who walked through his long tunnels of racks lit by fiber optic light, constantly tasting tomatoes and carrots and broccoli like a Punch making passes at lady puppets. Immediately he began to give his new apprentice lectures on taste control.

His Punch eyes bulged and his nose quivered when she was slow to learn the use of the mass chromatograph for her daily tests of nutrient composition. He made her sit down and balance chemical equations which didn't help her at all to understand the machines she had to deal with. He was mean and she was furious but when she finally caught on, he took her to a hidden room behind his office and selected a large strawberry reward.

She bit into it, without sugar, and her eyes lit up.

"Now that's a strawberry," he cackled. "I have the little buggers fooled that they are living on the slopes of a British Columbian mountain. Taste is everything. To hell with yield.

Yield we can leave to the Californians." Slowly his grin grew, showing his upper gums above his jagged teeth.

"May I have another?" she asked, knowing how to reach the soul of this man.

"One more." He picked it and brought it to her with the gentlest grip. "Now where would you ever find a taste like that? Only on the moon," he said. "We're the best ecological artists in the solar system. Tomorrow you start on the beetle meat farms. That's a polite name for slugs. I'm breeding them for taste. I'm the man you come to for your grub-steak."

She decided that her boss was crazy—not that what he *said* was crazy, but he had papered the wall of the small strawberry room with a fantastic view of a British Columbian valley, looking down from some mountain slope with other mountains in the background.

It didn't take her long to find out that everyone else was crazy, too. In the cafeteria with the construction workers she eavesdropped on a conversation beside her. Billy was sick, the men were lamenting. Poor Billy. Billy was going to die. He'd been anemic now for months. It was the first time Diana had ever conceived of anybody *dying* on her moon! Her soul filled with sympathy; poor man! She listened as the workers tried to cope with death, tried to comprehend. Billy's leaves, explained the worker to his companion, were drying around the edges. *His leaves?*

Byron's friend, Zimmerman, dropped around after work to play scrabble. Diana asked him. "What kind of fruitcake would name a lemon tree Billy?"

Zim nodded. "I hear Billy is pretty sick about it, too. How would you like to be stuck with a name like Billy? My tree, I named Hershel Ostropolier and he's never been sick."

Then there was the tiny cook who had a redwood tree called Paul Bunyan. Weird. What would they do when it went through the roof? But the cook was into bonsai so Diana supposed it might be all right. When she bought her own baby orange tree she decided it was *not* going to have a name. However . . . one evening when the conversation came around to Celtic worship of trees she toasted her tree with a local version of Irish Mist. She was just trying to be witty. "To my true Irish friend!" Henceforth her orange tree was invariably referred to as "the Irishman."

It wasn't easy living on the moon. The corridors were cramped. The rooms were small. There was no place to go. She missed hiking through the New Hampshire woods. There wasn't any view of the Pacific from emerald hills.

Worse, an enormous sense of loss began to plague her. She had no direction, no purpose to her life which had always known a fierce purpose. It was awful. It was like being a compass that has smashed its way through to the north magnetic pole and was now spinning, aimless. One night she dreamed about the truck driver who had taken her to Washington when she was twelve. In the dream he said with an ironic smile, "Better be careful what you want, kid—you may get it!"

Purpose. That was very important. A girl had to have purpose! The most important thing in her life became the study of plants and beetles. She decided to become a genius and bring life to the moon, tasty life and beautiful, too. She borrowed botany disks and began to memorize all the names, programming her computer to sort them out for her by picture. There were so many species, it scared her. She began to read biology and agricultural texts and call up every hydroponic book in the library of her boss. She studied beetles, appalled at their endless variety. Studying became an urgent compulsion. There wasn't even time to socialize, except with the trees, and finally no time to sleep.

One afternoon, looking for a scrabble game, Zimmerman found her wandering around the landing track control room passionately trying to explain a theory of life that no one could understand.

CHAPTER 60

I know for every truth there is a way for each to go,
And though you wander far,
    your soul will know that true path when you find it.
I will fear nothing for you day or night!
I will not grieve at all because your light
    is called by some new name;
Truth is the same!
Call it star or sun—
    All light is one.

UNKNOWN

Every time when Diana woke up and tried to get out of bed so she could go back to work, they held her down and shot her full of drugs again. Once she escaped and turned up for work in her pajamas. They brought her back and put her to sleep. This time she was going to be more cunning. She'd pretend to be asleep until the drugs were all worn off and *then* she'd get up and go to work.

She peeked.

"Ah, you're awake," said Charlie.

She opened her eyes in wide disbelief. "Charlie! What are you doing here?"

"The old man called me up. He told me to get off my ass and take care of you. It was like listening to a wire brush cleaning out the hole between my ears."

"Are you on *their* side?"

"I don't know from nothing. I got here an hour ago. I can't even walk straight. Tomorrow I'm out working on the track extension. The old man got me a job as a laborer, the rat."

"Get me out of here, Charlie. I have to go back to work."

"You're on a paid vacation and you're complaining?"

"They'll fire me." She was terrified.

He sat down gingerly because he didn't know how to sit yet, but when he was sure there was a seat under him he took her hand and held it between both of his. "Nobody is going to fire you with my old man backing you."

"What happened to me? They won't tell me."

"You were wandering around passionately trying to convince people that milkweed was going to save the moon. The flowers are edible or something."

"I wasn't! I don't believe you!" She hid under the covers in shame.

"Yeah, you were really around the bend."

"I don't understand," she said through the covers.

"Neither does the doctor. But I do. You ought to see the loonies wandering around MIT during final exam month. At some time in our life we're all afraid of failure. It drives us nuts."

"You'll take care of me?"

"Do you think I'll let you out of my sight again? You gave me the shock of my life. For a week I thought I was strong enough to dismiss you. Then a funny thing began to happen. The sweet flowered fields of New Hampshire dissolved away into the flowered fields of hell. And the moon up there in the sky began to take on a heavenly beauty. I used to just lie on the ground and watch it rise and set."

"Can I go back to work? I could finish the afternoon shift if I started now."

"Maybe tomorrow. We have to settle things between us. Like who is this Irishman you're living with?"

"That's not my Irishman! That's my orange tree!"

"I'm competing with an orange tree? Do you think I have a chance? They say they'll let you come with me if you're willing. You have to promise to do everything I say."

"I promise. As long as you keep your mouth shut."

She laughed as Charlie tried to walk her home. He needed low gravity locomotion lessons. Once he collided with one of the awkwardly placed potted trees. "Charlie! Excuse yourself to Jezebel." He looked at her askance as she patted the pear tree. "There, there, Jezebel. Everything is going to be all right." Then she burst into tears.

Select friends gave Diana a homecoming party. Her boss arrived with a bowl of strawberries so delicious they needed neither powdered sugar nor cream. Zimmerman leaned against the wall, a good position from which to steal more than his share of the berries. Louise was there and Captain Horrible Maltby brought his guitar and his regular copilot. The orange Irishman moved into one corner to make room for them all.

Later Charlie explained to her the profounder truths of the universe as he saw them. "Some unsolved problem starts to push you. You think that if you don't do what you have to do, the world will fall apart. A couple of weeks without sleep and the borderline between the real world and imagination begins to fuzz. You fall asleep on your feet. You begin to treat real people as if they were the ghosts of your dreams and that's when the guys in the white coats come after you. Happens all the time at MIT in May. So if you get eight hours of regular sleep, I'll let you go to work. Otherwise, no."

"Make love to me. That'll put me to sleep."

"Thanks!"

"Is that what happened to you at MIT?"

"Naw. I come from an old military family. We can sleep through anything. We can sleep in a muddy foxhole during a thundershower in the middle of an artillery barrage while our line is crumbling and a nail is working through our boot. I cracked up for a different reason. I was pushing to get my father's ass. It got to me. Haven't you ever wanted to slug your father?"

"Oh yes!" she said brightly.

He laughed. "I was going to get one hundred percent in every course my last year, just to rub that martinet's nose in the robot he'd made out of me. But no matter how much I strove I just couldn't make it as a robot. I couldn't get past ninety-eight percent. It drove me crazy. It was like continually jumping in front of my father's Buick to prove to him what a bad driver he was and always coming out between the wheels without a scratch."

"You're crazier than I am!"

"I owe it all to my father." He was smiling.

"I like Byron. I'd hate it if I disillusioned him."

"That's because you are an empty-headed woman." Charlie sighed. "Maybe one day I'll make peace with the old prick."

"You could have finished school. It was in your own best interest."

He shrugged. "I wasn't doing it for me."

"Why didn't you do more with your music?"

"My music was something they *didn't* want, so it was a reaction, too, I guess."

"What *do* you want, then?"

"You."

"Oh, Charlie! That's not enough and you know it!"

"Maybe it is. Men are more romantic than women. Women only pretend to be romantic because they know men like it and if they pretend to be romantic they get a nice safe nest."

"Are you calling me a fake?" she bridled.

"Naw. Not you. You made it very clear that what you wanted to do was sit on a peak 380 thousand kloms high and look down on the rest of us."

"Screw you!" She strode to the farthest corner of the room, which wasn't very far away, and sat with her arms crossed, confronting him belligerently.

"Hey, don't you think it's utterly romantic that I climbed a peak that high on my knees just to ask you to marry me?"

She smiled mischievously, still with her arms crossed. "You haven't passed the other tests yet. You have to learn how to work first. Then *maybe* I'll marry you."

Within two years Charlie worked his way to assistant chief construction engineer. He was known with awe as the one hundred percent man; the man who got the job done perfectly the first time. He lived with Diana and refused to take an SPS construction gig because it would take him away from her.

Diana began to write papers on taste in high yield crops. For a lark she sent some tomatoes to a California fair and won first prize. She had seven projects going at once. Some people suspected that she never slept. Then, when necessity moved the command center out of the original spartan diggings into much larger quarters, Diana made some frantic calls to Byron before someone else could find a use for the space. Charlie did the conversion design work. Zimmerman did the politicking. Ling, her old friend Ling, put up the money.

She decided to call her restaurant *Diana's Grove*. It was to be the first real salon and fine food establishment on the moon. She had big plans. Her own place!

CHAPTER 61

Had we but world enough, and time . . .

"To His Coy Mistress," Andrew Marvell

A restless urge can overtake a man. Byron begged off a camping trip with a girlfriend too young for him, pleading business, and three hours later was at his desk in Concord after flying in by commercial airline. He was not able to concentrate. Restlessly he rented a car and drove out to Stonefield.

He had no reason to be in Stonefield. The house had long been sold to a professor of English at the college. They invited him in for tea and made meaningless pleasantries. He was glad to break away. Instinctively, his walk in the woods took him to the sacred grave of Amanda's love letter, overgrown, invisible.

For a while he sat on his haunches talking to her with a cattail between his teeth. He had stopped writing to Amanda long ago—what was the use—she never replied.

Back on Stonefield's main street he entered Brady's, which was still there, and ordered a milkshake. Little Charlie used to drag him in here to slurp sundaes. Strange how he couldn't even carry on a conversation with Junie anymore.

His ex still smoked like a chimney and so did the hog she had married who ran a business from Florida shipping fresh fish to the midwest. Last year, in a randy moment of nostalgia at their pool, Byron had propositioned her for old times sake—anything to get a rise out of her. Of course, she was still shockable. Some things never changed. He didn't dare go back.

On the marble table at Brady's he unfolded his digiphone. Five minutes later he had hired a San Antonio detective.

From Stonefield he went directly to Amman, Jordan, and

checked into the Holiday Inn Hotel. He did his groundwork carefully. If a man was going to tackle the greatest screw-up love affair of his life he might as well be prepared. He visited Amanda's mound and took an American professor of archaeology with him to have the place surveyed. He talked to the right people in Jordan's Department of Antiquities. They were slow.

With a weekend on his hands, he revisited Petra, alone. It was different. Then the United States had been pitifully planetbound. Imperial Russia had only begun to build Mirograd. And he was a young and stupid and fast-reflexed flyboy on a fling with a charming woman, pondering his unpromising future.

Young men die violently and have no time to think about death. But if they survive they become slowly dying older men who have time to conceive magnificent tombs.

The tombs of Petra were marvels carved from the rock. An older Byron understood them. The Nabateans would have understood him, too, he thought. His tomb was vaster than all Petra, carved to last a billion years. Only in the chambers of Medea on the moon would Byron McDougall be remembered forever. But here on Earth in the awesome Khasneh lay the tomb of his greatest love, strangled in the full flower of youth.

For another week, he wandered aimlessly around Amman, sampling Lebanese cakes, taking a morning and an afternoon walk, squandering time. Then his San Antonian detective reached him with the message that Amanda's husband would be in El Paso until the third of next month.

The continents and oceans of Earth were as nothing to Byron. He knew where his heart was—and went. The light plane dropped onto the dusty ranch field in Texas, swiveled around and cut its engines. Before he was even oriented he spotted Amanda arriving in her truck, kicking up dust. He waited.

"Ah knew it was you—you're the only man around these parts who washes his plane; you stopped writing me." She hadn't even paused for breath, but paused now, gripping the wheel.

He climbed in. "You knew that if you didn't answer me, I'd eventually have to come visiting."

"Ah knew no such thing!"

It can be a shock to see someone after a long absence. The desert sun is hard on a woman who loves the outdoors; Amanda was tanned and her good-natured wrinkles showed. They didn't speak again until she parked and uncoiled her lanky frame at the house.

"You get taller every time I see you," he marveled.

"You're just not eating enough good Texas beef, Shorty."

"It's been a while since I was fed by a good Texas woman."

She yelled out some instructions to the hands, and then took him into the kitchen. "Ah'll have to cook you up something special—see if Ah can fatten up your flattery glands."

In the kitchen there was no sign that she had ever been an archaeologist except the small shelf of thousand year old pots from the cradle of civilization in which she kept her spices. She chatted about cattle and rainfall. He helped her chop vegetables. None of the magic was gone from the way they joked together. He had been afraid that so much time would distance them. And so it became a magnificent evening. He always fell in love with her all over again every time they met. She fussed like she was trying to impress a potential conquest.

The sun set. She lit old country candles. "If Ah remember right, you are a scotch man," she said, standing up to pour him a glass.

"Here's to many evenings like this one," he toasted.

That reminded her of a task undone. "Ah have a present for you Ah've been keeping hidden from my husband." She left the room and came back. It was his stack of letters bundled in ribbon. She handed them to him. "It's over, Byron," she said. "Ah don't want you ever to come back." She said it calmly, without any grief at all.

For a moment of terror his mind flashed on the image of his ex-wife bodily throwing him out of her Florida home after he had propositioned her.

"You don't just throw away your past like that," he said after collecting his wits.

"Ah clean my attic all the time of the clutter Ah'm never going to use."

"That's not true. Part of you is still an archaeologist," he countered.

"It's gone. Ah threw it out."

"Life is not an attic."

"We missed our chance, Byron."

"Those pots in the kitchen. You'll never give them up."

With a kind of fury she flew away and came back with a carton full of the tiny vessels still brimming with spices. "Take them."

He tried to decline. "What would I do with pots?"

"Ah don't care!"

"I suppose I could pass them to Professor Arnt." It was now or never. "You haven't even given me a chance to tell you why

I'm here. I just got back from Jordan. I found out they are going to dig your mound."

"My mound?"

"Yeah. They just surveyed it, and the Jordanian Department of Antiquities has given permission for the dig."

"Dig *my* mound!" she exclaimed indignantly.

"I told them that you knew more about that mound than any archaeologist alive. I came here to offer you the job."

"You asshole, Byron! A dig like that takes money. Ah tried for *eight years* to raise the money and couldn't do it."

"Professor Arnt has been having a hard time raising money, too. I told him I'd help out. What am I rich for if I can't be a patron of the arts?"

"Byron!"

"I forgot my ladder," he reminded himself.

"A ladder?"

"I was going to put my ladder up against your bedroom window so we could elope in style."

"Ah can't just leave like that!" she protested.

"Gotta clean out your attic *sometime*. Tell your husband you had an urgent call from Jordan."

"You're bamboozling me!" she accused.

Byron helped her pack. Halfway through she changed her mind again and began to unpack. "There's a catch!"

"Yeah. You have to marry me and spend some time with me on the moon."

She wouldn't let him put her red shoes back in the suitcase, tugging at them. "Ah'd be terrified to fly to the moon."

"I'll hold your hand." He stuffed the red shoes under her nightgowns.

"You've conned me with dreams! You're always conning me with dreams. Tell me one *good* reason Ah should go with you?"

"I've become a registered Democrat."

They skulked off to the plane with a suitcase, some Edomite pots and a packet of love letters. There was enough moonlight to take off.

"You haven't told me that you love me," she complained.

"You're my all time favorite chick." He noticed her staring at the brilliant Texas moon. "It's mine. I'll give it to you."

EPILOGUE

The place is called *Diana's Grove*. There are trees everywhere, not big trees, but what they lack in size they make up for in lushness. Some of them bear fruit—lemons and oranges and figs. There are vines and bamboo stands, even a brook called Camenae that flows in too dreamlike a manner to gurgle. The benches are real wood, sacred to the lunar Dryads. The food is the best in the solar system—just don't ask for real beef in your hamburgers. Nymphs with names like Callisto and Nephele and Hyale and Ranis and Psecas serve the tables wearing Roman hairdos and wispy gowns. The Moon Goddess is fiercely protective of the girls who work for her—Zeus beware!

If you've ever heard the music at *Diana's Grove* you know that her man Charlie has risen into the league of the greatest. He claims it is just an engineer's hobby but we know different. He has invented 43 new instruments and hardly a lunar day goes by when he has not composed a new DM piece. His compositions can be as simple as birds chattering in the morning from somewhere beyond the *Grove's* leaves—a heron's cry, a sightseeing flock southbound, a lone warbler—or it can be a conversation-stopping argument between the gods.

He's at his best when he tells stories: the nymph Canens wasting away to nothing more than a voice while she searches in vain for her lost husband who has been transformed into a woodpecker by the witch Circe. Listen to that among the trees.

When Diana comes to her mythical grove, she makes her appearance in a white tunic with quiver over her shoulder. She knows everyone. Often she has a dinner party in one of the alcoves, the Corycian Cave or the Gargaphie Vale, and brings people together who should be together, sometimes for major or minor politicking, sometimes because she delights in the clash of disparate views, sometimes because she is a secret matchmaker, sometimes for trivial reasons—an old professor of Charlie's needs company or one of her friends needs to discuss curtains.

It was Diana who argued with Limon Barnes when he arrived, unannounced, for a fortnight's stay on the moon, and began unilaterally to reorganize the lunar government. She said he was a damn meddler. He claimed to be taking a needed vacation from tinkering with the tradition-bound Russian soul. She scolded him for experimenting with *people* and he told her that it was an incredible pleasure to experiment with flexible subjects who didn't yet have a fixed tradition.

Traditionally the tables at *Diana's Grove* vibrate with political discussion. To stand out, Limon Barnes had to be more than outrageous. He took a perverse amusement in shaking the core assumptions of these transplanted Americans. Diana fought him all the way—but in a way which was very good for business. The *Grove* was full on the evenings of their battles.

"You just *think* you're Hari Seldon!" she accused him after he gave a talk on how to manipulate and subvert constitutions in order to end the general decay of government. (An older retired writer had to whisper to his companion that Hari Seldon was a pre-golden age pulp science-fiction hero who saved the galaxy by inventing the science of psychohistory, a latter-day Marx.)

Limon merely nodded, warily accepting the drink she brought with her, an *Amalthea* made out of goat's milk and honey and the stars only knew what else. He gave it such a strange look. Was he wishing that he had a "tester"?

"It was good enough for Zeus, so it's good enough for you!" Diana insisted.

She could make anyone smile and Limon toasted his hostess with his eyes. "When Hari Seldon got through with the galaxy, there was only *one* future left." He raised his glass. "When I'm through with the galaxy the situation will be much more confused than that." He leaned over conspiratorially. "You see, I'm introducing hundreds of futures that never previously existed."

"Thank the gods you're leaving us!"

And things did calm down at the *Grove* when Limon retreated back to Earth—but he left three men to manage a twenty-four hour computer bulletin board game called *Consensus* that held the full set of lunar colony laws, plus rules for updating those laws. To change them you had to be a very good player. It was a game of skill. Nobody understood the purpose of the game even if they liked to play; whatever changes you might manage to make in the laws with the help of the other players weren't *legally binding*. And yet . . . within a year, by consensus, there were no other lunar laws. No one even minded that eight year olds were allowed to play. If you had the skill to win, you had a "vote."

Yes. There is always excitement at *Diana's Grove*.

If you're a newcomer to Medea you won't remember the Big Party For Byron, but the whole citizenry took part. It started when Ray Armsiel visited the moon with his wife. Diana took them to the *Grove* to pay back an old debt she had picked up at a McDonald's in L.A. She cooked up her best grub hamburgers for Ray. "On Earth," she teased, "you're stuck with hamburgers made out of dead cow. Where else but the moon can you get *real* hamburgers made out of ground up beetle larvae?"

Ray sniffed at them.

"Aren't you the heavy terran!" snorted Diana. "Haven't you seen tomatoes and lettuce before? My hamburgers taste *better* than beef! You should see our breeding program!" She offered him a side dish of crisp grasshoppers in a goat's cheese dip.

And while his attention was occupied, Linda Armsiel, who was the great Sam Brontz's daughter, was gossiping about Byron. She whispered that he had been remarried secretly in Jordan by the American consul. To an archaeologist.

Five hours later the whole moon knew the story. Over the months spies began to add tidbits. Byron was going to try to smuggle her in as an immigrant! The lovebirds were going to pretend they weren't married and hardly knew each other! Each day more gossip trickled in. And then . . . they were to arrive at lunar sunset. Separately!

On Thursday (sunset day) the arrangements for the *Party* were barely hidden away. Signals were passed. A special computer center kept track of the couple's movements. And the word went out on a minute by minute countdown. . . . Byron had left his room . . . Byron was now in *Diana's Grove* alone, waiting . . . The tension mounted. Again the word went out. . . . Amanda was drifting toward the *Grove* herself . . . Even the men on the night shift in the new diggings had their earphones on. They were ignoring each other and forgetting to drill rock.

"Byron is starting to flirt with her," confided the announcer to all of Medea. "She's pretending to ignore him." The night staff at the anti-hydrogen factory put their machines on automatic so they could give their undivided attention to the blow by blow reports.

Now Amanda was accepting a drink with great reserve.

That was the signal. Into the *Grove* came Captain Horrible Bill Maltby dragging a string of tin cans. Diana's staff hurried out of hiding, banging pots. The lunacy lasted for two days. During the revelry a sentimental Charlie proposed to Diana again, for the twenty-seventh time.

And so it goes. Infrequently Charlie *still* proposes to his Diana. She smiles her teasing smile, even though they already have one child, and writes him out a new contract in a flourishing script that promises she will be faithful to him for at least the next fortnight. He grumbles that living with her is like being an untenured professor.

The solar power satellites are winking on all around the equator, eighty percent of their mass now coming from the moon. All of the oxygen used by the space fleet is manufactured on the moon. America is prosperous, for the moment, doing what it has always done best, selling high technology (and food) to the rest of the world. Her economy has achieved power independence and, perhaps, resource independence. When Byron McDougall isn't puttering around in the ancient cities of Jordan with his wife, he's plotting ways to snare a nickel-iron asteroid.

The investment in the leoport-lunar transportation system was considerable but it is, as yet, not well defended. People still talk about defense. No one has forgotten the Great Accidental War—and nuclear weapons have since become as cheap as homemade cruise missiles in a world whose numbers have crossed the eight billion mark, tens of millions more each year to eye each other with envy and hatred. Both McDougalls belong to an unofficial ministry which considers problems that the lunarians do not trust to Old Earth's archaic mentation. Serious decisions have to be made by someone to secure the high ground. Such duties take Charlie back to the homeworld once a year.

Diana never goes with him. She is a minor Earth diety who worked hard for her promotion to Moon Goddess and she is well content with her position.